WHITE WOLF

Also by David Gemmell

The Drenai books
Legend
The King Beyond the Gate
Waylander
Quest for Lost Heroes
Waylander II: In the Realm of the Wolf
The First Chronicles of Druss the Legend
The Legend of Deathwalker
Winter Warriors
Hero in the Shadows

The Jon Shannow books
Wolf in Shadow
The Last Guardian
Bloodstone

The Stones of Power books
Ghost King
Last Sword of Power
Lion of Macedon
Dark Prince

The Hawk Queen books
Ironhand's Daughter
The Hawk Eternal

The Rigante books
Sword in the Storm
Midnight Falcon
Ravenheart
Stormrider

Individual titles
Knights of Dark Renown
Drenai Tales
Morning Star
Dark Moon
Echoes of the Great Song

Anthologies
Drenai Tales
Drenai Tales Volume II
Drenai Tales Volume III

DAVID A. GEMMELL

WHITE WOLF

BANTAM PRESS

LONDON · NEW YORK · TORONTO · SYDNEY · AUCKLAND

TRANSWORLD PUBLISHERS
61–63 Uxbridge Road, London W5 5SA
a division of The Random House Group Ltd

RANDOM HOUSE AUSTRALIA (PTY) LTD
20 Alfred Street, Milsons Point, Sydney,
New South Wales 2061, Australia

RANDOM HOUSE NEW ZEALAND LTD
18 Poland Road, Glenfield, Auckland 10, New Zealand

RANDOM HOUSE SOUTH AFRICA (PTY) LTD
Endulini, 5a Jubilee Road, Parktown 2193, South Africa

Published 2003 by Bantam Press
a division of Transworld Publishers

A catalogue record for this book is available from the British Library.
ISBN 0593 044444 (cased)
0593 044568 (tpb)

Typeset in 11/14pt Sabon by Falcon Oast Graphic Art Ltd.

Printed in Great Britain by Clays Ltd
Bungay, Suffolk

1 3 5 7 9 10 8 6 4 2

White Wolf is dedicated with love to
Linda, Karl, Kate, Jade and Andrew,
for the joy of the barbecue, and the gift of family.
And also to two men I have never met,
Ken and Malcolm, the Gemmell brothers.

ACKNOWLEDGEMENTS

My thanks to Steve Saffel, whose advice inspired the creation of Skilgannon the Damned, to Selina Walker, my editor at Transworld, and to my test readers Jan Dunlop, Tony Evans, Stella Graham and Steve Hutt. Grateful thanks also to author Alan Fisher, for sharing his knowledge of the craft, to my copy editor, Nancy Webber, and to Dale Rippke for his work mapping the Drenai world.

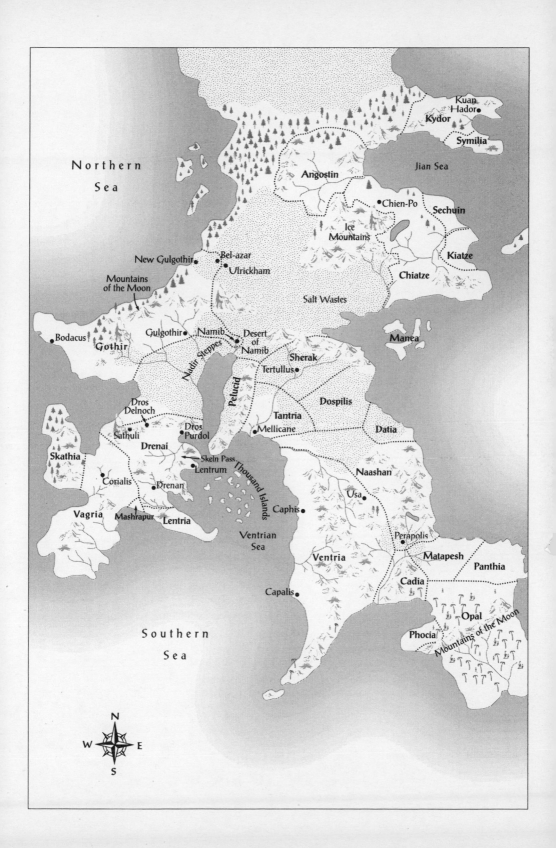

WHITE WOLF

PROLOGUE

CAPHAS THE MERCHANT WAS FRIGHTENED AS THE STRANGER approached his campfire in the woods to the north of the capital. Caphas had picked the spot with care, in a hollow away from the road, so that his fire would not be seen. Although the civil war was now ended, so great had been the losses on both sides that there were few troops left to patrol the wildlands, where renegades and deserters looted and stole. The merchant had thought long and hard about this journey, but with so many of his colleagues too terrified to enter the lands of Naashan he had seen an opportunity for huge profits from his goods: silks from Chiatze and spices from Sherak and Gothir. Now, as the full moon shone over the hollow, those profits seemed a long way away.

The rider emerged from the tree line above the camp, and angled his horse down the slope. The man's hairstyle – the lower part of the head shaved clean, the upper hair swept into a fierce crest – showed him to be a Naashanite swordmaster. Caphas began to relax. It was unlikely such a man would prove to be a robber. There were far better ways for skilled fighters to make money in this war-torn country than by waylaying travelling merchants. The man's clothes further reinforced this judgement. Though functional in appearance – a dark leather jerkin, the shoulders edged with chain mail, leather leggings and high riding boots also adorned

13

with mail – they were richly made. His black horse was Ventrian pure bred. Such beasts were rarely seen on the open market, but would sell privately for between two hundred and four hundred gold raq. The rider was quite clearly no thief. Thoughts of robbery drifted away, only to be replaced by a fear of another kind.

The man dismounted and walked to the fire. He moved with the grace common to all swordsmen, thought Caphas, who rose to greet him. Up close the rider was younger than Caphas had first thought. In his twenties. His eyes were a piercing sapphire blue, his face handsome. Caphas bowed. 'Welcome to my fire, sir,' he said. 'It is good to find company in such bleak surroundings. I am Caphas.'

'Skilgannon,' said the man, offering his hand.

A deep, sickening terror struck Caphas. His mouth was suddenly dry. Aware that Skilgannon was staring at him he managed to say: 'I . . . was about to prepare a small meal. You would be most welcome to share it.'

'Thank you.' Skilgannon's blue eyes scanned the campsite. Then he raised his head and sniffed the air. 'Since you are not the person wearing the perfume I suggest you invite the women to join us. There are wild beasts in the woods. Not as many wolves as once there were, but still some bears and the occasional panther.' He swung away from Caphas and walked to the fire. It was then that the merchant saw the strange ornament he carried slung across his back. It was around five feet in length, slightly curved, the centre polished black. At each end were set beautifully sculpted ivory sections. Ornate and exquisite, it would – had he not heard the man's name – have seemed to Caphas to serve no purpose.

Swinging the ornament from his back, the stranger placed it on the ground beside him as he sat down by the fire.

Caphas turned towards the dark woods. His heart was heavy. Skilgannon knew the girls were there, and if he intended rape or murder they would not escape him. 'Come in, Lucresis. Bring Phalia. It is all right,' he called, praying it was true.

A slender, dark-haired young woman moved out of the trees, holding the hand of a girl of around seven. The child broke clear of her sister's grip and ran to her father. Caphas put a protective arm around her, and drew her towards the fire. 'My daughters,

Phalia and Lucresis,' he said. Skilgannon glanced up and smiled.

'Always wise to be wary,' he said. 'The girls are very beautiful. They must take after their mother.'

Caphas forced a smile. 'Ah yes, she was the beauty. No doubt of it.' He was dismayed to see Lucresis staring boldly at the handsome young man. She tilted her head and ran her fingers through her long hair. She knew she was beautiful. So many young men had told her so.

'Lucresis! Come and help me fetch the pots and pans from the wagon,' he ordered, his voice showing his stress. Confused by his fear, the young woman followed him. As he reached the wagon he hissed at her, 'Stop making eyes at him.'

'He is very handsome, Father.'

'That is Skilgannon the Damned. You want nothing to do with him. We will be lucky to escape this with our lives,' he added, keeping his voice to a whisper. He handed her several pots.

Lucresis glanced back at the man by the fire. He was chatting to little Phalia, who was giggling at his words. 'He won't hurt us, Father.'

'Do not judge a man by his looks. If only ugly men committed crimes it would take no effort at all to find offenders. I have heard tales of his excesses. Not just on the battlefield. It is said he once had a large house, and all the servants were trained whores. He is not the sort of man I would want near my daughter – had I a choice in the matter. Which I don't,' he concluded miserably.

'I wish *I* had a choice,' said Lucresis.

Returning to the fire, Caphas prepared a broth. The smell of it hung in the air, rich and tempting. Occasionally he would stir the contents of the large pan, then take a sip before adding a little pepper and spice. Finally he sprinkled rock salt into the pot. 'I believe it to be ready,' he said.

After the meal Skilgannon put his plate to one side. 'You are a truly talented cook, Master Caphas.'

'Thank you, sir. It is a hobby of mine.'

'Why do you have a spider on your arm?' asked little Phalia, pointing to the black tattoo on Skilgannon's left forearm.

'Do you not like it?'

'It is very ugly.'

'Phalia, that was rude!' snapped Caphas. 'It is the mark of an officer, dear heart,' he added swiftly, realizing he had shocked the child. 'The fighting men of Naashan adorn themselves in this way. An officer who has . . . defeated . . . eight enemies in single combat is awarded the Spider. Generals have panther tattoos upon their chests, or eagles if their victories are great.' He knelt beside the child. 'But you should not make such comments.'

'I'm sorry, Father. But it *is* ugly.'

'Children say what they think,' said Skilgannon softly. 'It is no bad thing. Be calm, merchant. I mean you no harm. I shall spend the night in your camp and be on my way in the morning. Your life is safe – as is the honour of your family. And, by the way, the house you told your daughter of was not mine. It was owned by a courtesan who was, shall we say, a friend.'

'I did not mean to offend, sir.'

'My ears are very keen, merchant. And I am not offended.'

'Thank you. Thank you so much.'

They heard the sound of horses in the distance. Skilgannon rose and waited.

Within moments a column of cavalry rode into the clearing. Caphas, who had journeyed in Naashan throughout the years of civil war, knew them for the Queen's Horse, black-clad warriors in heavy helms. Each carried a lance, a sabre, and a small round shield decorated with a spotted snake. At the head of the column was a civilian he recognized: Damalon, the Queen's favourite. His hair was long and blond, his face lean. The fifty riders sat their mounts silently, while Damalon leapt lightly to the ground.

'It has been a long ride, general,' he said to Skilgannon.

'And why did you make it?' asked the warrior.

'The Queen wants the Swords of Night and Day returned.'

'They were a gift,' said Skilgannon. He shrugged. 'However, be that as it may.'

Lifting the curious ornament he held it for a moment, then tossed it to Damalon. In that moment Caphas saw a spasm of pain flicker on Skilgannon's face.

The handsome courtier glanced back to the soldiers. 'No need for you to stay, captain,' he told a tall man sitting a chestnut gelding. 'Our task here is concluded.'

16

The rider edged his horse forward. 'Good to see you again, general,' he said to Skilgannon. 'May the gods be with you.'

'And with you, Askelus,' answered Skilgannon.

The cavalry swung their mounts and rode from the clearing. All that remained were four riders, dark-garbed men carrying no swords. Long knives hung at their belts. They dismounted and walked to stand alongside Damalon.

'Why did you leave?' Damalon asked Skilgannon. 'The Queen admired you above all her generals.'

'For reasons of my own.'

'Most odd. You had it all. Riches, power, a palace a man might die for. You could have found another wife, Skilgannon.' Damalon curled his hand around one of the ivory handles, then pulled upon it. Nothing happened.

'Press the ruby stud on the hilt,' said Skilgannon. 'It will release the blade.' The moment Damalon pressed the stud a sword slid clear. Moonlight shone upon the silver steel and the runes engraved there. Caphas stared at the sword with undisguised avarice. The Swords of Night and Day were legendary. He idly wondered what they would fetch if offered to a king. Three thousand raq? Five thousand?

'Most beautiful,' said Damalon. 'It stirs the blood.'

'My advice to you – and your followers – would be to remount and leave,' said Skilgannon. 'As you say, your mission is concluded.'

'Ah, not quite,' said Damalon. 'The Queen was very angry when you left.'

'She will be angrier still if *you* do not return,' said Skilgannon. 'And I am tiring of your company. Understand me, Damalon, I do not wish to kill you and your creatures. I merely wish to ride away and leave this land.'

'Your arrogance is overwhelming,' snarled Damalon. 'I have your swords, and four men skilled with the blade, and you threaten me? Have you lost your wits?' He glanced at Caphas. 'Such a shame you were here, merchant. Fate, I suppose. No man can avoid it.' Damalon pressed an emerald stud on the second hilt. The black scabbard fell to the ground as a second blade slid clear. It shone like gold, bright and precious. For a moment the blond courtier stood very still, drinking in the beauty of the swords. Then he shook his head, as if coming out of a trance. 'Kill the old man and the child,' he said. 'The girl will prove an amusing distraction before we return to the capital.'

In that moment Caphas saw Skilgannon move towards Damalon. His hand flicked forward. Something bright and glittering flashed through the air. It struck Damalon lightly in the throat.

Blood sprayed from the severed jugular. What followed Caphas would never forget, not in the tiniest detail.

Skilgannon moved in on Damalon. As the dying courtier dropped the swords Skilgannon swept them up. The four black-garbed killers ran in. Skilgannon leapt to meet them, the sword blades shimmering in the firelight. There was no fight, no clash of steel upon steel. Within a matter of heartbeats five men were dead upon the ground – one virtually beheaded, another cut through from shoulder to belly. Caphas watched as Skilgannon cleaned the gold and silver blades before sliding them back into the single black scabbard, which he swung onto his back.

'Best you find new markets, Caphas,' he said. 'I fear Naashan will now be dangerous for you.'

The man was not even out of breath and there was no trace of sweat upon his brow. Turning from Caphas, he walked back and searched the ground around Damalon's body. Stooping, he picked up a small, circular piece of blood-smeared metal no more than two inches in diameter, and wiped it clean on Damalon's shirt. Caphas saw then that the metal had a serrated edge. He shivered. Skilgannon tucked the weapon into a sheath hidden behind his belt. Then he moved to his horse and saddled it.

Caphas approached him. 'They were going to kill us too,' he said. 'I thank you for saving my daughters and myself.'

'The child is frightened, Caphas. Best you go to her,' said Skilgannon, stepping up smoothly into the saddle.

Lucresis ran to his horse. 'I too am grateful,' she said, staring up at him wide-eyed. He smiled at her, then leaned down, took her hand and kissed it.

'Be lucky, Lucresis,' he said. 'It would have been most pleasant to spend a little more time in your company.' Releasing her hand he looked back at Caphas, who was holding his younger daughter

18

close. 'Do not stay here tonight. Prepare your wagon and head north at speed.'

With that he rode away.

Caphas watched him until he was lost among the trees. Lucresis sighed and turned to her father. 'I wish he had stayed.'

The merchant shook his head in disbelief. 'You just saw him kill five men. He is ruthless and deadly, Lucresis.'

'Perhaps, but he has beautiful eyes,' she replied.

CHAPTER ONE

SMOKE FROM THE BURNING BUILDINGS STILL HUNG IN THE AIR, BUT THE rioting mobs of yesterday had dispersed now, as the two priests walked slowly down the hill towards the town. Heavy clouds were gathering over the eastern mountains, promising rain for the afternoon, and a cool wind was blowing. The walk from the old monastery buildings to the little town was one that Brother Braygan usually enjoyed, especially with the sunshine glinting from the white buildings, and glittering on the rushing river. The chubby young priest loved to see the colourful meadow plants, so small and ephemeral against the backdrop of the eternal, snow-capped mountains. Not so today. Everything seemed different. The beauty was still there, but now an underlying sense of menace and real peril hung in the air.

'Is it a sin to be frightened, Brother Lantern?' he asked his companion, a tall young man with eyes of cold and brilliant blue, upon whom the pale robes of the acolyte seemed out of place.

'Have you ever killed a man, Braygan?' Lantern's reply was cold and disinterested.

'Of course not.'

'Or robbed, or raped or stolen?'

Braygan was shocked and stared up at his companion, his fears momentarily forgotten. 'No.'

'Then why do you spend so much time worrying about sin?'

Braygan fell silent. He never enjoyed working alongside Brother Lantern. The man said very little, but there was something about him that was wholly disturbing. His deep-set sapphire eyes were fierce, his lean face hard, his expressions unyielding. And he had sword scars upon his arms and legs. Braygan had seen them when they worked in the fields in the summer. He had asked about them, but Lantern had ignored him, as he ignored questions concerning the harsh and warlike tattoos upon his back, chest and arms: an eagle with outstretched wings and open talons between his shoulder blades, a large spider on his left forearm, and the snarling head of a panther upon his chest. When questioned about them Lantern would merely turn his cold eyes on the speaker and say nothing. Yet in all else he was an exemplary acolyte, working hard and never shirking his duties. He never complained, or argued, and attended all prayer and study meetings. When required he could quote verbatim from all sections of holy script, and knew also much of the history of the nations surrounding the Land.

Braygan turned his attention back towards the town, and his fear returned. The soldiers of the Watch had done nothing to stop the rioters. Two days ago the mob had attacked Brother Labberan and broken his arms when he went to teach at the church school. They had kicked and punched him, then struck him with rods of iron. Labberan was not a young man, and could easily have died.

The two priests came to the small bridge over the river. Braygan trod on the hem of his pale blue robe and stumbled. He would have fallen, but Brother Lantern's hand grabbed his arm, hauling him upright.

'Thank you,' said Braygan. His arm hurt from the iron grip and he rubbed it.

There were some people moving through the rubble. Braygan tried not to stare at them – or at the two bodies hanging from the branches of a tall tree. They looked like foreigners, he thought. 'I *am* frightened, Brother,' he whispered. 'Why do people do such hateful things?'

'Because they can,' answered the tall priest.

'Are you frightened?'

'Of what?'

The question seemed ridiculous to Braygan. Brother Labberan had been beaten close to death, and there was hatred everywhere. In the capital, Mellicane, a group known as the Arbiters had grown in power. Priests there had been murdered, or accused of treason and hanged. Now a representative of the Arbiters had arrived in Skepthia, touring taverns and meeting halls, speaking out against the church and its priests. And the terror continued to grow.

Crossing the bridge, Braygan and Lantern moved past the smouldering buildings and on to the main street. Braygan was sweating now. There were more people here, and he saw several dark-garbed soldiers standing in a group by a tavern door. Some of the townsfolk stopped to stare at the priests as they made their way to the apothecary's. One man shouted an insult.

Sweat dripped into Braygan's eyes and he blinked it away. Brother Lantern had reached the apothecary's door. It was locked. The tall priest tapped at the wooden frame. There was no answer. A crowd began to gather. Braygan tried not to look at the faces of the men. 'We should go, Brother Lantern,' he said.

Somebody spoke to Braygan, the voice angry. He turned to answer, but a fist struck him in the face and he fell clumsily to the ground. A booted foot caught him in the chest and he cried out, and rolled towards the wall of the apothecary's.

Brother Lantern stepped across him, and blocked the path of Braygan's attacker. 'Beware,' said Lantern softly.

'Beware of what?' asked the man, a heavily built and bearded figure, wearing the green sash of the Arbiters. It was the representative from Mellicane.

'Beware of anger, brother,' said Lantern. 'It has a habit of bringing grief in its wake.'

The man laughed. 'I'll show you grief,' he said. His fist lashed out towards Lantern's face. The priest swayed. The blow missed him. The attacker stumbled forward, off balance, and tripped over Lantern's outstretched leg, falling to his knees. With a roar of rage he surged upright and leapt at the priest – only to miss him and fall again, this time striking his face on the cobbles. There was blood upon his cheek. He rose more warily, and drew a knife from his belt.

'Be careful,' said Lantern. 'You are going to hurt yourself further.'

23

'Hurt myself? Are you an idiot?'

'I am beginning to think that I might be,' said Lantern. 'Do you happen to know when the apothecary will be arriving? We have an injured brother and are in need of herbs to reduce his fever.'

'You're the one who'll need the apothecary!'

'I have already said that I need the apothecary. Shall I speak more slowly?'

The man swore loudly then rushed in. The knife lanced for Lantern's belly. The priest swayed again, his arm seeming to brush against the charging man's shoulder. The Arbiter surged past Lantern and struck the apothecary's wall head first. Slumping down, he screamed as his knife blade gouged into his own thigh.

Lantern walked over and knelt beside him, examining the wound. 'Happily – though I suppose that is arguable – you have missed the major artery,' he said, 'but the wound will need stitching.' Rising, he turned towards the crowd. 'Does this man have friends here?' he called. 'He needs to be attended.'

Several men shuffled forward. 'Do you know how to treat wounds?' Lantern asked the first.

'No.'

'Then carry him into the tavern. I will seal the cut. And send someone to fetch the apothecary. I have many duties today and cannot tarry here long.'

Ignored by the crowd Braygan pushed himself to his feet, and watched as the injured man, groaning in pain, was carried to the tavern. Lantern glanced back. 'Wait for the apothecary,' he said. 'I will return presently.' With that he strolled towards the tavern, the crowd parting for him.

Braygan felt light-headed and vaguely sick. He took several deep breaths.

'Who was that?' asked a voice. It was one of the black-armoured soldiers, a thin-faced man with deep-set dark eyes.

'Brother Lantern,' answered Braygan. 'He is our librarian.' The soldier laughed. The crowd began to drift away.

'I do not think you will be further troubled today,' said the soldier.

'Why do they want to harm us? We have always sought to love all people, and I recognized many in the crowd. We have helped

24

them when they were sick. In the famine last year we shared our stores with them.'

The soldier shrugged. 'Not for me to say.'

'Why do *you* not protect us?' asked the priest.

'Soldiers obey their rule, priest. The martial code does not allow us to obey only those orders we like. Were I you I would leave the monastery and journey north. It will not be long before it is attacked.'

'Why would they attack us?'

'Ask your friend. He seems to be a man who knows which way the wind will blow.' He paused. 'During the fight I saw he had a dark tattoo upon his left forearm. What kind was it?'

'It is a spider.'

'I thought so. Does he perhaps also have a lion or some such upon his chest?'

'Yes. A panther.'

The soldier said nothing more, and walked away.

For three years now Skilgannon had sought to recapture that one perfect moment, that sense of total clarity and purpose. On rare occasions it seemed tantalizingly close, like a wispy image hovering at the corners of vision that danced away when he tried to focus upon it.

He had cast aside riches and power, and journeyed through the wilderness seeking answers. He had entered the priesthood here at the converted castle of Cobalsin, enduring three mind-rotting years of study and examination, absorbing – and largely dismissing – philosophies and teachings that bore no relation to the realities of a world cursed by the presence of Man.

And each night the dreams would haunt him. He would be wandering through a dark wood seeking the white wolf. He would catch a glimpse of its pale fur in the dense undergrowth and draw his swords. Moonlight would glisten on the blades, and the wolf would be gone.

Instinctively he knew there was a link between the swords and the wolf. The moment he touched the hilts the beast would disappear, and yet such was the fear of the wolf that he could not resist the lure of the blades.

The monk known as Lantern would awake with a start, fists clenched, chest tight, and roll from his narrow pallet bed. The small room with its tiny window would seem then like a prison cell.

On this night a storm was raging outside the monastery. Skilgannon walked barefoot along the corridor and up the steps to the roof, stepping out into the rain. Lightning blazed across the sky, followed by a deep rumble of thunder.

It had been raining that night too, after the last battle.

He remembered the enemy priest, on his knees in the mud. All around him were corpses, thousands of them. The priest looked up at him, then raised his thin hands to the storm. Rain had drenched his pale robes. 'The tears of Heaven,' he said.

It still surprised Skilgannon that he remembered the moment so powerfully. Why would a god weep? He recalled that he had laughed at the priest, and called him a fool. 'Find yourself a god with real power,' he had said. 'Weeping is for the weak and the powerless.'

Now on the monastery roof Skilgannon walked through the rain and stared at the undulating landscape, gazing out towards the east.

The rain eased away, the clouds clearing. A bright, gibbous moon illuminated the glistening land. The houses in the town below shone white and clean. No rioting crowds tonight, no rabble rousers. The fires in the merchant district had been doused by the storm. The mob will gather again tomorrow, he thought. Or the next day.

What am I doing here, he wondered? The fool in the town had asked whether he was an idiot. The question dogged his thoughts. He had looked into the man's eyes as he had stitched his wounded thigh. The glint of hatred shone there. 'We will sweep your kind from the pages of history,' the man had said.

Your kind.

Skilgannon had looked at him lying upon the tavern table, his face grey with pain. 'You might kill the priests, little man. It will not be hard. They do not fight back. But the pages of history? I think not. Creatures like you do not have such power. '

A bitter wind rippled across the rooftop. He shivered – then smiled. Pulling open his soaked robes, Skilgannon let them fall to the floor. Standing naked in the moonlight he stretched the muscles of his arms and back, then moved smoothly into the Eagle pose, the left foot hooked behind the right ankle, the right arm raised, the left arm wrapped around it, the backs of the palms pressed together. Motionless he stood, in perfect balance. In this moment he did not look like a priest. His body was well muscled and lean, and there were old scars upon his arms and chest, from sword and spear. His breathing deepened. Then he relaxed. The cold did not touch him now, and he began to move smoothly through the exercises that had sustained him in another life: the Shooting Bow, the Locust, the Peacock and the Crow.

His muscles stretched, his body loose, he began a series of dance-like movements, leaping and twirling, always in perfect balance. Warm sweat replaced the cold sheen of rain upon his naked flesh.

Dayan's face appeared in his mind. Not in death as he had last seen her, but bright and smiling as they swam together in the marble pool of the palace garden. His stomach tightened. His face betrayed no emotion, save for a tightness now around the eyes. Drawing in a deep breath he moved to the edge of the parapet and ran his hand along the foot-wide ledge. Water droplets clung to the smooth stone, making it greasy. The man known as Lantern vaulted to the ledge and stood some seventy feet above the hard rock upon which the monastery had been built. The narrow ledge ran straight for some thirty feet, before a sharp, right-angled turn.

He studied the ledge for a few moments, then closed his eyes. Blind now he ran forward then leapt high, twisting his body through a tight pirouette. His right foot landed firmly on the ledge and did not slip. His left caught the lip of the right angle. He swayed, then righted himself. Opening his eyes, he looked down once more on the rocky ground far below.

He had judged it perfectly. A small part of his mind wished that he had not.

Turning, he leapt lightly back to the roof and donned his robes.

If it is death you want, he told himself, it will be coming soon.

For two days the thirty-five priests remained mostly within the grounds of the old Cobalsin castle and its outbuildings, only venturing to the meadows east of the town. Here they tended the three flocks of rare sheep and goats from whose wool, and the garments they fashioned from it, the priests earned enough to support themselves and the headquarters of the church in the Tantrian capital, Mellicane.

The town itself remained ominously quiet. The bodies of the hanged foreigners were removed and the soldiers departed. Many among the priests hoped that the terror was at an end, and that life would soon return to normal. Spring was coming, and there was much to do, gathering the wild flowers to provide the dyes for cloaks and tunics, purchasing and preparing the secret blends of oils that would make the clothes they crafted waterproof, and help to maintain the depth of colour. The garments made here were highly prized by the nobles and the rich of the cities. Lambing season was also in full flow, and the spring cull was due. Merchants would soon be arriving to buy meat and deliver produce and supplies for the coming season.

The mood in the monastery was lighter than it had been for weeks, and the injured Brother Labberan had overcome his fever and – it was hoped – would soon be on the road to recovery.

Not everyone, however, believed the worst was over.

On the second morning Brother Lantern sought out the abbot.

'We should leave and head west,' he said. Abbot Cethelin, an elderly priest with wispy white hair and gentle eyes, beckoned Brother Lantern to follow him to his study in the high tower. It was a small room, sparsely furnished with two hard-backed chairs, a long writing desk and a single, narrow window, overlooking the town.

'Why do you wish us to leave, Brother?' asked the abbot, gesturing for Lantern to take a seat.

'Death is coming, Holy Brother.'

'I know this,' answered the abbot softly. 'But why do you wish us to leave?'

Brother Lantern shook his head. 'Forgive me, but your answer makes no sense. This is merely a respite. The storm is coming. Even now the rabble rousers will be encouraging the townsfolk to come here and massacre us. Soon – tomorrow or the next day – crowds will begin to form outside. We are being cast in the role of enemy.

We are being demonized. When they break through the gates they will cut us all down. They will rage through these buildings like a fire.'

'Once again, Younger Brother, I ask: why do you wish us to leave?'

'You want to die here?'

'What I *want* is not the concern. This is a place of spiritual harmony. We exist to offer love and understanding in a world too often bathed in blood and hatred. We do not add to that suffering. Our purpose is enlightenment, Younger Brother. We are seeking to enhance the journey of our souls as they yearn to be united with the Source of All Things. We have no fear of death; it is merely another step of the journey.'

'If this building was ablaze, Holy Brother, would you sit within it and wait for the flames to devour you?'

'No, Lantern. I would take myself to a place of safety. That, however, does not equate with the situation we are facing. Fire is inanimate and non-discerning. We are ordered to offer love in the face of hate, and forgiveness in the face of pain. We cannot run away when danger threatens. That would be like saying we have no faith in our own philosophy. How can we obey our teachings if we run in the face of hate?'

'It is not a philosophy I can share,' said Lantern.

'I know. That is one of the reasons you cannot find what you seek.'

'You do not know what I seek,' answered Lantern, a touch of anger in his voice.

'The White Wolf,' said the older man, softly. 'But you do not know what it is, or why you seek it. Until you do, what you seek will always be lost to you. Why did you come here, Younger Brother?'

'I am beginning to wonder that myself.' His keen blue eyes held to the abbot's gaze. 'How much do you know of me?'

'I know that you are a man rooted in this world of flesh. You have a keen mind, Lantern, and great intelligence. I know that when you walk through the town the women admire you, and smile at you. I know how hard it has been for you to obey the rule of celibacy. What else do you wish to hear?'

'I have tried to be a good priest,' said the tall man, with a sigh. 'I have immersed myself in this world of prayer and kindness. I thought that, as time passed, I would come to understand it. Yet I do not. Last summer we risked our lives in the plague to help these townspeople. Two of the men whose lives we saved took part in the beating of Brother Labberan. One of the women whose child we brought back from the brink of death was baying for her husband to break Labberan's face. They are scum.'

The abbot smiled. 'How simple love would be, Younger Brother, if we only had to bestow it on those who deserved it. Yet what would it be worth? If you gave a poor man a silver coin then that would be a gift. If you expected him to pay you back, then that would make it a loan. We do not loan our love, Lantern. We give it freely.'

'And what will be achieved if you let them kill you? Will that add one spark of love to the world?'

The abbot shrugged. 'Perhaps. Perhaps not.'

They sat in silence for a few moments. 'How did you know of the White Wolf?' asked Lantern. 'It is only in my dreams.'

'How do *you* know it *is* a wolf,' countered the abbot, 'when you have never seen it?'

'That does not answer my question.'

'I have a gift, Lantern. A small gift. For example, as we sit here now I can see you, but I also see glimpses of your thoughts and memories. They flicker around you. Two young women – very beautiful – one with golden hair, the other dark. They are opposites; one is gentle and loving, the other fierce and passionate. I see a slender man, tall with dyed yellow hair and a womanly face.' Cethelin closed his eyes. 'I see a weary man, kneeling in a garden, tending plants. A good man. Not young.' He sighed and looked at Lantern. 'You knew these people?'

'Yes.'

'And you carry them in your heart.'

'Always.'

'Along with the White Wolf.'

'It seems so.'

At that moment came the sound of the bell, heralding morning prayer. The abbot rose.

'We will talk again, Brother Lantern. May the Source bless you.'

'And you, Elder Brother,' answered Lantern, rising from his chair and bowing.

There was so much about the world that Braygan failed to comprehend. People mystified him. How could men gaze upon the wonders of the mountains, or the glories of the night sky, and not understand the pettiness of human ambition? Fearing death, as all men did, how could they so easily visit death upon others? Braygan could not stop thinking about the hanging bodies he had seen before the burning buildings. They had not merely been strung up by their necks. They had been beaten and tortured first. The young priest could not imagine how anyone could find pleasure in such deeds. And yet they surely had, for it was said there was much laughter in the crowd as the hapless victims were dragged to their places of execution.

The young priest sat at the bedside of Brother Labberan, spoon-feeding him vegetable broth. Occasionally he would stop and dab a napkin to Labberan's mouth. The left side of the older priest's face was swollen and numb, and the broth dribbled from his mouth to his chin.

'Are you feeling a little stronger, Brother?' asked Braygan.

'A little,' answered Labberan, his words slurred. Splints had been applied to both of his forearms, and his hands were also swollen and blue with bruises. There was an unhealthy sheen on the man's thin face. Close to sixty years old Labberan was not strong, and the beating had been severe. Braygan saw a tear form, and slowly trickle down the old priest's face.

'Are you in pain still, Brother?'

Labberan shook his head. Braygan put aside the bowl of broth. Labberan closed his eyes and drifted off to sleep. The young priest rose silently from the bedside and left the small room. He took the broth bowl to the lower kitchens and cleaned it. Several other priests were there, preparing the midday meal. Brother Anager approached him.

'How is he?' asked the little man. 'Did my broth sit well with him? It was always his favourite.'

'He ate well, Anager. I am sure he liked it.'

31

Anager nodded and seemed relieved. Small and round-shouldered, he had a nervous tic that caused his head to twitch as he spoke. It was most disconcerting to Braygan. 'It was the boys, you know,' said Anager. 'They hurt him the worst.'

'The boys?'

'His boys. From the church school.'

Braygan was nonplussed. Two days a week Labberan would travel in to the community hall, offering lessons in writing and arithmetic. He would also tell stories of the Source and His wonders. Teaching children was Labberan's joy. 'Our future lies with the young,' he would say. 'They are the foundations. Only through the young can we hope to eradicate hatred.'

'What about his boys?' asked Braygan.

'After Labberan was beaten by the mob some of the children came to where he lay and kicked him. You think it is over now, Brother Braygan?'

'Yes. Yes, I think so. Everything seems calmer.'

'It is these Arbiters, you know,' said Anager. 'They stir up trouble. Is it true that Brother Lantern thrashed one of them?'

'He did not thrash anyone. The man was clumsy and fell badly.'

'It is said that there have been many killings in the capital,' said Anager, blinking rapidly. He lowered his voice. 'It is even said they might loose the beasts. What if they come here?'

'Why would they allow the beasts to come here? The war is in the south and east.'

'Yes. Yes, you are right. Of course you are. They won't send beasts here. I saw one, you know. I went to the Games earlier this year. Ghastly. Huge. Four men went in against it. It killed them all. Horrible. Part bear, they said. Dreadful. A monstrosity. It is so wrong, Braygan. So wrong.'

Braygan agreed, and thought it best not to point out that priests were forbidden to watch blood sports.

He left the kitchens and made his way up to the lower hall and out into the vegetable gardens. Several of the brothers were working there. As Braygan arrived they asked after Brother Labberan. He told them he thought him a little better today, though a part of his mind considered that to be wishful thinking. Brother Labberan was a broken man in more ways than one. For an hour Braygan

32

worked alongside them, planting tubers taken carefully from large brown sacks. Then he was summoned to the abbot's study.

Braygan was nervous as he stood outside the door. He wondered which of his many errors had been pointed out to the abbot. He was supposed to have organized the mending of the chapel roof, but the new lead for the flashing had not arrived. Then there was the error with the dyes. It had not been his fault. The sack had split as he was adding the yellow. It should only have been two measures. More like ten had spilled into the vat. The result was a horrible, unusable orange colour, which had to be flushed away. It wouldn't have happened had Brother Naslyn not borrowed the measuring jug.

Braygan tapped at the door, then entered. The abbot was sitting by a small fire. He bade Braygan take a seat. 'Are you well, Younger Brother?' he asked.

'I am well, Elder Brother.'

'Are you content?'

Braygan did not understand the question. 'Content? Er . . . in what way?'

'With your life here.'

'Oh yes, Elder Brother. I love the life.'

'What is it that you love about it, Braygan?'

'To serve the Source and to . . . and to help people.'

'Yes, that is why we are here,' said the old man, looking at him keenly. 'That is what we are expected to say. But what do *you* love about it?'

'I feel safe here, Elder Brother. I feel this is where I belong.'

'And is that why you came to us? To feel safe?'

'In part, yes. Is that wrong?'

'Did you feel safe when the man attacked you in the town?'

'No, Elder Brother. I was very frightened.'

The abbot looked away, staring into the fire. He seemed lost in thought and Braygan said nothing. At last Cethelin spoke again.

'How is Brother Labberan faring?'

'He is not improving as fast as he should. His spirits are very low. His wounds are healing, though. I am sure that in a few days he will begin to recover.'

The abbot returned his gaze to the fire. 'Brother Lantern thinks we should leave. He believes the mob will gather once more and seek to do us harm.'

'Do *you* think that?' whispered Braygan, his heart beginning to pound. 'It cannot be true,' he went on, before the abbot could answer. 'No, it is getting calmer now. I think that the attack on Brother Labberan was an aberration. They will have had time to think about the evil of their deeds. They will understand that we are not enemies. We are their friends. Do you not think so?'

'You come from a large town, don't you, Braygan?' said the abbot.

'Yes, Elder Brother.'

'Did many people own dogs there?'

'Yes.'

'Were there sheep in fields close to the town?'

'Yes, Elder Brother,' replied Braygan, mystified.

'I came from such a town. Men would walk their dogs close to the sheep, and there would be no trouble. Occasionally, though, a few dogs would gather together, and run loose. If they went into a field of sheep they would suddenly turn vicious and cause great harm. You have seen this?'

'Yes, Elder Brother. The pack mentality asserts itself. They forget their training, their domesticity, and they turn . . .' Braygan stammered to a halt. 'You think the people in the town are like those dogs?'

'Of course they are, Braygan. They have come together and indulged in what they are led to believe is righteous anger. They have killed. They feel empowered. They feel mighty. Like the dogs they are glorying in their strength. Aye, and in their cruelty. These have been harsh years – crop failures, plagues, and droughts. The war with Datia has sapped the nation's resources. People are frightened and they are angry. They need to find someone to blame for their hardships and their losses. The church leaders spoke out against the war. Many have been branded as traitors. Some have been executed. The church itself is now accused of aiding the enemy. Of *being* the enemy. The mob will come, Braygan. With hatred in their hearts and murder on their minds.'

'Then Brother Lantern is right. We must leave.'

'You have not yet taken your final vows. You are free to do as you wish. As indeed is Brother Lantern.'

'Then *you* are not leaving, Elder Brother?'

'The Order will remain here, for this is our home and the people of the town are our flock. We will not desert them in their hour of need. Think on these things, Braygan. You have perhaps a few days to consider your position.'

CHAPTER TWO

ABBOT CETHELIN FELT HEAVY OF HEART AS THE YOUNG PRIEST, Braygan, left the study. He liked the boy, and knew him to be good-hearted and kind. There was no malice in Braygan, no dark corners in his soul.

Cethelin moved to the window, pushing it open and breathing in the cool Tantrian mountain air.

He could taste no madness upon it, nor sense any sorcery within it. Yet it was there. The world was slipping into insanity, as if some unseen plague was floating into every home and castle, every croft and hovel. A long time ago, close to his home, Cethelin recalled seeing a host of rodents scampering towards the distant cliffs. He and his father had walked to the clifftops, and watched as the rodents hurled themselves into the sea. The scene had amazed the boy he had been. He had asked his father why these little creatures were drowning themselves. His father had no answer. It happened every twenty or so years, he had said. They just do it.

There was something chilling in that phrase. *They just do it.*

Mass extinction should have a better reason. Now, at sixty-seven, Cethelin still pondered the reasons behind the madness – not, this time, of rodents, but of men. Had it begun when Ventria invaded the Drenai? Or had that merely been a symptom of the madness? War had spread like an unchecked bush fire through the heartlands of this eastern continent. Civil war still raged in Ventria, as a result of the Ventrian defeat at Skeln five years before. Rebellions had spread throughout Tantria, only to be followed by war with the country's eastern neighbours Dospilis and Datia – a war that continued still.

In Naashan to the southeast the Witch Queen's forces had invaded Panthia and Opal, and even the peaceful Phocians had been drawn in to help defend against the invaders. To the north-west the Nadir had spread into Pelucid, crossing the vast deserts of Namib to raze and plunder the cities of the coast. War was everywhere, and in its wake came the carrion birds of hatred, terror, plague and despair.

Cethelin felt the last worst of all. To spend a lifetime offering love to all, only to see it brutally transformed and twisted – obscenely reshaped into a blind, unreasoning hatred – was hard to bear. His thoughts swung to Brother Labberan. The children he had nurtured had turned on him, kicking and screeching.

Cethelin took a deep breath, and fought for calm.

Kneeling on the bare boards of the study floor the abbot prayed for a while. Then he rose and walked down to the lower levels and sat for an hour at Labberan's bedside. He spoke soothingly, but the old priest was not comforted.

Cethelin was tired by the time he climbed again to his own rooms, and he took to his narrow bed. It was still early afternoon, but Cethelin found that short naps at such times helped maintain his vigour. Not so today. He could not sleep, and lay upon his back, his mind unable to relax. He found himself thinking of Lantern and Braygan; opposites in so many ways. I should have sent Lantern across the water to found an order of the Thirty, he thought. He would have made a fine warrior priest.

A *fine warrior priest*.

A contradiction in terms, thought Cethelin sadly.

Unable to take comfort from rest he rose from his bed and made his way to the east wing of the monastery, moving past the kitchens and through the silent weaving rooms. Mounting the circular steps he climbed to the First Library. His right knee was aching by the time he reached the top, and he felt his heart thudding painfully.

There were several priests present, studying ancient tomes. They rose as he entered and bowed deeply. He smiled at them, and bade them continue with their reading. Moving through the aisles, he ducked beneath the last arch and entered the reconstruction room. Here also there were priests, meticulously copying decaying manuscripts or scrolls. So engrossed were they in their work they failed to notice him as he continued through to the eastern reading room. Here he found Brother Lantern sitting by a window. He was reading a yellowed parchment.

He glanced up and Cethelin felt the power in his sapphire gaze. 'What are you reading?' asked the abbot, sitting opposite the younger man. He winced as he sat, then rubbed his aching knee. Lantern noticed his pain.

'The apothecary said he would have some fresh juniper tisane for your arthritis within the month,' Lantern told him, then suddenly smiled and shook his head.

'We may yet have another month,' said Cethelin, sensing the irony that caused the smile. 'If the Source wills it.' He pointed to the parchment and repeated his question.

'It is a listing of little-known Datian myths,' replied Lantern.

'Ah. The Resurrectionists. I recall them. The stories are not Datian in origin. They come from the Elder Days, the days of Missael. The hero Enshibar was resurrected after his faithful friend, Kaodas, carried a lock of his hair and a fragment of bone to the Realm of the Dead. There the wizards grew Enshibar a new body and summoned his spirit back from the hall of heroes. It is a fine tale, and resonates through many cultures.'

'Most myths contain a grain of truth,' said Lantern warily.

'Indeed they do, Younger Brother. Is that why you carry a lock of hair and a fragment of bone within the locket round your neck?'

For a moment only Lantern's sapphire eyes glinted with anger. 'You see a great deal, Elder Brother. You see into men's dreams, and you see through metal. Perhaps you should be reading the dreams of the townsfolk.'

'I *know* their dreams, Lantern. They want food for their tables, and warmth in the winter. They want their children to have better and safer lives than they can provide. The world is a huge and terrifying place for them. They are desperate for simple answers to life's problems. They fear the war will come here and take away all that they have. Then the Arbiters tell them it is all our fault. If we were dead and gone everything would be fine again. The sun would shine on their crops, and all dangers cease. However, at this moment I am more interested in your dreams than theirs.'

Lantern looked away. 'You do not believe in this . . . this hidden temple of the Resurrectionists?'

'I did not say that I disbelieved. There are many strange places in the world, and a host of talented wizards and magickers. Perhaps there is one who can help you. On the other hand perhaps you should let the dead rest.'

'I cannot.'

'It is said that all men need a quest, Lantern. Perhaps this was always meant to be yours.' He leaned back in his chair. 'If I asked a favour of you would you do it?'

'Of course.'

'Do not be so swift, young man. I might ask you to put aside your search.'

'Anything but that. Tell me what you need.'

'As of this moment I need nothing. Perhaps tomorrow. Have you visited Labberan?'

'No. I am not much of a comforter, Elder Brother.'

'Go anyway, Younger Brother.' The abbot sighed and pushed himself to his feet. 'And now I will leave you to your reading. Try to locate the Pelucidian Chronicles. I think you will find them interesting. As I recall there is a description of a mysterious temple, and an ageless goddess who is said to dwell there.'

It was late when Skilgannon entered the small room where Brother Labberan was being tended. Another priest was already beside him. The man looked up and Skilgannon saw it was Brother Naslyn. The black-bearded monk had the look of a warrior. A laconic man, his conversation was mostly monosyllabic, which suited Skilgannon. Of all the priests he had to work alongside he found Naslyn the easiest to bear. The powerful brother rose, gently stroked Labberan's brow, then moved past Skilgannon. 'He's tired,' he said.

'I will not stay long,' Skilgannon told him.

Moving to the bedside he gazed down at the broken man. 'How much do you remember?' he asked, seating himself on a stool at the bedside.

'Only the hatred and the pain,' muttered Labberan. 'I do not wish to talk of it.' He turned his face away and Skilgannon felt a touch of annoyance. What was he doing here? He had no friendship with Labberan – nor indeed with any of the priests. And, as he had told Cethelin, he had never developed any talent as a comforter. He took a deep breath and prepared to leave. As he rose Labberan looked at him, and Skilgannon saw tears in the old man's eyes. 'I loved those children,' he said.

Skilgannon sank back to the stool. 'Betrayal is hard to take,' he said. The silence grew.

'I hear you fought one of the Arbiters.'

'It was not a fight. The man was a clumsy fool.'

'I wish I could have fought.'

Skilgannon looked into the old man's face and saw defeat and despair. He had seen that look before, back on the battlefields of Naashan four years ago. The closeness of defeat at Castran had seemed like the end of the world. Retreating soldiers had stumbled back into the forests, their faces grey, their hearts overburdened with fear and disillusionment.

Skilgannon had been just twenty-one then, full of fire and belief. Against all the odds he had regrouped several hundred fighting men and led them in a counter charge against the advancing foe, hurling them back. He gazed now into the tortured features of the elderly priest and saw again the faces of the demoralized soldiers he had rebuilt and carried to glory. 'You *are* a fighter, Labberan,' he said softly. 'You struggle against the evil of the world. You seek to make it a better and more loving place.'

'And I failed. Even my children turned against me.'

'Not all of them.'

'What do you mean?'

'When did you lose consciousness?'

'In the street, when they were kicking me.'

40

'Ah, I see,' said Skilgannon. 'Then you do not recall being dragged into the schoolroom?'

'No.'

'You were taken there by some of your pupils. They pulled you inside, and locked the door. One of them then ran here to tell the abbot of your injuries. Because of the riot we could not reach you immediately. You were tended by some of the children. They covered you with blankets. It was very brave of them,' he added. 'Brother Naslyn and I came to you before the dawn and carried you back. Several of the children had remained with you.'

'I did not know.' Labberan smiled. 'Do you know any of their names?'

'The boy who brought us to you was called Rabalyn.'

Labberan smiled. 'An unruly boy, argumentative and naughty. Good heart, though. Who else?'

'A slender girl with black hair and green eyes. She had a three-legged dog with her.'

'That would be Kalia. She nursed the hound back to health after it fought the wolves. We all thought it would die.'

'I do not recall the others. There were three or four of them, but they left when we arrived. But the boy, Rabalyn, had a swollen eye. Kalia told me he got it when he fought the other boys attacking you. He beat them off. Well, he and the three-legged dog.'

The old man sighed, then relaxed and closed his eyes. Skilgannon sat for a while, until he realized the old priest was sleeping. Silently he left the room and walked out into the night. As he crossed the courtyard he saw Abbot Cethelin standing below the arch of the gate. Skilgannon bowed to him.

'He feels better now, does he not?' said the abbot.

'I believe so.'

'You told him about the children who helped him?'

'Yes.'

'Good.'

'Why did you not tell him? Or someone else?'

'I would have, had you not. You still believe they are all scum, Lantern, these townspeople?'

Skilgannon smiled. 'A few children helped him. Good for them.

41

They will not however stop the mob when it comes here. But, no, I do not think they are all scum. There are two thousand people living in the town. The mob numbers some six hundred. I make little distinction, however, between those who commit evil and those who stand by and do nothing.'

'You were a warrior, Lantern. Such men are not renowned for understanding the infinite shades of grey that govern the actions of men. Black and white are your colours.'

'Scholars tend to overcomplicate matters,' said Skilgannon. 'If a man runs at you with a sword it would be foolish to spend time wondering what led him to such action. Was his childhood scarred by a cruel father? Did his wife leave him for another man? Was he perhaps misinformed about your intentions, and therefore has attacked you in error?' He laughed. 'Warriors need black and white, Elder Brother. Shades of grey would kill them.'

'True,' admitted the abbot, 'and yet a greater understanding that there *are* shades of grey would prevent many wars beginning.'

'But not all,' said Skilgannon, his smile fading. 'We are what we are, Elder Brother. Man is a hunter, a killer. We build great cities, and yet we live just like the wolf. The strongest of us dominate the weakest. We might call our leaders kings or generals, but the effect is the same. We create the wolf pack, and the very nature of that pack is to hunt and to kill. War, therefore, becomes inevitable.'

Cethelin sighed. 'The analogy is a sad one, Lantern – though it is true. Why then did you decide to remove yourself from the pack?'

'My reasons were selfish, Elder Brother.'

'Not entirely, my boy. I pray that time will prove that to you.'

At fifteen Rabalyn didn't care about wars and battles to the east, nor about who was right and who was wrong regarding the causes. These were enormous issues that concerned him not at all. Rabalyn's thoughts were far more focused. The town of Skepthia was all he had ever known, and he thought he had learned the rules of behaviour necessary to survive in such a place. True, he often broke those rules, stealing occasional apples from Carin's shop, or sneaking onto the estates of the absent lord to poach pheasants or hunt rabbits. If approached later and questioned he would also lie shamelessly, even though Brother Labberan taught that lies were a sin against Heaven. Broadly, however, Rabalyn had believed he understood how his small society operated. Yet in the last week he had witnessed appalling scenes that made no sense to him.

Adults had gathered in mobs, screeching and calling for blood. People who had worked and lived in the town were suddenly called traitors, dragged from their homes and beaten. The soldiers of the Watch stood by, doing nothing. Yet these same soldiers berated him for killing pheasants. Now they ignored the killing of people.

Brother Labberan was probably right to have called him an idiot. 'Stupid boy, are you incapable of learning?' It had always seemed such fun to irritate Brother Labberan. He would never raise a hand – not even to lightly slap a child. It did not feel like fun now in his memory.

Rabalyn rubbed at his swollen eye. It was still painful, but at least now he could see again, although bright sunshine still made the eye water. Todhe had caught him with a wicked blow just as he was pulling Bron away from the unconscious priest. With fury born of pain Rabalyn had pushed Bron to the ground, then swung and hammered a punch into Todhe's face. The blow had been a good one, and had smashed the other boy's lips against his teeth. Even so the powerful Todhe would have beaten him senseless had the dog not rushed in and bitten his calf. Rabalyn smiled at the memory. Todhe had screamed in pain. Kalia had called the dog back and Todhe had limped away with his friends. He had turned at the alleyway arch and screamed a threat back at Rabalyn: 'I'll get you for this – and I'll see the dog is killed too.'

He and Kalia and several others had pulled Brother Labberan into the small schoolroom and locked the door. The old priest was in an awful state. Kalia had begun to cry, and this perturbed the three-legged hound, which started to howl.

'What do we do when they come back?' asked Arren, a chubby boy from the northern quarter. Rabalyn saw the fear in his eyes.

'You ought to get home,' he said.

Arren fidgeted and looked uncomfortable. 'We can't leave Brother Labberan,' he said.

'I'll go to the castle,' said Rabalyn. 'The priests will come for him.'

'I can't fight Todhe,' said Arren. 'If he comes back he'll be very angry.'

'He won't come back,' said Rabalyn, trying to sound decisive. 'Keep the door locked behind me. I'll be back as soon as I can.'

'Did he mean what he said, do you think?' asked Kalia. 'About killing Jesper?'

'No,' lied Rabalyn. 'Wait for me. And find some blankets to cover old Labbers. He's shivering.'

With that Rabalyn set off through the town, heading out towards the old bridge and the long climb to the monastery. He heard the mob off to the west, and saw the flames starting. Then he ran like the wind.

He had been taken to the abbot, told him about old Labbers. The abbot ordered food brought for him and instructed him to wait. The hours wore on. A monk gave him a cold poultice to hold over his eye, and then at last a tall, frightening priest had come and sat beside him. Black-haired and hard-eyed, the man had introduced himself as Brother Lantern. He had questioned Rabalyn about the attack, then he and another monk had walked with Rabalyn back to the schoolroom, skirting the rioting mob.

That had been two days ago, and no-one had heard since whether old Labbers was alive or dead. Todhe and his friends had twice tried to ambush Rabalyn, but he had been too swift for them, darting away into alleyways and scaling walls.

Now he sat high on the northern hillside, near the old ruins of the watchtower. Kalia's crippled dog was squatting beside him. Todhe's father, the councilman Raseev, had put out an order for the hound to be killed. Kalia had brought Jesper to Rabalyn. The girl was distraught and Rabalyn had reluctantly agreed to hide the hound and brought him up to the watchtower. He didn't know what to do next. A three-legged dog was not easy to hide.

Rabalyn stroked the hound's large head, scratching behind its spiked ears. It pushed in towards him, licking his face, and laying the stump of its amputated right foreleg on Rabalyn's lap. 'You should have bitten him harder,' said Rabalyn. 'It was just a nip. Should have taken his leg off.'

From his high vantage point Rabalyn saw a group of youngsters emerging from the houses far below. One of them pointed up towards him. Rabalyn swore, then swiftly tethered a lead round Jesper's neck and led the hound off down the far slope.

If he skirted the town, and waded across the river at its narrowest point, he could reach the monastery by dusk. They'd protect Jesper, he thought.

Abbot Cethelin sat in his study, and in the lantern light pored over the ancient map. It was of thin hide, two feet square, the symbols and lines of mountains and rivers carefully etched in the leather and then filled with gold leaf. As with many pieces from the pre-Ventrian era, what it lacked in accuracy it more than made up for in beauty. As he stared at the map he found himself wishing he had been blessed with the gift of spiritual flight, like his old friend Vintar. Then he could have floated free of the monastery and up into the night sky, to stare down over lands he could now only imagine through the delicate tracing of gold upon leather.

But that was not his gift. Cethelin's talent was to dream visions, and to sometimes see within them faint threads – like the gold on the map. He could sense the malignant and the benevolent, constantly vying for supremacy. The large affairs of men, with their wars and their horror, were identical to the battles that raged in the valleys of each human soul. All men had a capacity for kindness and cruelty, love and hate, beauty and horror.

There were some mystics who maintained Man was little more than a puppet, his strings being tugged and manipulated by gods and demons. There were others who talked of fate and destiny, where every action of men was somehow pre-ordained and written. Cethelin struggled to disbelieve both these philosophies of despair. It was not easy.

In some ways he wished he could embrace the simplistic. Evil deeds could then be laid at the door of evil men. Unfortunately his intellect would not allow him to believe it. In his long life he had seen that, far too often, evil deeds were committed by men who deemed themselves good; indeed *were* good by the mores of their

45

cultures. The Emperor Gorben had built Greater Ventria in order to bring peace and stability to a region cursed by incessant wars. To do this he had invaded all the surrounding lands, razing cities and destroying armies, plundering farms and treasuries. In the end he had his empire, and it was at peace. He also had an enormous standing army that needed to be paid. In order to pay it he had to expand the empire, and had invaded the lands of the Drenai. Here his dreams had been crushed by the defeat at Skeln Pass. Now everything he had built was falling apart, and the region was descending once more into endless little wars.

No wonder the people of the town were frightened. Armies tended to plunder towns, and the war was getting closer. Only two months ago a battle had been fought not forty miles away.

Cethelin moved to the window and pushed it open. The night breeze was cool, the stars shining brightly in a clear sky. Flames were flickering again in the town's northern quarter. Some other poor soul was watching his house burn, he thought sadly.

A dog barked in the courtyard below. Cethelin leaned out of the window and gazed down. A dark-haired youth, in a pale linen shirt and black leggings, was squatting in the gateway, a black hound beside him. Cethelin threw a cloak around his thin shoulders and left his study, descending the long staircase to the lower levels.

As he walked out the hound turned towards him and growled. It lurched forward in a faintly comical manner, off balance and part hopping. Cethelin knelt and held out his hand to the beast. It cocked its head and eyed him warily. 'What do you want?' the abbot asked the youth, recognizing him as the young man who had helped Brother Labberan.

'Need a place for the dog, Father. Councillor Raseev ordered it put down.'

'Why?'

'It bit Todhe when he was kicking old Labbers . . . begging your pardon, Brother Labberan.'

'Did it hurt him badly?'

'No. Just a nip to the calf.'

'I'm glad to hear it. Now why did you think we could find a home for a three-legged dog?'

'Figured you owed him,' said the boy.

46

'For saving Brother Labberan?'

'Yes.'

'Is he useful?'

'He fights wolves, Father. He's not afraid of anything.'

'But you are,' observed Cethelin, noting that the youth kept casting nervous glances back through the open gate.

'Todhe's looking for me. He's big, Father. And he has friends with him.'

'Are you seeking sanctuary too?'

'No, not me. I'm too fast for them. I want to get back to my aunt's house. Looks like they've set fires again.'

'Who is your aunt?'

'Aunt Athyla. She comes to church. Big woman. Sings loud and out of tune.'

Cethelin laughed. 'I know her. Laundrywoman and occasional midwife. She has a sweet soul.'

'Aye, she does.'

'What of your parents?'

'They left to find work in Mellicane years ago. Said they'd send for me and my sister. They didn't. My sister died last year when the plague struck. Me and Aunt Athyla thought we'd get it, but we didn't. Brother Labberan gave us herbs and such. Told us to clean out the house and keep the rats away.'

'It was a harsh time,' said Cethelin.

'The Arbiters say the priests caused the plague.'

'I know. Apparently we also caused the war, and the harvest failures. Why is it that you don't believe the stories?'

The youth shrugged. 'Old Labbers, I expect. Always talking about love and such. Can't see him causing plagues. Makes no sense. Still, no-one cares what I think.'

Cethelin looked into Rabalyn's dark eyes. He saw strength there, and compassion. In that moment he also caught a glimpse of Rabalyn's memories: a woman being beaten by a harsh man, a small child fading towards death as Rabalyn sat by the bedside weeping. 'I care, Rabalyn. Old Labbers – as you call him – cares. I shall take care of the dog until such time as you return for him.'

'Jesper's not my dog. Belongs to Kalia. She brought him to me

47

and asked me to hide him. When all this blows over I'll get her to come and see you.'

'Walk with care, young man.'

'You too, Father. Best lock this gate, I'd say.'

'A locked gate will not keep out a mob. Goodnight to you, Rabalyn. You are a good lad.'

Cethelin watched as the boy sped off. The dog gave an awkward bound as if to follow him. Cethelin called to him softly. 'Here, Jesper! Are you hungry, boy? Let us go to the kitchen and see what we can find.'

Rabalyn returned the way he had come, wading across the shallows of the river and making his way through the trees and up the old watchtower hill. From here he could see the fires burning in the northern quarter. It was here that most of the foreigners had settled, including fat Arren and his family. There were merchants from Drenan, and a few shops run by Ventrian traders. The mob, however, were more concerned with those whose family ties were in the east, in Dospilis or Datia. Both these nations were now at war with Tantria.

Rabalyn squatted in the ruins, his keen eyes scanning the area at the base of the hill. He doubted Todhe and his friends would be waiting for him now, not with another riot looming. They would be out chanting and screaming at those they now dubbed traitors. Many of the houses in the northern quarter were empty. Scores of families had left in the last few days, heading west towards Mellicane. Rabalyn could not understand why any foreigners had chosen to stay.

A cool wind blew across the hilltop. Rabalyn's leggings and shoes were wet from wading the river and he shivered with the cold. Time to be getting home. Aunt Athyla would be worried, and she would not sleep until he was safe in his bed. The abbot had called her a sweet soul. This was true, but she was also massively irritating. She fussed over Rabalyn as if he was still three years old, and her conversation was absurdly repetitive. Every time he left the little cottage she would ask: 'Are you going to be warm enough?' If he voiced any concerns about life, schooling or future plans, she would say: 'I don't know about that. It's enough to have food on the table today.' Her days were spent cleaning other people's sheets and clothes. In the evenings she would unravel discarded woollen garments and create balls of faded wool. Then she would knit scores of squares, which would later be fashioned into blankets. Some she sold. Others she gave away to the poorhouse. Aunt Athyla was never idle.

The riots had unnerved her. When the first killings had taken place Rabalyn had run home and told her. At first she had disbelieved him, but when the truth was established Athyla refused to talk of it with the boy. 'It will all settle down,' she said. 'Best not to get involved.'

That evening she had sat with her balls of wool, looking old and grey. Rabalyn had moved alongside her. 'Are you all right, Aunt?'

'We don't have any foreign blood,' she said. 'It will be all right. Everything will be all right.' Her face was drawn and tight, just as it had been when Lesha had died – a mixture of bafflement and sorrow.

Rabalyn left the hilltop and made his way down towards the town.

The streets were deserted. He could hear the mob far off, chanting and screaming. The wind changed and he smelt smoke in the air. Pausing in a darkened alleyway arch he peered out across the short open stretch between the houses and his aunt's little cottage. No-one was in sight, but Rabalyn decided to take no chances. Squatting down in the shadows he scanned the area. There was a dry stone wall running along the north side of the cottage, and a line of scrub bushes around the gate. Rabalyn waited silently. Just as he was convinced there was no danger he saw someone rise briefly from behind the bushes and creep across to the wagon outside the baker's house. It looked like Todhe's friend Bron. A touch of anger flared in Rabalyn. He was hungry and tired, and his clothes were still wet. He wanted nothing more than to get inside the cottage and warm himself by the fire.

Backing down the alley he ran through Market Street, cutting through the smith's yard. Searching around he found a foot-long rod of rust-speckled iron in a pile of discarded metal. Hefting it he crept on, climbing a low wall and emerging between two lines of houses. From here he could see two young men crouched behind the miller's wagon. One was indeed Bron. The other was Cadras, whose father worked for Todhe's family as a general servant. Cadras was a decent enough lad, neither malicious nor vengeful. But he was malleable and followed Todhe's lead in everything. Rabalyn waited. After a while Bron ducked down and crept back to the hedge outside Aunt Athyla's cottage. Rabalyn saw Todhe emerge and haul Bron down. The iron rod felt heavy in Rabalyn's hand. It was comforting to be armed, and yet he did not want to use the weapon. Todhe's father, Raseev, virtually ran the council and any harm to his son would be swiftly, and harshly, punished.

Rabalyn decided to outwait them.

Which might have worked had a fourth youth not crept up behind Rabalyn and leapt upon him, pinning his arms.

'He's over here!' shouted the youth. Rabalyn recognized the voice as that of Archas, Bron's older brother. Rabalyn leaned forward, then threw his head back into Archas's face. The hold round his chest loosened. Rabalyn squirmed clear, then spun and hit Archas across the cheek with the iron rod. The youth was thrown from his feet.

Rabalyn could hear the others pelting towards him. He should have run, but his blood was up now, and a raging fury swept through him. With a cry he leapt to meet them. The iron rod cracked against Bron's skull, causing the youth to stumble. Rabalyn ducked to his right and swung the rod again – this time at Todhe. The big youth threw up his arm to protect his head. The rod hammered against the upraised limb causing Todhe to scream in pain. A fist struck Rabalyn in the back. He stumbled and swung towards the new assailant. It was Cadras. Rabalyn hit him in the belly, then leapt in and head-butted him. Cadras cried out and fell. Rabalyn backed away from them, holding the rod high. Todhe was already running away. Bron had struggled to a sitting position and was looking dazed. Suddenly he leaned forward and vomited. Cadras pushed himself to his knees and put a hand to his smashed nose. Blood was running over his mouth and chin. Rabalyn stood looking at them both. Beyond the injured pair Archas was lying unconscious. Dropping the iron rod Rabalyn moved to where the youth lay on his face. Gently turning him he was relieved to hear Archas groan. 'Lie still,' said Rabalyn. 'Gather your wits.'

There was blood on Archas's face, and a huge lump over his left eye.

'I feel sick,' said Archas.

'Best you sit up,' said Rabalyn, helping the youth to the wall. Bron struggled over, then slumped down beside his brother. Neither of the young men spoke and Rabalyn left them there.

He had tackled four attackers and defeated them. He should have felt uplifted and empowered. Instead his heart was heavy, and fear of retribution clung to him.

Skilgannon made his way to the high battlements, and felt a moment of irritation when he saw that he was not alone. Brother Naslyn was already there, leaning on the crenellated wall. He was a big man, wide-shouldered and powerful. Turning, he saw Skilgannon and nodded a greeting. 'A fine night, Brother Lantern,' he said.

'What brings you to the old tower?' asked Skilgannon.

'I wanted to think.'

'Then I shall leave you to your thoughts.' Skilgannon turned away.

'No, do not leave, Brother. I was hoping you would come. I have seen you here exercising. I know some of the moves. We practised them in the Immortals.'

Skilgannon looked at the man. It was not hard to imagine him in the black and silver armour of the Emperor's elite regiment. Invincible in battle, they had carried Gorben to victory after victory for decades. They had been disbanded after the defeat at Skeln. 'Were you there?' asked Skilgannon. Such was the awesome reputation of that dreadful battle, and its aftermath, that the question could have referred to nothing else.

'Aye. I was there.' He shook his head. 'The world ended,' he said, at last.

Naslyn was a quiet, solitary man. He needed to talk now, but only in his own time. Skilgannon began to stretch, easing the muscles of his shoulders and back. Naslyn joined him, and together they quietly moved through the familiar routines of the Shooting Bow, the Locust, the Peacock and the Crow. It had been some time since Naslyn last practised the moves, and it took him a while to

51

rediscover his balance. Then they faced one another, bowed, and began to shadow fight, spinning and leaping, hands and feet lancing out, the blows landing on target areas lightly. Skilgannon was faster than the heavier man, but Naslyn moved well for a while until fatigue overtook him. At the last he stepped back, and bowed once more. Sweat covered his face and dripped from his short black beard. They stretched once more, then sat quietly on the battlements.

'I still dream of it,' said Naslyn, after a while. 'It was one of those impossible moments where, when you replay it in your mind, you are convinced the outcome will be different.' He turned towards Skilgannon. 'We couldn't lose, Lantern. We were the best. Not only that but we outnumbered the enemy ten – perhaps twenty – to one. There was no way they could stand against us. No way.'

'The Drenai are fine warriors, they say.'

'Aye, they are,' snapped Naslyn. 'But that's not why they won. Three men were responsible for our downfall that day. And the odds against what happened are so enormous they are incalculable. The first was Gorben, bless him. I loved that man – even though the madness was on him at the end. We had taken losses in the eastern battles and he promoted fresh recruits to our ranks. One of these was a young soldier named Eericetes – may his soul be cursed to wander for eternity, the coward.' He fell silent and stared out at the silhouetted mountains.

'Who was the third?' asked Skilgannon, though he knew the answer.

'The Silver Slayer. Druss. They call him Druss the Legend now. Man, but he earned it that day. We struck their line like the hammer of Heaven. It buckled and damn near broke. And then – just as victory was in our grasp . . .' Naslyn shook his head in remembered disbelief '. . . Druss charged. One man, Lantern. One man with an axe. It was the pivotal moment. He was unstoppable. The axe blade clove into our ranks and men fell. He couldn't have stood for long. No one man could. But then the coward Eericetes threw down his shield and ran. Around him other new recruits panicked and did the same. Within a dozen heartbeats the line broke and we were all retreating. Unbelievable. We were the Immortals, Lantern. We didn't run. The shame of it burns like fire in my heart.'

52

Skilgannon was intrigued. Tales of Druss the Legend had abounded in Naashan, ever since the death of the champion Michanek. 'What was he like? Is he a giant?'

'No taller than me,' said Naslyn, 'but more heavily built. It wasn't his size, though. It was the sheer power he radiated. Him and that damned axe.'

'They say he fought alongside the Immortals years ago,' said Skilgannon.

'Before my time, but there were some who remembered him. They told incredible tales of his skill. I didn't believe them then. I do now. The retreat was awful. Gorben went totally mad and demanded his generals kill themselves for the dishonour. Instead they killed him. Ventria was finished then. And look at us now, tearing ourselves apart.'

'Why did you become a priest?'

'I was sick of it all. The slaughter and the battles.' Naslyn laughed grimly. 'I thought I could put right the evils of my youth.'

'Perhaps you can.'

'I might have. But I didn't survive Skeln to be slaughtered by angry peasants. They'll be coming, you know. With clubs and scythes and knives. I know what I'd do. I'd fight, by Heaven. I don't want that.'

'So what will you do?'

'I'm thinking of leaving. I wanted to talk to you first.'

'Why me? Why not the abbot?'

'You don't talk much, Lantern, but I know a warrior when I see one. You've been in battles. I'll wager you were an officer – and a good one. So I thought I'd get your advice.'

'I have none to give, my friend. I am still undecided.'

'You are thinking of staying, then?'

Skilgannon shrugged. 'Maybe. I truly do not know. When I came here I gave my swords to the abbot to dispose of. I had no wish to be a fighter any more. In the town yesterday I wanted to kill a loudmouthed braggart who struck Braygan. It took all of my control to hold back. Had my swords been close to hand I would have left his head on the cobbles.'

'We are not such good priests, are we?' offered Naslyn, with a smile.

'The abbot is. Many of the others are. I do not want to see them slaughtered.'

'Is that why you are thinking of staying, so that you can defend them?'

'It is in my mind.'

'Then I will stay too,' said Naslyn.

CHAPTER THREE

CETHELIN AWOKE WITH A START, THE COLOURS OF THE VISION filling his mind. Lighting a lantern he moved to his small writing desk, spread open a section of parchment and took up a quill pen. As swiftly as he could before the vision faded he wrote it down. Then he sat back, exhausted and trembling. His mouth was dry and he filled a goblet with water. In the days of his youth he could hold the visions in his head, examining them until all was revealed. Now he could barely sketch out the broadest lines of them before they dissolved.

He stared down at what he had written. *A gentle hound, scarred by fire, had become a snarling wolf, dangerous and deadly. The beast had lifted its head and lightning had forked up from its mouth, striking the sky with great power and causing a massive storm. The sea reared up in a huge tidal wave and swept towards a rocky island. Atop the island was a shrine.* The last word Cethelin had scrawled was *Candle.* He remembered then that a single candle was burning on the beach of the island, its tiny flame bright against the onrushing darkness of the colossal wave.

Cethelin could make no sense of the hound-wolf, but he knew that the tide always represented humanity. The angry sea was the mob in the town, and the shrine was the church. Lantern was right.

The mob would be coming with hatred in their hearts. Could a candle of love turn them from thoughts of murder? Cethelin doubted it.

The three-legged hound limped in from the bedroom and sat beside the abbot. Cethelin stroked its head. 'You are not a wolf, my boy,' he said. 'And you have chosen a poor place to seek safety.'

Rabalyn entered the small cottage and closed the door quietly, inserting the wooden plug that locked the latch. He wandered through to the small living room. Aunt Athyla was dozing in the chair by the fire. In her lap were several balls of brightly coloured wool, and by her feet lay around a dozen knitted squares. Rabalyn moved through to the kitchen and cut himself some bread. Returning to the fire he took up the brass toasting fork, thrust a slice of bread onto it, and held it close to the coals. There had been no butter for some weeks now, but the toasted bread still tasted fine to a young man who had not eaten that day. He glanced across at Aunt Athyla as he ate. A large woman in her late fifties, she had never married, and yet she had been a mother to two generations of the family. Her own parents had died when she was just fifteen – only a little younger than Rabalyn was now. Athyla had worked to raise four sisters and a brother. They were all gone now, and only rarely did she hear from any of them. Rabalyn's own mother had deserted the family eight years ago with her husband, leaving two children in the care of the time-worn spinster.

He gazed fondly at the sleeping woman. Her hair was mostly grey, and her legs were swollen with rheumatism. Her knuckles too were slightly deformed by arthritis, yet she laboured on daily without complaint. Rabalyn sighed. When he was younger he had dreamed of becoming rich and repaying Aunt Athyla for her kindness, perhaps buying her a fine house, with servants. Now he knew such a gift would bring her no joy. Athyla did not desire servants. He wondered if she truly desired anything at all. Her long life had been filled with duties and responsibilities she had not asked for, yet had accepted. She had only one piece of jewellery, a small silver pendant that she unconsciously stroked when worried. Rabalyn had asked her about it and she just said someone had given it to her a long time ago. Aunt Athyla did not engage in long conversations and her reminiscences were abrupt and to the point. As were her criticisms. 'Just like your mother,' she would say, if Rabalyn left any food upon his plate. 'Think of those starving children in Panthia.'

'How do you know they are starving in Panthia?' he would ask.

'Always starving in Panthia,' she would say. 'It's a known fact.'

Old Labbers had later explained that forty years earlier a severe drought had struck the nations of the southeast. Cadia, Matapesh and Panthia had suffered crop failures and there had been great hardship. Scores of thousands had died in Panthia, the worst hit of all. Now, however, the Panthians were among the richest of nations. Aunt Athyla listened as Rabalyn explained all this to her. 'Ah, well, that's nice,' she said. Some days later, when he refused to finish a meal that contained a disgusting green vegetable he loathed, she shook her head and said: 'Those little children in Panthia would be glad of it.'

It had irritated him then, but he smiled as he thought of it now. It was easy to smile and think fond thoughts when Athyla was asleep. As soon as she was awake the irritation would return. Rabalyn couldn't stop it. She would say something stupid and his temper would flare. Almost daily he made promises to himself not to argue with her. Most altercations ended the same way. His aunt would begin to cry and call him ungrateful. She would point out that she had beggared herself to raise him, and he would reply: 'I never asked you to.'

His leggings were still damp, and he stripped them off and hung them over a chair near the fire. Returning to the kitchen, he filled the old black kettle with water from the stone jug and carried it back to the living room. He added fuel to the coals, then hung the kettle over the flames. Once the water was boiling he made two cups of elderflower tisane, sweetening them with a little crystallized honey.

Athyla awoke and yawned. 'Hello, dear,' she said. 'Have you had something to eat?'

'Yes, Aunt. I made you some tisane.'

'How is your eye, dear? Better now?'

'Yes, Aunt. It's fine.'

'That's good.' She winced as she leaned forward towards where Rabalyn had left her tisane. Swiftly leaving his chair he passed her the cup. 'Not so much noise tonight,' she said. 'I think all this unpleasantness is over now. Yes, I'm sure it is.'

'Let us hope so,' said Rabalyn, rising from his chair. 'I'm going to bed, Aunt. I'll see you in the morning.' Leaning over he kissed her cheek, then made his way to his own room. It was tiny, with barely space enough for the old bed and a chest for his clothes.

Too weary to undress, he lay on his bed and tried to sleep. But his thoughts were all of Todhe and the revenge he would seek. Rabalyn had always avoided trouble with the councillor's son. Todhe was malicious and vengeful when he failed to get his own way, and merely surly and unpleasant to those he deemed not important enough to draw into his inner circle. Rabalyn was no fool and had remained wholly neutral in the only area where they were forced to come together – the little schoolroom. When Todhe spoke to him, which was a rare occurrence, Rabalyn was always courteous and careful to avoid giving offence. He didn't think of it as cowardice – though he was scared of Todhe – but more as good common sense. On occasions when he witnessed the bullying of other boys – like fat Arren – he had convinced himself it was none of his business and walked away.

However, the beating of old Labbers had been brutal and sickening, and Rabalyn found that he did not regret the punch that had begun this enmity with Todhe. His regret was that he had not had the courage to rush in on the adults who began the beating. No matter how much he thought about the dreadful incident he could make no sense of it. Old Labbers had never done anything to harm anyone in the town. Quite the reverse. During the plague he had gone from house to house ministering to the sick and the dying.

The world was indeed a strange place. As he lay on his bed Rabalyn thought about the lessons he had attended. He hadn't taken much notice of them, save for the stories about heroic battles and mighty warriors. Rabalyn had formed the impression that wars were fought by good people against evil people. The evil people were always from foreign countries. Yet was it not evil for a score of healthy men to beat an elderly priest almost to the point of death? Was it not evil for women in the crowd to jeer and scream for them to 'kick his ugly face' as Marja, the baker's wife, had?

'She always was a sad and sour woman,' Aunt Athyla had said – which was a remarkable thing to hear from her. Aunt Athyla never spoke badly of anyone.

It was all most unsettling. Rabalyn had heard the gossip that travellers brought to the town. In the capital, Mellicane, huge crowds were said to have burned churches and hanged priests. The King's adviser, the Lord Ironmask, had ordered the arrests of scores of ministers, who had then been executed and their lands forfeited to the state. As the government began to crumble Ironmask had appointed Arbiters, and these had travelled all across Tantria, rooting out 'foreign inspired' traitors.

When Rabalyn had first heard of these events he had thought them generally to be good. Traitors *should* be rooted out. Now, however, he had seen old Labbers branded a traitor, and he was confused.

Then there were the constant tales of battles fought between loyal troops and the vile enemy from Dospilis and their evil allies, the Datians. These battles were always won by Tantria, and yet each battle seemed to get closer. He had asked old Labbers about this one day. 'How can it be that when we win we draw back, and the defeated enemy moves forward?'

'A little more reading might be in order, young Rabalyn,' said Labbers. 'In particular I would refer you to the historical works of Appalanus. He wrote: "Truth in war is like a maiden pure. She must be protected at all times within a fortress of lies." Does that help?'

Rabalyn had nodded and thanked him, though he had no idea what the old man was talking about.

As he lay on his bed he could smell the smoke from the hearth. He would have to borrow Barik's brooms and clear the chimney of soot. Pulling a blanket over his shoulders he closed his eyes and tried again to sleep.

His mind was too full. He kept thinking of Todhe. Perhaps if he just accepted a beating from Todhe and his friends it would all blow over. Like for like. Rabalyn doubted it. He had raised the stakes when he assaulted them with the iron rod. Perhaps the Watch would arrest him for it. This was a new and frightening thought. Uncomfortable now, and newly afraid, he sat up and opened his eyes. Immediately they began to sting. Smoke was everywhere. Rabalyn climbed off his bed and opened the door. The living room was filled with oily smoke, and he saw flames outside the window.

Coughing and gasping, he ran across the living room and pushed open the door to Aunt Athyla's bedroom. The fire was eating through the window frame, and he could now hear it roaring through the thatched roof above. Stumbling to the bedside, he shook his aunt by the shoulder.

'Aunt Athyla!' he shouted. 'The house is on fire.' His knees buckled, his lungs hot and smoke-filled. Grabbing a chair, he hammered with it at the burning shutters. They would not give. Dragging a blanket from the bed he wrapped an edge of it round his hands and tried to lift the blazing wooden locking bar. The fire had warped it too badly. Pulling all the covers from Aunt Athyla he grabbed her by the arm and hauled her from the bed. Her body hit the floor, and she gave a groan.

'Wake up!' he screamed. On the verge of panic he began to haul her back into the living room. Fire was now bright here also, and a section of the roof fell into the far corner. The heat was intense. Leaving Athyla he ran to the door, lifted the bar and pushed it. The door would not open. Something had been wedged against it from the outside. Rabalyn could scarcely breathe. Staggering to the one window in the living room he lifted the shutter bar and pushed open the shutters. Flames were licking at the wood. Scrambling up onto the sill he threw himself out onto the path beyond. Jumping to his feet he ran back to the front door. A wooden bench had been lodged against it. Grabbing it, he hauled it clear, then pulled open the door.

The flames were high now inside and as he tried to enter he felt the ferocity of the heat. Sucking in a deep breath he gave a yell and hurled himself forward. Fire was all around him as he reached the unconscious woman. Grabbing her arm he began to drag her across the floor. Her nightdress caught alight, but he could not stop to put it out. Flames licked at his arms and the backs of his legs, and he could feel his clothing charring. Still he would not let go. He screamed in pain but struggled on. Once into the doorway he heard a great groan from the timbers above. They suddenly sagged and burning thatch showered down over Aunt Athyla. Rabalyn hauled the woman out onto open ground.

Her nightdress was ablaze and he knelt by her side, beating out the flames with his hands, and wrenching the garment clear of her body. In the brightness of the fire he could see burns all over her legs. Pulling her even further from the blazing building he left her for a moment and ran to the well, dropped the bucket, and then hauled it up. It seemed to take an age. Carrying the bucket to Aunt Athyla, he tore off his shirt and dipped it into the water. Then, squatting naked beside her, he gently dabbed the drenched shirt to Athyla's smoke-smeared face. Suddenly she coughed, and his relief was total.

'It's all right, Aunt. We're all right.'

'Oh dear,' she said. Then there was silence.

People began to arrive, rushing forward to surround Rabalyn.

'What happened, boy?' asked a voice.

'Someone set fire to the cottage,' he said. 'They blocked the door to stop us getting out.'

'Did you see anyone?'

Rabalyn did not answer. 'Help my aunt,' he said. 'Please help my aunt.'

A man knelt down beside the still form, and held a finger to her throat. 'She's gone, boy. Smoke did for her, I reckon.'

'She just spoke to me. She's going to be all right.' His voice was breaking as he began to shake Aunt Athyla by the shoulders. 'Wake up, Aunt. Wake up.'

'What happened here?' asked a new voice.

'Someone fired the cottage,' said the man beside Rabalyn. 'The boy says they blocked the front door.'

Rabalyn looked up and saw Councillor Raseev. He was a tall man, with greying blond hair and a wide handsome face. His voice was smooth and deep. 'What did you see, boy?' he asked.

'I woke up with the flames and the smoke,' said Rabalyn. 'I tried to get Aunt Athyla out, but someone put a bench against the front door. I had to climb out of the window to move it. Will someone help my aunt!'

A woman knelt beside Athyla. She also felt for a pulse. 'There is nothing to be done,' she said. 'Athyla is gone, Rabalyn.'

'I asked what you saw, boy,' repeated Raseev. 'Could you identify the villain who did this?'

Rabalyn pushed himself to his feet. He felt light-headed, as if it all were but a dream. The pain from the burns on his hands, arms and legs faded away. 'I saw no-one,' he said. He looked around at the faces of the gathered townsfolk. 'But I know who did it. I only have one enemy.'

'Speak the name, boy!' ordered Raseev.

Rabalyn located Todhe in the crowd, and saw no fear in his eyes. If Rabalyn named him nothing would be done. No-one had seen him torch the cottage. He was the son of the most powerful man in the town. He was immune from the law. Rabalyn turned away and dropped down to his knees beside his aunt. Reaching out, he stroked her dead face. Guilt was heavy on his heart. Had he not made an enemy of Todhe, Aunt Athyla would still be alive. 'Who is your enemy, boy?' demanded Raseev.

Rabalyn kissed his aunt's cheek, then rose to his feet. He turned to Raseev. 'I didn't see no-one,' he said. He swung towards the crowd. 'But I know who did it. He'll pay. With his bastard life!' He looked straight at Todhe – and this time there was real fear in the youth's eyes.

Todhe ran forward and grabbed his parent's arm. 'He is talking about me, Father,' he said. 'He is threatening me!'

'Is this true?' thundered Raseev.

'Did he torch my aunt's house?' asked Rabalyn.

'Of course he did not!'

'Then he has nothing to fear, does he?'

Rabalyn walked away. In that moment Todhe broke away from his father and drew a knife from his belt.

'No, son!' yelled Raseev. The burly youth leapt at Rabalyn. Hearing the cry Rabalyn turned. Todhe's knife flashed towards his face. Rabalyn swayed back. The blade missed him by inches. He hammered an overhand right to the side of Todhe's jaw. The bigger youth, off balance, staggered. Rabalyn ran in and kicked Todhe in the stomach. Todhe dropped the knife and fell to his knees. Without thinking Rabalyn swept up the blade and plunged it into Todhe's neck. The blade thudded against bone then sliced through the youth's jugular. Blood gushed over Rabalyn's hand. Todhe gave a strangled cry and tried to stand. His knees gave way and he fell to his face on the ground. Raseev shouted: 'No!' and ran to his son's side. Rabalyn stood there, the knife in his hand dripping blood.

For a moment nothing was said. The crowd stood stunned into silence. Then Raseev looked up. 'Murder!' he shouted. 'You all saw it! This vile creature has murdered my son!'

Still no-one moved. But then two soldiers of the Watch pushed themselves through the crowd. Rabalyn dropped the knife and ran, vaulting the low wall round the burning cottage, and sprinting through the streets.

He had no idea where he was going. All he knew was that he had to escape. The punishment for murder was public strangulation, and there was no doubt in his mind that he would be found guilty at trial. Todhe had dropped the knife. He was unarmed when Rabalyn slew him.

Panicked now, the pain from his burns forgotten, the naked youth ran for his life.

Raseev Kalikan's view of himself was complex and distorted. People saw him as honest and a loyal worker for the good of the town and its people. Therefore, in his own mind, that was what he was. The fact that he misappropriated town funds for his own benefit, and awarded building contracts to those of his cronies who paid him bribes, did not alter his own view of himself. On those rare occasions when his conscience pricked him he would think: 'But this is how the world works. If I didn't do it someone else would.' He used words like honour and principle, faith and patriotism. His voice was rich and deep and persuasive, and when he used those words in his public speeches he would often see tears in the eyes of the townsfolk, who loved him. It was most moving, and, caught up in the moment, he would become quite emotional himself. Raseev Kalikan truly believed only in what was good for Raseev Kalikan. He was his own god and his own ambition. In short, Raseev Kalikan was a politician.

His greatest talent was an innate feeling for which way the political wind was blowing.

When the King's armies had suffered defeats, and the ruler had turned on his advisers, the day of the Arbiters had dawned. Until now the Arbiters had been a minor force in the political life of Tantria, raging against what they saw as the malign influence of foreigners living within Tantria's borders. Now they were pre-eminent. All the ills that had befallen the new nation were laid at the door of foreigners from Dospilis or Naashan or Ventria. Even the few Drenai merchants in the capital were viewed with deep suspicion. The irony was that the new leader of the Arbiters was himself a foreigner: Shakusan Ironmask, the Captain of the Warhounds, the King's mercenary bodyguard. Raseev had greeted the Arbiter emissaries to the town warmly, and made them welcome in his own home. He had embraced their cause and pictured himself rising through the ranks, and perhaps moving on to a greater role in the future in Mellicane.

When the Arbiters had spoken against the church Raseev had spotted an opportunity not only to advance himself politically, but also to wipe away his debts. The church owned much of the property in the town, and also lent money to aid local businesses. Raseev had taken out three large loans in the past four years, in order to promote and build his business interests. Two of his ventures – timber felling and mining – had failed miserably, leaving him facing large losses. The church men were doomed anyway, so why should he not turn their destruction to his financial benefit?

The problem was that he had not been able to stir up the people sufficiently to attack the church directly. Many of them recalled how the priests had helped them during the time of plague and drought. The attack on the old teacher by some of Raseev's hired men had been viewed with distaste by many – though no-one had spoken out directly. And when that other priest had caused the Arbiter to stab himself some had even laughed at his misfortune.

But now there was a way forward.

People's sympathies were with Raseev following the death of Todhe, and word had been spread that the killer had taken refuge in the church, and that the abbot had refused to hand him over to the authorities for trial. It was not true, but it was believed to be, and that was what counted.

Raseev stayed in his house that night, the body of his son laid out in a back room and dressed in his best clothes. He could hear his wife weeping and wailing over the stupid lout. How strange women are, he thought. Todhe was useless in every way. He was dull, vicious and a constant trial to Raseev. At least in death he could achieve something.

Several of Raseev's most trusted supporters were out now, stirring the crowds, calling for the church to be stormed and the killer taken.

Antol the Baker was a bitter, vengeful man, and he would lead the crowd. Others who worked closely with Raseev would have weapons hidden, which would be drawn as soon as they were in the church buildings. Once the killings began the mob would rage through the environs of the monastery. Those priests who were not slain would flee. Then Raseev would locate the Order's treasury and seize its assets. It would also be a good time to find and destroy their records.

He took a deep breath and began to work on a speech. The murders of the priests could not be overlooked, and he would be forced to speak out against the dangers of hatred, and to have the speech recorded and placed in the council records. Political winds had a habit of changing and, at some point in the future, Raseev could then point out that he had been against the violence.

Taking up a quill pen, he began to make notes. 'The deaths of so many scar us all,' he wrote. Then he paused. From the back room the sound of sobbing increased.

'Will you stop that wailing!' he shouted through the wall. 'I am trying to work in here.'

For Skilgannon the night had been long and sleepless, his mind haunted by painful memories, and laden with the guilts of his life. He had led men into battle – and for this he felt little shame – but he had also taken part in the razing of towns, and the awful butchery that accompanied it. He had allowed himself to be swept along on a tide of hatred and vengeance, his sword dripping with the blood of innocence. Those memories would not go away.

When the Queen had addressed her troops before the last battle – the dreadful storming of Perapolis – she had ordered that no-one should be left alive, not one man, woman or child within the besieged city. 'All are traitors,' she said. 'Let their fate be an example for all time.'

The troops had cheered. The civil war had been long and bloody and victory was at hand. Yet it was one thing to say the words, and quite another to be part of the slaughter. As a general Skilgannon had not needed to bloody his sword. And yet he had. He had run through the alleys of Perapolis, slashing and killing until his clothes and armour were drenched in blood.

The following day he had walked through the now silent streets. Corpses were everywhere. Thousands had been killed. He saw the bodies of children and babes, old women and young girls. His heart had been sickened beyond despair at the sight.

On the high tower wall Skilgannon stared up at the fading stars. If there was a supreme being – and this he doubted – then his sins would never be washed away. He was a damned soul, in a damned world.

'Where were you when the children were being slaughtered?' he asked, looking up into the vast blackness. 'Where were your tears that day?'

Something glinted in the distance and he saw another fire in the town. Some other poor soul was being tortured and killed. An empty anger swept through Skilgannon. Idly he touched the locket on the chain round his neck. Within it was all that was left of Dayan.

Three days they had shared after his return from the war. Her pregnancy had not yet begun to show, but there was more colour in her cheeks, and a silken sheen to her golden hair. Her eyes were bright and sparkling, and the joy of her condition made her radiant. The first signs of problems began on a bright afternoon as they sat in the garden, overlooking the marble pool and the tall fountain. Sweat was gleaming on her pale features, and Skilgannon suggested they move to the shade. She had leaned heavily on him, then groaned. He had swept her into his arms and carried her inside, laying her down on a long couch. Her face had taken on a waxy sheen. She reached up and pressed her fingers into her

66

armpit. 'So painful,' she said. Opening her dress he saw the skin of her left armpit was swollen and bruised. It seemed as if a large cyst was forming. Lifting her once more he carried her upstairs to the main bedroom, and helped her undress. Then he sent for the surgeon.

The fever had begun swiftly. By the late afternoon large purple swellings had appeared in her armpits and groin. The surgeon arrived just before dusk. Skilgannon would never forget the man's reaction when he examined Dayan. Full of quiet confidence, shrewd and resourceful, he had stepped inside the room and bowed to Skilgannon. Then he had walked to the bedside and drawn back the covers. It was in that moment that Skilgannon knew the worst. The surgeon had blanched, and taken an involuntary step backwards. All confidence fled from him. He continued to back away towards the door. Skilgannon grabbed him. 'What is it? What is the matter with you?'

'The Black Plague. She has the Black Plague.'

Pulling himself free of the shocked Skilgannon the surgeon had fled the palace. The servants had followed within hours. Skilgannon sat beside the delirious Dayan, placing water-cooled towels on her feverish body. He did not know what else to do.

Towards dawn one of the huge purple swellings under her arm burst. For a time her fever dropped, and she awoke. Skilgannon cleaned away the pus and the blood, and covered her with a fresh sheet of white satin. 'How are you feeling?' he asked her, stroking the sweat-drenched blond hair back from her brow.

'A little better. Thirsty.' He helped her drink. Then she sagged back to the pillow. 'Am I dying, Olek?'

'No. I will not allow it,' he said, forcing a lightness of tone he did not feel.

'Do you love me?'

'Who could not, Dayan? All who meet you are enchanted by you.' It was true. He had never known anyone of such gentle disposition. There was no malice in Dayan, no hatred. She even treated the servants as friends, and chatted with them as equals. Her laughter was infectious, and lifted the spirits of all who heard it.

'I wish we had met before you knew her,' she said. Skilgannon's heart sank. He took her hand and kissed it. 'I have tried not to be jealous, Olek. But I cannot help it. It is hard when you love someone with all your heart, and yet you know they love another.'

He did not know how to answer her, and sat quietly, holding her hand. Finally he said: 'You are a finer woman than she can ever be, Dayan. In every way.'

'But you regret marrying me.'

'No! You are my wife, Dayan. You and I together.' He sighed. 'Until death.'

'Oh, Olek. Do you mean that?'

'With all my heart.' She squeezed his hand, and closed her eyes. He sat with her through the dawn, and into the day. She awoke again towards dusk. The fever had returned and she cried out in pain. Once more he bathed her face and body, trying to reduce the inflammation. Her beautiful face took on a sunken look, and her eyes were dark-rimmed. A second swelling burst at her groin, staining the sheet. As night came on Skilgannon felt a dryness in his throat, and sweat began to drip from his brow into his eyes. He felt tenderness in his armpits. Gently he probed the area. Already the swellings had begun. Dayan sighed, then took a deep breath. 'I think it is passing, Olek. The pain is fading.'

'That is good.'

'You look tired, my love. You should get some rest.'

'I am fine.'

'I have good news,' she said, with a smile, 'though now is probably not the time to share it. I was hoping to be sitting in the garden with you, watching the sunset.'

'This is a fine time for good news.' Skilgannon tried to drink some water, but his throat was swollen and inflamed, and it was difficult to swallow.

'Sorai cast the runes for me. It will be a boy. Your son. Are you happy?'

It was as if a white hot iron had been plunged into his heart. Sorrow threatened to overwhelm him. 'Yes,' he said. 'Very happy.'

'I hoped you would be.' She was silent for a while, and when she spoke next the delirium had returned. She talked of lunching with her father, and what a fine time they had had. 'He bought me a necklace in the market. Green stones. Let me show you.' She struggled to sit up.

'I have seen it. It is very pretty. Rest, Dayan.'

'Oh, I am not tired, Olek. Can we go for a walk in the garden?'

'In a little while.'

She chattered on, and then, in mid-sentence, stopped. At first he thought she was sleeping, but her face was utterly still. Reaching out, he gently pressed her throat. There was no pulse. A searing pain lanced his belly and he doubled over. After a while it passed. He gazed down at Dayan, then lay down beside her, drawing her into an embrace. 'I did not choose to fall in love with Jianna,' he said. 'If I could have chosen it would have been you. You are everything a man could desire, Dayan. You deserved better than me.'

He lay there for some hours, as the fever grew. Finally delirium took him. He tried to fight it, forcing himself from the bed and falling to the floor. Then he had staggered to the gardens, and out into the meadows beyond.

Skilgannon remembered little of what followed, save that he had tumbled down a steep incline, then crawled towards a distant building. He seemed to recall voices, and then gentle hands lifting him.

He had awoken to a silent room in a church hospital. His bed was beside a window, and through that window he saw a cloudless sky, rich and blue. A white bird had glided across his field of vision. In that moment everything froze and Skilgannon experienced . . . what? He still did not know. For a single heartbeat he had felt something akin to perfection, as if he and the bird, and the sky, and the room were somehow one and bathed in the love of the universe. Then it passed and the pain returned. Not just the physical pain from the huge, lanced cysts and the terrible toll they had taken on his body, but the agony of loss as he remembered that Dayan was gone from the world, no longer to hold his hand, or to kiss his lips. No more to lie beside him on still summer evenings, her hand stroking his face.

Despair clung to his heart like a raven.

A young priest visited him on that first day and sat at his bedside. 'You are a lucky man, general. Aye, and a tough one. By all rights you should be dead. I have never seen any man fight off the plague as you did. At one point your heart was pounding so fast it was beyond my ability to keep count.'

'Was the plague contained to our area?'

'No, sir. It is sweeping through the kingdom and beyond. The death toll will be awesome.'

'The revenge of the Source for our sins,' said Skilgannon.

The priest shook his head. 'We do not believe in a god of revenge, sir. The plague was spread by man's error and greed.'

'What do you mean?'

'In the northeast there is a tribe, the Kolear. You have heard of them?'

'Kin to the Nadir and the Chiatze. They are nomads.'

'Indeed, sir. One of their customs is that if they see a dead marmot – small furry creatures that live in the lowlands – they move on. According to their beliefs the marmots contain the souls of Kolear wise men. That is why the Kolear do not hunt the creatures. A dead marmot is seen as a sign that the wise spirits have moved away and that the tribe should seek fresh pastures. During the war many of the Kolear sided with the Queen's enemies, and were driven from their lands, or slain. Other non-Kolear residents moved in. They saw the marmots and decided to trap them for their fur. It is good fur. What they did not realize was that the marmots carried the seeds of a plague. At first the hunters and trappers fell sick. Then their families. Then travellers and merchants who bought the fur. Then it struck the eastern cities, and people fled, carrying the plague with them. Strange, is it not, that the backward Kolear had, within their simplistic theological beliefs, a way to avoid the plague, yet we – more civilized and knowledgeable – gathered it and spread it?'

Skilgannon was too weary to debate the point and drifted off to sleep. Often now, though, he thought back to the priest's words. It was not strange at all. One of the first of the Prophets wrote: *The Tree of Knowledge bears fruit of arrogance.*

Skilgannon sighed, and once more became Brother Lantern. He stripped off his clothing and began to exercise. Slowly he freed his mind of all tension, then smoothly ran through the repertoire of stretching and balance. Finally he began a series of swift, sudden moves, his hands lancing out, slashing the air, his body twirling and leaping, feet kicking high. Sweat-drenched, he pulled on his robes, and knelt on the stone floor.

For the first time in many days he thought of his swords, and wondered what the abbot had done with them. Had he sold them, or merely cast them in a pit? Giving up the Swords of Night and Day had been harder than he could ever have imagined. Even the act of passing them to Cethelin had caused his hands to tremble and his heart to flutter in panic. For weeks afterwards he had struggled against a desire to retrieve them, to hold them again. He had felt physically sick for days, unable to hold down solid food. It was the opposite of the exhilaration he had experienced when the Queen gave them to him. When his hands first touched the ivory handles a sense of strength and purpose had flowed through his limbs. It seemed incomprehensible then that they had been created by the loathsome hag in the faded red gown who had stood alongside the young Queen. Mostly bald, wisps of straggly white hair clung to her skull like mist on rock. Once she would have been heavily built, but now the wrinkled skin of her face hung loose over the folds of her neck. Her eyes were rheumy, and one was marred by a grey cataract.

'Are they pleasing to you, Olek?' she had asked. Her dry voice raised gooseflesh on the back of his neck, and he looked away as she smiled, showing rotted teeth.

'They are very fine,' he said.

'My swords are blessed,' she told him. 'I made one for Gorben many years ago. With it he almost conquered the world. Now I have made more. Mighty weapons. They enhance the strength and speed of the wielder. The blades you carry now are fit for a king.'

'I have no wish to be a king.'

The Old Woman laughed. 'Which is why the Queen grants them to you, Olek Skilgannon. You are loyal – and that is a quality so rare as to be priceless. You will win many battles with these swords. You will win back the lands of Naashan for your Queen.'

Later, as he sat alone with the young Queen, Skilgannon voiced his disquiet. 'The Old Woman is evil,' he said. 'I do not wish to use her swords.'

The Queen had laughed. 'Oh, Olek! You are too rigid in your thinking.' She had sat beside him, and he had smelt the perfume of her raven hair. 'She is everything you say – and probably more. But we must win Naashan back and I will use every weapon I can gather.' She drew a knife from her belt and held it up to the light. It was long and curved, the blade exquisitely engraved with ancient runes. 'She gave me this. Is it not beautiful?'

'Aye, it is.'

'It is the Discerning Blade. It enhances wisdom. When I hold it I can see so many things. And so clearly. The Old Woman is evil, but she has proved herself loyal. Without her you and I would have been killed on that awful night. You know that. I need her strength, Olek. I need to rebuild the kingdom. As a vassal state to Gorben we could not grow. Now he is dead we can fulfil our own destiny. Take the swords. Use them. Use them for me.'

He had bowed his head, then lifted her hand to his lips. 'For you I would do anything, majesty.'

'Not anything, Olek,' she said softly.

'No,' he agreed.

'Do you love her more than you love me?'

'No. I will never love anyone that much. I did not know I was capable of loving with such intensity.'

'You could still come to my bed, Olek,' she whispered, sliding in close to him and kissing his cheek. 'I could be Sashan again. Just for you.'

He rose from the couch with a groan. 'No,' he said. 'If I did that it would rip away all my reasoning. We would destroy everything we have fought for. Everything your father died for. You have my heart, Jianna. You have my soul. I loved you as Sashan, and I love you now. But it cannot be! There is nothing more I can give. Dayan is my wife. She is sweet, and she is kind. And soon she will be the mother of my child. I will be loyal to her. I owe her that.'

Then he had taken the Swords of Night and Day, and ridden back to the war.

Now alone in his small room Skilgannon placed his hand over the locket round his neck. 'If the temple exists, Dayan,' he whispered, 'I will find it. You will live again.'

He stayed for a while kneeling upon the floor, lost in thoughts of the past. Had he been a coward to refuse the demands of his heart? Was his love for Jianna so great, or not great enough? Could he

72

have defeated the princes as well as the Ventrian overlords and their supporters? His mind told him no. He and Jianna would have been dragged down and betrayed. His arrogance whispered the opposite. 'You could have beaten them all, and been as one with the woman of your soul's desire.'

Such thoughts were reinforced by what had happened following the gift of the swords. During the next two years all enemies had fallen before him. One by one the cities held by Ventrian supporters had been taken, or had surrendered to his conquering armies without a fight. Yet, as Jianna's power grew, she had begun to change. Their relationship cooled. She took many lovers, men of power and ambition, then leached away their strength before tossing them aside. Poor, demented Damalon had been the last. He had followed at her heels like a puppy, begging for scraps.

Jianna had sent Damalon away on that last night, after the massacre of Perapolis, and had entertained Skilgannon in her battle tent. He had arrived with the blood of the slaughtered on his clothes. Jianna, dressed in a gown of shimmering white, her black hair braided with silver wire, looked at him disdainfully. 'Could you not have bathed before coming into my presence, general?'

'A tidal wave could not wash this blood from me,' he said. 'It will be upon me all my days.'

'Is the mighty Skilgannon growing soft?'

'It was wrong, Jianna. It was evil on the grandest scale. Babies with their skulls smashed against walls, children with their guts torn out. What kind of a victory was this?'

'*My* victory,' she snapped. 'My enemies are dead. Their children are dead. Now we can rebuild and grow without fear of revenge.'

'Aye, well, you'll have no need of a soldier now. So, with your leave, I'll return to my home and do my best to forget this awful day.'

'Yes, go home,' she said, her voice cold. 'Go to your Dayan. Rest for a few weeks. Then return. There will always be a need for good soldiers. We have retaken the cities of Naashan, but I wish to re-establish the old borders that were in place when my father was king.'

'You will invade Matapesh and Cadia now?'

'Not immediately – but soon. Then Datia and Dospilis.'

'What has happened to you, Jianna? Once we talked of justice and of peace and prosperity and freedom. These are the virtues we fought for. We had only contempt for the vanity of Gorben and the desire of conquerors to build empires.'

'I was little more than a child then,' she snapped. 'Now I have grown. Children talk of silly dreams. I now deal in realities. Those who support me I reward. Those who stand against me die. Do you no longer love me, Olek?'

'I will always love you, Sashan,' he said simply.

Her features softened then, and for a moment she was the girl he had saved in the forest of Delian. Then the moment passed. Her dark eyes narrowed and held his gaze.

'Do not seek to leave me, Olek. I could not allow it.'

Pushing aside all dreams of the past Skilgannon climbed upon his narrow bed. He fell asleep.

And dreamed of the White Wolf.

It was a beautiful dawn, the sky bathed in gold, the few clouds drenched in colour: rich red at the base and glowing charcoal at the crown. Cethelin stood on the high tower, absorbing the beauty with all his being. The air tasted sweet and he closed his eyes and sought to still the trembling of his hands.

He did not lack faith, but he did not want to die. The distant town was quiet, though once more smoke hung in the air over ruined buildings. Soon the mob would begin to gather, and then, like the angry sea of his dream, it would surge towards the church buildings.

Cethelin was old, and had seen such events too often in his long life. Always they followed a pattern. The majority in the mob would, at first, merely stand around, awaiting events. Like a pack of hunting hounds, held on invisible leashes. Then the evil among them – always so few – would initiate the horror. The leashes would snap, the pack surge forward. Cethelin felt another stab of fear at the thought.

Raseev Kalikan would be the ringleader. Cethelin tried to love all those he met, no matter how petty or cruel they might appear. It was hard to love Raseev – not because he was evil but because he was empty. Cethelin pitied him. He had no moral values, no sense of spirituality. Raseev was a man consumed by thoughts of self. He was too canny, however, to be at the forefront of the mob. Even with plans of murder already in place he would be looking to the future – to show that his hands were clean. No, it would be the vile Antol and his ghastly wife, Marja. Cethelin shivered and berated himself for such judgemental thoughts. For years Marja had attended church, making herself responsible for organizing functions and gathering donations. She saw herself as holy and wise. Yet her conversations inevitably led to the judgement of others. 'That woman from Mellicane, Father. You know she is having an affair with the merchant, Callian. She should not be welcome at our services.' 'You must have heard the dreadful noise that the washerwoman, Athyla, makes during evensong. She cannot hit a note. Could you not ask her to refrain from singing, Father?'

'The Source hears the song from the heart, not from the throat,' Cethelin had told her.

Then had come the awful day when – after a fundraising for the poor – Brother Labberan discovered that Marja had 'borrowed' from the fund. The sum had not been great, some forty silver pieces. Cethelin had asked her to return the money. At first she had been defiant, and denied the charge. Later, with proof offered, she maintained that she had merely borrowed the sum and had every intention of returning it. She promised it would be replaced the following week. She had never since attended any service. Nor had the money been repaid. Brother Labberan had requested the matter be brought before the Watch, but Cethelin had refused.

Since then both Marja and her husband had joined the ranks of the Arbiters, and had spoken against the church. The attack on Brother Labberan had been orchestrated by Antol, and Marja had stood by, screaming for them to kick him and make him bleed.

These two would be at the forefront of the mob. They would be the ones baying for blood.

The door to the tower was pushed open. Cethelin turned to see which of the priests had disturbed his meditations, but it was the dog, Jesper. It limped forward, then sat looking up at him. 'The world will go on, Jesper,' he said, patting the hound's large head.

'Dogs will be fed, and people will be born, and loved. I know this, and yet my heart is filled with terror.'

Raseev Kalikan was in the front rank of the crowd as it moved over the old bridge and onto the slope before the old castle buildings. Alongside him was the burly bearded figure of Paolin Meltor, the Arbiter from Mellicane. His injured leg was healing well, but walking any distance still caused him pain. Raseev had urged him to stay behind, but the Arbiter had refused. 'It will be worth a little discomfort to watch those traitors die.'

'Let us not talk of death, my friend. We are merely looking to see them hand over the boy who killed my son.' There were others present during the conversation and Raseev ignored the look of shock and surprise on the face of Paolin Meltor. 'If they refuse to do their honest duty then we must enter the monastery and arrest them all,' he continued. Taking Paolin by the arm he led him away from the listening crowd. 'All will be as you wish it,' he whispered. 'But we must think of the future. We must not be seen to go to the church as a murdering mob. We seek justice. A few angry men will lose their heads and a regrettable – deeply regrettable – massacre will take place. You understand?'

'Whatever!' snapped Paolin. 'I care nothing for this . . . this subterfuge. They are traitors and they deserve to die. That is enough for me.'

'Then you must do as your conscience dictates,' said Raseev smoothly.

Paolin moved away to walk alongside Antol and Marja. Raseev hung back just a little.

He glanced around at the crowd. It was some three hundred strong. It seemed to Raseev likely that the priests would bar the gates, but they were of wood and would burn swiftly enough. Antol had made sure some of the men were carrying jugs of oil and there was dry wood aplenty on the slopes before the castle. Barring the gates would suit Raseev. It would give the crowd time to grow angry.

The captain of the Watch, Seregas, approached Raseev as they moved on. Seregas was a canny northerner who had been stationed in Skepthia for the last two years. He had reorganized the Watch, increasing foot patrols in the more wealthy areas and the merchant district. For this service Seregas levied extra monies from shopkeepers and businessmen. It was purely voluntary. No-one was forced to pay, or threatened if they did not. Curiously, those who did not pay were certain to see their businesses or homes robbed. Taverns and eating places whose owners chose to remain outside the levy saw fights and scuffles break out, and a significant decrease in their turnover as customers stayed away from their troubled premises.

Seregas was a tall, thin man, with deep-set dark eyes and a thin mouth, partly hidden by a thick beard. The previous day he had come to Raseev's home. Raseev had taken him to his study and poured him a goblet of wine. 'You know the boy's tracks led away from the church, Raseev,' he had said. It was not a question.

'The slope is rocky. He probably doubled back.'

'Doubtful at best.'

'What are you saying?'

'It is quite simple, councillor. You will ask them to surrender a boy they do not have. Therefore they must refuse. I am sure that this misunderstanding will lead to bloodshed.'

Raseev looked at him closely. 'What is it that you want, Seregas?'

'There is a wanted man at the church. There is a small reward for him. I'll take his body.'

'Wanted by whom?'

'That is none of your affair, councillor.'

Raseev had smiled. 'You are becoming rich, Seregas. A small reward would interest you not at all. It occurs to me that – if matters get out of hand – all the bodies will be burned. Mobs and fire, Seregas.'

Seregas sipped his wine. 'Very well, councillor, then I shall be more open with you. One of the priests is worth a great deal of money.'

'As I asked before: to whom?'

'To the Naashanite Queen. I have already sent a rider to Naashan. It should take him around five days to reach the border, and another two weeks, perhaps, for my letter to reach the capital.'

'Who is this priest?'

'Skilgannon.'

'The Damned?'

'The very same. We will need to keep his body for viewing. If we remove the inner organs then cover the corpse with salt it will dry and remain largely intact. Enough for them to see the tattoos. He has a spider on his forearm, a panther upon his chest and an eagle upon his back. In all other respects he also matches the description: dark-haired, tall with eyes of brilliant blue. After he arrived here the abbot sold a Ventrian pure bred black stallion for more than three hundred raq. It is Skilgannon.'

'How much is she willing to pay?'

Seregas chuckled. 'The question is, councillor, how much must I pay you?'

'Half.'

'I think not. You are organizing murders. Times change, as do political ideologies. You might well need someone in authority to give evidence of your good will in these troubled times.'

Raseev refilled the goblets. 'Indeed so, captain. Then what do you suggest?'

'One third.'

'And that sum would be?'

'A thousand raq.'

'Sweet Heaven! What did he do to her? Slay her firstborn?'

'I do not know. Are we agreed, councillor?'

'We are, Seregas. But tell me, why did you not merely arrest and hold him?'

'Firstly, he has committed no crime here. More importantly he is a deadly killer, Raseev – with or without weapons. I don't doubt that many of the tales are exaggerated, but it is well known that he entered the forest of Delian alone and slew eleven warriors who had captured the rebel princess – as the Queen then was. You also heard how he dealt with the Arbiter. I saw that, Raseev. The skill was extraordinary.'

'You think he will fight tomorrow?'

'It will not matter against three or four hundred. He is not a god. Sheer weight of numbers will drag him down.'

In the bright light of morning Raseev walked with the crowd, Seregas beside him, three other soldiers of the Watch close by. As they approached the old castle Raseev saw that the gates were open. The abbot, Cethelin, was standing beneath the gateway arch, two priests alongside him. One was tall and lean, the other black-bearded and heavily built.

'The tall one is Skilgannon,' whispered Seregas. Raseev held back, allowing other people to pass him.

'Very wise,' said Seregas.

CHAPTER FOUR

FOR BRAYGAN IT WAS THE SINGLE MOST TERRIFYING MOMENT OF HIS life so far. He had become a priest to escape the horrors of a world threatened by wars and violence, droughts and starvation. Now, before he was even twenty, death was marching towards him.

More than twenty of the thirty-five priests were already fleeing through the rear gates, running out towards the sheep paddocks and the woods beyond. He saw Brother Anager emerge from the main building, a canvas sack upon his shoulder. Braygan stood very still as the cook came alongside him. 'Come with us, Braygan. It is futile to die here.'

Braygan so wanted to obey. He moved several steps towards the paddock, then glanced back to where Abbot Cethelin was standing beneath the gateway arch.

'I cannot,' he said. 'Fare you well, Anager.'

The other priest said nothing. Hoisting his sack to his shoulder he ran out to the paddock. Braygan watched him labouring up the green slope.

In that moment a feeling of peace descended on the young acolyte. He took a deep breath and walked slowly to where the abbot waited. Cethelin turned as Braygan arrived. He smiled and patted the young priest on the arm. 'I saw a candle in my dream, Braygan. It stood against the onrushing darkness. We will be that candle.'

The crowd were closer now, and Braygan saw the tall, lean figure of Antol the Baker, his dark hair held in place by a bronze circlet, his protruding eyes wide and angry. Beside him was the Arbiter who had punched Braygan to the ground, and then been stopped by Brother Lantern. Braygan flicked a glance at Lantern, who was standing very still, his face impassive.

'Bring out the criminal Rabalyn,' shouted Raseev Kalikan. 'Or face the consequences.'

Cethelin stepped closer to the milling crowd. 'I do not know of what you speak,' he said. 'There are no criminals here. The boy Rabalyn is not within these walls.'

'You lie!' bellowed Antol.

'I never lie,' Cethelin told him. 'The boy is not here. I see you have officers of the Watch with you. They are free to search the buildings.'

'We don't need your permission, traitor!' yelled the Arbiter. The crowd began to move forward. Cethelin raised his thin arms. 'My brothers, why do you wish us harm? Not one of my brethren has ever caused you ill. We live to serve . . .'

'*This* is for traitors!' shouted Antol, suddenly running forward. Sunlight glinted from the long knife in his hand. Cethelin turned towards him. Brother Lantern leapt across Braygan's line of sight. Cethelin staggered and Braygan saw blood on the knife blade. A woman shouted from the crowd. 'Spill his guts to the ground!' Braygan recognized the voice of Marja, Antol's wife.

Braygan caught Cethelin as he fell. The abbot had been stabbed just above his left hip, and blood was soaking through his blue robes. Antol tried to reach him for a second thrust, but Lantern caught his arm and twisted it savagely. Antol screamed and dropped the knife. Lantern caught it with his right hand, then twisted Antol round to face the crowd.

Then Lantern spoke, his voice harsh and powerful. 'Death is what you came here for, you maggot-ridden scum, and death is what you will have.' He looked towards Marja, a round-faced, plump woman with short-cropped greying hair. 'You called for guts to be spilled, you hag. Then here they are!'

Antol's back was towards him and Braygan did not see the terrible strike with the knife. But he heard Antol scream, and he

81

saw something gush from his belly and flop to the ground. The sound that screeched from the disembowelled man was barely human, and chilled Braygan to the depths of his soul. Then Brother Lantern dragged the man's head back and slashed the knife across his throat. Blood spurted over the blade.

'No!' screamed Marja, stumbling to where her husband's body lay. Brother Lantern ignored her and strode towards the crowd. 'Is that enough pleasure for you, or do you desire more? Come, you gutless worms. More can die.'

They backed away from him – all save two black-garbed officers of the Watch who ran forward, sabres in their hands. Lantern moved to meet them. He swayed as the first blade lanced for his heart. The soldier stumbled back. Braygan saw that Antol's knife was now embedded in the man's throat. And somehow Lantern had the dying officer's sabre in his hand. He parried a thrust from the second soldier, rolled his blade, then plunged it through the man's chest. The soldier cried out and staggered back. The sabre blade slid clear.

Lantern stepped back from the man and swung away. Braygan thought he was about to return to where Cethelin lay, but he suddenly spun on his heel, the sabre flashing through the air. It took the officer in the side of the neck, cleaving through skin, tendon and bone. The young soldier's head struck the ground while his body stood for several seconds. Braygan saw the right leg twitch and the headless corpse crumple to the earth.

There was not a sound now from the crowd. Lantern had both sabres in his hands and he walked along the line of waiting men and women. 'Well?' he called out. 'Are there no more fighting men among you? What about you, Arbiter? Are you ready to die? I have stitched your wounds – now let me give you another. Come to me. Here, I shall make it easy for you.' So saying he plunged both sabres into the ground.

'You cannot kill all of us!' shouted the Arbiter. 'Come on, men, let's take him!'

He rushed forward with a great shout. Lantern stepped in to meet him. His left hand caught the Arbiter's knife wrist and twisted it. The Arbiter grunted in pain and dropped the weapon. Lantern moved his foot beneath the falling weapon, flicking it back into the air. He caught it with his left hand, then rammed it through the Arbiter's right eye socket.

As the body fell he stepped back and swept up the sabres. 'The man was an idiot,' he said. 'But he was quite right. I cannot possibly kill you all. Probably no more than ten or twelve of you. Do you wish to draw lots, peasants? Or will you rush me all at once and check the bodies later?'

No-one moved. 'What about you?' asked Lantern, pointing the sabre at a broad-shouldered young man standing close by. 'Shall I spill your guts to the ground next? Well, speak up, worm!' He suddenly moved towards the man. The townsman cried out in fear and forced himself further back into the crowd. 'What about you, councillor?' Lantern raged, making towards Raseev Kalikan. 'Are you ready to die for your beloved townsfolk? Or do you think there has been enough entertainment for today?'

He advanced on the hapless Raseev, who stood blinking in the sunlight. The crowd moved back from the terrified politician.

'There has been enough . . . bloodshed,' whispered Raseev, as the blood-covered sabre touched his chest.

'Louder! Your miserable flock cannot hear you.'

'Don't kill me, Skilgannon!' he pleaded.

'Ah, so you know me then. No matter. Talk to your flock, Raseev Kalikan, while you still have a tongue to use. You know what to say.'

'There has been enough bloodshed!' shouted Raseev. 'Return to your homes now. Please, my friends. Let us go home. I did not want anyone hurt today. Antol should not have attacked the abbot. He has paid for it with his life. Now let us be civilized and pull back from the brink.'

'Wise words,' said Skilgannon.

For a moment the crowd did not move. Skilgannon turned his ice-blue gaze upon the nearest man, and he backed away. Others followed his lead, and soon the mob was dispersing. Raseev made to follow them.

'Not yet, councillor,' said Skilgannon, the sabre blade tapping at Raseev's shoulder. 'Nor you, captain,' he added, as Seregas backed away. 'How long have you known?'

'Only a few days, general,' said Seregas smoothly. 'I spotted the tattoo when you thrashed the Arbiter.'

'And you sent word to the east.'

'Of course. There is three thousand raq on your head.'

'Understandable,' said Skilgannon. Then he returned his attention to Raseev. 'I will not be here after today,' he told the councillor. 'But I will hear of all that happens after I am gone. Should any harm befall my brothers I shall come back. I will kill you in the old way – the Naashanite way. One piece of you will die at a time.'

Skilgannon turned his back on the two men and moved towards where Braygan knelt, cradling Abbot Cethelin. As he approached them Marja reared up from alongside the body of her husband. 'You bastard!' she screamed and ran at Skilgannon. Spinning on his heel he swayed aside. Marja stumbled and fell face first to the earth.

'By Heaven, I never did like that woman,' said Skilgannon.

Dropping to one knee he examined the wound in Cethelin's side. Antol's knife had slashed the skin above the hip, but had not penetrated deeply. 'I will stitch that wound for you,' he said.

'No, my son. You will not touch me. I feel the hatred and the anger radiating from you. It burns my soul. Braygan and Naslyn will take me to my chambers and attend me. You will join me there in a while. I have something for you.' Braygan and Naslyn lifted him to his feet. The old priest looked at the bodies and shook his head.

Skilgannon saw tears in his eyes.

Skilgannon stood silently as the two priests helped Cethelin across the open courtyard and into the buildings opposite. His hands were sticky with blood. Wiping them on his robes, he moved to a stone seat in the gateway arch and sat down. The woman, Marja, stirred and struggled to her knees. Skilgannon ignored her. She looked around, saw her dead husband and began to sob. The sound was pitiful. She stumbled over to the corpse and knelt beside it. Her grief was real, but it did not touch Skilgannon. She was one of those people who never gave thought to consequences. Marja had screamed for guts to be spilled. And they were.

Four more souls had been despatched on the long, dark journey.

Two years of suppressed rage had been released in a few terrifying heartbeats. Brother Lantern was a role he had tried so hard to play. His father's face appeared in his mind, as he always saw it, the broad features framed in a bronze helm, a transverse horse hair plume of white glinting in the sunlight.

'*We are what we are, my son.*'

Skilgannon had never forgotten those words. His father, Decado, had not been wearing the armour of a mercenary when he had spoken them. He had been on one of his rare visits home, recovering from a wound to his upper thigh and a broken wrist. Skilgannon had been sent home from school in disgrace after fighting two boys and knocking them both senseless. 'Blood runs true in our family line, Olek. We are warriors.' Decado had chuckled. 'People are like dogs, boy. There's the little, tubby fat ones everyone likes to pet, and the tall, rangy ones we watch race and bet upon. There's all kinds of house dogs with wagging tails. Then there's the wolf. It is strong. It has powerful jaws, and it is ferocious when roused. We are what we are, my son. And wolves is what we are. And all them little waggy-tail beasts best walk wary around us.'

Two months later his father was dead.

Trapped on a ridge by two divisions of Panthian infantry Decado had led a last charge down the slope. The few survivors talked of his incredible courage, and how he had almost reached the Panthian King. When the main body of the army arrived at the battlefield they found all but one of the corpses impaled on stakes. Decado was still sitting his horse, which had been tethered nearby. At first the relief force had thought him to be alive. When they reached him they saw he had been strapped to his saddle, his back held upright by three lengths of wood. His swords had been sheathed at his side, his rings still upon his fingers. In one closed fist they found a small gold coin, bearing the Panthian crest.

A rider brought the coin to Skilgannon. 'It is the toll for the Ferryman,' he told the boy. 'The Panthians wanted to ensure that he crossed the Dark River.'

Skilgannon had been horrified. 'Then what will he do now? You took the coin from him.'

'Do not worry, lad. I buried him with another coin – one of ours. It is still gold and the Ferryman will accept it. I wanted you to have this one. The Panthians honoured him, and this is the symbol of that honour.'

'We are what we are, my son. And wolves is what we are.'

Skilgannon the Damned was who he was, and who he would always be.

Hearing movement behind him he looked back, and saw the runaway priests returning, moving sheepishly back into the main building. It is all a nonsense, he thought. In all likelihood only Cethelin truly believed in the all-healing power of love. The rest? Naslyn wanted redemption, Braygan safety. Anager and the other runaways had probably chosen the priesthood as one might choose between being a tailor or a bootmaker. It was just a profession.

He could not find it in himself to hate Raseev Kalikan or the captain Seregas. At least there was purpose in their actions.

Skilgannon had stood beside Cethelin, and almost convinced himself that he would stand passively by and let the mob do as they would. The world would not be a poorer place without me, he had thought. Yet when the foul baker had stabbed Cethelin something had snapped inside Skilgannon. The darkness had been released.

Brother Anager crept alongside him, saw the bodies before the gates and made the sign of the Protective Horn. 'What happened here, Brother?' he whispered.

'I am not your brother,' said Skilgannon.

He walked back to his room and pulled the narrow chest from beneath the bed. From it he took a cream-coloured shirt of linen edged with white satin. It was collarless and sleeveless. He draped it across the bed and pulled clear a pair of leather leggings and a broad brown belt. These he laid alongside the shirt. Stripping off his blood-drenched robes, he tossed them to the floor and put on the clothes from the chest. He tugged on a pair of knee-length brown riding boots, then stood and stamped his feet. The boots felt tight after two years of wearing open sandals. Lastly he lifted clear a riding jacket of greased buckskin. This was also sleeveless, but long leather fringes, tipped with silver, had been placed over both shoulders. The silver was tarnished now and black, as were the silver rings – five on each side – which decorated the outer sides of

86

his boots from knee to ankle. Donning the jacket, he strolled from the room without a backward glance.

Brother Braygan was waiting in the courtyard. 'It was a nasty gash,' he told Skilgannon. 'Naslyn stitched it. I think he will be fine.'

'That is good.'

'You are leaving us?'

'How can I stay, Braygan? Even without the deaths they know who I am. Hunters will come, killers seeking bounty.'

'So you really are the Damned?'

'I am.'

'It is hard to believe. The stories must be . . . exaggerated.'

'No, they are not. Everything you have heard is true.'

Moving away from him Skilgannon mounted the steps to Cethelin's chambers. He found him upon his bed, Naslyn beside him. The black-bearded priest rose as he entered and left quietly. Skilgannon approached the bed and looked down at the grey face of the elderly abbot.

'I am sorry, Elder Brother.'

'As am I, Skilgannon. I thought my dream meant a candle of love. It did not. It meant a warrior's flame. Now everything we set out to do here is sullied. We are the priests who killed to save ourselves.'

'Would you sooner have died out there?'

'Yes, Skilgannon, I would. Or rather the priest that I am would. The man that I am is grateful for a few more days, months or years of life. Go to the closet over there. At its base you will find a bundle wrapped in an old blanket. Fetch it here.'

Skilgannon did as he was bid. As he touched the bundle he knew instinctively what was hidden within it. His pulse began to race. 'Open it,' ordered Cethelin.

'I do not want them.'

'Then take them from here and see them destroyed. When first you gave them to me I felt their evil. I hoped that you would become free of the dark power. I watched you suffer, and I took pride in the strength you showed. But I could not discard them, or sell them as you suggested. It would have been like loosing a plague on a troubled world. They are yours, Skilgannon. Take them. Take them far from here.'

Laying the bundle on a nearby table Skilgannon loosed the thongs that bound it and lifted clear the blanket. Lying there were the Swords of Night and Day. Sunlight from the window gleamed on the carved ivory handles, and glinted upon the single polished black sheath. Taking hold of the silver-edged baldric connecting both ends of the sheath he swung the weapons to his back. There was something else in the bundle, a bulging leather pouch. He hefted it.

'There are twenty-eight golden raq in that pouch,' said Cethelin. 'All that remains of the money from the stallion I sold for you. The rest was used to purchase food for the poor during the drought year.'

'Did you know who I was when I came here, Elder Brother?'

'Yes.'

'Why then did you let me stay?'

'No man is beyond redemption. Even the Damned. It is our duty to love the unlovable, and by so doing open their hearts to the Source. Do I regret it? Yes. Would I do it again? Yes. You recall I asked you if you would grant me a favour? Do you still hold to that?'

'Of course.'

'I am sending Braygan to the elders in Mellicane. Go with him and see him safely into their charge.'

'Braygan is a pure soul. Do you not think he might be corrupted by my evil?'

'Perhaps. Yes, he is pure and unsullied. He is also untried and understands little of the harshness of this world. If he can walk with you to Mellicane and remain pure then he will be a better priest for it. If he cannot then he should seek a future outside the church. Farewell, Skilgannon.'

'I preferred it when you called me Brother Lantern.'

'Brother Lantern died outside these walls, Skilgannon. He fled when the blood flowed. One day he may return. I will pray for that day. Go now. The sight of you offends me.'

Skilgannon said no more. Turning away from the old priest he moved to the door and stepped outside. Naslyn was waiting. Reaching out, he gripped Skilgannon's arm. 'I thank you, Brother,' he said.

'For your life?'

'For giving me the courage to stay.' Naslyn sighed. 'I am no philosopher. Maybe Cethelin is right. Maybe we should just offer our love to the world and let the world rip our hearts out. I have no answers, man. But given the choice between having Cethelin in this world, or that foul baker, Antol, I know which I'd choose.' He looked Skilgannon in the eye. 'You are a brave man, and I respect you. Where will you go?'

'First to Mellicane. After that? I do not know.'

'May the Source be with you, wherever you journey.'

'He and I are not on speaking terms, I fear. Take care, Naslyn.'

CHAPTER FIVE

RABALYN LAY VERY STILL, KNOWING THAT IF HE MOVED THE DRAGON would see him. He could feel the fire of its breath on his arm, his chest, and the left side of his face. The pain was searing. The youth did not look at the dragon. He lay with his eyes closed, using all his strength not to cry out. His body began to shake. The dragon's fire ceased, and then a terrible cold settled over him. He knew then that the dragon had been replaced by a Frost Demon. Aunt Athyla had spoken of such creatures in the far north. They would creep close to homes and chill the bones of the sick and weak. If anything the cold was worse than the dragon's heat. It ate into his flesh.

Rabalyn opened his eyes and struggled to his knees. He was in a small hollow, surrounded by trees and bushes. Weak sunlight was filtering through the branches overhead. His hand touched a thick fallen branch. He grabbed it and wielded it like a club. Then looked around for the Frost Demon. Sweat was dripping into his eyes.

There was no demon. No dragon. His throat was awfully dry, and his arms and face prickled with pain.

'Dreaming,' he said aloud. The trembling grew worse. His naked body was soaked with sweat and dew and the light breeze blowing through the woods felt like a winter blizzard. Rabalyn rose on unsteady legs and made it to a thick bush. Crouching down, he groaned as fresh pain flared from his thigh. He glanced down and saw that the skin was puckered and raw. He lay down. It seemed warmer here, and, for a few moments, he felt almost normal. The warmth grew. And grew. Sweat bathed his features and dripped from his face.

He saw again the knife slam into Todhe's neck, and Aunt Athyla's body lying before the burning house.

The dragon returned. This time Rabalyn looked at it, uncaring and unafraid. Its body was golden and scaled, its head long and flat. The fire that burned Rabalyn did not come from its mouth, but from its eyes. So bright they were that it pained the youth to look upon them. 'Go away,' he whispered. 'Leave me be.'

'He is delirious,' said the dragon.

'The burns are festering,' said another voice.

Rabalyn drifted into strange dreams. He was floating upon a clear lake. The water was cool upon his skin, save for where the sun beat down on his face and arm. He tried to lower himself further into the cold liquid, but it was impossible. Aunt Athyla was there, sitting in an old chair. He realized then that he was not in a lake at all, but in a shallow bath. 'Where have you been, child?' asked Aunt Athyla. 'It is very late.'

'I'm sorry, Aunt. I don't know where I've been.'

'Do you think he will die?' someone asked Aunt Athyla.

Rabalyn could not see the speaker. Aunt Athyla did not answer. She was unravelling a ball of wool. Only it wasn't wool. It was fire. A ball of fire. 'I shall make you a cloak,' she said. 'It will keep you warm in the winter.'

'I don't want it,' he said.

'Nonsense. It will be a lovely cloak. Here, feel the wool.'

She rubbed the fire against his face and he screamed.

Darkness swamped him. When the light came again he found himself looking at the strangest sight. A man was kneeling over him, but floating above the man's shoulders were two curious faces. One was dark, with wide, slanted golden eyes, like a wolf; the other was pale, the mouth a long gash filled with pointed teeth. The eyes were slitted, like those of a cat. Both faces shimmered, as if shaped from woodsmoke. The man seemed

91

oblivious of the smoke creatures. 'Can you hear me, Rabalyn?' he asked.

The face was familiar, but he could not place it in his memory, and drifted off into more dreams.

When at last he awoke the pain from his burns was more bearable. He was lying on the ground, a blanket covering him. There was a bandage over his left arm. Rabalyn groaned. Immediately a man came and knelt beside him. He recognized him as one of the priests.

'I know you,' he said.

'I am Brother Braygan,' said the man, helping Rabalyn to sit and offering him a drink of water. Rabalyn took the copper cup and drained it. 'How did you come by these burns?'

'Todhe set fire to my aunt's house.'

'I am sorry. Is your aunt all right?'

'No. She died.'

Another figure moved alongside. At first Rabalyn failed to recognize him. He was wearing a fringed jacket, and his arms were bare. A black spider had been tattooed upon his forearm. Rabalyn looked into the man's pale eyes. He realized it was the priest, Brother Lantern. 'They are hunting you, boy,' said Lantern. 'You cannot go back to the town.'

'I know. I killed Todhe. I wish I hadn't.'

'He'll have to come with us,' said Brother Braygan.

'What will he do in Mellicane?' snapped Lantern. 'Become a beggar on the streets?'

'My mother and father are there,' said Rabalyn. 'I shall find them.'

'There, that is settled then,' said Braygan. 'You rest for now. I have applied herbal poultices to the burns on your legs and arms. They will be painful for a while, but they will heal, I think.'

Rabalyn drifted off to sleep – and slowly sank into a lake of dreams. When he awoke it was dark. The dreams drifted away like mist on the breeze.

Save for one. He remembered a terrible axe, and a man with eyes the colour of a winter sky. Rabalyn shivered at the memory.

In the morning Brother Lantern took a spare shirt and breeches from his pack and gave them to Rabalyn. The shirt was of a soft cloth Rabalyn had never seen before. There was a sheen to it that caught the light. It was pale blue, and upon the breast was a small snake, embroidered in gold thread. It was coiled and ready to strike. 'My burns will stain the cloth,' said Rabalyn. 'I don't want to ruin such a fine shirt.'

'It is just an item of clothing,' said Lantern dismissively. The breeches were of a thin, black leather, and too long for the youth. Braygan knelt at his feet, folding the leather up and over Rabalyn's ankles. From his own pack Braygan took a pair of sandals. Rabalyn tied them on. They were an almost perfect fit.

'There, that should suffice,' said Braygan. 'You look like a young nobleman.'

The next few days proved difficult for Rabalyn. The burns did not heal swiftly, the flesh puckering and splitting. Even the new skin, when it formed, was tight and easily broken. The pain was constant. He tried not to complain, for he realized that the tall warrior, who had been Brother Lantern, did not want him around. The man rarely spoke to him. On the other hand he didn't speak much to Brother Braygan either. He just strode on ahead, sometimes disappearing from view. Whenever they passed through areas of hills he would run up the tallest slope and study their back trail.

On the morning of the fourth day the warrior – as Rabalyn had come to think of him – ushered them off the road and into thick undergrowth. There they crouched behind a screen of bushes as five horsemen came into sight, riding hard. Rabalyn recognized the lean figure of Seregas, the Captain of the Watch.

After the horsemen had passed Rabalyn felt close to tears. His wounds were painful. He was travelling with strangers, one of whom did not like him, and the officers of the Watch were still hunting him. What if they followed him all the way to Mellicane, and reported him as a murderer?

The warrior led them deeper into the woods to the left of the trail, and for most of the day they travelled over rough country. By evening Rabalyn was exhausted. The warrior found a hidden hollow and lit a small fire. Rabalyn did not sit too close to it. His wounds could not tolerate heat.

Brother Braygan brought him a bowl of broth. 'Are you feeling a little better?' he asked.

'Yes.'

'You are sad because of your aunt. I see it in your eyes.'

Rabalyn felt ashamed. He had been more concerned with his own plight, and guilt at his selfishness bore down on him. 'She was a good woman,' he said, unwilling to lie outright.

The warrior had vanished into the night, and Rabalyn felt more comfortable in his absence. 'I wish he'd just go away,' he said aloud.

'Who?' asked Braygan. Rabalyn was immediately embarrassed. He had not meant to voice the thought.

'Brother Lantern. He frightens me.'

'He will do you no harm, Rabalyn. Lantern is a . . . good man.'

'What happened back at the church? Did the mob go there?'

'Yes.'

'Did they burn everything?'

'They burned nothing, Rabalyn. Tell me about your parents. Do you know where they live now?'

Rabalyn shook his head. 'Don't suppose they'll want me around. They left me and my sister with Aunt Athyla years ago. They never sent word or anything. They don't even know Lesha is dead. Truth is they're both worthless.'

Now it was Braygan who looked uncomfortable. 'Never say that, my friend. We all have weaknesses. No-one is perfect. You must learn to forgive.'

Rabalyn did not respond. Aunt Athyla had never spoken badly of his parents, but as he grew older he heard stories. His father had been a lazy man, twice dismissed and once jailed for a year for stealing from his employers. He was also a drunkard, and Rabalyn's one clear memory of him was seeing him strike his mother in the face after a row. She had been hurled back against a wall, half stunned. Rabalyn had been six years old at the time, and he had run to his mother, in tears. That was when his father kicked him. 'How is a man supposed to make something of himself?' his father had shouted. 'Bad enough trying to earn enough to get by, without having to feed and clothe ungrateful brats.'

Rabalyn hated weakness. And he had never understood why his mother had deserted her children to go off with a man so lacking in virtue. He had only told the priests about his parents' being in

Mellicane so that they would not leave him to his fate. He had no intention of seeking them out. Let them rot wherever they are, he thought.

Braygan moved to the small fire, and added several dry sticks. 'So what happened when the mob went to the church?' asked Rabalyn.

'I don't really want to talk about it.'

'Why?'

'It was ugly, Rabalyn. Horrible.'

The priest's face showed his sorrow, and Rabalyn watched him sitting quietly and staring into the fire. 'Is Jesper all right?' asked the boy.

'Jesper?'

'Kalia's dog.'

'Oh, yes, the dog is fine. Abbot Cethelin is looking after him.'

'Why is Brother Lantern not dressed like a priest?'

'He has left the Order. Like me he is . . . was . . . an acolyte. He had not taken his final vows. Would you like something to eat?'

'I'd like to know what happened at the church,' said Rabalyn. 'What was so horrible?'

Braygan sighed. 'Men died, Rabalyn. The abbot was stabbed.'

'Brother Lantern stopped them, didn't he?'

Braygan glanced at the boy. 'How would you know that?'

'I don't *know* it. Just guessed really. I saw him knock over that Arbiter attacking you. He didn't seem afraid. Then he just ordered the crowd to carry the Arbiter into the tavern. I guessed he'd do the same if the mob came to the church. Who did he kill?'

'As I said, I do not want to talk about it. Perhaps you should ask Lantern when he returns.'

'He won't talk about it. And he doesn't like me.'

Braygan smiled sheepishly. 'He doesn't like me much either.'

'Then why are you travelling together?'

'The abbot asked him to see me safely to Mellicane.'

'What will you do when you get there?'

'Deliver letters to the church elders, and then take my vows before the bishop.'

'Is it a long way?'

'Just over a hundred and fifty miles. Lantern thinks the journey will take another twelve, perhaps fifteen days.'

'What about the war? Will we see soldiers?'

'I do hope not,' said Braygan, suddenly fearful. 'There are several settlements between here and the capital. We will purchase provisions from them and keep away from the major roads.'

'Have you ever been to the capital?'

'No. Never.'

'Kalia has. She said they have huge beasts there, who fight in the arena. And Kellias the Pedlar told us that some of them were going to be fighting in the war. He said they were called Joinings, and that the King had promised an army of them to fight off our evil enemies.'

'I do not like to speak of such things,' said Braygan, attempting a stern tone, and failing miserably.

'I'd like to see one,' added Rabalyn.

'Be careful of what you wish for, boy,' said Lantern, silently emerging from the trees. 'The Joinings are a curse, and anyone who seeks to use them is a fool.'

On the morning of the sixth day, tired and hungry, their provisions almost exhausted, they arrived at a waystation just outside a small village nestling in the hills. Skilgannon scanned the area. There were three wooden structures and a corral containing no horses. Smoke was drifting lazily from the chimney of the largest building. Beyond the waystation there was no sign of movement in the village, save for a fox that darted across the main street, disappearing into an alley.

Skilgannon told Rabalyn and Braygan to wait at the edge of the trees, then strode down to the corral. As he approached it a burly man appeared from the main building. He was tall and round-shouldered, his hair close-cropped, but his brown beard thick and shaggy.

'Good morning to you,' he said.

'And to you. Where are your horses?'

'Soldiers took them. The station is closed until further notice.'

Skilgannon glanced towards the silent village. 'All gone,' said the man. 'The Datians are less than a day from here. So people grabbed what they could and fled.'

'But not you.'

The man shrugged. 'Nowhere to go, son. This is my home. There's still food left, so if you and your friends want breakfast you are welcome.'

'That is kind of you.'

'Glad to have the company, tell you the truth. My name is Seth,' he said, stepping forward and extending his hand. Skilgannon shook it. Seth glanced down at the spider tattoo. 'There's men looking for you,' he added. 'They were here yesterday. Big reward, they said.'

'Huge,' agreed Skilgannon.

'Best you don't stay too long then,' said Seth, with a grin. 'Expect they'll be back.' Then he turned and walked back inside.

Skilgannon summoned the others. Most of the space within the building was taken up by a storage area, now empty, but several tables and a dozen chairs had been set by the western wall. Seth seated them, then wandered away to the kitchen. Skilgannon rose and followed him. The big man took up a frying pan and placed it atop a large stove. Wrapping a cloth around his hand, he pulled clear the iron cover and moved the pan to the flames. Then from the larder he took a large chunk of smoked ham, and carved eight slices. As they were placed in the pan they began to sizzle. Skilgannon's stomach tightened as the smell of frying bacon filled the air.

'You don't need to worry about me, son,' said Seth. 'I'm not interested in bounties.'

'Where did the villagers go?'

'Some headed for Mellicane, others went south. Some headed up into the high hills. The war is lost. No doubt of it. The soldiers who stole the horses were deserters. They told me that only the capital still holds out against the Datians.' Seth flipped the bacon slices with a long knife. 'You are a Naashanite?'

'No, but I was raised there.'

'Word was that the Witch Queen would send an army to help us. Never came.' The bearded man pushed the bacon to the side of the large pan. From the larder he took a bowl of eggs, and, one by one, cracked six of them. Three of the yolks split, the golden centres seeping over the congealing mess in the pan. 'Never was much of a cook,' he said, with a grin. 'It will still taste good, though. Fine hens. Trust me.'

Skilgannon relaxed and smiled. 'How long have you been here?'

'Twelve years this summer. Not a bad place, you know. People are friendly, and – before the war – the station was pretty busy. Postal riders and travellers. I built the sleeping quarters myself. At one time I was even turning business away. Twenty beds, full for a month. Thought I was going to get rich.'

'What would you do if you were rich?'

Seth laughed. 'No idea, man. I've no taste for finery. Having said that, there was a fancy whorehouse in Mellicane that I always hankered to try. There was a woman there who charged ten gold raq for a single night. Can you believe that? She must have been something.' He glanced down at the mess in the pan. 'Well, I think it's ready.'

He served the meal onto four wooden platters. He and Skilgannon carried them back into the dining area, and they ate in silence – after Braygan had offered a prayer of thanks.

When they had finished Seth leaned back in his chair. 'Second breakfast of the day for me,' he said. 'Damned if it didn't taste better than the first.'

'How will you survive here on your own?' asked Braygan.

'I have my hens, and I know how to hunt. There's also quite a bit of grain hidden close by. I'll do well enough – if this war ends by the summer. People will start coming back then. Business will pick up.'

'Wouldn't it be safer to go to Mellicane?' asked Braygan.

Seth looked at the priest and smiled. 'Nowhere is truly safe in a war, young man. Mellicane is a city under siege. If it falls the slaughter will be terrible. Look what happened in Perapolis when the Damned took it. He killed everyone, men, women, babes in arms. No, I think I'll stay here in my home. If I'm to be killed it'll be in a place I love.'

An uncomfortable silence fell. Braygan looked away.

'I'd like to purchase some supplies from you, Seth,' said Skilgannon.

For the next five days the travellers moved northwest, ever downwards into lush valleys and low woodland. The temperature rose sharply, and both Braygan and Rabalyn found the going increasingly hard. Sweat itched and tingled on Rabalyn's healing burns, and Braygan, unused to such sustained exercise, stumbled along on painful legs. Occasionally he would suffer severe cramps in his calves and be forced to sit until the agony passed. They saw few people in this time, though occasionally glimpsed riders in the distance.

On the morning of the sixth day they came across the smoking ruins of a small farm. Five bodies lay on the open ground. Crows were feasting on dead flesh. Braygan shepherded Rabalyn from the scene, while Skilgannon moved to where the bodies lay. As he approached the crows flew away a little distance and waited.

There were three adults, one man and two women, and two small girls. Skilgannon examined the ground around them. The earth was churned by the hooves of many horses, though it was impossible to tell how many. At least twenty, he thought. The bodies were all close together, so it was likely they were led from the building and murdered. Otherwise – if they had tried to run – they would have been slain further apart. There was no indication that the women had been raped. They were fully clothed. Skilgannon rose to his feet. A cavalry group had ridden in, looted the farmhouse, then murdered the family who lived there. The farm had then been torched. In the distance Skilgannon could see other farms. Those had not been set ablaze.

Calling to Braygan and Rabalyn, he walked across the ploughed fields towards the next farmhouse. It was deserted.

'Why did they kill that family?' asked Braygan.

'Any number of reasons,' Skilgannon told him. 'The most likely is that such an act would spread terror. All the other families in this area, seeing the smoke, and perhaps even witnessing the killings, have fled. My guess is that by terrorizing the rural areas the Datians are forcing more and more people to seek refuge in Mellicane.'

'I don't understand.'

'Food, Braygan. Wars are not won merely by defeating enemies on the field of battle. Mellicane is a fortress city. Everyone there needs to eat. If you swell the numbers then food will run out more swiftly. Without food they cannot resist an enemy. The city might then surrender, and save the need for a sustained siege.'

Skilgannon left Braygan and Rabalyn at a deserted farmhouse, then set out to scout the area.

There were few farm animals anywhere. Skilgannon saw two pigs and several hens, but any sheep or cattle had been driven away, probably to feed the armies converging on Mellicane.

Pausing at a well, he drew up a bucket of water and drank deeply.

Seth had talked of a Naashanite army that was supposed to come to the aid of the Tantrian King. It would come, Skilgannon knew, but intentionally too late. Centuries ago Tantria, Datia and Dospilis had been part of the Naashanite empire. The Queen desired those lands again. Better to let the three nations tear each other apart first, then move in to conquer them all.

He sat on the wall of the well and wished that he could just walk away, find a horse and head north towards Sherak. If the Temple of the Resurrectionists existed he would find it, then bring back to life the woman who had married him. 'I wish I could have loved you more,' he said aloud. Closing his eyes he pictured Dayan's face, her golden hair bound in a braid of silver wire, her smile bright and dazzling. Then, without warning, another face appeared, long dark hair framing features of singular perfection. Dark eyes looked into his own, and full lips parted in a smile that clove his heart.

Skilgannon groaned and surged upright. Even now he could not picture Dayan without summoning the memory of Jianna.

'Do you love me, Olek?' Dayan had asked, on the night of their wedding.

'Who could not love you, Dayan? You are everything a man could desire.'

'Do you love me with all your heart?'

'I will try to make you happy, and I will take no other wives, nor concubines. That is my promise to you.'

'My father warned me about you, Olek. He said you were in love with the Queen. That all men knew this. Have you lain with her?'

'No questions, Dayan. The past is gone. The future is ours. This is our night. The servants are gone, the moon is bright, and you are the most beautiful woman in all the world.'

His thoughts were interrupted by the sound of horses' hooves. Glancing to the west he saw three riders approaching. They were soldiers, bearing white crests upon their helms. Skilgannon stood quietly as they approached. They were carrying small, round, unadorned shields, and he could not identify which army they fought for.

The lead rider, a tall man with a wispy blond beard, drew rein. He said nothing, but stared at Skilgannon with cold, blue eyes. His comrades drew alongside, waiting for orders. 'Are you from this village?' asked the leader, after a few more moments of silence. The voice was low, with a soft burr that suggested the east. Probably Datian, thought Skilgannon.

'I am passing through.'

'A refugee then?'

'Not yet.'

'What does that mean?'

'It means I see no reason to run and hide. Feel free to water your horses.'

A touch of anger showed in the rider's eyes. 'I *am* free to water my horses. I need no permission from you.'

'Were you in the group that murdered the farmer and his family?' asked Skilgannon, gesturing towards the blackened farmhouse in the distance.

The man leaned back in his saddle, crossing his hands on the pommel horn. 'You are very cool, stranger.'

'I am merely enjoying the sunshine and a sip of water from a well. I am at war with no-one.'

'The whole world is at war,' snapped one of the riders, a young beardless man with long black hair, wrapped tightly into two braids.

'Tantria is not the world,' said Skilgannon. 'It is merely a small nation.'

'Shall I kill him, sir?' asked the rider, looking towards the blond warrior. The man's eyes held to Skilgannon's gaze.

'No. Water the horses,' he said, dismounting and loosening his saddle girth. Skilgannon walked away from them and sat quietly on a fence rail. The leader, leaving his horse with the black-haired rider, moved to join him. 'Where are you from?' he asked.

'South.'

'Where are you heading?'

'Mellicane.'

'The city will fall.'

'I expect you are right. I'll not be there long.'

The rider eased himself up onto the fence rail, and glanced back towards the smouldering farmhouse. 'I was not with that group,' he said. 'Though I could have been. What is your business in Mellicane?'

'I am escorting a priest who wishes to take his vows there, and a boy seeking lost parents.'

'Not a Naashanite messenger then?'

'No.'

'I see you sport the Spider on your arm. Naashanite custom, is it not?'

'Yes. I served the Queen for a number of years. Now I do not.'

'You realize I should either kill you or take you back to our camp?'

'You do not have enough men with you to attempt it,' said Skilgannon softly. 'Otherwise that is precisely what you would do.'

The rider smiled. 'Exactly so. Would you explain to me how a warrior like yourself became engaged in so small a mission?'

'A man I owed asked it of me.'

'Ah, I see. A man should always honour his debts. We are nothing without honour. There is talk of a Naashanite army preparing to come against us. You think there is truth in the rumour?'

Skilgannon looked at the man. 'You know there is.'

'Aye,' muttered the soldier sadly. 'The Witch Queen has played us all for fools. Together we could have withstood her. Now we have more than decimated our armies. And for what? Datia and Dospilis together are not strong enough to hold Tantria. How soon will they come, do you think?'

'As soon as Mellicane falls,' said Skilgannon. 'It is no more than a guess. I have no contact now with Naashan.'

The soldier stretched, then climbed to his feet and replaced his horsehair-crested helm. He tightened the chin strap then offered his hand to Skilgannon. 'Good luck with your mission, Naashanite.'

Skilgannon stepped down from the fence and accepted the handshake. The rider gripped him hard. Then his left hand swept out from behind his back. A thin-bladed dagger flashed upward towards Skilgannon's throat. Instead of trying to pull away Skilgannon threw himself forward, his forehead slamming into the bridge of the soldier's nose. The dagger thrust missed Skilgannon's throat, the blade causing a shallow cut to the skin at the back of his neck. Still gripping the rider's right hand Skilgannon spun to his left, lifting the trapped arm and twisting it. The man cried in pain. Skilgannon dropped him, leapt back and drew the Swords of Night and Day.

The other two soldiers ran forward, swords drawn. Their captain scrambled to his feet.

'You are a skilled fighter, Naashanite. You realize that I had to make the attempt to kill you? My men here would have reported me had I merely let you go. No hard feelings, eh?'

'You are a stupid man,' Skilgannon told him, his voice trembling with suppressed rage. 'I had no wish to kill you. You could have lived. Your men could have lived.' Even as he spoke he leapt forward. The first of the soldiers – the young man with black, braided hair – managed to parry the thrust from the golden blade, but the silver sword opened his throat to the bone. The second soldier charged in – only to have his chest skewered by a single thrust. Skilgannon dragged clear his blade and stepped back as the body toppled towards him.

The leader backed away. Skilgannon cleaned his blades and sheathed them. Then he looked at the rider. Slowly the man drew his cavalry sabre.

'I have struggled for years to put this vileness behind me,' said Skilgannon. 'A man like you can have no understanding of how hard that was.'

'I have a wife and children,' said the man. 'I don't want to die. Not here. Not so uselessly.'

Skilgannon sighed. 'Then walk away,' he said. 'I will take your horses. By the time you send men after us we will be long gone.' With that he walked past the rider towards the waiting mounts.

For a moment it seemed the soldier would let him go. Then, seeing Skilgannon's back, he raised his sabre and darted forward.

Skilgannon spun. A shining circle of serrated metal tore through the rider's throat. Blood gouted from the wound. The man choked and stumbled, falling to his knees.

With scrabbling fingers he tried to close the wound. Skilgannon walked past him, gathered up the circle of steel, then returned to kneel by the dying man. The fallen rider began to tremble violently, then with one last gasp he died.

Skilgannon wiped the steel weapon clean on the dead man's sleeve, then rose and walked to the horses.

'You seem very sad,' said Rabalyn, moving to sit opposite Braygan at the dining table. The deserted house was cheerless, as if yearning for the people who had fled it in fear.

'I am sad, Rabalyn. It hurts my heart to see such violence. That family back there were not soldiers. They grew crops and they loved one another. I cannot understand how people can commit such acts of evil.'

Rabalyn said nothing. He had killed Todhe, and killing was evil. Even so he now *knew* how such acts began. Rage, grief and fear had propelled him into the murder of Todhe. And Todhe himself had been angry with him, which is why he had set fire to the house . . . Lost in thought Rabalyn sat quietly at the table.

Braygan stared around the large room. It had been carefully constructed, originally of logs, but the inner walls had been plastered. The floor was hard-packed earth, but someone had etched designs upon it, spirals and circles that had then been dusted with powdered red clay, creating crimson patterns. Everything about the room spoke of care and love. The furniture had not been crafted by a trained carpenter, but had been carved and adorned by someone trying hard to master the skills; someone willing to add small individual touches to the pieces. A clumsy rose had been carved into the back of one of the chairs, and what might have been an ear of corn had been started on another. A family had tried to make a life here, filling the room with evidence of their love. Initials had been carved into the beam above the hearth. 'I think I would like the people who lived here, Rabalyn,' he said. 'I hope they are safe.'

Rabalyn nodded, but still said nothing. He didn't know these people, and, truth to tell, he didn't much care if they were safe or not. Rising, he wandered about the house, seeking any food that might have been left behind. In a deep larder he found some pottery jars with cork stoppers. Removing one he looked inside. It was filled with honey. Rabalyn dipped his finger into it and licked it greedily. The silky sweetness on his tongue was beyond pleasurable. Aunt Athyla had used honey in her baking, but Rabalyn's favourite snack was to toast stale bread over the fire, then smear it with honey. Finding a wooden spoon, he sat down in the kitchen and scooped out several spoonfuls. After a while the sweetness began to cloy on his tongue. Putting aside the jar he walked outside to the well, and drew up a bucket of water. Drinking deeply, he washed away the sugary taste. Then he saw Brother Lantern riding towards the house. He was leading two other horses.

Rabalyn walked out to meet the warrior. The horses looked huge, quite unlike the shaggy ponies to be seen back in Skepthia. Rabalyn stepped aside as they passed. They loomed above him and he reached out to stroke the flank of the nearest. Its chestnut-coloured coat gleamed and its powerful muscles rippled under his hand.

Skilgannon rode past Rabalyn without a word and dismounted at the house, tethering the horses to a post. Rabalyn followed him as he walked inside. Braygan looked up. 'Did you discover any more victims?' he asked.

'No. We have horses. Do you ride?'

'I once rode a pony around a paddock.'

'These are not ponies. These are war horses, highly trained and intelligent. They will expect equal intelligence from you. Come outside. It will not be safe to stay here long, but we will risk a short training period.'

'I would just as soon walk,' said Braygan.

'There are three dead Datians back there,' said the warrior, 'and they will be discovered before long. Walking is no longer an option. Follow me.'

Once outside he gestured to Rabalyn, and helped him mount the chestnut gelding the boy had stroked moments earlier. 'Kick your feet from the stirrups,' said Skilgannon.

Rabalyn did so, glancing down as the warrior adjusted the height of each stirrup. 'Gently take hold of the reins. Remember that the horse's mouth is tender, so no savage jerking or pulling.' He led the horse away from the others, then glanced back at Rabalyn. 'Do not grip with your legs. Sit easy. Now merely walk him around for a while.' Releasing his hold on the bridle Skilgannon moved back to where Braygan was standing.

'These horses don't like me,' said Braygan.

'That is because you are standing there staring at them. Come forward. Keep your movements slow and easy.' He helped the priest to mount, then adjusted his stirrups, repeating the advice he had given to Rabalyn.

Lastly Skilgannon sprang easily into the saddle of a steeldust gelding and rode alongside the two nervous novices. 'The horse has four gaits,' he said, 'walk, trot, canter and gallop. Walking, as we are now doing, is simple. You just sit lightly in the saddle. The trot is not so simple. The horse will break into what is known as a two-time gait.'

'What does that mean?' asked Braygan.

'The horse will step from one diagonally opposite pair of legs to the other. Near-fore and off-hind together, then off-fore and near-hind. This will create a bouncing effect and your backsides will be pummelled until you learn to move with the rhythm. Stay tall in the saddle. Do not slouch.'

They spent an hour in the open fields behind the farmhouse. Rabalyn learned swiftly, and even cantered his mount briefly at one point. For Braygan the entire exercise was a nightmare.

'If I strapped a dead man to the saddle he'd show more rhythm than you,' said the warrior. 'What is wrong with you?'

'I am frightened. I don't want to fall off.'

'Kick your feet from the stirrups.' Braygan did so. 'Now let go of the reins.' Once more Braygan obeyed him. Skilgannon suddenly clapped his hands and yelled. Braygan's horse reared then broke into a run. The movement was so sudden that the priest fell backwards, turning a somersault before striking the soft earth. Shakily he climbed to his feet. 'There,' said the warrior. 'Now you have fallen off. As ever the fear of it was not matched by the actuality.'

'You could have broken my neck.'

'True. The one certainty about riding, Braygan, is that – at some time – you will fall off. It is a fact. Another fact you might like to consider, in your life of perpetual terror, is that you will die. We are all going to die, some of us young, some of us old, some of us in our sleep, some of us screaming in agony. We cannot stop it, we can only delay it. And now it is time to move on. I'd like to reach those far hills by dusk. We can find a campsite in the trees.'

CHAPTER SIX

RABALYN ENJOYED THE DAY'S RIDE MORE THAN HE COULD EXPRESS. HE knew that he would always remember it with enormous affection. If he was lucky enough to live until he grew old he would look back to this day as one of the great, defining moments of his life. It was an effort not to let the horse have its head and ride off at ferocious speed towards the distant hills. As he sat in the saddle he could feel the power of the beast beneath him. It was awesome. As Brother Lantern had instructed him he chatted to the gelding, keeping his voice low and soothing. The gelding's ears would flick back as he spoke, as if listening and understanding. Rabalyn patted its sleek neck. At one point he drew rein and let the others ride on for a while, then gently heeled the gelding into a run. Exhilaration swept through him as he settled into the saddle, adjusting his rhythm so that there was no painful bouncing. He and the horse were one – and they were fast and strong. No-one could catch them.

As he approached the others he tried to rein in. But the gelding was at full gallop now and swept on by them, ignoring his commands. Even then, with the horse bolting, Rabalyn felt no fear. A wild excitement roared through him. Dragging on the reins he began to shout: 'Whoa, boy. Whoa!' The horse seemed to run even faster.

Brother Lantern's steeldust came galloping alongside. 'Don't drag on the reins, boy,' he shouted. 'It will only numb his mouth. Gently turn him to the right. As he turns keep applying gentle tugs to the reins.' Rabalyn followed the orders. Slowly the gelding began to angle to the right. He slowed to a canter and then a trot. Finally, at the gentlest of tugs the gelding halted, alert and waiting for the next instruction.

'Well done,' said the warrior, drawing rein a little way from Rabalyn. 'You will be a fine rider.'

'Why did he bolt? Was he frightened of something?'

'Yes, but he doesn't know what. You have to understand, Rabalyn, that a horse in the wild uses its speed to avoid danger. When you pushed him to the gallop ancestral memories took over. He was running fast, therefore he was in danger. Panic can set in very fast in a horse. That is why the rider must always be in control. When he broke into that run you relaxed and gave him his head. Thus, left to his own devices, he panicked.'

'It was a wonderful feeling. He is so fast. I bet he could have been a racer.'

'He is a young war horse,' said the man, with a smile, 'skittish and a little nervous. A Ventrian pure blood would leave him for dead in a flat race. On a battlefield the Ventrian would be a liability. It is not as agile and its fleetness can be a hazard. But, yes, he is a fine mount for a young man in open country.'

'Should I give him a name, Brother Lantern?'

'Call me Skilgannon. And, yes, you can call him what you will. If you have him long enough he will come to recognize it.'

Braygan approached them at an awkward trot, the young priest bouncing in the saddle, his arms flapping. 'Some men are not made to ride,' said Skilgannon softly. 'I am beginning to feel sorry for that horse.' With that he swung his mount and continued on their way.

By late afternoon they were climbing ever higher into wooded hills. Through breaks in the trees, Rabalyn could see a vast plain below them to the northwest. He saw also columns of people walking, and occasionally mounted troops. They were too far away to identify as friend or foe. Rabalyn didn't care which they were. His gelding was faster than the winter wind.

109

That night they camped at the base of a cliff. Skilgannon allowed no fire, but the night was warm and pleasant. A search of the saddlebags produced two wooden-handled brushes and Skilgannon showed Braygan and Rabalyn how to unsaddle the mounts and then groom them. Lastly he led the horses out a little way to where the grass was thick and green. Then, with short ropes also from the saddlebags, he hobbled them and left them to feed.

Braygan was complaining about his sore legs and bruised backside, but Skilgannon paid no attention, and soon the young priest wrapped himself in a blanket and settled down to sleep. The night sky was clear, the stars brilliantly bright. Skilgannon walked a little way from the camp and was sitting alone. Normally Rabalyn would not disturb him, but the man had – for the first time – spoken in a friendly way after Rabalyn's horse bolted. So, with just a hint of trepidation, Rabalyn walked across to where the warrior was sitting. As he came up Skilgannon glanced round. His gaze was once more cold and distant.

'You want something?'

'No,' said Rabalyn, instantly turning away.

'Come and join me, boy,' said Skilgannon, his voice softening. 'I am not the ogre I appear.'

'You seem very angry all the time.'

'That would be a fair judgement,' agreed Skilgannon. 'Sit down. I'll try not to snap at you.' Rabalyn sat on the ground, but could think of nothing to say. The silence grew, and yet Rabalyn found it comfortable. He looked up at the warrior. He no longer seemed so daunting.

'Is it hard being a monk?' he asked, after a while.

'Is it hard being a boy?' countered Skilgannon.

'Very.'

'I fear that answer could be given by any man, in any position. Life itself is hard. But, yes, I found it especially difficult. The studies were easy enough, and quite enjoyable. The philosophy, on the other hand, was exquisitely impenetrable. We were ordered to love the unlovable.'

'How do you do that?'

'You're asking the wrong man.'

'That is blood on your neck,' said Rabalyn.

110

'A scratch from an idiot. It is nothing.'

'What will you do when you get to Mellicane?'

Skilgannon looked at him, then smiled. 'I shall leave as soon as possible.'

'Can I go with you?'

'What about your parents?'

'They don't care about me. Never did, really. I only said I was looking for them so you wouldn't leave me behind.'

'Ah,' said Skilgannon. 'Very wise – for I would have.'

'What will you do now you are not a monk?'

'You are full of questions, Rabalyn. Are you not tired after a day in the saddle?'

'A little, but it is very peaceful sitting here. So what *will* you do?'

'Head north towards Sherak. There is a temple there – or it might be there. I don't know. But I will seek it.'

'And become a monk again?'

'No. Something even more foolish.'

'What?'

'It is a secret,' said Skilgannon softly. 'All men should have at least one secret. Maybe I will tell you one day. For now, though, go and sleep. I need to think.'

Rabalyn pushed himself to his feet and walked back to where Braygan lay. The young priest was snoring softly. Rabalyn lay down, his head resting on his arm.

And dreamed of riding through clouds on the back of a golden horse.

Skilgannon watched the lad walk away, and, for the first time in many weeks, felt a sense of peace settle on his troubled soul. He had not been so different from Rabalyn. As a youngster his mind was also full of questions, and his father had rarely been home to answer them. Why did men fight wars? Why were some people rich and some poor? If there was a great god watching over the world why were there diseases? Why did people die so unnecessarily? His mother had died in childbirth, bearing a sickly daughter. Skilgannon was seven years old. The baby had followed her two days later. They were buried in the same grave. Then – as now – Skilgannon had no answers to his questions.

He was tired, and yet he knew sleep would not come. Lying down on the soft earth he stretched out on his back, his arms behind his head, his hands pillowing his neck. The stars were brilliantly bright, and a crescent moon shone. It reminded him of the earring Greavas wore. He smiled at the memory of that sad, strange man, and recalled the winter evenings when Greavas had sat by the fireside and played his lyre, singing songs and ballads of glorious days gone by. He had a sweet, high voice, which had served him well in his days as an actor, playing the part of the heroine.

'Why don't they just have women playing women?' the boy Skilgannon had wanted to know.

'It is unseemly for women to perform in public, my dear. And if they did what would have become of my career?'

'What *did* become of it?' asked the eleven-year-old.

'They said I was too old to play the lead, Olek. Look at me. How old do I look?'

'It is hard to tell,' the boy had said.

'I could still pass for twenty-five, don't you think?'

'Except for the eyes,' said the boy. 'Your eyes look older.'

'Never ask a child for flattery,' snapped Greavas. 'Anyway, I gave up the playhouses.'

Decado had hired Greavas to teach Skilgannon to dance. The boy had been horrified.

'Why, Father? I want to be a warrior like you.'

'Then learn to dance,' Decado had told him, on a rare visit home.

Skilgannon had become angry. 'All my friends are laughing at me. And at you. They say you've brought a man-woman to live with you. People see him walking with me in the street and they shout out insults.'

'Whoa there, boy. Let's deal with this one thing at a time,' said Decado, his expression darkening. 'First the dancing. If you want to be a swordsman you'll need balance and co-ordination. There is no better way of honing that than to learn to dance. Greavas is a brilliant dancer and a fine teacher. He is the best. I always hire the best. As to what your friends say, why should either of us care about that?'

'But I *do* care.'

'That is because you are young, and there is a great deal of foolish pride in the young. Greavas is a good man, kind and strong. He is a friend to this family, and we will brook no insults to our friends.'

'Why do you have such strange friends? It embarrasses me.'

'When you speak like this it embarrasses *me*. You listen to me, Olek. There will always be men who select their friends for reasons of advancement, either socially, militarily or politically. They will tell you to avoid a certain man's company because he is out of favour, or his family is poor. Or, indeed, because his life is lived in a manner some people find unbecoming. As a soldier I judge my men by what they can do. By how much guts they have. When it comes to friends all that matters is whether I like them. I like Greavas. I think you will come to like him too. If you don't that is too bad. You will still learn to dance. And I will expect you to stand up for him with your friends.'

'I won't have any friends left if he stays,' snapped the eleven-year-old.

'Then you won't have lost anything worthwhile. True friends stand with you, regardless of the ridicule of others. You'll see.'

The following weeks had been hard for Skilgannon. At eleven years old the respect of his peers was everything to him. He responded to the jeers and the jibes with his fists, and soon only Askelus remained his friend. The boy he most admired, the thirteen-year-old Boranius, tried to reason with him.

'A man is judged by the company he keeps, Olek,' he said, one afternoon, in the physical training area. 'Now people think you are a catamite, and that your father is a pervert. The reality is immaterial. You must decide what means most to you – the admiration of your friends, or the loyalty of a servant.'

At that tender age Skilgannon longed to be able to side with his peers. Yet the most important person in his young life was his father, whom he loved. 'Will I lose your friendship also, Boranius?'

'Friendship carries responsibilities, Olek. Both ways. A true friend would not wish to put me in a position to be scorned. If you ask me to stand alongside you, then of course I will.'

Skilgannon had not asked him, and had avoided the young athlete's company after that.

Askelus remained. Dark-eyed and brooding, he said nothing about the situation. He called at Skilgannon's home, and together they walked to school.

'Are you not ashamed to be seen with me?' asked Skilgannon one day.

'Why would I be?'

'Everyone else is.'

'Never liked the others much anyway.' It was then that Skilgannon discovered that – apart from the loss of Boranius – he felt the same. Added to this, his father proved to be right. He had begun to appreciate and like Greavas. And this despite the man's mocking tone during dance lessons. He had taken to calling Skilgannon 'Hippo'.

'You have all the inherent grace of a hippopotamus, Olek. I swear you have two left feet.'

'I am doing my best.'

'Sadly I believe that is true. I had hoped to complete your studies by the summer. I now see I have taken on a lifetime commitment.'

Yet week by week Skilgannon had improved, and the exercises Greavas set him strengthened his legs and upper body. Soon he could leap and twirl and land in perfect balance. The dancing also improved his speed, and he won two races at school. The last was his greatest joy, for his father was there to see him, and he beat Boranius in the half-mile sprint. Decado had been delighted. Skilgannon's joy was tempered by the fact that Boranius had run with his ankle heavily strapped, following an injury sustained the previous week.

That evening Decado had once more set off to the Matapesh borders, and Skilgannon had sat with Greavas in the west-facing gardens. Two other servants had sat with them.

Sperian and his wife, Molaire, had served Decado for five years then. Molaire was a large, middle-aged woman, with sparkling eyes and deep auburn hair, touched now with silver. Constantly good-natured she would, at times like this, chatter on about the flowers and the brightly coloured birds that nested in the surrounding trees. Sperian, who maintained the gardens, would sit quietly staring out over the blooms and the pathways, making judgements about which areas to prune, and where to plant

114

his new seedlings. Skilgannon enjoyed these evenings of quiet companionship.

On this night Sperian commented on the medal Skilgannon wore. 'Was it a good race?' he asked.

'Boranius had an injured foot. He would have beaten me otherwise.'

'It is a lovely ribbon,' said Molaire. 'A very pretty blue.'

'I fear he does not care about the colour of the ribbon, my dear,' said Greavas. 'His mind is on the victory, and the defeat of his opponents. His name will now be inscribed on a shield hung in the school halls. Olek Skilgannon, Victor.'

Skilgannon had blushed furiously. 'No harm in a little pride,' said Sperian softly. 'As long as you don't get carried away by it.'

'I won a prize once,' said Greavas. 'Ten years ago. I was playing the maiden, Abturenia, in *The Leopard and the Harp*. A wonderful piece. Comic writing at its very best.'

'We saw that,' said Molaire. 'Last year in Perapolis. Very amusing. I don't remember who played Abturenia, though.'

'Castenpol played it,' said Greavas. 'He wasn't bad. The delivery was a little halting. I would have been better.'

Sperian chuckled. 'Abturenia is supposed to be fourteen years old.'

'And?' snapped Greavas.

'You're forty – at the least.'

'Cruel man! I am thirty-one.'

'Whatever you say,' replied Sperian, with a grin.

'Did you ever see me perform?' Greavas asked, switching his attention to Molaire.

'Oh, yes. It was the second time we stepped out, wasn't it, Sperian? We went to see a play at the Taminus. Something about a kidnapped princess and the errant king's son who rescues her.'

'*The Golden Helm*,' said Greavas. 'Difficult part to play. All that screaming and wailing. I remember it. I had a beautiful wig made just for me. We played forty successive nights to full houses. The old King himself complimented me. He said I was the best female lead he had ever seen.'

'No mean feat for a two-year-old,' said Sperian, with a wink at Skilgannon. 'That being twenty-nine years ago this spring.'

'Leave the poor man alone,' said Molaire. 'He doesn't need your teasing.'

Sperian glanced at Greavas. 'I tease him because I like him, Mo,' he said, and the moment passed. Greavas smiled and fetched his lyre.

Skilgannon often remembered that evening. The night was warm, the air scented with jasmine. He had the victor's medal round his neck, and he was with people who loved him. A new year was about to begin, and the future seemed bright and full of hope. His father's successes against the forces of Matapesh and Panthia had brought peace to the heartlands of Naashan, and all was well with the world.

Looking back now, with the jaded eyes of manhood, he shivered.

Where joy exists despair will always beckon.

Skilgannon was moving through a dark forest. His legs felt heavy and weary. Danger was close. He could sense it. He paused. He heard the stealthy sound of something moving through the undergrowth. He knew then it was the White Wolf.

Fear surged through him, and his heart fluttered in panic. The trees were silent now. Not a breath of wind stirred in the forest. He wanted to draw his swords. He could almost feel them calling to him. Clenching his fists he tried to quell the terror. 'I will meet you without swords!' he shouted. 'Show yourself!'

In that moment he felt its hot breath upon his back. With a cry he spun round. For a moment only he caught sight of white fur. Then it was gone – and he realized the Swords of Night and Day were once more in his hands. He could not recall drawing them. A voice came to him then – as if from a great distance. He recognized it as the boy, Rabalyn.

Skilgannon opened his eyes.

'Are you all right?' asked Rabalyn.

Skilgannon sat up and took a deep breath. 'I'm fine.'

'Was it a nightmare?'

'Of a kind.' The sky was pale with the pre-dawn, and Skilgannon shivered. Dew had seeped through his clothes. He rose and stretched.

'I had good dreams,' said Rabalyn brightly. 'I dreamed I was riding a golden horse through the clouds.'

Skilgannon moved across the open ground to where Braygan was preparing a fire. 'Best move that beneath a tree,' said the warrior. 'The branches will disperse the smoke. Make sure the wood is dry.'

'There is very little food left,' said Braygan. 'Perhaps we should seek a village today.' The little priest looked tired and drawn, and his blue robes were now filthy. The beginnings of a beard were showing on his chin, though his cheeks were still soft and clear.

'I doubt we will find anyone living in a village so close to the war. Tighten your belt, Braygan.'

Skilgannon took up his harness and carried it out to where the horses were hobbled. Wiping down the back of his steeldust gelding, he bridled and saddled it. As he mounted the horse gave several cursory bucks and leaps, jarring Skilgannon's bones. Rabalyn laughed.

'They won't all do that, will they?' asked Braygan nervously.

'Do not eat too much,' said Skilgannon. 'I'll scout ahead and be back within the hour.'

Heeling the gelding forward he rode away from the pair. In truth he was relieved to be alone, and looked forward to the time he could part company for good. A mile from the camp he dismounted just beneath the crest of a tall hill. Leaving the gelding with trailing reins he crept forward to the top and scanned the countryside below. There was a wooded valley, but he could see a ribbon of road, with many refugees upon it. Some were pulling carts, but most were walking, bearing what little they could carry in sacks or packs. There were few men, the majority being women with children. They were still days from Mellicane.

The sky darkened. Skilgannon looked up. Heavy black clouds were looming over the mountains. Lightning forked across the sky. A rumble of thunder followed almost instantly. His gelding snorted and half reared. Skilgannon patted its sleek neck, then stepped up into the saddle. 'Steady now,' he said, keeping his voice soft and soothing. The rain began, light at first. Skilgannon unstrapped his hooded cloak from the back of the saddle and settled it into place, careful to stop the cloth billowing and spooking the horse. Then he swung back towards the south.

Within minutes he had to pick out a different trail. The rain was slashing down now, drenching the ground, and making the simple slopes he had ridden treacherous and slippery. It took more than an hour to reach the campsite. He found Braygan and Rabalyn huddling against the cliff face, beneath a jutting overhang of rock. There was nothing to be done now but wait out the storm. Skilgannon could not risk two inexperienced riders tackling the hill slopes with thunder booming and lightning blazing. He dismounted and tethered the gelding, then pulled his hood over his head and squatted down with the others. Conversation was impossible and Skilgannon leaned against the rock face and closed his eyes. He slept for a while. Within the hour the storm passed, drifting towards the east. The sun broke through the clouds, bright and glorious. Skilgannon rose and glanced down at Braygan. The little priest looked utterly miserable.

'What is wrong?'

'I am wet through, and now I have to mount that fearsome beast.'

Skilgannon felt a flicker of irritation, but he quelled it. 'We should reach the outskirts of Mellicane within two days,' he said. 'Then you can put your time as a rider behind you.'

This thought seemed to cheer Braygan and he pushed himself to his feet. Rabalyn was already hefting his saddle towards his horse.

Two hours later they were riding along a ridge within half a mile of deep woods which masked the trail through the mountains. Below, a straggling line of refugees were trudging slowly on.

Skilgannon was about to heel his horse down the slope when he saw a group of cavalrymen coming from the east. 'Are they our soldiers?' asked Braygan.

The warrior did not answer. The advancing riders spurred their mounts. There were five of them, three with lances and two carrying sabres. The refugees saw them and began to run. One elderly woman stumbled. As she struggled to rise a lance clove between her shoulder blades. 'Oh, sweet Heaven!' cried Braygan. 'How can they do this?'

The refugees were fleeing in terror now, streaming towards the woods. A few small children, their parents panicked and gone, stood where they had been left.

Skilgannon reached for his swords.

As he did so a black-garbed figure emerged from the trees below. He was powerfully built, wearing a sable leather jerkin, with shining silver steel upon the shoulders. On his head was a black helm, also decorated with silver. In his hands was a glittering double-bladed axe. He ran onto the open ground. The horsemen saw him and wheeled to charge. The first of the lancers bore down on the warrior. He did not run away. Instead he ran directly at the galloping horse. Throwing up his hands he shouted at the top of his voice. Unnerved, the horse swerved. The warrior moved in, and the great axe smashed into the chest of the rider, hurling him from the saddle. A second horseman rode in. The axeman leapt to the rider's left, away from the deadly lance. Then the axe hammered into the neck of the horse. Instinctively it reared – then fell. The rider tried to scramble free of the saddle, but the blood-smeared axe clove into his temple, shattering both helm and skull.

'By Heaven, now *that* is a fighting man,' said Skilgannon.

Heeling his horse forward, he rode down the slope. Two more of the riders had closed in on the axeman. Both carried sabres. The remaining lancer held back, waiting for his moment. That moment would never arrive. Hearing the thundering hooves of Skilgannon's gelding he swung his mount. The lance came up. Skilgannon rode past on the rider's left, the golden Sword of Day slicing through his throat. Even as his victim fell from the saddle Skilgannon was bearing down on the riders circling the axeman. His aid was not needed.

The axeman charged in. One horse went down. Hurdling the rolling beast the warrior suddenly hurled his axe at the second rider, the upper points of the twin blades piercing his chest and shattering his breastbone. The rider of the fallen horse lay on the ground, his leg pinned beneath the saddle.

Ignoring him, the axeman dragged his weapon clear of the corpse and stared up at Skilgannon. The warrior was not young, his black beard heavily streaked with silver. His eyes were the colour of a winter sky, grey and cold. The warrior glanced back to the lancer Skilgannon had killed, but said nothing.

Behind him the last rider had freed himself, and was now on his feet, a sword in his hand.

'You have one enemy left,' said Skilgannon. The axeman turned. The swordsman blanched and took a backward step.

'Run away, laddie,' said the axeman, his voice deep and cold. 'And remember me the next time you think of killing women and children.'

The soldier blinked in disbelief, but the axeman had already turned away. He glanced back towards the east, then swung towards where the four children still stood, horrified and un-moving. The warrior, his axe resting on his shoulders, strolled over to them.

'Time to be moving on,' he told them, his voice suddenly gentle. Scooping up a small girl he sat her on his hip and walked off towards the dense woods. The three other children waited for a moment. 'Come on,' he called.

And they followed him.

Skilgannon sat his horse watching the man. The remaining rider sheathed his blade and walked to a riderless horse. Stepping up into the saddle he cantered away.

Braygan and Rabalyn came down the slope. 'That was in-credible,' said Rabalyn. 'Four of them. He killed four of them.'

A group of women came running from the trees, knives in their hands.

'They are attacking us!' screamed Braygan. The sudden noise startled his horse and it reared. Braygan clung to the saddle pommel. Skilgannon helped him steady the mount.

'They are starving, you idiot!' Skilgannon told him. 'They're coming for meat.'

'Meat?'

'The dead horses. Now let's get into the woods. The enemy could return at any time.'

They camped a half-mile inside the woods. All around them refugees began to prepare fires. The women looked gaunt and hungry, the children listless and silent. Skilgannon found a spot a little away from the nearest refugees. Braygan slumped to the ground and began to ferret inside the food sack, drawing out some salt biscuits. 'Put them back and give me the sack,' said Skilgannon.

'I'm hungry,' said the priest.

'Hungrier than them?' asked Skilgannon, gesturing towards where several women were sitting with their children.

'We don't have much left.'

Skilgannon looked at him, then sighed. 'We are only days from the church, little man. Have you lost your faith so swiftly? Give me the sack.'

Braygan looked crestfallen. 'I am sorry, Brother Lantern,' he said. 'You are right. A little hardship has made me forget who I am. I will take the food to them. And gladly.' Braygan pushed himself to his feet, dropped the salt biscuits back into the sack, and walked across to the nearest refugees.

'Shall I unsaddle the horses?' asked Rabalyn.

'Yes. Then give them a rub down. After that resaddle them. We may need to leave here swiftly.'

'Braygan is a good man,' said the youth.

'I know. I am not angry at *him*, Rabalyn.'

'Then why are you angry?'

'That is a good question.' He suddenly smiled. 'I failed in the one career I desired, and was too successful in the one I hated. A woman who loved me with all her heart is dead. A woman I love with all *my* heart wants *me* dead. I own two palaces, and lands you could not ride across in a week. Yet I am hungry and weary and soon to sleep on a wet forest floor. Why am I angry?' He shook his head and laughed. 'The answer eludes me, Rabalyn.'

The light was beginning to fade. Skilgannon patted the youth on the shoulder and started to walk away. 'Where are you going?' asked Rabalyn.

'Look after the horses. I'm going to scout a while.'

He wandered away through the trees, heading back the way they had come. After a while he left the refugees behind, though if he glanced back he could still see the twinkling light of their campfires.

The crescent moon was bright in a cloudless sky as he climbed the last hill before the valley. In the bright moonlight he could see the stripped carcasses of the dead horses. There was no sign of any pursuit. He sat down at the edge of the trees and stared out towards the east.

'I don't think they'll come tonight, laddie,' said a deep voice.

121

'You move silently for a big man,' said Skilgannon, as the axeman emerged from the shadows of the trees.

The man chuckled. 'Used to make my wife jump. She swore I always crept up on her.' He sat down beside Skilgannon, laying his great double-bladed axe on the ground. Removing his helm he ran his fingers through his thick black and silver hair. Skilgannon glanced down at the helm. It had seen much use. The folded iron sections showed many dents and scratches, and the silver motifs, two skulls alongside a silver axe blade, were worn down. A small edge of one of the silver skulls had been hacked away.

'If the enemy had come did you plan to take them all on by yourself?' asked Skilgannon.

'No, laddie. I guessed you'd be along.'

'Aren't you a little old to be tackling cavalrymen?'

The axeman glanced at Skilgannon and grinned. But he did not reply, and they sat for a while in companionable silence. 'Your accent is not Tantrian,' said Skilgannon at last.

'No.'

'Are you a mercenary?'

'I have been. Not now. You?'

'Just a traveller. How long do you plan to wait?'

The axeman thought about the question. 'Another hour or two.'

'I thought you said you didn't think they'd come.'

'I've been wrong before.'

'They'll either send no-one, or a minimum of thirty men.'

'Why thirty?' asked the axeman.

'The survivor is unlikely to admit his party was defeated by one old man with a big axe. No offence intended.'

'None taken.'

'He'll say there were a group of soldiers.'

'If that is true why would they choose to send no-one – which was the first of your predictions?'

'They are driving refugees towards Mellicane. That is their main purpose. To swell the numbers in the city, and create food shortages. They don't need to hunt down enemy soldiers here.'

'Makes sense,' admitted the axeman. 'You sound like an officer. I see you have a Naashanite tattoo. I'll bet there's a panther or some such on your chest.'

Skilgannon smiled. 'You know our customs well.'

'We old folk are an observant bunch.'

The young warrior laughed aloud. 'I think you lied when you said no offence was taken.'

'I never lie, laddie. Not even in jest. I *am* old. Damn little point in getting upset when someone mentions it. I turn fifty in a couple of months. Now I get aches in the knees and aches in the back. Sleeping on hard ground leaves me stiff.'

'Then what are you doing sitting here waiting for thirty cavalrymen?'

'What are *you* doing here?' countered the axeman.

'Maybe I came to find you.'

'Maybe so. I think, though, that you came because you don't like seeing women and children hunted by cowards on horses. I think you came here to show them the error of their ways.'

Skilgannon chuckled. 'You would have liked my father,' he said. 'There were no shades of grey with him, either. Everything was black and white. You remind me of him.'

'Is he still alive?'

'No. He led a suicidal charge against a Panthian regiment. It allowed some of his men to escape. My father didn't try to escape. He rode straight at the Panthian King and his bodyguard. His was the only body the enemy did not mutilate.'

'They strapped him to his horse, and left a gold coin in his hand,' said the axeman softly.

Skilgannon was surprised. 'How did you know?'

'I've lived most of my life among warriors, laddie. The talk around campfires is mostly about everyday matters, a good horse or dog. Sometimes it's about the farms we'll all have one day when the fighting is done. When a hero dies, though, the word comes to those campfires. Your father was Decado Firefist. I've met men who served with him. Never heard a bad word said about him. I never met him – though we both served in Gorben's army. He was cavalry and I've never liked horses overmuch.'

'Were you with the Immortals?'

'Aye, for a while. Good bunch of lads. No give in them. Proud men.'

'Were you at Skeln?'

123

'I was there.'

Another silence deepened. Skilgannon saw the axeman's eyes narrow. Then he sighed. 'Past days are best laid to rest. My wife died while I was at Skeln. And my closest friend. It was the end of an era.' He picked up his helm, wiped his hand round the rim and donned it. 'Think I'll find a place to sleep,' he said. 'I'm beginning to sound maudlin. And damn I hate that.' Both men rose. The axeman put out his hand. 'My thanks to you, youngster, for coming to an old man's aid.'

Skilgannon shook his hand. 'My pleasure, axeman.'

Then the warrior swept up his axe and walked away.

Skilgannon stayed where he was. The meeting with the axeman, with its easy camaraderie, had warmed him. It had been a long time since he had relaxed so much in the company of another human being. He wished the man had stayed longer.

He sat quietly on the slope. Hearing his father's nickname of Firefist had opened long locked doors in the halls of his memory. The days immediately after news of Decado's death reached them had been strange. Skilgannon, at fourteen, had at first refused to believe it, convincing himself it was a mistake, and that his father would ride home at any moment. Messages of condolence arrived from the court, and soldiers visited him, talking of his father's greatness. At the last he had to accept the truth. It tore a gaping hole in his heart, and he felt he would die of it. He had never been so alone.

Decado left a will, instructing Sperian and Molaire to share custody of the boy until his coming of age at sixteen. He had also left two thousand raq – a colossal sum – lodged with a Ventrian merchant he trusted, who had invested it for him. Sperian, who had always been poor, suddenly found himself with access to capital beyond his dreams. Lesser men would have been tempted to appropriate some of it. Decado, however, had always been a fine judge of character. Sperian proved himself worthy of that trust from the start.

Untutored in economics, and unable to write, he engaged Greavas to help him manage the funds, and also tried to take an interest in Skilgannon's schooling. This was difficult for him, since he understood little of what the boy had to study. Skilgannon did not make it easy at first. His heart was full of bitterness, and he would often rail at Sperian or Greavas, ignoring their instructions. His studies began to suffer, and he was, at the end of the term, demoted to the second class. Instead of accepting that this was a result of his own folly, he shouted at Greavas that he was being victimized because one of his guardians was a freak. Greavas had packed his bags and left the same night.

Skilgannon had stormed around the house, his anger uncontrollable. Sperian found him sitting in the garden. The servant was furious.

'You should be ashamed of yourself,' he said.

Skilgannon had sworn at him. In that moment Sperian did something no adult had ever done. Stepping in, he backhanded Skilgannon in the face. The boy was half stunned. The gardener, though slim, was a powerful man. 'And *I* am ashamed of you,' he said. Then he walked away.

Standing in the garden, his face burning, Skilgannon felt a terrible rage swell in his heart. His first thought was to find a dagger and stab Sperian to death with it. But then, as swiftly as it had come, his rage died. He sat down beside the small ornamental pond Sperian had built. The man was right.

Molaire found him there an hour later, still lost in his thoughts. 'I brought you some fruit bread,' she said, sitting down beside him.

'Thank you. Do you know where Greavas went?'

'I expect he's at the Park Gates tavern. They have rooms.'

'He'll hate me now.'

'What you said *was* hateful, Olek. It hurt him dreadfully.'

'I didn't mean it.'

'I know. Best you learn from this. Never, in anger, say what you don't mean. Words can be sharper than knives, and the wounds sometimes never heal.'

An hour later, with the moon high, Skilgannon entered the Park Gates tavern. Greavas was sitting at a corner table alone. Even to the fourteen-year-old he seemed strangely out of place. Most of the men here were labourers or craftsmen, burly and bearded, toughened by years of labour. In his blue silk flared-sleeve shirt, grey roots showing in his dyed yellow hair, the slim former actor stood out like a beacon.

Skilgannon approached him. He saw the sorrow in Greavas's eyes, and felt the burden of his guilt drag down like a rock on his heart. 'I am so sorry, Greavas,' he said, tears in his own eyes.

'Perhaps I am a freak. Don't worry about it.' Greavas turned away and stared out of the window.

'You are not a freak. You are my friend and I love you. Forgive me and come home. Please forgive me, Greavas.'

The actor relaxed. 'Of course I forgive you, stupid boy,' he said, rising from his chair.

It was then that Skilgannon realized that a silence had fallen over the small crowd in the tavern. He looked round to see a lean, sharp-faced man staring at him. His eyes were glittering with malice. 'Bad enough to have the likes of him in here,' he said to the company, 'without having him parade his little bumboys in front of us.'

Skilgannon was stunned. Greavas came alongside him. 'Time to go, Olek. I'll come back for my things later.'

'What you need is a thrashing,' said the man, suddenly pushing himself towards Greavas.

'And what you need is a bath,' said Greavas. 'Oh, yes, and perhaps to eat fewer onions. Your breath would fell an ox.'

The man's fist lashed out. Greavas swayed, the blow sailing harmlessly past him. Off balance, the man stumbled into Greavas's outstretched leg and fell heavily against the table, striking his chin, and hitting the floor. He struggled to rise and fell again.

Greavas led the boy outside. 'Can you teach me to do that?' asked Skilgannon.

'Of course, dear boy.'

Once they reached the house gates Skilgannon paused. 'I really am sorry, Greavas. Molaire says that sometimes word-wounds don't heal. This will heal, won't it?'

Greavas ruffled the boy's hair. 'This has already healed, Olek. How did you get that bruise on your face?'

'Sperian hit me.'

'Then perhaps you should apologize to him too.'

'He hit me!'

'Sperian is the kindest of men. Hitting you would have hurt him more deeply than that bruise hurts you. Go and find him. Make your peace.'

Sperian was in the garden, watering seed trays, when Skilgannon found him.

'Did you bring him back?' he asked.

'Yes. I apologized and he forgave me.'

'Good boy. Your father would be proud of that.'

'I wanted to say . . .'

Sperian shook his head. 'You don't have to say anything to me, lad. Here, give me a hand with these trays. I want them placed where the morning sun can warm the soil. We'll put them on the well wall.'

'I will never let you down again, Sperian. Not ever.'

The gardener gazed at him fondly, and said nothing for a moment. Then he patted his shoulder. 'You take those two trays there. Be careful now. Don't want the dirt spilling out.'

Ten years later the memory of that night still brought a lump to his throat. Rising from the hillside Skilgannon took one last look out across the lowlands, then strolled back to where his companions waited.

Braygan was asleep, but the boy Rabalyn was sitting by the horses, his hands clutching the reins. 'You can sleep now,' said Skilgannon. 'Did anyone try to steal the horses?'

'No. I've kept watch, though. All the time.'

Skilgannon sighed. 'You did well, lad. I knew I could trust you.'

CHAPTER SEVEN

RABALYN SLEPT FOR A WHILE, AND THEN AWOKE, GASPING, FROM A nightmare. His face was cold. Reaching up he touched his cheek. It was clammy and wet. A little rain had fallen and his clothes were damp. The healing skin on his face and leg began to itch and burn. Ignoring the pain, he got to his feet. Skilgannon was sitting with his back to a tree. The hood of his cloak was raised and his head was bowed. Rabalyn could not tell whether he was asleep or not. Carefully and silently he moved towards the warrior. Skilgannon's head came up. In the moonlight it seemed his eyes were the colour of burnished iron.

'I can't sleep,' said Rabalyn lamely.

'Bad dreams?'

'Yes. I don't remember them now, but they were frightening.'

'Come and sit,' said Skilgannon. Rabalyn brushed wet leaves from a flat rock and settled himself down upon it. Skilgannon tossed him a folded blanket and the boy gratefully wrapped it round his shoulders.

'That man with the axe was incredible,' he said. 'He's so old and yet he beat all those men.'

'He's a former Immortal. Tough men,' agreed Skilgannon. 'Hard to believe any army could have defeated them.'

'Who defeated them?' asked Rabalyn.

'The Drenai – at a place called Skeln Pass. Five years ago now. That's where Gorben died.'

'I remember when the Emperor died,' said Rabalyn. 'We had a week of mourning back in Skepthia. We all had to have ashes in our hair. It was really itchy. Everyone said he was a great man. Then a little while later everyone said he was a terrible man. It was really confusing. Which one was he?'

'Both, I guess,' said Skilgannon. 'When he died he was the Emperor of all the lands of the east. No-one knew then whether his heirs would prove as capable. So people were careful with their opinions. They praised the dead Emperor. Then, when the civil wars broke out, and nations like Tantria and Naashan broke away from the empire, they became more daring, talking of him as a conquering tyrant.'

'Did you know him?' asked the lad. 'Was he a tyrant?'

'No, I did not know him. I saw him once. He came to Naashan – two thousand Immortals with him. There was a massive parade. Flowers were strewn along the Great Avenue, thousands of them. And tens of thousands of people gathered to watch him ride by. He was a fine-looking man, broad-shouldered, keen of eye. A tyrant? Yes. He killed any who opposed him, and even killed those he *thought* would oppose him. And their families. His devoted followers maintained he was driven by a desire to see peace across all the lands of the empire. For a while, once he had conquered, there was peace. So he was both. Great and terrible.'

'Were you a soldier then?'

'No. I was little older than you. I went to the parade with my friend Greavas.'

'Why did the Emperor come to Naashan?'

'For the coronation of a new king. His puppet king. It's a long story, and I'm too tired to tell it all. In brief he had invaded Naashan and made it a part of his empire. The Naashanite Emperor was dead, killed in battle, and Gorben put his own man on the throne. His name was Bokram. At first most of the people were content. The war was over and peace looked immensely attractive.'

Rabalyn yawned. All this talk of history was tiring and confusing. War bringing peace, peace bringing war. Yet he did not

129

want to sleep. There was something reassuring, even comforting, about sitting in the night silence and talking to Skilgannon. 'Did he have a great horse?' he asked.

Skilgannon smiled. 'Yes, let us talk of truly important matters. He had a wonderful horse. Seventeen hands tall, and black as deepest night. The bridle was decked with gold – as was the saddle. It was a war horse the like of which I have never seen since.'

'I would like a horse like that.'

'What man wouldn't?'

'Did the Immortals have good horses?'

'No. They were foot soldiers, heavily armoured. They marched in perfect unison. They wore ceremonial armour of black and gold. Handsome men, with fierce, proud eyes. I watched them. I was awestruck. The name they carried was a fitting one – for they seemed like gods to me.'

'Why were they called Immortals?'

'After every battle the Immortals who died would be replaced by men promoted from other regiments. Therefore there were always ten thousand of them. In that way the regiment itself was immortal. You follow? But the name came to mean something else. The Immortals were unbeatable. Like gods, they never lost.'

'But they *did* lose.'

'Aye, they did. Once. And that was the end of them.'

Rabalyn eased himself off the rock and lay down. The blanket felt warm on his shoulders. Resting his head on his arm he closed his eyes. 'How did you become a soldier?' he asked sleepily.

'I was born to it,' said Skilgannon. 'My father was Decado Firefist. His father was Olek the Horse Lord. His father was Decado the Smiter. A line of warriors, Rabalyn. Our family has fought battles throughout time. Or that's what my father used to say.' Rabalyn heard the man sigh. 'Always other men's battles. Always dying in one lost cause after another.'

'Will your son be a warrior?'

'I have no sons. Perhaps that is just as well. The world needs no more warriors. It needs fine young men like you; men who can become teachers, or farmers, or surgeons. Or actors or gardeners or poets.'

Skilgannon fell silent. Rabalyn wanted to ask him more questions concerning Gorben's horse. But as he tried to think of them he drifted into a dreamless sleep.

Skilgannon stared at the sleeping Rabalyn. For the merest moment he felt a touch of emotional warmth towards the lad. Then it passed. Skilgannon had no place in his heart for such feelings. Friendship weakened a warrior. A man comes into this world alone, and he is alone when he leaves it. Far better to rely on no-one, to love no-one. He sighed. Easy to say. He could even believe it – until thoughts of Jianna seeped into his mind.

The Witch Queen.

It remained baffling how one so beautiful could have become so cold and deadly.

Weariness washed over him. Leaning back against the tree he closed his eyes.

The parade had been remarkable to the fifteen-year-old Skilgannon. It was the first time he had seen elephants. Standing alongside Greavas, he had been totally stunned by the majesty and power of the six beasts. Silver chain mail had been fitted to their foreheads and chests. It glittered in the morning sunshine. And the tusks! At least four feet long, they gleamed like white gold. Wooden towers had been placed upon their enormous backs, each protecting four Ventrian bowmen.

'The beasts are less useful than they look,' said Greavas. 'They can be panicked and turned. Then they will stampede back through their own lines.'

'But they are magnificent.'

'Indeed. Wondrous creatures.'

Then had come the new Naashanite lancers, loyal to Bokram, the soon to be crowned king. Bokram himself rode at their head, a slim man, thin-faced and sharp of eye. He wore a tall, curved silver helm and breastplate, but his chain mail, elaborately fashioned, was of white gold. 'Oh, how the fallen are mighty,' whispered Greavas.

All Naashanites knew of Bokram's history. Stripped of his titles three years before, Bokram had been banished by the old Emperor, only to flee to Ventria and enter the service of Gorben. Soon after that the Ventrians had invaded western Naashan. For two years the

Naashanites had held out, but then the Emperor himself had fallen in battle, his body pierced by the iron swords of the Immortals. It was whispered that, as the Emperor lay dying, Bokram had run to his side and spoken to him, before slowly pushing a dagger through the old man's eye. With the Naashanite army in flight, Bokram advanced into the capital. Today he would be crowned king in the presence of the true ruler, Gorben of Ventria.

'You shouldn't speak against Bokram,' Skilgannon warned Greavas. 'He is a harsh man, and they say all whispers reach his ears eventually.'

'I expect they are right – whoever *they* are,' said Greavas. 'There have been many arrests among the noble classes. Others have fled. There is even a death warrant against the Emperor's widow, and his daughter, Jianna.'

'Why would they want to kill women?'

'It is the normal practice, Olek. All members of the old blood royal must die. That way there will be no men to rise against Bokram and his new dynasty – and no women to birth new enemies for the future.'

'I hope they don't find them then.'

'So do I,' muttered Greavas. 'She is the sweetest child. Well, when I say child, she is almost sixteen and about to be dazzlingly beautiful.'

'You have seen her?'

'Oh, yes, many times. I have been teaching her poetry and dance.'

Skilgannon was amazed. He said nothing, though, for at that moment the Emperor Gorben came into sight, riding the most magnificent war horse. He was a powerful man, his hair and beard jet black and gleaming. Unlike Bokram he wore no gilded chain mail. His armour was of the highest quality, but designed for use rather than ornament. Behind him marched two thousand Immortals. 'Now there is the *real* power,' said Greavas. 'Look closely upon him, Olek. He is – at this moment – the most powerful man in the world. He has it all. Charm, strength, charisma and enormous courage. He is adored by his men and he has a purpose. There is only one flaw.'

'And what is that?'

'He has no children. His empire is built, therefore, on shifting sand. He is the mortar which binds the castle walls. If he dies the building will crumble.'

They stood and watched as the parade passed, then eased their way back into the crowds and headed along the broad avenue towards home.

'Did you see Boranius?' asked Greavas.

'No. Where was he?'

'Riding just behind Bokram. He is a captain of the Lancers now. Not bad for an eighteen-year-old – though it helps if the new king is your uncle, I suppose. Now we best move swiftly or you will be late for your appointment with Malanek.'

'Are you coming to watch?'

Greavas shook his head. 'I have matters to attend to. I will see you this evening. Best run, Olek. Malanek is not a man to keep waiting.'

Greavas waved a farewell and walked across the avenue. Skilgannon watched him go. The man had been most secretive of late, disappearing sometimes for days without explanation. Now Skilgannon had learned he had been tutoring the princess Jianna. Skilgannon grinned. Greavas had spent much of his adult life portraying princesses on stage, so who better to instruct her?

Following Greavas's advice he began to run through the streets, cutting through the alleyways, and up the steep Hill of the Cedars. Priests in yellow robes were leaving the domed temple, and he darted between them, continuing on to the old academy buildings. They had been sold several years before, and the barracks had been refashioned into apartments for rich visitors to Naashan. Close to the palace, they made ideal temporary homes for visiting courtiers and ambassadors.

One of the guards at the gate waved at Skilgannon as the youth ran by. They had long since ceased to ask him for his pass. This both pleased and disturbed the lad. It made access to Malanek more swift, yet it was sloppy. Many of the residents of the Old Academy were powerful men. As Decado had once explained, all powerful men have enemies. It was a natural law. If the guards became complacent, then one day the wrong person would be allowed in, and blood would flow.

However, it was not his problem. Skilgannon ran up the stone stairs to the former dining hall. It was now an indoor exercise area, equipped with climbing ropes, vaulting frames, baths and massage areas. There were targets for bowmen and javelin throwers, and a long rack of swords, some of wood, but others of sharp iron. A separate rack held smaller projectile weapons: knives and shimmering circular pieces with serrated edges.

Malanek was waiting by the far sword rack, testing the balance of a matched pair of sabres. Skilgannon paused to watch the swordmaster. He was tall and, though appearing slender, was powerfully built. The lower part of his head had been shaved up to the ears and around to the temples. The dark hair of his crown was cropped short into a wedge-shaped crest at the front, while at the back it fell away like a horse's tail. He was naked from the waist up. Upon his chest was a tattooed panther and both forearms were also tattooed, one with a spider, the other with a snake that wound around his arm, the head emerging on his right shoulder. The swordmaster did not acknowledge the boy's presence. Instead he walked out to the centre of the hall.

He swung the sabres gently, then, with increasing pace, he began to leap and twirl, loosening his body. Malanek had incredible grace. Skilgannon waited in excited anticipation for the finale. He always enjoyed it. Malanek flipped the blades into the air, then launched himself into a forward roll. As he came to his feet he raised his arms, his fingers closing on the hilts of the spinning swords. Skilgannon clapped. Malanek bowed, but did not smile. Without a word he flung one of the blades towards Skilgannon. The razor sharp sword spun through the air. Skilgannon focused on it, then swiftly stepped to the side, his hand snaking for the hilt. He almost had it, but it slipped from his fingers. The blade clattered down, glancing from his bare leg. A little blood began to flow.

Malanek strolled forward and examined the shallow cut. 'Ah, it is nothing,' he said. 'It will seal itself. Go and prepare.'

'I almost had it.'

'Almost doesn't count. You tried to think it into your hand. Can't do that, boy.'

For two hours Malanek pushed Skilgannon through a gruelling

134

set of exercises: running, climbing, vaulting and lifting. Every ten minutes or so he would allow one minute of rest, then begin again. At the last he took the two sabres, handed one to Skilgannon, then launched into a sudden attack. Skilgannon was surprised. Normally he was told to buckle on the padded leather chest armour, and the arm protectors. Often, when the practice was intense, Malanek would insist he also wear a head guard. Now he had nothing. He defended himself as best he could. Malanek was also devoid of armour, and Skilgannon made no attempt to pierce his guard. The swordmaster stepped back. 'What do you think you are doing?' he asked coldly.

'Defending myself, sir.'

'And the best method of defence is?'

'Attack. But you are wearing . . .'

'Understand me, boy,' snapped Malanek. 'This session will end with blood. Either mine or yours. Now raise your blade, or place it on the floor and leave.'

Skilgannon looked at the man, then placed his sabre on the floor, and swung towards the stairs.

'Are you frightened?' hissed Malanek. Skilgannon turned.

'Only of hurting you, sir,' he said.

'Come here.' Skilgannon walked back to the swordmaster. 'Look at my body. See the scars. This one,' he said, tapping his chest, 'was a lance I thought had killed me. And this was a dagger thrust. And this,' he went on, pointing to a jagged cut alongside the snake head on his shoulder, 'was given to me by your friend Boranius during a practice. I bleed and I survive. We can play in this room with our blades for an eternity and you will never be a warrior. Because until you face a genuine threat you cannot know how you will cope with it. Follow me.' The swordmaster walked to the far wall. There was a shelf there. Upon it he had laid bandages, a curved needle and a length of thread, a jug of wine and a jar of honey. 'One of us will bleed today. The likelihood is that it will be you, Olek. Pain and suffering. If you are skilled when we fight the wound will be small. If not, it may be serious. You might even die.'

'This makes no sense,' said Skilgannon.

'And war does?' countered Malanek. 'Make your choice. Leave or fight. If you leave I never want to see you again in my training hall.'

Skilgannon wanted to leave, but, at fifteen, he could not have borne the shame of such a withdrawal. 'I shall fight,' he said.

'Then let us do it.'

Sitting now in the woods Skilgannon remembered the pain of the stitches. The cut on his chest was some seven inches long. He had bled like a stuck pig. The wound had pained him for weeks. The fight had been intense, and somewhere within it, he had forgotten that Malanek was his teacher. As the blades whirled and clashed Skilgannon had fought as if his life depended on the outcome. At the last he had risked death to send a deadly lunge at Malanek's throat. Only the speed and innate skill of the swordmaster had allowed him to duck and sway away from the death stroke. Even so the point had opened his cheek, spraying blood into the air.

Only in that moment did Skilgannon realize that – even as he avoided the death thrust – Malanek's blade had sliced across his chest. He stepped back as the blood began to flow. Malanek had turned his own blade at the last possible second, merely scoring the skin. Had he wished he could have plunged the sabre through Skilgannon's heart.

The two combatants had looked at one another. 'I hope one day to have half your skill,' the boy had said.

'You will be better, Olek. One more year and I will have nothing more to teach you. You will be a fine swordsman. One of the best.'

'As good as Boranius?'

'Hard to say, boy. Men like Boranius are rare. He is a natural killer, with faster hands than any man I've ever known.'

'Could you beat him?'

'Not any more. His skills surpass mine. Already he is as good as Agasarsis, and they don't come much better than that.'

By mid-morning the travellers had made some eleven miles, emerging from thick forests and out onto rolling farmland. They rode along the column of refugees, hundreds of weary people trudging towards a place they hoped would offer at least transient security.

Heavy clouds masked the sun, and the day was grey and cool. Braygan had at last managed to find his rhythm in the saddle – at least for the trot. The canter saw him bounce awkwardly and grip the saddle pommel. Skilgannon took to riding ahead, scanning the land for sign of hostile riders. He saw several cavalry patrols, but none approached the refugees.

As afternoon faded towards dusk the clouds cleared, and bright sunshine shone on the column. It lifted the spirits of the fleeing people. Far ahead Skilgannon saw that the refugees had stopped walking. They were milling around. The news that had halted the column flowed back faster than a brush fire.

Mellicane had fallen. No-one knew what had become of the Tantrian King, or the remnants of his army. All they knew was that their journey to safety now had no purpose. There were no walls to shelter behind. People sat down on the ground. Some wept. Others merely stared vacantly over the landscape. They had left their homes in terror. They feared to go back, and yet now there was no going forward.

Skilgannon galloped his horse towards the northwest, dismounting where the largest group of refugees had gathered. Here he saw several armoured lancers, wearing the yellow cloaks of the Tantrian army, trying to respond to a host of shouted questions, most of which they could not answer. Sitting his gelding Skilgannon gleaned what information there was. The King had killed himself – or been killed by those he believed loyal. The gates had been thrown open. The Datians had ridden in uncontested. There had been some looting and stories of attacks on the populace, but the city was now under martial law. The worst incidents had occurred when the arena beasts had been set free. The creatures had moved out into the populated areas, killing indiscriminately until hunted down. Skilgannon rode back to where Braygan and Rabalyn were waiting. 'What are we to do?' asked the little priest.

'Go on to the city. That is why we came.'

'Is the war over then?'

'No,' Skilgannon told him. 'Only the first stage. Now the Naashanite army will invade.'

'I don't understand,' said Braygan. 'The Naashanites were our allies. Why did they not come earlier?'

'The sheep made an alliance with the wolf, Braygan. The Queen desires to rule these lands. And those of Datia and Dospilis. The Tantrian King is dead. Now the Queen will come as an avenging liberator, and accept the grateful thanks of a frightened people.'

'Does she have no honour then?' asked Rabalyn.

'Honour?' answered Skilgannon, with a harsh laugh. 'She is a ruler, boy. Honour is a cloak she wears when it suits her. You remember the old adage: "The louder they spoke of their honour, the faster we counted the spoons"? Do not look for ordinary virtues among rulers.'

'Will it be safe in the city?' enquired Braygan.

Skilgannon shrugged. 'I cannot answer that. It will be safer than it was yesterday, though we will have to release the horses and walk in.'

'Why?' asked Rabalyn.

Skilgannon saw the hurt on the youth's face. 'We have no choice. They are branded, Rabalyn. We took them from dead Datian lancers. You think it wise to ride into a conquered city on stolen horses? We will keep them until the far hills above the city. Then we will let them go. No harm will come to them. Now let us be moving on.'

Swinging his horse, Skilgannon skirted the refugees and cut across the fields. The fall of the city was – at least for Skilgannon – a blessing. With this phase of the war over entry to – and exit from – Mellicane should prove somewhat simpler. Supplies would be more accessible, and the journey north towards Sherak and the deserts of Namib should be less troublesome. The armies of Naashan would be entering from the south. The armies of Datia and Dospilis would be forced to march in that direction to oppose them. There would be little military activity, therefore, in the north.

They rode on in silence for several hours. The land here was deceptive, apparently flat, and yet filled with concealed gullies and dips. Skilgannon rode slowly and carefully. His trained eyes scanned the area. This would be one place to ambush an invading army. A large force could be hidden in these gullies, or in the reeds alongside the streams. Skilgannon had planned many such surprise attacks during the early days of the Naashanite uprising.

Once more they came upon refugees, ever more weary as they plodded on towards an uncertain future. They were wading through a sea of reeds, trying to create a shortcut to the hills. The ground below the horses' hooves was waterlogged and spongy, and, with the mass of people heading northwest, the going was slow. On horseback Skilgannon could just see over the tops of the reeds. They went on for close to another half-mile. Swarms of midges rose up, clustering around the faces of the riders and their mounts. The horses tossed their heads and flicked their ears. The heat rose, and Skilgannon felt sweat trickling down his back.

From somewhere ahead came a scream of pure terror. Skilgannon reined in his mount. Across the top of the reeds he saw a body fly up, and twist in the air. Then came another scream – harshly cut off in mid-cry.

People began streaming back past Skilgannon, running for their lives. This sudden movement startled the horses. Skilgannon's mount reared and he fought for control. Braygan was dumped from the saddle, his horse turning and galloping back towards the south. Rabalyn's horse bolted past Skilgannon, the boy wrestling with the reins.

A slight breeze began to blow through the reeds. Skilgannon's horse caught the scent. Despite the skill of its rider the gelding suddenly trembled, reared again and swung away, bolting after Braygan's riderless mount.

Skilgannon had little choice but to let his horse run for a while, keeping a light but constant pressure on the reins. As it reached firmer ground Skilgannon spoke to it in a gentle voice, and sat back in the saddle. 'Whoa now, boy!' he said. Clear of what it perceived as the initial danger the gelding heeded the commands, dropped back into a lope and finally halted. Skilgannon patted its long neck, and swung it back towards the north.

He scanned the reeds, now some quarter of a mile distant. People were still running in every direction.

Then he saw the beast.

It was around seven feet high, covered in black fur. For a moment Skilgannon thought it to be a bear, but then it turned. The body tapered down from powerful shoulders and long arms to a slimmer waist and long legs. The head was huge and hunched forward on a massive neck, the jaws elongated like a wolf's. Blood stained its teeth and throat. The great head swung from side to side, then the beast darted forward, the speed impressive for something so large. Bearing down on a fleeing woman it leapt to

139

her back, its fangs crunching down on her skull. The woman collapsed, instantly dead. Another beast, its fur a mottled grey, emerged from the reeds, and ran at the first. Rearing up, they struck at each other. The black beast gave way, moving back, and the grey newcomer moved in to feed.

Skilgannon had heard of the arena beasts, but never seen one. It was said they were created by renegade Nadir shamen in the pay of the Tantrian King. He had heard talk of bizarre rites where prisoners were dragged from their dungeons and magically melded with wolves, bears or dogs.

At that moment he saw Braygan stumble from the reeds, some two hundred yards from the feeding beast.

Skilgannon swore, and heeled the gelding into a run. The grey-coated creature looked up, but ignored both the horseman and the staggering priest. Not so the black-furred one, who had been robbed of his feed. Dropping to all fours he charged at Braygan.

The gelding, at full run, bore down on the priest. Skilgannon glanced back. There would be no room for error now. Braygan had seen the wolf creature and was trying to run away. Skilgannon leaned over in his saddle and guided the gelding alongside the fleeing man. Grabbing his robe he hauled him from his feet, throwing him over the pommel. Braygan landed with a grunt. The gelding continued to run. Skilgannon turned him, heading back towards the hills. He glanced over his shoulder. The beast was gaining.

The gelding thundered on. Braygan, the pommel horn digging into his ribs, tried to wriggle clear of it.

'Keep still, idiot!' yelled Skilgannon.

The gelding jerked and whinnied. Skilgannon looked back. The beast had dropped to its haunches and given up the chase. But there was blood on the gelding's hindquarters, and the bloody marks of talons upon its back.

It had been close.

Skilgannon rode on. The terrified gelding struggled up the slope. At the top Skilgannon unceremoniously dumped Braygan from its back. Then he dismounted and checked the horse's wound. There were three parallel slashes, but they were not deep.

The black creature watched them from some three hundred yards distant, then turned and ambled back towards the reeds.

Braygan came to his knees, his hands clasped in prayer. 'I thank thee, Great Lord in Heaven,' he said, his voice breaking. 'I thank thee for this life, and for sparing me upon this day.'

'The day is not over,' observed Skilgannon.

They sat upon the hillside for almost an hour, until the light began to fail. Then Skilgannon saw movement to the south. Another large group of refugees came into sight, emerging from a fold in the land. They were walking towards the reeds.

'Sweet Heaven!' said Braygan. 'They will be torn to pieces.'

Rabalyn became aware of pain in his head. It began as a soft thumping, then grew alarmingly. A feeling of nausea swept through him and he groaned and opened his eyes. He was lying on the grass, a little way from a line of trees. With another groan he sat up and looked around. Some distance away he could see the edge of the reed marsh. Beside him there was a splash of blood on the surface of a flat rock. He stared at it for a moment, then reached up to his head. His hand came away sticky. He wiped his fingers on the grass, leaving a red smear.

Then he remembered the horse bolting, racing along the edge of the marsh. He had clung to the pommel horn, fighting to stay in the saddle. That was when the horror had surged from the reeds. Rabalyn had only caught a glance as the horse raced by, but what he saw was enough to chill his heart. The beast was massive, with slavering jaws. It stood upright like a bear, but its head was that of a wolf. The creature lunged at the horse and struck it. Rabalyn was hurled to his left, but clung on as the horse stumbled. Then it righted itself and sped away. It had galloped for some minutes, then had stumbled again. At the last its neck dipped and Rabalyn was hurled through the air. His head had obviously struck the rock.

The youth struggled to his feet and turned. The dead horse lay some fifteen feet distant. Rabalyn cried out in anguish, and ran to it. There was a deep and bloody wound in its flank. Flesh and sinew hung from it, trailing down into a deep, congealing pool of blood.

The pain in his head forgotten, Rabalyn knelt down and stroked the horse's mane. 'I am so sorry,' he said.

From the distance came a weird and blood-chilling howl.

Rabalyn scrambled to his feet. The horse was dead, but the scent of its blood would carry on the wind. He had to get as far from it as possible. Turning, he stumbled up the hill and into the trees. He had no idea where he was going, only that he needed to put distance between himself and the carcass. His head began to pound again. Falling to his knees, he vomited. Then he struggled on. The undergrowth was thick, and he skirted it, looking for a tree which he could climb. But his limbs felt leaden, and he did not know if he had the strength to haul himself into the branches.

The dreadful howling sounded again. Rabalyn could not tell if it was closer now, but in his terror he believed it was. Coming to a large oak, he began to climb. His foot slipped and he fell back, landing with a jarring thud on the ground. As he tried to rise a shadow loomed over him. Panic swept through him.

'Easy, laddie,' said a deep voice. 'I'll not harm you.'

Rabalyn blinked. Before him stood the ancient axeman who had killed the lancers. Up close he seemed even more fearsome, with his glittering pale grey eyes. His beard was black and silver, and he wore a black leather jerkin, reinforced at the shoulders with shining steel. Upon his head was a round black helm, edged with silver. Rabalyn's eyes were drawn to the huge axe he carried. The blades looked like butterfly wings, flaring up into two points. The haft was black, and runes were embossed there in silver. 'What happened to your head?' asked the axeman, kneeling down, and placing his axe on the ground.

'I fell off my horse.'

'Let me look.' The axeman probed the wound. 'I don't think you've cracked your skull. Looks like a glancing blow. Torn the skin a bit. Where are your friends?'

'I don't know. My horse bolted when the beasts attacked.' Fear returned and Rabalyn scrambled up. 'We must climb a tree. They are coming.'

'Be calm, laddie. *What* is coming?'

Rabalyn told the axeman what he had seen, and how his horse was dead, half its belly ripped open by sharp talons. 'They may have killed my friends,' he said.

The axeman shrugged. 'Maybe. I doubt the swordsman is dead. He seemed a canny man to me.' Glancing up at the darkening sky he rose. 'Let's find a place to camp. We'll light a fire and you can rest awhile.'

'The beasts . . .'

'They'll either come or they won't. Nothing I can do about that. Come on.' Reaching out, he pulled Rabalyn to his feet, then took up his axe and walked back through the trees. Rabalyn followed him. A little while later the axeman reached a natural clearing. Two old oaks had fallen, creating a partial wall to the west. With his boot the axeman scraped away twigs and tinder, clearing a spot for a fire. He told Rabalyn to gather dry wood, and, when the boy had done so, took out a small tinder box and struck a flame.

The darkness deepened. Rabalyn sat down beside the fire. He still felt a little sick, but his headache was passing.

'Brother Lantern said you were with the Immortals.'

'Brother Lantern?'

'The swordsman who helped you.'

'Ah. Yes, I was for a while.'

'Why did you attack those soldiers?'

'What do you mean?'

'Well, I thought at first you were protecting your family, or some friends. But you are travelling alone. So why did you fight?'

'Good question. What is your name?'

'Rabalyn.'

'And why are you heading for Mellicane, Rabalyn?'

The youngster told him about the attack on his house, and the death of Aunt Athyla. At the last he also admitted the killing of Todhe, and the shame he felt.

'He brought it on himself,' said the axeman. 'No point losing sleep over it. All actions have consequences. I used to argue all the time with a friend of mine. He'd talk endlessly of what he called the potential of Man. He'd say even the most evil were capable of good. He'd witter on about redemption, and such like. Maybe he was right. I don't bother myself with such thoughts.'

'Have you killed lots of people?' asked Rabalyn.

'Lots,' agreed the axeman.

'Were they all evil?'

'No. Most were soldiers, fighting for their own cause. As I was

143

fighting for mine. It is a harsh world, Rabalyn. Get some sleep. You'll feel better come morning.'

'You didn't say why you attacked those soldiers,' the youngster pointed out.

'No, I didn't.'

Rabalyn stretched out and looked up at the forbidding figure seated beside the fire. He noticed then that the axeman was not facing the flames, but was looking out into the gathering darkness.

'You think they will come?' asked the boy.

'If they do they'll regret it. Go to sleep.'

For a little while Rabalyn forced himself to stay awake. The axeman did not speak, and the boy lay very still, staring up at the seated figure. The glare from the flickering fire made the axeman appear even older. The lines on his face were deep. Rabalyn saw him pick up his axe. The muscles on his forearm rippled as his huge hand curled round the haft. 'Have you ever been frightened?' asked Rabalyn.

'Aye, once or twice. My wife had a weak heart. Several times she collapsed. I knew fear then.'

'Not now, though?'

'There's nothing to be frightened of, laddie. We live. We die. A wise man once told me that one day even the sun will fade, and all will be darkness. Everything dies. Death isn't important. What counts is how you live.'

'What happened to your wife?'

'She's gone, boy. Five years now.' The axeman threw a chunk of wood to the fire and the flames rippled over it. Then he rose to his feet, and stood statue still. 'Time to climb your tree, I think,' he said softly. Rabalyn scrambled to his feet. 'That one there,' said the axeman, pointing to a tall oak close by. 'Do it now!'

Rabalyn ran to the tree and leapt for the lowest branch, hauling himself up. He climbed to a fork and sat down, staring back at the campfire. The axeman was still standing quietly, his axe in his hands. Rabalyn scanned the area. He could see nothing, save moonlit undergrowth and trees. Then a shadowy figure flitted across his line of vision. He tried to focus on it, but there was nothing to be seen. Another shape moved to the right. Rabalyn found himself trembling. What if they could climb?

He felt ashamed of himself. One old man was about to face these creatures, while he hid in a tree. Rabalyn found himself wishing he had a weapon, so he could aid the axeman. Down below he saw the man lift the axe above his head and slowly stretch from side to side, loosening his muscles.

For a while nothing moved. Rabalyn became aware of his heart thumping like a drum. He felt a little dizzy and clung on tight to the branch. The moon disappeared behind a cloud, and darkness fell over much of the clearing. Rabalyn could just make out the axeman, by the glint of reflected flames on his axe and helm. He heard the snapping of branches, then a feral growl. A black shadow fell across the axeman, and Rabalyn could see nothing for a moment. A strangled cry sounded. Something tumbled across the fire, scattering sparks. Now it was even darker. Rabalyn could hear something moving through the undergrowth, its breathing harsh.

The moon emerged, bright silver light bathing the clearing. The axeman still stood. Across the fire lay the body of a huge beast. Smoke wreathed it, and Rabalyn caught the smell of charred fur and flesh. Another beast leapt over a fallen tree, hurling itself at the axeman. He spun on his heel, the axe thudding into the creature's massive neck. As the beast half fell the axeman wrenched his weapon clear and struck again. The axe blades crunched through the creature's shoulder, biting deep. Two more beasts ran in. Tearing his axe clear the axeman turned to face them. They backed away, circling him. One rushed forward, then sprang away as the axe rose. The second darted in, but also swerved aside at the last moment. Rabalyn saw one of them look up at the sky. The boy followed its gaze. More clouds were looming, and he realized the creatures were waiting for darkness.

The axeman leapt at the first beast. It sprang away. Rabalyn wished there was something he could do to help the man. Then it came to him. He could distract them. Taking a deep breath he shouted at the top of his voice. Startled, one of the creatures half turned. The axeman charged in, his weapon cleaving through the beast's ribcage. It screamed and fell back, tearing the weapon from the man's hand. The second creature sprang through the air. The axeman spun and hammered a right cross into its jaws. The weight of the beast bore the axeman back, and they fell together, rolling

145

across the clearing. Rabalyn scrambled down the tree and jumped from the lowest branch. He ran to the body in which the axe was embedded and grabbed the haft with both hands, trying to pull it free.

The beast was not dead. Its golden eyes flared open and it roared. Rabalyn threw his full weight back. The axe wrenched clear. The beast gave an ear-splitting scream. It half rose, then slumped back, blood pumping from the great wound in its chest. The axe was heavier than Rabalyn had imagined. Struggling with it, he hefted it to his shoulder and stumbled to where the axeman was wrestling with the last creature. The old man's helm had been knocked from his head, and blood was flowing from a gash in his temple. His left hand was locked to the creature's throat, straining to hold the snapping fangs from his face. His right was gripping the left wrist of the monster.

Holding the axe in both hands Rabalyn raised it high. It tipped backwards, almost making him lose balance. Righting himself, he hacked the axe downwards. It thudded into the beast's back between the shoulder blades. A hideous screech came from the creature. It arched up, dragging the axeman with it. Releasing the beast's wrist the axeman thundered a punch to its head. Behind the creature Rabalyn grabbed for the axe haft, trying to tear it clear. The beast spun. Its taloned arm lashed out, striking Rabalyn in the chest and sending him hurtling through the air. He landed heavily. Half stunned, he struggled to his knees. The old warrior had his axe once more in his hand. The beast backed away, then turned and fled into the trees.

The warrior watched it go, then walked over to Rabalyn. 'My, but you are a game lad,' he said. Reaching out, he hauled Rabalyn to his feet.

'You killed three of them,' said Rabalyn. 'It was incredible.'

'I'm getting old,' replied the axeman, with a grin. 'Was a time when I wouldn't have needed my axe to deal with such puppies.'

'Truly?' asked Rabalyn, amazed.

'No, laddie, I was making a joke. Never was much good at jokes.' He lifted his helm, wiped his hand around the rim, then settled it back on his head. A low snarl sounded from one of the bodies. The axeman walked back to the creature. Its legs were twitching. The axe swept up, then down into its neck. All movement ceased. Returning to Rabalyn, the axeman thrust out his hand. 'I am Druss. I thank you for your help. I was beginning to struggle a mite with that last one.'

'It was my pleasure, sir,' answered Rabalyn, feeling proud as he shook the old man's hand.

'Now I want you to climb that tree again.'

'Are there more of them?'

'I don't know. But I need to leave you here for a short while. Don't worry. I'll be back.'

Rabalyn climbed to the original fork and settled down. His fears returned once Druss had left the clearing. What if the man left him here? He banished the thought instantly. He did not know the axeman well, but he instinctively knew he would not lie about coming back.

Time passed, and the sky cleared. Wedged against the fork in the branches Rabalyn dozed a little. He awoke to the smell of roasting meat.

Down in the campsite the axeman had hauled the dead beasts from the clearing and had rekindled the fire. He was sitting before it, a thick strip of flesh held on a stick before the flames. Rabalyn climbed down to join him. The aroma of the food made his senses swim. He squatted down beside the axeman. Then a thought struck him. 'This is not from those creatures, is it?' he asked.

'No. Though were I hungry enough I'd try to cook them. Smells good, doesn't it?'

'Yes, it does.'

'Where did you get it?'

'From the dead horse.'

'*My* horse?' asked Rabalyn, horrified.

'There's only one dead horse, boy.'

'I can't eat my horse.'

The axeman turned to look at him. 'It's just meat.' He sighed, then chuckled. 'I know what Sieben would say. He'd tell you that your horse is now running in another place. He'd say the sky is blue there, and the horse is galloping across a field of green. All that's left behind is the cloak it wore.'

'Do you believe that?'

'That horse carried you from danger – even after it was mortally wounded. In some cultures they believe that to eat the flesh of a great beast is to absorb some of its qualities into yourself.'

'And do you believe *that*?'

The axeman shrugged. 'I believe I am hungry, and that what I don't eat the foxes will devour, and the maggots will thrive on. It's up to you, Rabalyn. Eat. Don't eat. I'm not going to force you.'

'Maybe your friend was right. Maybe he is running in another world.'

'Maybe.'

'I think I'll eat,' said Rabalyn.

'Hold on to this for a moment,' said Druss, handing Rabalyn the toasting stick. Then he rose and took his axe to a nearby tree. With two swift chops he cut away sections of bark, which he carried back. 'They'll make do for plates,' he said.

Later, after they had eaten, Rabalyn stretched out on the ground. He felt almost light-headed, as if in a dream. His stomach was full. He had helped defeat monsters, and he was sitting by a fire in the moonlight with a mighty warrior. 'How can you be so good when you are so old?' he asked.

The axeman laughed aloud. 'I come from good stock. Truth is, though, I am not as good as I was. No man can resist time. I used to be able to walk thirty miles in a day. Now I'm tired at half that, and I have an ache in my knee and my shoulder when the winter comes, and the rain falls.'

'Have you been fighting in the war?'

'No,' answered Druss. 'Not my war. I came here looking for an old friend.'

'Is he a warrior like you?'

Druss laughed. 'No. He is a fat, frightened fellow with a fear of violence. A good man, though.'

'Did you find him?'

'Not yet. I don't even know why he came here. He's a long way from home. He may have returned to Mellicane. I'll find out in a day or two.' A tiny trickle of blood was still seeping from the gash in the old man's temple. Rabalyn watched as he wiped it away.

'That should be stitched or bandaged,' he said.

'Not deep enough for that. It will seal itself. And now I think I'll get some sleep.'

'Shall I keep watch?'

'Aye, laddie. You do that.'

'You think the beast might come back?'

'I doubt it. That was a deep cut you gave it. He's probably hurting too much to think of feeding. But if he does then two great heroes like us should be able to deal with him. Don't worry overmuch, Rabalyn. I am a light sleeper.'

With that the axeman stretched himself out and closed his eyes.

With Braygan clinging on behind him Skilgannon urged the tired horse down the slope towards the refugees. The steeldust was almost at the end of its strength and stumbled twice.

As he rode Skilgannon scanned the land. He could see no sign of the beasts. Transferring his gaze to the refugees he saw two swordsmen walking at the head of the column. Both were tall, with close-cropped black hair, and both were heavily bearded. They paused as he rode up. Leaping from the saddle, Skilgannon approached them. 'Are you in charge here?' he asked the first warrior. The man cocked his head and looked confused, then swung to the other swordsman.

'Are we in charge, Jared?'

'No, Nian. Don't worry about it. What is it you want?' he asked Skilgannon. People were milling around now, anxious to hear whatever news the newcomers had brought.

'There is great danger here,' Skilgannon told Jared. 'It will be upon us at any moment.' Turning away from him Skilgannon pulled Braygan from the saddle, and slapped the rump of the horse. Surprised, it began to run towards the reeds. It had travelled no more than a hundred yards before it swerved to the right. A Joining reared up from the long grass and leapt at it. The horse bolted. Screams of shock came from some of the refugees.

'Be silent!' roared Skilgannon, his words booming out. The power in his voice cowed the crowd. They stood silently awaiting instructions. 'Gather together. Get into as tight a circle as you can. Now! Your lives depend upon it!' As the crowd began to move Skilgannon shouted again. 'Every man here with a weapon come to me.' Men began to shuffle forward. Some had swords, others knives. Several had wooden clubs, or scythes. Turning to the swordsman, Jared, he said: 'Move to the other side of the circle. Stay on the outside of it. Do it now!' Skilgannon turned his attention to the gathering men. 'There are beasts abroad – Joinings who have escaped from the arena in Mellicane. Already they have killed many refugees. Spread yourselves around the circle, facing outwards. When the beasts come make as much noise as you can. Scream, shout, clash your weapons. Do not be drawn away from the circle.'

There were less than twenty armed men. Not enough to form a protective ring round the refugees. Skilgannon called out to the women. 'We need more for the fighting circle,' he said. 'Do any women here carry weapons?' Around a dozen women moved forward. Most had long knives, but one had a small hatchet. 'Move alongside the men,' Skilgannon told them. 'Everyone else sit down. When the attack comes, take hold of the person closest to you. Keep low to the ground. Do not let any children panic or run. And do not break the circle.'

Braygan stood where he was, staring anxiously towards the reeds, no more than four hundred yards distant. Skilgannon grabbed him by the arm. 'Go and sit with the women and children,' he said. 'You can do nothing here.'

The little priest did as he was bid, easing his way into the huddled refugees and sitting down. He gazed around the circle. It was some thirty feet in diameter. All around it stood the warriors, both men and women, Skilgannon had gathered. Braygan was still in shock. He had seen Brother Lantern fight, but this was a man he had never seen. He watched as Skilgannon moved around the outer edge of the circle, issuing orders. People were hanging on his every word. He radiated power and authority.

The light was beginning to fail. A weird howling arose from all around them. Children screamed in panic and some people began to rise, ready to run.

'Be still!' bellowed Skilgannon. Braygan saw him draw his swords.

A huge Joining reared up and ran at the circle. Skilgannon leapt to meet it. The beast sprang at him. The golden sword in

Skilgannon's right hand flashed out, slicing across the Joining's belly. Ducking under a sweep of its taloned arm Skilgannon spun. The silver blade in his left hand clove deep into the beast's neck. It fell to all fours, blood gouting from its wounds. The swordsman, Nian, charged in, bringing his long, two-handed broadsword down onto the Joining's skull. The creature slumped dead to the ground.

'Do not break the circle!' shouted Skilgannon. 'Hold your line.'

All around them now the beasts were gathering.

'Stand firm!' the priest heard Skilgannon shout. His voice was all but drowned out by a dreadful howling that chilled the blood.

Braygan squeezed shut his eyes and began to pray.

CHAPTER EIGHT

SITTING BY THE FIRE, THE SOFT SCENT OF WOODSMOKE HANGING IN the night air, Rabalyn felt suddenly free of fear. In its place came a sweet melancholy. He found himself thinking of Aunt Athyla, and softer, safer days when she would mix stale bread with milk, dried fruit and honey and bake a pudding. They would sit in the evenings by the fire and cut deep slices, savouring each mouthful. In those days Rabalyn dreamed of being a great hero; of striding across the world carrying a magical sword. Of freeing maidens in distress and earning their undying love.

Now he had fought a beast, alongside a *truly* great warrior. He gazed down at the sleeping man. Druss had come seeking a friend. A kind of quest. Just like old Labbers had said. Warriors were always on quests, according to Labbers. Mostly they were hunting for magical jewels, or other items of sorcery. Or they were really kings in disguise. Rabalyn had loved the stories – even the stupid ones. He could never understand why a succession of otherwise sensible rulers would always send their eldest son on a quest. Surely they knew the first to go always died or got captured. The second eldest would go. He'd fall down a pit, or get eaten by wolves, or seduced by witches. Finally the king would send his youngest, most inexperienced son. He would finish the quest, find the princess, and live happily ever after. If Rabalyn was a king he would send the youngest son first. He had often giggled during story time. Labbers had grown frustrated. 'What is so funny, child?'

Rabalyn could never explain. He would just say: 'Nothing, sir.'

Sometimes the king had no sons. Only daughters. These stories were great favourites among the other children. Rabalyn didn't like them. The king would be looking for a suitor for his prettiest daughter. Every handsome, rich nobleman would ride in. Of course, they were doomed to failure. The man who would win the hand of the princess would be a kitchen lad, or a stable boy, or a young thief. He would naturally have to prove himself by slaying a dragon, or some such, and he would do it in a sneaky way that the children loved. Rabalyn's dislike for those tales centred on the endings. It always turned out that the stable lad was the secret son of a great king, or a wizard. Princesses, it seemed, just didn't fall in love with common folk.

Beside him the axeman was snoring softly. 'You are not really a light sleeper,' whispered Rabalyn.

'Don't let appearances fool you,' answered the axeman. Rabalyn laughed, and added a chunk of wood to the fire. Druss sat up and yawned.

'Were you the youngest son?' asked Rabalyn.

The old warrior shook his head and scratched at his black and silver beard. 'I was the only son.'

'Did you ever fall in love with a princess?'

'No. My friend Sieben was the man for loving princesses. Well, princesses, duchesses, maids, courtesans. Anyone, really. He ended up marrying a Nadir warrior woman. That's when he started to lose his hair.'

'Did she put a spell on him?'

The axeman laughed. 'No, boy, she just wore him out.' For a while they talked. The fire was warm, the night peaceful. Rabalyn told the axeman about his Aunt Athyla and their little house, and how he had always dreamed of being a great warrior.

'All boys want to be warriors,' muttered Druss. 'That's why so many of them die young. We don't achieve anything, you know, Rabalyn. At best we fight so that other men *can* achieve something. We're not even important.'

153

'I think you are important,' objected Rabalyn.

The axeman laughed. 'Of course you do. You're young. A farmer ploughs the land, and grows crops. The crops feed the cities. In the cities men make laws, so that youngsters like you can grow in peace and learn. People marry and have children, and they teach them to respect the land and their fellow citizens. Philosophers and poets spread knowledge. The world grows. Then along comes a warrior, with a shining sword and a burning brand. He burns the farm and kills the farmer. He marches into cities and rapes the wives and maidens. He plants hate like a seed. When he comes there are only two choices. Run away – or send for men like me.'

'But you are not like the killers and the rapers.'

'I am what I am, boy. I try to make no excuses for my life. I wasn't strong enough to be a farmer.'

This confused Rabalyn, who had never seen a stronger man. No farmer could have stood against the beasts as this man had. Rabalyn threw some sticks on the fire and watched them blaze.

'How did the Immortals lose at Skeln?' he asked.

'They faced better fighters on the day.'

'Better fighters than you?'

'You are a bottomless pit of questions.'

'There's so much I don't know.'

'Ah, well, we are not so unalike then, Rabalyn. There is so much I don't know.'

'But you are old and wise.'

The axeman stared hard at the boy. 'I'd be happier if you stopped talking about my age. Bad enough living this long, without there being constant reminders.'

'I'm sorry.'

'And I'm not wise, Rabalyn. Had I been wise I would have stayed home with the woman I loved. I'd have farmed and planted trees. I'd have raised cattle, and sold them at market. Instead I found wars and battles to fight. Old and wise? I've met wise men who were young, and stupid men who were old. I've met good men who did evil things, and evil men who tried to do good. It's all beyond my understanding.'

'Did you have children?'

'No. I regret that. Though I have to say that I get tense around

154

the very young. The screaming and the squalling grates on me. I'm not a great lover of noise. Or people, come to that. They irritate me.'

'Do you want me to stop talking?'

'Laddie, you came down that tree and probably saved my life. You can talk as much as you like. Sing and dance if you want to. I may be cantankerous, but I'm never ungrateful. I owe you.'

Rabalyn felt a surge of pride. He wished he could hold on to this moment for ever. The silence grew. Rabalyn listened to the crackle of burning wood, and felt the night breeze blowing against his skin. He looked back at the axeman. 'If you truly are like those killers who attack cities then why did you help those people when the soldiers were killing them?'

'Had to, laddie. It's the code.'

'I don't understand,' said Rabalyn.

'That's the only difference between me and the killers. They see what they want and they take it. They have become just like those beasts we slew tonight. Outwardly they look like the rest of us. Under the skin they are savage and cruel. They have no mercy. That beast is in me too, Rabalyn. I keep it chained. The code holds it.'

'What is the code?'

The axeman gave a grim smile. 'If I tell you, then you must swear to live by it. Do you really want to hear it? It could be the death of you.'

'Yes.'

The axeman leaned back and closed his eyes. When he spoke it was as if he was reciting a prayer. The words hung in the air. '*Never violate a woman, nor harm a child. Do not lie, cheat or steal. These things are for lesser men. Protect the weak against the evil strong. And never allow thoughts of gain to lead you into the pursuit of evil.*'

'Did your father teach you that?' asked Rabalyn.

'No. It was a friend. His name was Shadak. I have been lucky with my friends, Rabalyn. I hope you are too.'

'Is it Shadak you are looking for?'

Druss shook his head. 'No, he died a long while back. He was more than seventy. He was knifed in an alleyway by three robbers.'

'Were they caught?'

'Two were caught and hanged. One escaped. He fled to a settlement in the high hills. A friend of Shadak's tracked him down and killed him, and the gang that he had joined.'

'So who are you looking for?'

'The young Earl of Dros Purdol. He came to Mellicane two months ago, and then went missing.'

'Perhaps he's dead,' said Rabalyn.

'Aye, the thought had occurred to me. I hope not. He's a good man, and he has an eight-year-old daughter, Elanin, who is a constant joy. Whenever I see her she makes daisy chains I have to wear in my hair.'

Rabalyn laughed, as he pictured the grim warrior with a crown of flowers. 'I thought you said you got tense around the young?'

'I do. Elanin is an exception. Last year on my farm a wild dog ran at her. Most children would have panicked. The dog was large and it would have savaged her. Even as I ran to ward it off she picked up a stick and thumped it across the nose. It yelped and fled.'

'And you like her because she's brave?'

'I admire courage, boy.' The old man sighed. 'I expect she's back in Dros Purdol now worried sick about her father. To see the two of them together lifts the heart.'

'Can I travel with you to Mellicane?' asked Rabalyn.

'Of course. But your friends will come for you.'

'I don't think so. We were scattered when the beasts attacked. I expect they'll just go on without me.'

Druss shook his head. 'As you get older you'll learn to judge men better. The man with the swords would never leave a friend behind. He'll keep looking until he finds you.'

'Unless the beasts killed him.'

'That *would* surprise me,' said the axeman. 'Trust me. He would be a hard man to kill. Now you should get some sleep. I'll sit for a while and – with your leave – enjoy a little silence.'

'Yes, sir,' said Rabalyn, with a smile. Settling down by the fire he tried to stay awake. He wanted to savour this night, to fill his mind with it so that not even the smallest detail would ever be lost to him.

'Was your father a king?' he asked sleepily.

'No. He was a common man, like me.'

'I'm glad.'

Rabalyn was almost asleep when the wind changed. He heard distant howling, and what sounded like a scream of pain.

'There's others fighting tonight,' said Druss. 'May the Source be with them.'

The sound of the old man's voice comforted the youth.

And he slept.

Elanin was a bright child, and, until recently, happy and contented. When her mother arrived for one of her infrequent visits to Dros Purdol she had been pleased to see her. When Mother said she was going to take her on a trip to sea, to meet her father in Mellicane, she had been delighted. She hoped, as children do, it meant that Mother and Father were getting back together, and would be friends again.

But it had all been a lie.

Father hadn't been in Mellicane. Instead Mother had brought her to a huge palace, and there she had met the awful Shakusan Ironmask. The meeting had not, at first, been frightening. Ironmask was a big man, wide-shouldered and powerful. He was not wearing the mask that gave him his name. His face was handsome, though strangely discoloured from the bridge of his nose down to his chin. One of the servants back at Dros Purdol had a purple birthmark too, on the side of his face. But this was far worse.

Mother said that he was going to be her new father. This was just so silly, and Elanin had laughed. Why would she need a new father? She loved the one she had. Mother had said that Father didn't want her any more, and had instructed she was now to live with her mother. At this Elanin became angry. She knew in her heart this was yet another lie and she had told her mother so. It was then that Ironmask had struck her on the face with the flat of his hand. No-one had ever hit her before, and Elanin had been more shocked than hurt. The force of the blow knocked her to the floor. Ironmask loomed over her. 'In my home you will treat your mother with respect,' he said. 'Or you will suffer for it.' Then he had left.

Mother had knelt by her, helping her to her feet, and stroking her blond hair. 'There, you see,' she said. 'You mustn't make him angry. You must *never* make him angry.' It was then that Elanin saw her mother was frightened.

'He is a horrible man,' she said. 'I don't want to stay here.'

Mother looked suddenly terrified, and swung to see if the comment was overheard. 'Don't speak like that!' she said, her voice breaking. 'Promise me you never will again.'

'I won't promise you. I want my father.'

'Things will get better. Trust me, they will. Oh, please, Elanin. Just try to be nice to him. He can be charming and wonderful and generous. You'll see. It is just that he has a . . . terrible temper. There is a war, you see, and he is under a great deal of strain.'

'I hate him,' said Elanin. 'He hit me.'

'Listen to me,' said her mother, drawing her in close. 'This is not Drenai land. The customs here are different. You must be polite to Shakusan. If not he will hurt you. Or me.' The fear in her mother's voice reached through Elanin's anger.

In the days that followed she was careful around Ironmask, avoiding contact where possible, and remaining quiet and softly spoken where not. Before long she began to notice how timid the servants were. They did not joke and laugh as her own servants did back in Purdol. They moved silently, bowing whenever they saw her or her mother. One of the serving girls brought her some break-fast on the fifth day. Elanin saw that the girl – who could have been no more than fifteen – had lost two fingers from her right hand. The stump of one was covered by a badly stitched flap of skin and there was dried blood around it. The girl was quiet and avoided eye contact, so Elanin did not ask her about her injury. The same day she noticed that several of the servants had lost fingers.

That night she was awoken by the sound of screaming coming from far below. Elanin scrambled from her bed and ran into the room Mother shared with Ironmask. He was not there, and Mother was sitting up in bed, hugging her knees and weeping.

'Someone is screaming, Mother!' cried Elanin. Mother had hugged her, and said nothing. Later, when they heard Ironmask approaching, Mother sent Elanin running back to her own room.

She had lain in her bed, dreaming of being rescued. Much as she loved Father she knew that Orastes was not strong enough to take her and Mother from Ironmask. He was a wonderful man, but so much of his life was spent in fear. The officers at Dros Purdol bullied him, and treated him with contempt. Even Mother, when she visited, would talk disparagingly of him when others were present. This always hurt him, but he did nothing to stop her. None of this mattered to Elanin, who loved him more than she could express. No, when she dreamed of rescue in those early days, she thought of Uncle Druss. He was the strongest man in the world. Last year, when she and Father visited him on his farm in the mountains, he had straightened a horseshoe for her with his hands. It was like a magic trick, and when she returned to Purdol no-one believed her. No-one was that strong, she was assured.

She hoped that Father would send Uncle Druss to Mellicane.

When Rabalyn awoke the sky was bright and clear, a glorious blue that lifted the heart. He yawned and stretched. The axeman looked at him and grinned. 'I tell you, laddie, if sleeping ever catches on as a sport I'll wager everything I have on you becoming champion.'

Rabalyn rubbed sleep from his eyes. 'Did you sleep?' he asked.

'I dozed a mite.' Druss looked away, towards the trees, his eyes narrowing.

'Is there something out there?' asked Rabalyn, fear rising.

'Not something. Someone. Been there a while now,' answered Druss, his voice low.

'I can't see anyone.'

'She's there.'

'She?'

Druss swung back to the youth. 'When she comes in don't question her. Sometimes she's a strange lass.' The axeman added fuel to the fire, then rose and stretched his huge arms over his head. 'Damn, but my shoulder aches,' he said. 'Must be rain coming.' As he spoke a young woman emerged from the trees. Over one shoulder she carried a small pack, and in her hand, held by the ears, were two dead hares. Rabalyn watched her. She was tall and slim, her movements graceful. Her long honey-gold hair was pulled back from the brow and bound into a single braid that hung between her shoulders. Her clothes were dark, an ankle-length cloak over a jacket of sleek black leather, the shoulders adorned with beautifully fashioned mail rings, blackened to prevent them gleaming in the light. Her trews were also of leather, though dark brown. She wore knee-length, fringed moccasins, and a short sword in a black scabbard. Rabalyn looked at her face. She was strikingly attractive, though her expression was grim and purposeful. Striding to the fire she dropped her pack, and tossed the hares to the ground. Without saying a word she drew a small curved knife and began to skin them. Druss wandered away into the trees, leaving Rabalyn alone with the woman. She ignored him, and continued to prepare the meat. From the pack she took a small pan, laying it by the fire. Rabalyn sat quietly as she sliced meat into it. Druss strode in, carrying his helm upturned. Walking to the fire he offered it to the woman. Rabalyn saw it was full of water. Taking it, the woman emptied the contents into the pan, and placed it over the fire.

Then she settled back and glanced at the bodies of the beasts. 'The fourth one is dead,' she said. Rabalyn jerked as she broke the odd silence. 'We killed it last night.' Her voice was hard and cold. 'We were lucky. It was already wounded and weak.'

'The boy struck it with my axe,' said Druss.

The woman turned her gaze on Rabalyn for the first time. Her eyes were a smoky grey. She tilted her head as she looked at him, her expression unchanging. Rabalyn felt himself reddening. Then she looked back at Druss. Finally she stood and wandered over to the dead beasts, examining them, and then the ground around the campsite. At last she returned to the fire. 'Now you know,' said Druss.

'Yes.'

'Thought you would.'

The woman unclipped her cloak and let it fall to the ground. Then she lifted clear a narrow leather baldric from which hung a small black double-winged crossbow. Rabalyn had never seen a weapon like it before. He leaned forward. 'May I look at it?' he asked.

The woman ignored him. 'Your axe became lodged in one of the beasts. The boy pulled it clear as you wrestled with the last,' she said to Druss. 'The boy hid in that tree until then.'

160

'Exactly. Now show him your bow, Garianne,' said the axeman softly. 'He's a good lad and means no harm.'

Lifting the weapon, she passed it to Rabalyn without glancing at him. The bow was around a foot in length, with two bronze triggers, and a sharply curved grip. He turned it in his hands, trying to see how the lower bolt could be inserted. It was a clever mechanism. The top bolt was merely placed in a groove in the main shaft; the second was loaded below it, through an opening in the side. Rabalyn curled his hand around the grip and extended his arm. The weapon was lighter than it looked. An image appeared in his mind, of a tall man, dark-eyed and lean. Then it was gone. Rabalyn placed the crossbow on the ground. Garianne moved to the cookpot, stirring the contents with a wooden spoon. From the pack she took a small sack of salt, and added several pinches. Then, from another muslin package, she sprinkled dried herbs into the broth. A savoury scent filled the air.

Time passed, and Rabalyn became uneasy at the lack of conversation. The woman said nothing. The axeman seemed unconcerned. Finally Garianne lifted clear the pot, and set it on the ground to cool. Occasionally she would stir it. 'I'll buy you a meal in Mellicane,' said Druss.

'We are not going to the city. We're heading north. We want to see the high country.'

'There's some sights to see,' agreed the axeman. 'If you change your mind I'll be staying at the Crimson Stag on the west quay.' She seemed not to be listening, then Rabalyn saw her cock her head to one side, and nod.

'I don't like cities,' she said, staring upwards. Then there was a pause. 'Easy for you to say,' she continued. Then another pause. 'But I can hunt what we need.' Finally she shrugged and said: 'As you wish.'

Now Rabalyn was totally confused. The axeman seemed to take the entire one-sided conversation in his stride. Moving to the pan he lifted the spoon, and stirred the contents. 'Smells good,' he said.

'Eat,' said Garianne. Druss ate several spoonfuls, then passed the pot and spoon to Rabalyn. The broth was thick and tasty, and he too ate. At last he pushed the pot towards Garianne. She sighed. 'I am not hungry now,' she said, replacing her baldric and clipping her cloak back into place. 'We will see you in Mellicane, Uncle.'

'I'll bring your pot with me,' he said.

She walked off into the trees without another word.

Druss finished the last of the broth. 'Who was she talking to?' asked Rabalyn.

The axeman shrugged. 'I don't know. I've learned there is more in this world than I can see. I like her, though.'

'Are you her uncle?'

'I can imagine worse nieces. But no, I'm not her uncle. She started calling me that after I nursed her through a fever last year.'

'I think she's mad,' said Rabalyn.

'Aye, I can see why you would.'

'Why didn't she wait for you to finish the broth? Then she would have had her pot.'

'She's uncomfortable around people. You made her nervous.'

'Me? How?'

'You asked her a question. I did warn you, laddie. She doesn't take well to questions.'

'I only asked to see her crossbow. I was being polite.'

'I know. She's a strange lass. But she's got heart, and she uses that crossbow like a master.'

'What does her family think of her running around dressed like a man?' asked Rabalyn.

Druss laughed aloud. 'I'm forgetting you come from a small community, laddie. She doesn't have any family – not that I know of. She sometimes travels with a pair of twins. Good lads. One's a simpleton. I have never heard her speak of family, though. My guess is they were probably killed. That, or some other shock unhinged her. She is not always as you saw her today. A little wine inside her and she'll sing sweeter than a songbird. Aye, and dance and laugh. It's only when the voices come that she . . . well, you saw,' he concluded lamely.

'How did you meet her?'

'Do you never run out of questions, laddie?' replied Druss, pushing himself to his feet. 'Come on, it's time to be moving. I have a feeling we'll be meeting your friends before long.'

With the coming of the dawn Braygan was more exhausted than at any other time in his life. The bright sunshine hurt his eyes, and he felt as if he was walking through a dream. A small boy was sleeping beside him, his terrified mother stroking the child's hair. Other women and children were huddled together at the centre of the circle. A girl of around three began to cry. Braygan reached out to comfort her, but she backed away from him. A woman called to the child, who scrambled over to her, sobbing. Braygan pushed himself to his feet and eased his way to the outer circle where Skilgannon stood, with around a dozen surviving men, and the same number of strong women. Some of the women in the circle were armed with knives. The remainder held thick lumps of wood, which they had used as clubs when the beasts attacked.

'Have they gone for good this time?' asked Braygan, glancing down at the dried blood on Skilgannon's blades.

Skilgannon looked at the priest and shrugged. Just beyond the circle lay the giant body of a hideous creature. Braygan tried not to look at it, but his eyes were drawn to its massive jaws. The little priest had seen those fangs crunch into the skull of a man, ripping the head from the shoulders, before Skilgannon had leapt in, cutting a gaping hole in the beast's throat. The headless body of the man was no longer in sight. Other creatures had dragged it away into the darkness, along with the corpses of other Joinings.

Braygan swung to look back at the crowd of people huddled together inside the circle. There were some fifty or more, half of them children.

'How many of us did they get?' asked Braygan.

'Ten . . . fifteen,' answered Skilgannon wearily. 'I had no time to keep count.'

The two brothers, Jared and Nian, broke away from the outer circle and approached Skilgannon. Both carried longswords, with double-handed hilts. 'You think we should try to get away now it's light?' asked Jared.

'Wait a while,' said Skilgannon. 'They may have retreated back into the reeds, and be watching for just such a move.'

'I counted eighteen of them,' said the young man. 'I think we killed five at least, and wounded four others.'

'I cut the head from one,' said Nian. 'Did you see that, Jared? Did you see me cut its head?'

'I saw. You did well. Very brave, Nian.'

'Did you see?' the man asked Skilgannon. 'Did you see me cut its head off?'

'Your brother is right. You are very brave,' said Skilgannon. Braygan saw the simpleton give a crooked smile, then reach out and take hold of the long blue sash that hung from his brother's belt. He stood there, sword in one hand, sash in the other.

'We cannot just wait here all day,' said Skilgannon. 'Either they have gone, or they are waiting. We need to know which.'

'What are you thinking?' asked Jared.

'I'm going to take a stroll to the reeds.'

'We'll keep you company.'

Skilgannon glanced past Jared, at his brother. 'Might be best if Nian remains behind – to look after the women and children.'

Jared shook his head. 'He couldn't do that, my friend. He needs to be close to me.'

'Then you both remain here,' said Skilgannon. With that he sheathed his swords and strolled away towards the northwest.

Braygan watched him go, and felt his heart sink. A murmur began among other people in the circle, as they watched Skilgannon move away towards the reeds. 'Hold the circle!' shouted Jared, moving away from Braygan. 'He's just scouting. He'll be back. Stay watchful!'

A flicker of resentment flared in Braygan, and he was immediately ashamed. How swiftly Skilgannon had become important in these people's lives. He was their saviour and their hope. What am I, wondered Braygan? I am nothing. If these people survive they will not remember the chubby little priest who cowered at the centre of the circle, begging the Source to keep him alive. They will recall the dark-haired warrior with the twin swords who took command, forming the circle that saved them. They will remember him to the ends of their lives.

'There's one!' The shout was full of terror, and a wail went up from the children.

Braygan swung round, eyes wide and fearful. A dark shape emerged from the tall grass. It was a golden-haired woman in a dark cloak. Braygan's relief was immense.

'It's Garianne! It's Garianne!' shouted the simpleton, Nian. Still holding to his brother's sash he walked towards the woman. Jared grabbed his arm.

'Don't pull me,' he said gently. 'She's coming here.'

Nian waved. 'Over here, Garianne. We're over here.'

The woman was beautiful, her eyes a soft flecked grey, her braided hair gleaming in the sunlight. She approached the two brothers. Nian moved towards her, and, dropping his sword, lifted her into a hug. She kissed his cheek lightly. 'Put me down,' she said, 'and be calm.' Then she swung towards Jared. 'We are glad to see you alive,' she said, her voice flat and emotionless. She did not smile.

'It is good to see you, Garianne,' Jared told her. 'Did . . . ?' He cleared his throat. 'We were wondering if the beasts were still close by.'

'Some moved northeast in the night. We killed one. Old Uncle and his friend killed three more.'

'I cut the head off one,' said Nian. 'Tell her, Jared.'

'He did. He was very brave, Garianne. It would be good if you could stay awhile and help us fight off the creatures. There are many children here.'

'We are going to Mellicane. Old Uncle is buying us a meal.'

'We are all heading to Mellicane, Garianne. Nian would be happy if you came with us.'

'Yes, yes, come with us, Garianne,' insisted Nian. Suddenly the woman smiled. Braygan found the moment breathtaking. In that instant she moved from attractive to stunningly beautiful. Stepping towards Nian, she reached up and curled her arm round his shoulder.

'I wish I had seen you cut its head off,' she said, kissing his cheek.

'Three whacks it took. Is Old Uncle coming too?'

Her smile faded and she stepped away from Nian.

'No questions, Nian,' said Jared softly. 'Remember?'

'I'm sorry, Garianne,' muttered Nian. Her smile returned briefly, and she seemed to relax.

'Old Uncle is coming. Maybe an hour. Maybe less,' she told them.

Jared swung to Braygan. 'Old Uncle is a warrior named Druss.

165

You have heard the name?' Braygan shook his head. 'He is Drenai, and, like your friend, he is deadly. With Garianne and Druss we have more than a chance against any beasts.'

Skilgannon walked towards the swaying bank of reeds, his movements smooth and unhurried, scanning the stalks for any sign of movement not caused by the breeze. He was exactly as he seemed to those who watched him from the circle, relaxed and strolling, his swords sheathed.

Malanek had called it *the illusion of elsewhere*; where the mind floats free and surrenders control of the body to the instincts and the senses. As he walked Skilgannon allowed his thoughts to roam far, even as his eyes watched for danger.

He thought of Malanek, and the tortuous training, the endless exercises and the harsh regime of physical stress. He remembered Greavas and Sperian, and the increasing tension of the days after Bokram's coronation. Arrests were sudden. Houses were raided, the occupants dragged away. No-one spoke of the departed. Known followers of the dead Emperor disappeared, or were publicly executed in Leopard Square.

Fear descended on the capital. People watched each other with suspicious eyes, never knowing who might inform on them for a hasty word, or a suggested criticism. Skilgannon worried about Greavas, and his connections to the royal family, and, indeed, the former actor often went missing for days before returning without a word as to his previous whereabouts. Skilgannon asked him one evening where he had been. Greavas sighed. 'Best you don't know, my friend,' was all he would say.

One night, around three weeks after the coronation, armed soldiers arrived at the house. Molaire was beside herself with fear, and even the normally resolute Sperian was ashen and afraid. Skilgannon was sitting in the garden when the officer marched out. It was the golden-haired former athlete, Boranius. Skilgannon rose from his chair. 'Good to see you,' he said, and meant it.

'And you,' answered Boranius coolly. 'However, I am here on official business.'

'I shall have refreshments served for you,' said Skilgannon, gesturing towards the pale-faced Sperian. The man gratefully withdrew. Skilgannon glanced at the two soldiers standing in the garden doorway. 'Please make yourselves comfortable,' he told them. 'There are chairs for all.'

'My men will stand,' said Boranius, lifting his scabbard, and seating himself on a wicker chair. He still looked every inch the athlete Skilgannon had so admired.

'Do you still run, Boranius?'

'No, I have little time for such pursuits. You?'

Skilgannon laughed. 'I do, but it is not the fun it was, for I have no-one to test me. You were my inspiration. You set the standard.'

'And you beat me.'

'You had an injured ankle, Boranius. However, I did enjoy getting the medal.'

'The days of school medals are behind me now – and you too soon. Have you considered your future?'

'I shall be a soldier like my father.'

'That is pleasing to hear. We need good soldiers. Loyal soldiers.' The blond officer leaned back in his chair. 'These are difficult times, Olek. There are traitors everywhere. They must be hunted down and exterminated. Do you know any traitors?'

'How would I recognize them, Boranius? Do they wear odd hats?'

'This is not a subject for jests, Olek. Even now someone is sheltering the Emperor's concubine and her bastard daughter. Bokram is king by right and by blood. Those who speak or act against him are traitors.'

'I have heard no-one speak against him,' said Skilgannon. There was a tightness around Boranius's blue eyes, and the man seemed constantly on edge.

'What about the pervert who lives here? Is he loyal?'

Skilgannon felt a coldness settle in his belly. 'You are a guest in my home, Boranius. Do not speak ill of any of my friends.'

'I am not a guest, Olek. I am an officer of the King. Have you heard Greavas speak against the King?'

'No, I have not. We do not discuss matters of politics.'

'I need to question him. Is he here?'

'No.'

Sperian returned carrying a tray of drinks, the mixed juices of apple and apricot in silver goblets. Skilgannon glanced up at him. 'Where is Greavas?' he asked.

'He is visiting friends, sir, in the north of the city.'

'When will he be returning?'

'Tomorrow, perhaps, or the next day, sir. He did not say.'

Skilgannon thanked the man and waved him away. 'I shall tell him you need to speak with him when he returns,' he said, 'though I fail to see how a retired actor could be of help to you.'

'We shall see,' said Boranius, rising. 'There is also a warrant for the arrest of your friend, Askelus.'

Now Skilgannon was truly shocked. 'Why?'

'Like his father he is also a traitor. His father was disembowelled this morning in Leopard Square.'

'Askelus is no traitor,' said Skilgannon, also rising. 'We have spoken often. He is a huge admirer of the Emperor Gorben, and he has talked, like me, of serving in Bokram's army. Not once have I heard him say a word of criticism against the King. Quite the reverse, in fact.'

'Then – sadly – he will perish for the sins of his father,' said Boranius coldly.

Skilgannon had stared then at the young man who had been his hero. The young athlete of his memory disappeared. In his place stood a cold-eyed soldier, bereft of emotion, save perhaps malice. Memories flooded Skilgannon then, moments that had seemed insignificant at the time, but now shone bright in the glow of sudden understanding. The casual discarding of friendships, the sarcastic comments, the meanness of spirit. Skilgannon had seen Boranius through the golden gaze of hero worship. Now here was the reality. Boranius held the power of life and death, and he revelled in it. Anger swelled in Skilgannon's heart, but he quelled it, and smiled. 'I have much to learn, my friend,' he said. 'I thank you for taking the time to visit me.'

Boranius chuckled then and slapped Skilgannon on the shoulder. 'When you have your final papers – assuming they are Firsts – come and see me. I will find a place for you in my regiment.'

'You do me great honour.'

With that he walked Boranius and his men to the front door, and waited as they mounted their horses and rode away.

Sperian came out and breathed a sigh of relief. 'I thought we were all to be arrested,' he said.

'The man is a viper,' said Skilgannon.

'Aye, your father thought that. Never liked the family.'

'Can you get a message to Greavas tomorrow?'

'Yes.'

'Tell him not to come home for a while. Go through the market. Tomorrow is auction day. There will be hundreds there. You should be able to slip through unnoticed.'

Sperian looked uncertain. 'You think I might be followed?'

'It is a possibility.'

'My eyes aren't good, Olek. I am not skilled at this sort of thing.'

'No, of course you aren't. Foolish of me. I will take it myself.'

Now Sperian looked even more worried. 'He doesn't want you involved, sir. He would be most put out if I told you where he was.'

Skilgannon put his hand on the retainer's shoulder. 'If he comes out into the open he will be arrested. Probably executed. Most certainly tortured. I don't think you should concern yourself with his annoyance at your disclosure.'

'It's not just that, sir. It's who he's with.'

'Tell me.'

'He has the Empress and her daughter hidden. He's looking for a way to get them out of the city.'

Skilgannon was jerked from his memories as the reeds rustled and shook. The Swords of Night and Day flashed from their scabbards. A small dog darted by him, sniffed the ground, then ran on towards the circle. A little girl called out a name and the dog barked and scampered over to her. Skilgannon let out his breath, and continued his walk.

There was no sign of the beasts. Turning back towards the refugees, he saw the massive figure of the axeman emerge from the long grass. Beside him was the boy, Rabalyn.

CHAPTER NINE

SKILGANNON ORGANIZED THE EIGHTY OR SO REFUGEES INTO A TIGHT column, which moved slowly through the reeds. He took point and moved ahead of the column, while Druss and Garianne walked at either side of the centre. The two brothers brought up the rear. Other surviving fighters kept to the outsides of the column, and walked warily, swords and knives at the ready.

There was only one moment of anxiety during the morning, when an old bull pushed its head through the reeds, causing children to scream and scatter. Other than this they passed through the countryside without incident.

For a time Rabalyn walked with Braygan at the centre, then he dropped back to where the brothers travelled. They were an odd pair, he thought, noting how the bearded Nian constantly held on to the blue sash at Jared's waist. Druss had said they were fighting men, and Rabalyn believed it, despite their odd appearance.

Towards afternoon the column halted at the base of a low hill. There was a stream close by, and many of the women gathered water and prepared their meagre rations. Druss had wandered off with Skilgannon, and the strange girl was sitting alone on the hillside, staring out towards the northwest.

Rabalyn hunkered down with the brothers. 'Have you known Druss long?' he asked.

170

'A long time,' said Nian. 'More than a year. Chop chop. That's Old Uncle. Then they all ran away.'

'Who ran away?'

'All the bad men. We killed some too, didn't we, Jared?'

'Aye, we did.'

'And Garianne shot their leader through the head. Right through the head. He looked really silly. He tried to pull it out. Then he was dead. It was funny.'

The story made no sense to Rabalyn. He gave Jared a quizzical glance. 'We were paid to guard a village,' said Jared. 'About a dozen of us. We were informed there were some twenty bandits. But it was a far bigger group, around sixty men, half of them Nadir outcasts. Vicious bastards. They attacked just before dusk. We should have been overrun. No question about it.'

'Chop chop,' said Nian happily.

'Druss just charged into the middle of them, his axe cleaving left and right. You'd have thought they'd have borne him down with weight of numbers. Nian and me rushed in. So did some of the others – and some of the villagers, armed with scythes and sticks. Garianne was coming down with the sickness then, but she staggered out and sent a bolt straight through the forehead of the outlaw leader. That finally broke them. At the end there wasn't a scratch on Druss. Knives and swords had bounced off his gauntlets and his shoulder guards – even his helm. But nothing had touched him. Amazing,' he said, awe in his voice. 'He was covered in blood. None of it his.' Jared shook his head at the memory of it. 'Thing is, in a fight, he's always moving, never still. Always attacking. Having seen that I now know what happened at Skeln.'

'Skeln?' queried Rabalyn. 'But we lost at Skeln.'

'Yes, we did.'

'I don't understand. How could we lose with Druss on our side?'

Jared laughed. 'Are you mocking me, boy?'

'No, sir. Brother Lantern told me Druss was at Skeln, with the Immortals.'

'I think you misheard, lad. Druss *was* with the Immortals once. At Skeln he fought with the Drenai. It was Druss who broke the last charge and turned the battle. He broke the Immortals, by God. That's not just a man we're talking about. That's Druss the Legend.'

'Does that mean he's our enemy?' asked Rabalyn, concerned.

Jared shrugged. 'Not mine. Neither Nian nor me would be here had it not been for Druss. And I certainly don't want him for an enemy. I'm pretty good with this longsword, son. I'd fancy myself against just about anyone. Not against Druss, though. Nor that Skilgannon either, come to that. How did you come to be travelling with him, Rabalyn?'

Rabalyn told them the story of the riot at the church, and of how Brother Lantern had quelled it.

'There's no accounting for people,' said Jared. 'Who would have thought it? The Damned became a priest. There's always something to surprise you in this life.' Beside him Nian began to moan. Rabalyn glanced at the man. His face was grey, and sweat was gleaming on his skin.

'Hurts, Jared,' he whimpered. 'Hurts bad.'

'Lie down. Come on, just lie down for a while.' He swung to Rabalyn. 'Get some water.'

Rabalyn ran off and borrowed a small bucket from a family. He filled it at the stream, then made his way back to the twins. Jared dipped a cloth in the water and began to bathe his brother's head. Then he opened a pouch at his side, took a pinch of pale grey powder, and sprinkled it into Nian's mouth. Drenching the cloth, he squeezed drops of water onto Nian's lips. After a while the groaning ceased and the man slept.

'What's wrong with him?' asked Rabalyn.

'He's dying,' said Jared. 'Go tell Skilgannon we'll have to wait here at least another hour.'

People had begun to gather around the unconscious Nian. Some women from the column enquired what was wrong, but Jared waved them away. Garianne came over and sat beside Nian, gently stroking his cheek. Rabalyn hesitated for a moment, watching her, but then he stood and walked away, up the hillside to where Skilgannon and Druss were talking.

The older warrior looked round as Rabalyn approached, and smiled at him. 'Is it Nian? Don't look so downcast, boy. He'll come round.'

'Jared says he's dying.'

'Aye, but not today.'

'What is wrong with him?'

'There is a sickness in his head,' said Druss. 'A surgeon told Jared there's a cancer growing there. It is destroying Nian's mind.'

'Couldn't they give him medicine, or something?'

'That's why they're heading for Mellicane. There's said to be a healer there.'

Rabalyn turned to Skilgannon. 'Jared says we have to wait until Nian wakes up.'

'Aye. He'll sleep for an hour – maybe two,' added Druss.

'It will be dusk by then,' said Skilgannon. 'I have no idea how far the beasts have moved, or whether they'll come back after nightfall.'

'I was thinking that myself. We're no more than two hours from Mellicane now. Give him an hour. If he hasn't woken I'll carry him. The boy can take my axe and walk beside me.'

Skilgannon offered no objection. 'I'm going to make a sweep to the north and see how the land lies,' he said. 'If I am not back in an hour then lead them on towards the city. I'll meet you on the way.'

With that he loped off down the hillside. Rabalyn watched him go. 'What if there are any beasts out there?' he asked Druss.

'Well, Rabalyn, he'll either kill them or die.'

As he approached the trees around a half-mile from the base of the hill Skilgannon slowed. The short run had warmed and loosened his muscles, but he had no wish to race headlong into a pack of the beasts. His eyes felt gritty, his body weary. It was more than twenty-four hours since he had last slept, and the previous night had been long and bloody.

The attacks by the beasts had been sustained and cunning. The creatures had darted in from different directions, as if operating to a plan. Several times during the night he had seen the colossal grey one he had first spotted emerging from the reeds the previous afternoon. It seemed to Skilgannon that this one beast was directing the others. After a while he had watched for it. If he glimpsed it to the south of the circle, then it would be from that direction the next attack would come.

Looking back on the night of terror Skilgannon realized that the beasts had not set out to kill all of the refugees. They had been hunting food, and once they had gathered enough bodies they had withdrawn. Like a wolf pack.

He pushed on into the trees, and climbed towards a hilltop, scanning the ground as he moved. There were many deep paw prints, but all were heading away from the city. At the top of the hill were several tall oaks. He climbed one of them and scanned the land. To the far north he could just make out the spires of Mellicane, and the tents of the besieging armies of Datia and Dospilis. Out towards the east he saw riders. There was no sign of Joinings. A great weariness settled over him, and he wedged himself against two thick branches, rested his head against the tree trunk and closed his eyes.

He was walking through a moonlit forest. The White Wolf was near. He could hear its stealthy movements in the undergrowth. Skilgannon's heart was beating fast. He clenched his fists to avoid reaching for his swords. A low snarl came from behind him. Spinning on his heel he swung to face the threat.

There was nothing there. Then he saw that – once again – he had unconsciously drawn the Swords of Night and Day, the blades glittering in the moonlight. Casting them from him he cried out: 'Where are you?'

Then he awoke.

The sun had scarcely moved in the sky. He had not slept for more than a few minutes. Even so he felt refreshed, and considered rejoining the refugees. But it was peaceful here, high in the tree, and he realized how much he had missed his own company. There was a time he had enjoyed having people close by; the days when Greavas, Sperian, and Molaire had cared for him, when Malanek had taught him the dance of blades. Long painful years had flowed by since then. The days of Bokram and the terror. The days of Jianna.

The horror had been ahead of him on the morning he set off to find Greavas. The sun had shone bright in a clear, cloudless sky, and the strength and arrogance of youth had filled him with confidence.

Skilgannon, at sixteen, had begun the day by walking to the Royal Park. During the stroll through the lanes and shops of

174

the city centre he had taken time to pause at the stalls and – while appearing to study merchandise – had identified the men following him. There were two, one tall, lean and sandy-haired, the other shorter, with a long, dark moustache that overran his chin. Skilgannon, upon reaching the park, had stretched his muscles and begun to run. The paths through the park were beautifully paved with white stone, angling through flower beds, and past artificial lakes and statue gardens. Many people were strolling, or sitting on the stone benches. Some had even spread blankets and were picnicking. Skilgannon continued on at an even lope. As the path bent he had glanced back to see the two men toiling after him. There was no sense of danger. It was like an adventure for the young man. He took them through four miles of slow jogging, and then steadily increased the pace. At the last he came almost full circle, back to the marble gymnasium and bathhouse set beside the western gates of the park. Here he slowed and finally sat upon a wide bench. The two followers, sweat-drenched and weary, stumbled to where he sat.

'Good morning,' said Skilgannon.

The man with the drooping moustache nodded at him. The taller man forced a smile.

'A hot day for a run,' said the youth. 'Are you in training?'

'Always,' said the sandy-haired man.

'I am Olek Skilgannon.' Rising, he offered his hand.

'Morcha. This is Casensis.' Both men seemed uneasy. Skilgannon guessed they had been told to follow at a distance and not be seen.

'I am about to enjoy a bath and a massage,' Skilgannon told them. 'Nothing like it after a warming run.'

'We're not members,' said the burly Casensis, his eyes narrowing. 'These places are for the rich.'

'And for the sons of soldiers who have served the nation,' said Skilgannon smoothly. 'My father was given honorary membership, which has passed to me. I am also allowed to bring guests. Will you join me?'

He led the surprised men inside. The marble hallway was cool and scented. Skilgannon signed the register and the three men were led through to a cedar-panelled changing room, where they were given soft white robes and towels. Then, having stripped off their clothing and donned their robes, they made their way through two archways and into a huge area with a vaulted ceiling. Enormous windows had been set into the walls, many with stained glass. Trees were growing here, and hot water gushed over rocks to fill a series of artificial pools that had been created on different levels. Rose petals floated on the water, and the air was rich with scent. Only two of the pools were being used. Skilgannon laid his robe and towels on a stone bench and walked down the marble steps, wading into the upper pool, close to the gushing water. Stretching out, he floated on the surface, closing his eyes. The two spies followed him.

Skilgannon swam across the centre of the pool, away from the waterfall, and sat back with his arms on the stone lip. The sandy-haired Morcha swam to join him, while Casensis waded across. Two serving women, bare-breasted but wearing long, clinging skirts, moved from the shadows bearing goblets of cold spring water. Both women had the traditional dyed yellow hair, streaked with red at the temples, that marked them as pleasure servants. They also sported gold torques upon their necks, signifying they were several ranks above the cheaper whores who worked the streets and the marketplaces.

Casensis stared up at them, unable to tear his gaze from their naked breasts. One of them smiled at him. Then they moved away.

'Are they free also?' asked Casensis.

'For massage, yes,' said Skilgannon. 'All other services are negotiable.'

'What do they charge?'

'Ten silver pieces.'

'That's three months' wages!' said Casensis, outraged.

'And for what do you earn these wages?' Skilgannon asked.

'We are soldiers of the King,' said Morcha swiftly.

'Ah, I see why you were running today. It is important to stay strong and able. I too am hoping to join the King's army soon.'

They sat in silence for a while, enjoying the cool drinks and the warm water. Morcha turned towards Skilgannon. 'This has been good of you, sir. It will be something to remember.'

'My pleasure, my friend. But you must enjoy a massage before you go. The girls here are highly skilled. They will soothe away all aches and pains, and you will doze and dream beautiful dreams. It is my favourite part of the day. Then perhaps you will join me for a meal in the dining area.'

'That is most kind of you,' said Morcha.

With the bath finished the three men climbed out. Immediately blonde women moved forward, leading each of them into a separate candlelit room.

Once Skilgannon was clear of the men he thanked the girl and declined a massage. 'I shall leave a handsome tip for you,' he told the surprised masseuse. 'When my friends have been suitably relaxed tell them I was called away, but that I have arranged for them to dine at my expense.'

'Yes, sir,' she said.

He dressed swiftly in the changing room and then left the building. Leaving the park, he moved quickly through the streets, pausing once more at shops and stalls, just in case there were other followers. Satisfied at last that he was alone, Skilgannon followed the directions Sperian had given and headed into the north of the city.

The house he was seeking was new, built on the outskirts, and close to an army barracks. It was a small three-roomed property, with a roof of roughcast red tiles. There were some twenty similar buildings constructed for the wives and children of workers at the barracks: cooks, carpenters and blacksmiths. Sperian had described the house, saying that a bougainvillaea bush was growing on the western wall alongside the front door. There was something about the location that spoke of Greavas. Only a man with his keen sense of irony would hide the most wanted pair in the capital within a stone's throw of one of the largest barracks. And yet even as the thought occurred Skilgannon realized there was also great intelligence in the decision. All the buildings in the city's richest quarter had been searched, as well as outlying estates. No-one would dream of seeking the Empress and her daughter in a hastily built dwelling so close to a centre for the new King's loyal troops.

Skilgannon tapped at the door, but there was no reply. Moving around to the back of the house he tried the small gate leading to the tiny patch of garden. This was locked. Glancing round to see if he was observed from any of the other houses, Skilgannon scaled the wall and leapt down into the garden.

As he landed he caught a glimpse of movement to his left. Something flashed for his head. Ducking, he hurled himself to his right, landed on his shoulder and rolled to his feet. Even as he came upright a sandal-shod foot thudded against his temple. He rolled with the blow, throwing up his arm to prevent a second high kick exploding against his head. His assailant was blonde and female, her dyed hair streaked red at the temples. She launched another attack, her left hand slashing towards his face. Grabbing her wrist he twisted it savagely, trying to turn her. Instead of resisting she threw herself forward, aiming a head butt at his face. It thudded painfully against his collar bone. Angry now, he threw her to the ground. She rolled expertly to her feet and advanced on him again, her pretty face masked by fury, her eyes narrowed.

'Enough! Enough!' yelled Greavas, running from the doorway, and grabbing the girl by the waist. 'This is a friend – though a stupid one. What are you doing here?' he demanded of Skilgannon.

'Not a subject I think we should discuss in the presence of a whore,' he snapped.

'A whore you cannot afford,' she responded. 'And if you could you still wouldn't be man enough.'

The venom in her voice stunned him. Never had a pleasure girl spoken so to him. Always they were deferential, never making eye contact. Added to which this girl had used moves that Malanek had taught *him*. Unheard of for a woman. Skilgannon looked more closely at her, then back at Greavas. A middle-aged woman appeared in the rear doorway, her eyes fearful. 'Is everything all right?' she asked.

'Everything is fine,' said Greavas. 'Unless of course you were followed here,' he added, swinging to Skilgannon. 'Then we are all dead.'

'I was not followed – though two men were assigned to the task. I left them at the bathhouse.'

'Let us hope there were no others.'

'There were no others,' said Skilgannon, his temper flaring. 'I came to warn you not to return to the house. Boranius is seeking you.'

178

'No more than I expected. I had not intended to return. If that is all you have to tell me, Olek, then you had best leave now.'

'I thought you would need help.'

'Aye, I do need help,' said Greavas. 'But this is not a boy's game. This is not some schoolboy adventure. The stakes here are high. Torture and death await failure.'

Skilgannon said nothing for a moment, calming himself. He looked again at the yellow-haired girl he had taken for a prostitute, then back at the fearful woman in the doorway. 'The disguise is a good one,' he said. 'It still leaves you with the problem of smuggling a mother and her daughter from the city, when soldiers have been given your description.'

'I intend to cut my hair and dye it black,' said Greavas, 'but you are right. They are searching for a woman and her young daughter. Nothing I can do about that.'

'Of course there is. You can separate them. As a whore the princess can travel anywhere without suspicion. Without her daughter the Empress can travel as your wife.'

'All the gates are guarded,' replied Greavas, 'and there are faithless former retainers stationed at all of them, ready to betray the royal family for gold. There is no escape, Olek. Not yet.'

'They should still separate,' said Skilgannon. 'And I *do* have a plan.'

'*This* I would love to hear,' said the princess.

Ignoring the contempt in her voice he pressed on. 'If I get back to the bathhouse swiftly the men who followed me will still be there. I shall do as I proposed and buy them a meal. If the princess is outside the bathhouse in three hours, and approaches me as a whore, they will see her. They will also see me engage her services and take her home. They will make their report. Olek Skilgannon is not linked with traitors. He is more interested in playing with whores. She will be invisible to them – well, invisible as a princess, anyway.'

Greavas sat down at a small wooden table and rubbed his chin. 'I don't know,' he said.

'It is a good plan,' said the princess. 'I like it.'

'It has dangers,' Greavas told her. 'First you must get to the bathhouse. The road there is packed with men. You will be accosted all the way. Secondly there are already whores at the bathhouse. They will defend their territory – harshly. They will want no strangers coming in and stealing their trade. Thirdly you do not sound like a whore. Your voice is refined. And lastly you might still be recognized, despite the disguise, and that will lead to your capture and death, and the death of Olek.'

'The alternative is to sit in this appalling closet of a house until we are discovered, or we die of boredom,' said the princess. 'And do not concern yourself about my refined speech. I spent enough time with my father's soldiers to know how to speak roughly. And Malanek trained me well enough. I can deal with angry whores. I assure you of that.'

Greavas looked uncertain, but he nodded. 'Very well. Olek, you get back as swiftly as you can. And may the Source watch over you both. I will get a message to you when it is safe to move. Go now.'

Skilgannon sped back to the bathhouse. Less than an hour had passed, but he was still worried that Morcha and Casensis might have left. He located the girl he had spoken to and asked her if she had passed on his message. She said she had not, for they were still in the booths with the body maidens. Relieved, Skilgannon thanked her and settled down to wait. Morcha emerged first, arm in arm with a buxom blonde girl. Leaning down he kissed her cheek. She smiled at him and walked away.

'By the Source,' said Morcha, 'this is a day I shall remember fondly.' He sat down and leaned back against the wall, fingering the thick, soft cloth of his robe. 'How the rich live,' he said.

'I am ashamed to say I had not considered it,' said Skilgannon, with sincerity.

'Not your fault you are rich, lad. Gods, I don't blame you for it.'

Casensis emerged from another booth. The girl curtsied to him, but did not smile as she left. He wandered out, looking sour and unhappy, and asked Morcha if he had bedded his girl. 'Indeed I did,' said Morcha happily. 'And she did not charge me.'

Casensis swore. 'Knew I should have chosen her,' he said.

'Some men have no luck,' said Morcha, with a wink at Skilgannon.

'Join me for a meal,' Skilgannon offered. Both men accepted

180

and, once they had donned their clothes, he led them up the stairs to the dining hall. An hour later, having devoured several roast pheasants in a berry sauce, plus consuming a tankard of fine wine, the two soldiers were in good spirits. Even Casensis had a smile on his surly features.

As they left the building by the main entrance Skilgannon felt tense, and, for the first time that day, uncertain. The plan had seemed so good when he had thought of it. But Greavas was right. This was no schoolboy game. What if the princess was recognized by Morcha or Casensis? What if she could not play the role? Added to which he himself had now become a traitor to the new order. What future would there be for him as a result? Be calm, he told himself, remembering his father's advice. 'A man should stand by his friends – unless they do evil – and hold always to what he believes in.' Could Greavas's actions in protecting two women from death be considered evil? Skilgannon doubted it. Therefore there was only one course of action.

There were around a dozen whores in the marble square. One of them was sitting down, nursing a cut lip and a swollen eye. Others were clustered together, staring malevolently at a slim, beautiful newcomer. As the three men emerged several of the whores moved towards them, smiling provocatively. Casensis stopped to chat to them, while Morcha stood back.

The slim girl approached Skilgannon. She walked with a subtle sway of the hips. Her head tilted and she smiled at him. It was as if he had been struck in the chest by a hammer. Gone was the violent, scornful girl in the garden. Here was the most devastatingly attractive woman he had ever seen. 'You look like a man in need of a little company,' she said, linking her arm in his. Her voice was rough and uncultured, and her smile full of dark promise. Skilgannon's mouth was dry, and he could think of nothing to say. Morcha laughed good-naturedly.

'I'd take her up on it, lad. I may not be the sharpest arrow in the quiver, but she looks like something special to me.'

Skilgannon was about to speak when the girl slipped her hand under his tunic, fondling him. He leapt backwards and almost fell. 'Be careful with him, darling. He's young and I'd reckon a little inexperienced,' said Morcha.

'My home is close by,' was all Skilgannon could say. He felt like an idiot, and knew he was blushing.

'Can you afford me? I don't come cheap.'

'I don't think I can,' he said, 'but I'll sell the house.'

'That's the way, boy,' said Morcha, with a booming laugh. 'Damn, but I wish I hadn't sported in the bathhouse now. This is a girl I'd willingly fight you for. Go on, go off with you!'

The princess took his arm and led him away. He glanced back to see Morcha and Casensis watching him. Morcha waved. Casensis looked sour.

And so it was that Skilgannon met the love of his life, and took her home.

Sitting in the tree, overlooking the distant city of Mellicane, Skilgannon recalled the day. Despite the horror and death that had followed that meeting he found he could not regret it. Before that afternoon, it seemed to him, the sky had been always grey, and after it he had experienced the beauty of the rainbow.

Jianna shone like the sun, and sparkled like a jewel. She was unlike anyone he had ever met. He still recalled the scent of her hair as they walked together arm in arm. He sighed at the memory. Then she had been a beautiful young woman, no older than he. Now she was the Witch Queen and wanted him dead.

Pushing such sombre thoughts from his mind, he climbed down from the tree.

Cadis Patralis had been a captain in the army of Dospilis for a mere four months. His father had purchased his commission, and he had taken part in only one action, the routing of a small group of Tantrian archers at a bridge some twenty miles from Mellicane. Now, it seemed, the war was over, and for young Cadis the prospect of glory and advancement was receding by the hour.

Instead of fighting the enemy, and earning respect, admiration and elevated rank, he now led his forty lancers across the hills, seeking escaped arena beasts. There was no glory to be had in hunting down these abominations, and Cadis was in a foul mood. It was not helped by the sergeant who had been foisted on him. The man was insufferable. The colonel had assured Cadis that the sergeant was a sound fighter and a veteran of three campaigns. 'He will be invaluable to you, young man. Learn from him.'

Learn from him? The man was a peasant. He had no understanding of philosophy or literature, and he swore constantly – always a sign of ill breeding.

At nineteen Cadis Patralis cut a handsome figure in his tailored cuirass and golden cloak. His chain mail glistened, and his padded helm fitted to perfection. His cavalry sabre had been made by the greatest swordsmith in Dospilis, and his thigh-length boots, reinforced around the knee, were of finest shimmering leather. By contrast Sergeant Shialis looked like a vagabond. His breastplate was dented, his cloak – once gold, but now a pale urine yellow – was tattered and much repaired. And his boots were beyond a joke. Even his sabre was standard issue, with a wooden hilt, strongly wrapped with leather strips. Cadis glanced at the man's face. Unshaven, his eyes red-rimmed, he looked ancient and worn out. How such a man could have fooled the colonel was beyond the understanding of Cadis Patralis.

Leaning forward in the saddle Cadis heeled his grey gelding up a slope, pausing at the crest and scanning the land. Some quarter of a mile to the south he saw a group of refugees struggling across a valley.

'Rider coming, sir,' said Sergeant Shialis. 'It's one of the scouts.'

Cadis swung in his saddle. A small man riding a pinto pony rode up the hill, drawing rein before the officer. 'Found 'em,' he said. 'Wish I hadn't.' Cadis fought to control his temper. The man was a private citizen, paid to scout, and therefore not obliged to salute or follow military protocol. Even so the lack of respect in his manner was infuriating.

'Where are the others?' he asked tightly.

'Dead. I would have been too, if I hadn't stopped to piss.'

'Dead?' echoed Cadis. 'All three of them?'

'Rode into a trap. They come from all sides. Tore down the horses, then butchered the men. I was behind, but they almost had me. I grabbed the pommel of me saddle and let the pinto drag me clear of them.'

'How could beasts have sprung a trap?' snapped Cadis. 'It is preposterous.'

'I agree with you, general. I wouldn't have believed it myself unless I'd seen it.'

'I am not a general, as you well know, and I will not tolerate insubordinate behaviour.'

'Tolerate what you like,' replied the man. 'I'm quitting anyway. There's no amount of money that would take me back to those creatures.'

'How do you know it was a trap?' asked Sergeant Shialis.

'Trust me, Shialis. Four of them were crouched down in the long grass. Didn't emerge until the others had ridden by. It's the grey one. I tell you, he's smart, that one. When the others attacked he just stood back and watched. Gives me the shivers just to remember it.'

'How many were there?' asked the sergeant.

'If you don't mind I will conduct this interrogation,' said Cadis, glaring at the soldier. A silence grew. He stared hard at the scout. 'Well?'

'Well what?'

'How many were there?'

'Fifteen – counting the grey one.'

'And where was this?'

'Twenty miles northeast, just where the land rises towards the mountains.'

'There were more than twenty reported missing,' said Cadis.

'Aye. We found three of them dead back in the woods to the south. Looked like they'd been struck by an axe – or a damn big sword. Don't think there's no live ones around here now.'

'Twenty miles northeast, you say. That is out of our jurisdiction,' said Cadis. 'I'll report this back to the colonel. You will make yourself available for his interrogation.'

At that moment the first of the refugees began to emerge onto the hill crest. Cadis stared at them. Many of the women and children were glancing nervously at him and his men. A child began to cry. The sound was shrill and spooked Cadis's mount. 'Shut that brat up!' he snarled, jerking on the reins. The horse reared. Cadis fell back, his feet slipping from the stirrups. He landed on the ground with a bone-jarring thud. Furious, he lurched to his feet, the sound of hastily curbed laughter from his soldiers adding fuel to the flames of his rage. 'You stupid cow!' he yelled at the frightened woman, who was trying to comfort the child.

A tall man stepped between them. 'Control yourself,' he said softly. 'These people are frightened enough.'

Cadis blinked. The man was wearing a fringed buckskin jacket, obviously well made and expensive, and good quality leggings and boots. The officer looked into the man's eyes. They were startlingly blue and piercing. Cadis stepped back a pace. The silence grew. Cadis became aware that his men were waiting for him to say something. He felt foolish now – and this brought back his anger.

'Who do you think you are?' he stormed. 'You don't tell me to control myself. I am an officer in the victorious army of Dospilis.'

'You are a man who fell off your horse,' said the newcomer, his voice even. 'These people have been attacked by beasts, and also by men who behaved like beasts. They are weary, frightened and hungry. They seek only the shelter of the city.' Without another word the man walked past Cadis and approached Sergeant Shialis. 'I remember you,' he said. 'You led a counter attack on a bridge in Pashturan five . . . six years ago. Took an arrow in the thigh.'

'Indeed I did,' said Shialis. 'Though I don't remember you being there.'

'It was a brave move. Had you not held that bridge your flanks would have been turned and what was merely a defeat would have become a rout. What is it that you do here?'

'We're hunting beasts.'

'We fought them last night. They moved off towards the north.'

Behind the two men Cadis Patralis had almost reached breaking point. He had fallen from his horse, been laughed at, and now he was being ignored. Gripping the hilt of his cavalry sabre he made to move forward. A huge hand descended on his shoulder, stopping him in his tracks.

'Been a soldier long, laddie?' Cadis turned and looked into eyes the colour of a winter sky. The face that framed them was old, deep lines carved on the features. The man had a black and silver beard, and wore a black helm, emblazoned with an axe, flanked by grinning silver skulls. 'I've been a soldier most of my life,' continued the man. 'I've carried this axe across . . . well, I don't rightly know how many lands.' The warrior raised the weapon and Cadis

185

found himself looking at his own reflection in the shining blades. 'Never learned as much as I should. One truth, though, that I have found, is that it's always best to leave anger at home. Angry men are stupid men, you see, laddie. And in wars it's usually the stupid who die first. Not always, mind. Sometimes the stupid ensure that others die first. But the principle remains. So, how long have you been a soldier?'

Cadis felt a trembling begin in his stomach. There was something about the man that was leaching away his courage. He made one last attempt to regain control of the situation. 'Unhand me,' he said. 'Do it now.'

'Ah, laddie, if I do that,' said the man amicably, his voice low, 'then within a few heartbeats you'll be dead. And we don't want that, do we? You'll insult that fine young fellow talking to your sergeant, and he'll kill you. Then matters will turn ugly and I'll be obliged to use old Snaga on your troops. They seem like good boys, and it would be a shame to see so much unnecessary bloodshed.'

'There are forty of us,' said Cadis. 'It would be insane.'

'There won't be forty at the close, laddie. However, I am now done talking. What happens now is up to you.' The huge hand lifted from Cadis's shoulder and the massive figure stepped away.

The young man stood for a moment, then took a deep breath. A cool breeze touched his skin and he shivered. He looked across at the woman and the child, saw the fear in her eyes, and felt the first heavy touch of shame. He walked over to them, offering a bow. 'My apologies, lady,' he said. 'My behaviour was boorish. I am sorry if I frightened your child.' Then he walked to his horse and stepped up into the saddle. Angling his mount he approached his sergeant. 'Time to leave,' he said.

'Yes, sir.'

Cadis led the troop back down the hill and off towards the northwest and the waiting city.

'What did he say, sir?' asked Shialis, riding alongside.

'Who?'

'Druss the Legend.'

Cadis felt suddenly light-headed. '*That* was Druss? *The* Druss? Are you sure?'

'I knew him, sir. Years ago. No mistaking him. What did he say? If you don't mind me asking?'

'I don't mind, sergeant. He gave me some advice about soldiering. Said to leave anger at home.'

'Good advice. You mind if I say something else, sir?'

'Why not?'

'That was a noble gesture, when you apologized to the mother. A lesser man wouldn't have done that.' Shialis suddenly smiled. 'Advice from Druss the Legend, eh? Something to tell the kids one day.'

There would be no children to tell.

Four months later Cadis Patralis would die fighting, back to back with Shialis, against the invading army of the Witch Queen.

Rabalyn missed the company of the twins. They had said goodbye at the city gates, and had left with Garianne, heading for the southern quarter. He had enjoyed talking to them. Jared treated him like an adult, never speaking down to him. And Nian, though simple, was always warm and friendly.

His feeling of loss soon evaporated, replaced by a sense of wonder. Having never before seen a city Rabalyn could scarce believe his eyes. The buildings were monstrously large, towering and immense. There were temples, topped by massive statues, and houses boasting scores of windows and balconies. Rabalyn had always believed that the three-storey home of Councillor Raseev had been the height of magnificence. Here it would look like a tiny hovel. Rabalyn stared at one palace as they passed, and counted the windows. Sixty-six. It was hard to believe that any family could have grown so large as to *need* a home like this.

Beyond these magnificent buildings they came to narrower streets, the houses close packed and tall, the roads of cobbled stone. Rabalyn stayed close to Skilgannon, Druss and Braygan, and wondered how so many people could live in such a place without becoming lost. Roads met and intersected, flowing around the buildings like rivers. There were people everywhere, and many soldiers with bandaged wounds. Most of the shops were empty of produce, and people gathered in crowds to barter or beg for what food there was to be had.

The axeman led them out along a broad avenue, and down through a long stretch of parkland. It must have been beautiful before the war, thought Rabalyn, for there were statues and pathways, and even a fountain at the centre of a lake. Now, however, tents had been pitched on the grassy areas and hundreds of downcast and weary people were milling around them.

'They are so sad,' said Rabalyn. Skilgannon glanced at him.

'They'd have been sadder still if they'd had better leaders,' he said.

'How can that be true?' asked the youth.

'Think on it a while,' replied the former priest.

They walked on for more than a mile, coming at last to a gated area, before which stood two tall guards, dressed in red cloaks and silver helms. One of them saw Druss and smiled. He was tall and slim, and sporting a black trident chin beard. 'Surprised to see no-one's killed you yet, axeman,' he said.

'Heaven knows they've tried,' answered Druss, with a grin. 'They just don't breed them tough any more. Milkmaids in armour now. Just like you, Diagoras.'

'Aye, you ancients always say things were better in the old days,' replied the man. 'I don't think it's true, though. I reckon young warriors look at you and are reminded of their grandfathers. Then they can't possibly fight you.'

'Maybe so,' agreed the axeman. 'At my age I'll take any advantage I can get. Any word on Orastes?'

The guard's expression changed, the smile fading. 'Not exactly. His servant has been found. He's alive, but barely. He was in the arena dungeons. The Datians discovered him there when they opened the prisons.'

'In the dungeons? That makes no sense. Where is he now?'

'Being cared for at the White Palace,' Diagoras told him. 'I'll arrange a pass for you tomorrow. Where are you heading?'

'The Crimson Stag on the west quay. Do they still have food?'

'Aye, but not the menu they had. Things will ease now the Datians have lifted the blockade. Six ships have already unloaded. Old Shivas will have been prowling the dock to restock his larders. I'll come by after my Watch and help you down a flagon or ten.'

'Ah, laddie,' chuckled Druss, 'in your dreams. One sniff of a

188

wine cork and youngsters like you slide under the table. However, you buy the wine, and I'll teach you how it should be drunk.'

'Let's say that the last person standing can forget the bill,' offered Diagoras.

'That's what I did say.'

Rabalyn watched the exchange. As the two men spoke he saw the Drenai soldier's eyes constantly flick towards Skilgannon, who was standing some distance away, chatting to Braygan.

'Will your companions be travelling with you to the Crimson Stag?' asked Diagoras.

'Not all of us. The little priest is heading for the Street of Vines, and his church elders. Is there a problem?'

'The warrior with him. I have seen him before, Druss. I was stationed in Perapolis for two years. We left just before the end. The Naashanites granted the embassy and its staff safe passage through their lines. I saw the Damned as we rode through. Not a man I'd soon forget.' Druss glanced back at Skilgannon.

'Maybe you are wrong.'

'I don't believe so. I'll let him through if you vouch for him.'

'Aye, I'll do that. Best you report his presence to your superiors, though.'

Diagoras nodded, and pushed open the gates. 'I'll see you after dark.'

'Bring enough coin to pay the bill.'

'I'll bring a pillow too, so that your old head can rest on it as you sleep under the table.'

Druss clapped the man on the shoulder and strolled through the gates. Skilgannon and Braygan followed him, Rabalyn bringing up the rear.

The light was fading as they reached a second set of gates, blocking the way across an arched bridge over a river. Here there were more guards, powerful men with blond beards and pale blue eyes. They were wearing long mail-ring tunics and horned helms.

Druss spoke to them, and once more the gates were opened. 'The Street of Vines is across the bridge and the first turning on the left,' Druss told Braygan. 'Your church building is a short way along.' The little priest thanked him, then swung to Skilgannon, offering his hand. The warrior shook it.

'Thank you for all you have done for me, Brother,' said Braygan. 'May the Source be with you on your travels.'

Skilgannon smiled wryly, but did not answer. 'Will you take your vows?' he asked after a moment.

'I think that I will. Then I will return to Skepthia, and try to be of service.' Braygan offered his hand to Rabalyn. 'You are welcome to come with me,' he said. 'The elders may know the whereabouts of your parents. If not they can give you shelter while you try to find them.'

Rabalyn shook his head. 'I don't want to find them.'

'If you change your mind I shall be here for some days.' With that the little priest walked through the gates. He paused once on the bridge to look back and wave. And then he was gone.

CHAPTER TEN

THE CRIMSON STAG TAVERN WAS AN OLD BUILDING, L-SHAPED AND double-storeyed, constructed close to the west quay, overlooking the harbour and the sea beyond. It had long been the haunt of Drenai officials and soldiers stationed in the embassy quarter of the city. Such was its reputation for food, wine and ale that even Vagrian officers used it. Normally the antipathy between soldiers of Vagria and Drenan would have precluded any such common ground. Though none now living could recall the Vagrian–Drenai wars the ancient enmity between the peoples continued. Occasionally there were even border skirmishes.

There were, however, no fights at the Crimson Stag. Not one man from either camp would risk being barred by Shivas, the sour-faced owner. His cooking was as sublime as his temper was dark. Added to which his memory was known to be long indeed, and a man refused custom once would never be forgiven.

Druss and Skilgannon sat at a table overlooking the moonlit harbour. Despite the coming of night, ships were still being unloaded at the quayside, and wagons were drawn up to ferry food back out into the hungry city.

Skilgannon sat quietly watching the dockers. His heart was heavy. He had not expected to miss the little priest. Yet he did.

191

Braygan was the last link to a gentle life Skilgannon had tried so hard to embrace.

'*We are what we are, my son. And wolves is what we are.*'

The tavern was filling up. By the far wall a group of Vagrian soldiers were drinking and laughing. Skilgannon glanced across at them. Many still wore their tunic-length mailshirts, and one still had on his horned helm of reinforced brass. Elsewhere soldiers and officials of other races were sitting quietly, some already eating, others enjoying a goblet of wine or a tankard of ale. 'How many nations are stationed in the embassy quarter?' he asked the axeman. Druss shrugged.

'Never counted them.' He glanced around the tavern. 'Mostly I only know those from Lentria and Drenan. There must be more than twenty embassies. Even one from Chiatze.'

Druss lifted his wine goblet and drained it. Skilgannon looked at him. Without his helm and steel-reinforced jerkin the axeman looked what he was – a powerful fifty-year-old man. He could have been a farmer, or a stonemason. Save for the eyes. There was something deadly in that iron gaze. This was a man – as the Naashanites would say – who had looked into the eyes of the Dragon. 'Are you the Damned, laddie?' asked Druss suddenly.

Skilgannon took a deep breath, and met Druss's gaze. 'I am,' he replied.

'Do they lie when they talk of Perapolis?'

'No. There is not a lie which could make it any worse.'

Druss signalled a serving maid. The menu was not extensive and the axeman ordered eggs and salt beef. He glanced at Skilgannon. 'What are you eating?'

'The same will be fine.'

When the serving maid had departed Druss refilled his goblet from a flagon and sat quietly, staring out of the window. 'What are you thinking?' asked Skilgannon.

'I was thinking of old friends,' said Druss. 'One in particular. Bodasen. Great swordsman. We fought side by side all across this land. No give in the man. A fine soldier and a true friend. I think of him often.'

'What happened to him?'

'I killed him at Skeln. Can't change it. Can't help regretting it.

The boy tells me you were a priest for a while. Brother Lantern, I think he said.'

'A man should always try new things,' said Skilgannon.

'Don't make light of it, laddie. Were you touched by faith, or haunted by guilt?'

'Probably more guilt than faith,' admitted Skilgannon. 'Are you intending some subtle lecture at this point?'

Druss laughed, the sound unforced and full of genuine humour. 'In all my long life no-one has ever accused me of that, boy. A man who uses an axe doesn't generally build a reputation for subtlety. You want me to lecture you?'

'No. There is nothing anyone could say to me that I haven't already told myself.'

'Are you still with the Naashanite army?'

Skilgannon shook his head. 'The Queen wishes me dead. I am outlawed in Naashan. I'm told there is a large price on my head.'

'Then you are not here as a spy?'

'No.'

'Good enough.' Druss topped up his goblet. Skilgannon smiled.

'Rabalyn tells me you are to be involved in a drinking contest later. Shouldn't you hold off on that wine?'

'A few sips to prepare the belly. This is Lentrian red. I've not tasted a drop for two months. Are you not a drinker?'

Skilgannon shook his head. 'It tends to make me argumentative.'

Druss nodded. 'And a man with your skills can't afford meaningless arguments. I understand that. I have heard tales of you and the Witch Queen. It is said you were her champion.'

'I was. We were friends once – in the days when she was hunted.'

'It is said you loved her.'

Skilgannon shook his head. 'That doesn't come close. Thoughts of her fill my waking hours, and haunt my dreams. She is an extraordinary woman, Druss; courageous, clever, witty.' He fell silent for a moment. 'Compliments like this fall so far short of the actuality that they seem like insults. I say she was courageous, but it does not paint the reality. I never met anyone more brave. At the battle of Carsis, with the left in rout and the centre crumbling, her generals advised her to flee the field. Instead she donned her armour and rode to the centre where

193

all could see her. She won the day, Druss. Against all the odds.'

'Sounds like you should have married her. Or did she not feel the same way towards you?'

Skilgannon shrugged. 'She said she did. Who can know? But it was politics, Druss. Back in those dangerous days she needed allies. The only treasure she possessed then was her blood line. Had we been wed she could never have gathered enough troops to win back her father's throne. The princes and earls who fought under her banner all hoped to win her heart. She played them all.'

The meal arrived and the two men ate in silence. Finally Druss pushed away his plate.

'You did not mention your own actions at Carsis. The story I heard was that you rallied the broken left flank and led a counter charge. It was *that* which turned the battle.'

'Yes, I've heard that story,' said Skilgannon. 'It came about because *men* write the histories. They find it hard to praise a woman in a man's world. I am a soldier, Druss. It is in my blood. Had Jianna not ridden to the front and given the men fresh courage, no action of mine would have made a jot of difference. Bokram's forces had broken the left. Men were fleeing through the forest. When the Queen arrived Bokram saw her, and pulled back half the cavalry giving chase on the left flank. He turned them back towards the centre. It wasn't a foolish move. Had he succeeded in killing Jianna he could have hunted down the deserting warriors at his leisure. As it was I had a little time to regroup some of the fleeing men. And, yes, it was the counter attack that sundered Bokram's army. Had the Usurper had more courage he would still have won the day. Such is the way of history, though. Ultimately the coward rarely succeeds.'

'The same is true in life,' said Druss. 'So why does she now want you dead?'

Skilgannon spread his hands. 'She is a hard woman, Druss.' He suddenly smiled and shook his head. 'She doesn't take well to disappointment. I left her service without her permission. She sent her lover to find me, to seek the return of a gift she made me. He came with a group of killers. I don't know whether she ordered him to kill me. Perhaps not. In the end, though, it was her lover who lay dead. After that there was a price on my head.'

194

'Well, laddie, you've been a soldier and a priest. What now?'

'Have you ever heard of the Temple of the Resurrectionists?'

'Can't say as I have.'

'I mean to find it. It is said they can work miracles. I need such a miracle.'

'Where is it?'

'I do not know, Druss. It could be in Namib, or the Nadir lands, or Sherak. It could be nowhere. Just a legend from the past. I shall find out.'

The far door opened. Skilgannon glanced round. 'Ah, your drinking opponent has arrived,' he said, as the tall young soldier with the trident beard strolled over to the table. 'I'll leave you to talk. I shall take a stroll and breathe in the sea air.'

Diagoras moved into the seat vacated by the Naashanite killer and glanced at the half-empty flagon of Lentrian red. 'I do believe you started without me, old fellow,' he said, lifting it and filling a goblet.

'You need all the help you can get, boy.'

Diagoras watched as the Naashanite left the tavern. 'You are mixing with dark company, Druss. He is a butchering madman.'

'I have been called that myself,' Druss pointed out. 'Anyway, I like him. He came to my aid a few days ago. An evil man would not have risked himself. And he helped a group of refugees against the arena beasts. There's more to Skilgannon than tales of butchery. Did you report his presence?'

'Yes. Gan Sentrin is unconcerned. It seems the Damned is no longer an officer of Naashan. The Witch Queen has put a price on his head. He is an outlaw.'

'Aye, he told me.' Druss settled back in his chair, then rubbed at his eyes. Diagoras thought he looked tired. There was more silver in his beard than there had been at Skeln. Time, as the poet once said, was a never ending river of cruelty. Diagoras sipped his wine. He wanted to say more about the vile Skilgannon. He wanted to ask how a hero like Druss could find anything to like about him, but he knew Druss well enough to recognize when the older man was finished with a conversation. His grey eyes would become bleak, and his face harden. Diagoras understood this aspect of him well. In a world of shifting shades of grey Druss the Legend struggled to see everything in black or white. A man was good or evil in Druss's eyes. It was, however, hard to comprehend how he could hold to that view in this case. Druss was no fool. Diagoras sat quietly. The wine was good, and he always enjoyed the company of the older axeman. He might be naïve in his view of life, thought Diagoras, but there was always a sense of certainty around him. It was reassuring. After a while he spoke again.

'Did you hear that Manahin is now serving in Abalayn's government?' he asked. 'One of the heroes of Skeln. He always has his campaign medal on his cloak.'

'He earned it,' replied Druss. 'Where is yours?'

'Lost it in a dice game a couple of years ago. To be honest, Druss, I lost too many friends there to want to be reminded of it. And I'm sick of people telling me they wish they could have been there with me. Damn, but I'd give a sack of gold *not* to have been there.'

'You'll get no argument from me, laddie. I lost friends on both sides. It would be good to think it was all worthwhile.'

The comment shocked Diagoras. 'Worthwhile? It kept us free.'

'Aye, it did. But because of it these eastern lands were plunged into war. It never ends, does it?' Druss drank deeply, then refilled his goblet. 'Ah, don't mind me, Diagoras. Sometimes the wine brings a darkness to my mind. What news of Orastes's servant?'

'The surgeon gave him something to help him sleep. He was hard used, Druss, and greatly terrified. As far as we can ascertain he was in that dungeon around two months. It is likely Orastes was with him.'

'Imprisoned? It makes no sense. Why?'

'I can't answer that. The situation here has been chaotic. No-one knew what was going on. For the last few weeks we've kept all the embassy quarter gates locked. There have been riots, and murders, and hangings. The King went insane, Druss. Utterly. Word is that he ran around his own palace attacking his guards with a ceremonial sword, shouting that he was the God of War. He was cut down by his own general, Ironmask. That's when the Tantrians surrendered and opened the gates to the Datians. Just as well, in the end. You know what would have happened had the city fallen by storm?'

'Rape, plunder and butchery,' said Druss. 'I know. Skilgannon said it earlier. If the Tantrians had been better led they'd have suffered more. So, why would Orastes have been imprisoned?'

'We can make little sense of it, Druss. All I have been able to learn is that his reasons for coming to Mellicane were personal and not official. Every day he went out into the city, sometimes with his servant, sometimes without. You'll need to speak to the man, but be aware, my friend, that Orastes is probably dead.'

'If he is,' said Druss coldly, 'I'll find the men who did it, and the men who ordered it.'

'Well, if you're still here in four days I'll join you,' said Diagoras. 'My commission runs out then and I'm leaving the army. I'll help you find out what happened, then I'll head back to Drenan. Time I got married and sired a few sons to look after me when I'm in my dotage.'

'I'll be glad to have you, laddie. Put enemies in front of me and I know just how to deal with them. But this search has me foxed.'

'There was a rumour Orastes was seen heading southeast about a month ago. It must have been put out by those who had him imprisoned. Is that where you've been?'

'Aye. He was said to be riding his white gelding, and accompanied by a group of soldiers. It turned out to be a merchant who bore a passing resemblance to Orastes, tall, plump and fair-haired. The soldiers were his bodyguards. I caught up with them in a market village sixty miles from here. The gelding had belonged to Orastes. The merchant had a bill of sale, signed by the earl. I know his handwriting. It was genuine.'

'Well, tomorrow – hopefully – we'll be able to speak with the servant. Now, are you ready for that drinking contest?'

'No, laddie,' said Druss, 'tonight the meal and the drinks are on me. We'll sit and do what old soldiers are renowned for. We'll talk about past days and old glories. We'll discuss the problems of the world, and – as the wine flows – we'll come up with a hundred grand ideas to put everything to rights.' He chuckled. 'And when we wake tomorrow with aching heads we'll have forgotten all of them.'

'Sounds good to me,' said Diagoras, raising his hand and summoning the tavern girl. 'Two flagons of Lentrian red, my dear, and some larger goblets, if you please.'

Skilgannon wandered along the dock, skirting the quays where weary men were still unloading cargo. The sounds of the sea lapping against the harbour walls was soothing, as was the smell of seaweed and salt air.

Mellicane had been lucky this time. They had surrendered early. There had been little time for simmering angers to build into blind hatreds among the besieging troops. The longer a siege went on, the more the darkness swelled in the hearts of the besiegers. Men would lose friends, or brothers, to sniper fire or accident. They would stare at the ramparts, anger building, and dream of revenge. Once the walls were breached the invaders would swarm through the city like avenging demons, hacking and killing until the insanity of rage was purged from their hearts.

He shivered, recalling the horrors of Perapolis. The people of Mellicane probably felt themselves safe now, with this small war at an end. Skilgannon wondered how they would feel when the armies of Naashan descended upon them.

I will be long gone by then, he decided.

Walking out to a deserted jetty he stood and watched the reflected moon, lying broken upon the waves. Jianna would probably already have men searching for him. One day they would find him. They would step from a darkened alleyway, or emerge from the shadows of the trees. Or they would come upon him as he was sitting quietly in a tavern, his mind on other matters. It was unlikely they would announce their presence, or seek to fight him, man to man. Even without the Swords of Night and Day Skilgannon was deadly. With them he was almost invincible.

He heard stealthy footfalls on the planks behind him and turned. Two men were moving towards him. They were dressed in ragged clothes, which were wet through. Both carried knives in their hands. He guessed they had entered the water below the embassy quarter gates and had swum through to the docks. Both were thin, haggard and middle-aged.

Skilgannon watched them as they approached. 'Give us your coin,' demanded the first, 'and you'll not get hurt.'

'I will not be hurt anyway,' said Skilgannon. 'Now best you be on your way, for I have no wish to kill you.' The man's shoulders sagged, but his comrade pushed past him and rushed at Skilgannon. The warrior blocked the knife thrust with his forearm, hooked his foot behind the man's leg and sent him crashing to the deck. As his assailant struggled to rise Skilgannon trod on his knife hand. The attacker cried out in pain, the knife slipping from his fingers. Skilgannon scooped it up. 'Stay where you are,' he told the fallen man, then turned to his comrade. 'This is not an enterprise to which you are suited,' he said. 'What do you think you are doing here?'

'There's no food,' said the man. 'My children are crying with hunger. All of this,' he added, waving his arm at the food ships being unloaded in the distance, 'is going to the homes of the rich. I'll not watch my children starve. I'd sooner die myself.'

'And *that* is what you will do,' said Skilgannon. 'You will die.' With a sigh he tossed the knife to the deck, then dipped his hand into his money pouch, producing a heavy golden coin. 'Take this to the tavern and purchase some food. Then go home and forget this foolishness.'

The second man lurched to his feet, knife in hand. 'No need to take crumbs from this bastard's table, Garak,' he said. 'Look at his money pouch. It's bulging. We can have it all. Let's take him!'

'You have a decision to make, Garak,' said Skilgannon. 'Here is a coin honestly offered. With it you can feed your family for a month. The alternative is never to see them again in this world. I am not a forgiving man, and I offer no second chances.'

The knifemen exchanged glances. In that moment Skilgannon knew they would attack, and he would kill them. Two more lives would be wasted. Garak's children would lose their father, and Skilgannon would have two more souls upon his conscience. Then, as always, his mind cleared. He could feel the weight of the scabbard on his back, the need to draw the Swords of Night and Day, to feel his fingers curl round the ornate ivory handles, to see the blades slice through flesh, and blood gushing from severed arteries. Skilgannon made no effort now to quell the growing hunger.

'Brother Lantern!' came the voice of Rabalyn. Skilgannon did not turn, but kept his eyes on the two men. He heard the youth walking along the jetty, and saw Garak's gaze flick towards him.

As the deadly moment passed Skilgannon's anger rose. He fought for control.

'I'll take the coin, master,' said Garak, sheathing his knife. The haggard man sighed. 'These are terrible times. I am a furniture maker. Just a furniture maker.'

Skilgannon stood stock still, then drew in a deep breath. It took every effort of his will not to cut the man down. Silently he handed him the coin. Garak gestured to his comrade, who stood for a moment, staring malevolently at Skilgannon. Then both men walked along the jetty, past Rabalyn.

Skilgannon moved to the jetty rail and gripped it with trembling hands.

'Druss told me you had gone for a walk. I am sorry if I disturbed you,' said Rabalyn.

'The disturbance was a blessing.' The blood lust began to fade. Skilgannon glanced at the lad. 'So, what are your plans, Rabalyn?'

The youth shrugged. 'I don't know. I wish I could go home. Perhaps I shall stay in the city and seek work.'

Skilgannon saw the boy staring at him, and knew that he was waiting for an invitation. 'You cannot come with me, Rabalyn. Not because I do not like your company. You are fine and brave. I like you greatly. But there are people hunting me. One day they will find me. I have enough death on my conscience without adding you to the list. Why don't you take Braygan's advice, and join him at the temple?'

The youth's disappointment showed. 'Maybe I will. May I keep the shirt? I have no other clothes.'

'Of course you may.' Skilgannon fished another coin from his pouch. 'Take this. Ask the priests to exchange it for silver and copper coins. Then you can purchase another tunic and some leggings that fit more closely. What is left will allow you to pay the priests for your lodgings.'

Rabalyn took the coin and stared at it. 'This is gold,' he said.

'Aye, it is.'

'I have never held gold. One day I will pay you back. I promise.' He stared hard at Skilgannon. 'Are you all right? Your hands are trembling.'

'I am just tired, Rabalyn.'

'I thought you were going to fight those men.'

'It would not have been a fight. Your arrival saved their lives.'

'Who were they?'

'Just men, seeking to find food for their families.' A cool breeze whispered across the water.

'Do you have a family?' asked Rabalyn.

'I did once. Not now.'

'Doesn't it make you lonely? I have felt lonely ever since Aunt Athyla died.'

Skilgannon took a deep, calming breath. He felt his body relax, and the trembling in his hands ceased. 'Yes, I suppose it does.'

Rabalyn moved alongside Skilgannon and rested his arms on the jetty rail. The moon shone broken on the lapping sea. 'I never thought about it before. I used to get really annoyed with Aunt Athyla. She'd fuss over me constantly. Once she had . . . gone I realized there wasn't anyone who'd fuss over me again. Not in the same way, if you know what I mean?'

'I know. After my father died I was raised by two kindly people, Sperian and Molaire. Molaire would worry constantly about whether I had eaten enough, or was getting enough sleep, or wearing warm enough clothes in the winter to fend off the chill.'

'Yes, exactly,' said Rabalyn, smiling at the memories. 'Aunt Athyla was like that.' His smile faded. 'She deserved better than to die in that fire. I wish I could have done something more for her while she was alive. Bought her a nice gift, or a . . . I don't know. A house with a real garden. Even a silk scarf. She always said she liked silk.'

'She sounds a good woman,' said Skilgannon softly, seeing the youth's distress. 'I expect you gave her more than you think.'

'I gave her nothing,' said Rabalyn, an edge of bitterness in his voice. 'If only I had killed Todhe earlier she would still be alive.'

'That may be so, Rabalyn, but there is no more futile phrase than *if only*. If only we could go back and live our lives again. If only we hadn't said the unkind words. If only we had turned left instead of right. *If only* is useless. We make our mistakes and we move on. In my life I have made decisions that cost the lives of thousands. Worse than that, through my actions those who loved me died horribly. If I allowed myself to walk the path of *if only* I would go mad. You are a fine, strong young man. Your aunt raised you well. She gave you love, and you will repay that love by loving others. A wife, sons, daughters, friends. That is the greatest gift you can give her.'

They stood in silence for a while, listening to the water lapping against the jetty.

'Why are people hunting you?' asked Rabalyn, after a while.

'They have been sent by someone who wants me dead.'

'He must hate you very much.'

'No, she loves me. Now I need to be alone, my friend. I have much to think on. You go back to the tavern. I will join you there later.'

It still seemed strange to Skilgannon that of all the moments he had shared with Jianna, through all of the violence, fear and excitement, he should recall so vividly their walk home together from the bathhouse.

Having fooled the men sent to spy on him they strolled together, her arm hooked in his. He had glanced at her, his eyes drawn to the flimsy yellow tunic dress she wore. Her breasts were small and firm, her nipples pushing at the fabric. She was wearing a cheap scent that dazzled his senses. He found himself wishing with all his heart that she could have been what she pretended to be. Skilgannon had discovered the joys of sex at the bathhouse the previous summer, but never had he wanted anyone the way he desired the girl holding his arm.

'What is your plan now?' she asked, as they walked together. He could not think clearly, aware of an uncomfortable tightness in his belly. 'Well?' she persisted.

'We will go to my home. We will talk there,' he said, trying to buy time.

'What will you tell your servants?'

This was a good question. Sperian was close-mouthed and spoke to few people. He was a solitary man, who could be trusted. Molaire, on the other hand, was a chatterbox. 'Where was Greavas intending to take you?' he asked. 'Once he got you from the city.'

'East, into the mountains. There are tribes there who are still loyal. Will you stop looking at my breasts? It is making me uncomfortable.'

He jerked his gaze from her. 'My apologies, princess.'

'Probably best if you don't call me that,' she pointed out.

He paused, and turned towards her. 'I am not usually this much of a dullard,' he told her. 'Forgive me. You are the most beautiful girl I have ever seen. It is muddling my senses.'

'My name will be Sashan,' she said, ignoring his comment. 'Try it. Say it.'

'Sashan.'

'Good. Now about your servants?'

'I shall tell them both I met you at the bathhouse, and that your name is Sashan, and you will be staying with me for a while. I will get Sperian to give you an allowance. Thirty silver pieces a week. That should help allay suspicion. You should take the money, and go to the market. Buy yourself . . . whatever you like.'

'I see that you know the going price for whores, young Olek.'

'Indeed I do, Sashan. And so should you.'

She laughed, the sound rich and throaty. 'Were I a whore, you could not afford me.'

'If you were a whore I'd sell everything I had for a night with you.'

She took his arm again. 'And you would not regret it. Not a copper coin of it. However, I am not a whore. What sleeping arrangements do you have in mind?'

'Oh, we have many spare rooms.'

'And how will that look to your servants? You bring a whore home and then do not sleep with her? No, Olek, we must share a room. But that is all we will share.'

Back at the house he introduced Sashan to Sperian and Molaire. The gardener said nothing, but Molaire was outraged. She swung to Sperian. 'Are you going to allow this?'

'The boy is three weeks from his majority. It is his choice.'

'I think it disgraceful,' said Molaire, ignoring Jianna, and storming from the entrance hall. As the princess wandered through to the living room Sperian looked hard at Skilgannon.

'Is that who I think it is?' he whispered.

'Yes. Say nothing to Molaire.'

'She is very convincing in that yellow tunic.'

'Aye, she is.'

Jianna came back into the hallway and smiled at Sperian. 'I fear your wife does not like me.'

'More a problem for me than you, Sashan,' Sperian told her. 'It will be like having a wasp in my ear tonight. I doubt I'll get any rest. Why don't you and Olek go out into the garden. I'll bring a little food and drink.'

After the servant had gone Skilgannon led Jianna through to the garden. The sun was setting beyond the western wall, and it was cool in the shade. She sat down in a deep chair, her long legs stretched out. Skilgannon tore his gaze from her thighs, and stared hard at the blooms in the garden. 'He knows, doesn't he?' said Jianna.

'Yes. But then he already knew that Greavas was hiding you – and *he* sent me to Greavas. I guessed we wouldn't fool Sperian. He will say nothing. Not even to Molaire.'

'He would be wise not to. Trusting that fat sow with a secret would be like trying to carry water in a fish net.'

'She is a good woman,' said Skilgannon sharply. 'You will not speak ill of her.'

A look of surprise touched the girl's face, immediately followed by a flash of anger that made her grey eyes glint with a cold light. 'You forget who you are talking to.'

'I am talking to Sashan the whore, who is living in my house for thirty silvers a week.'

She looked away, and he studied her profile. It seemed to him that her face was beautiful from any angle. Even with the badly dyed yellow hair, and the red ringlets at the temple, she was stunning. 'How long must I stay here?' she asked.

'At this moment soldiers are scouring the city, and all the gates are manned. In three weeks the Festival of Harvest begins. Farmers and merchants will be coming here from all over Naashan. Once the festival is over they will return. There will be huge numbers leaving the city. That will be the time, I think.'

'A month then?'

'At least.'

'It will be a long month.'

Skilgannon had not known just how long a time a month could be. He began to realize it that first night, as he and Jianna retired to his west-facing room above the garden. The bed was wide, and made for two. Even so he lay awake, feeling the warmth emanating from her. The scent from her hair wafted to him every time the night breeze blew. In the night she awoke and moved silently from the bed. He saw her naked body silhouetted against the window. His arousal was swift and painful. She stretched her arms above her head, and ran her fingers through her hair. Skilgannon drank in the lines of her, the sleekness of her waist, and the long perfection of her legs. She padded across the room and poured herself a goblet of water. Skilgannon closed his eyes, and tried to force the image of her from his mind. It was a useless exercise. He felt her slide in alongside him once more.

'Are you awake?' she asked.

He thought of ignoring her and pretending sleep. 'Yes,' he said, 'I am awake. Is the bed uncomfortable? Is it stopping you sleeping?'

'No. I was thinking of my mother. I was wondering if I will ever see her again.'

'Greavas is a clever man. I am sure he will succeed.'

'She carries poison, you know. Hidden in a ring. If they come for her she will swallow it.'

'Do you have poison?'

'No. I shall escape. I will avenge my father, and I will see Bokram dragged down.'

'No easy task, Sashan. He has the support of the Emperor. Even if you raised an army to match Bokram, you would still have to face the Immortals. They have never been beaten.'

'Gorben will fall,' she said. 'His ambition is too great, his pride colossal. My father understood this, but his timing was wrong. Gorben will not stop. He will continue to enlarge his empire. One day he will take a step too far. Against the Gothir perhaps, or the Drenai.'

'What if he doesn't fall?'

She rolled towards him. 'Then I shall find a way to woo him. None of his wives have given him sons. I shall give him sons. Then I will drag Bokram down.'

'You do not lack confidence,' he said. 'I do not believe, though, that Bokram is quaking in his boots at this moment.'

'I hope that he is not,' said Jianna. 'He seeks two women who are, at worst, a nuisance. His only fear is that I will escape and be wedded to a prince with power. Even that will not worry him unduly, for there is no single prince with the fortune or the army to overthrow him.'

'Then how can you succeed?'

'There are at least fifty princes and chieftains who would like to wed me. Combine them and we have an army to sweep across the land.'

'You plan to wed fifty princes? I think playing the whore has gone to your head.'

'Malanek said you were intelligent, and quick-witted. Was he wrong?'

'Strangely my wits are not enhanced by lying so close to a naked woman.'

She laughed. 'The story of men everywhere. And now I shall sleep.' She rolled away from him.

Somewhere in the night he managed to doze a little, but every time she moved he would awake and feel restless. Once she turned and her arm fell across his chest, her head close to his shoulder.

Just after the dawn he awoke, bleary-eyed and weary. Jianna still slept. Dressing in a simple grey tunic and sandals he went downstairs. Molaire was already in the kitchen, cleaning vegetables for a broth. She gave him a look which was meant to be scornful. Crossing to her he kissed her cheek. 'Your father would not approve of this,' she said, blushing.

He gazed at her round, honest face. 'Perhaps he would not,' he admitted.

'And you look dreadful this morning. Totally debauched.'

Skilgannon laughed and left the room, wandering through to the garden. Sperian was already there, kneeling in one of the flower beds, dead-heading blooms and clearing away weeds. For a while Skilgannon helped him, then both men walked back to the house, scrubbed the dirt from their hands and sat down to breakfast. Molaire left them and moved off to the laundry room. Skilgannon told Sperian about the thirty silvers that would need to be paid to Sashan.

'Aye, that's wise. Though I am not sure about her going to the market. I doubt she's done any haggling in her life.'

'I think she'll do well enough. Are there watchers outside the house?'

'Aye. Two men. They were here most of the night. They've been replaced this morning. Have you thought what you'll say if Boranius returns? Has he ever met her?'

The question caused a tightness in Skilgannon's stomach. 'I don't know. I'll ask her.'

Sperian cut some fresh bread and several thick slices of cheese, which he placed on a tray. 'You want to take this up to her?'

Skilgannon returned to the bedroom. Jianna was awake, but still lying in the bed. 'I brought you some breakfast,' he said. She sat up, the sheets falling away and exposing her breasts. Skilgannon swore. 'Could you at least dress?' he snapped.

'My, you are feeling tetchy this morning, Olek. Did you not sleep well?' Reaching out, she took the food, then sat and quietly ate. Pushing the tray aside she rose from the bed. Skilgannon turned his back, and heard her laughter. 'You may look at me now, my prudish friend,' she said. She had slipped on the yellow tunic dress and was sitting in a wicker chair by the window.

'Have you ever met Boranius?' he asked.

She shrugged. 'The name means nothing.'

'Tall and handsome, with golden hair. He was a student of Malanek's.'

'Ah, yes, now I recall him. Eyes the colour of emeralds, and an arrogant mouth. Why do you ask?'

'He may come here. It would be best if he did not see you.'

'Ah, Olek, you worry too much. The only time we met I was dressed in silks and satins. My hair was dark and I wore a tiara with seventy diamonds upon it. My face was painted, and he merely bowed his head to kiss my hand, then turned his attention to my father – whom he was desperate to impress.'

'Even so. Boranius is no fool. He has men still watching the house.'

'Then I should let them see me. I shall go to the market. You will give me coin. I shall buy a necklace, and a new dress.'

'You seem to be enjoying yourself,' he said.

Her smile faded. 'What would you prefer, Olek? That I simpered and trembled in this room, waiting for strong men to save me? I will succeed – or I will be captured and killed. No man on this earth will ever terrify me. I will not allow it. Yes, I shall enjoy going to the market. It is something I have never done. I will walk in the sunshine and I will revel in my freedom. I am Sashan, the whore. And Sashan the whore has nothing to fear from Boranius or anyone else.'

He stood watching her for a moment. Then he nodded and bowed. 'You are an exceptional woman,' he said.

'Yes, I am. Tell me about the market.'

They sat and talked for some time about the art of haggling, and how no-one ever paid the first price mentioned. He also warned her against the places women were not allowed to enter: gambling halls, private taverns, and public temples.

'A woman cannot enter a temple?' she queried.

'Not by the main door. At the side there are entrances leading to galleries. Women cannot approach the altar, or sit in the altar hall.'

'Ridiculous!' she stormed.

'Nor once inside the building are they allowed to speak,' he told her, with a smile.

Her grey eyes narrowed. 'I shall change *that* once I have my throne.'

Skilgannon recalled with great fondness watching her walk away from the house. The sun was shining on her bleached hair, and turning the cheap yellow tunic to glowing gold. She had subtly exaggerated the sway of her hips, and had smiled broadly at the men passing by. It was a fine performance, born of arrogance and courage.

Alone on the jetty Skilgannon glanced up at the moon. 'There never was a woman like you, Jianna,' he whispered.

The day had been long and tense for Jianna, Queen of Naashan. It had begun just after dawn, reading lengthy reports from the various southeastern war fronts in Matapesh, Panthia and Opal. Casualties had been heavy, especially in the jungles of Opal, but her forces had captured the three main diamond mines. Shipments of these precious stones would enable Jianna to purchase more iron from Ventria, and weapons from established Gothir armourers. She had breakfasted with four princes from northern Naashan, who had promised men for the coming battles in Tantria. After that she had met councillors and advisers, checking reports on tax incomes and the condition of the treasury.

It was now after dusk, and she was not yet tired as she strode with her bodyguard through the royal gardens, lit now by lanterns on tall iron poles. Behind her walked the Captain of Horse, Askelus, a tall, forbidding man, and alongside him the wiry figure of Malanek the former swordmaster. Both men had their hands on their sword hilts as they came into the open. Jianna laughed. 'They say lightning does not strike twice in the same place,' she said.

'You take too many risks, Highness,' offered Malanek. Moonlight cast shadows on his face, making the lines of age seem even deeper. No longer a fighting swordsman he had grown his hair, though he still sported the elaborate raised crest and pony tail that had marked him as the King's champion. His hair was dyed black – a small conceit, which the Queen did not mind. She was fond of the old warrior.

'I cannot avoid all risks, Malanek,' she said. 'And look, am I not wearing the mail rings you had made for me?'

'Aye, and they look very fine on you, Highness,' he said. 'Which is, I think, why you wear them.'

Jianna did not reply, but walked on. He was right, of course. The thigh-length silver mail tunic, with its backing of soft lambskin, and its wide embossed belt, emphasized the slimness of her waist. It shimmered as she moved. Jianna strode on, sensing the tension in the two men as they approached the Lake of Dreams, a large marble pool on which sat a statue of a fabulously attractive woman. Her arm was raised towards the sky, and entwined around it was a snake. The statue was of Jianna. Often the Queen would wander her gardens, always stopping to gaze upon her own image.

Ten days ago two assassins had leapt from the undergrowth close by. Both were dressed as palace servants. Only Malanek had been with her on that night. Despite his age he had acted with great speed, drawing his sabre and darting in to block their assault. He had killed the first, but the second barged past him and ran at

Jianna, knife raised. Leaping high she had hammered her booted foot into his face, hurling him back. Malanek had stabbed him through the lower back. The man screamed and fell. Unhappily the wound was deep and mortal, and he had died under questioning without revealing who had sent him.

It was the fourth assassination attempt in two years.

Jianna gazed at the statue. 'She will be beautiful when I am ancient and a crone,' she said wistfully.

'Aye,' agreed Malanek, 'but she will never ride a horse, nor see a sunset. Nor will she ever know the adoration of a people.'

'Adoration comes and goes,' said Jianna. 'The people threw flowers at the Ventrians and garlanded Bokram's horse. They are fickle.'

They came at last to the new gates and the high walls of Jianna's private quarters. The two guards, both handpicked by Askelus, saluted and bowed. 'Who is within?' Askelus asked one of them.

'Four of the Queen's councillors, five royal handmaidens, the blind harpist, and a rider from Mellicane. The Ventrian ambassador has requested an audience. His messenger is waiting outside the gallery.'

The guards pushed open the gates and Jianna walked through. 'Shall I send them all away?' asked Malanek.

'Ask Emparo to stay. I would like to hear his harp later. The Ventrian ambassador I will see tomorrow morning, before the council meeting. Have him brought here. We will breakfast together.' She arrived at the door to her chambers. 'I'll see the rider from Mellicane now. Askelus, you will stay with me.'

The tall warrior nodded, and opened the doors to the Queen's apartments. Lanterns had been lit within, the light shimmering on silk-covered couches and ornately fashioned chairs. The five hand-maidens, all dressed in gowns of white silk, stepped forward and curtsied as the Queen entered. 'You may all go to your beds,' said Jianna, with a wave of her hand. The women curtsied once more, and departed. Malanek strode off after them, returning with a round-shouldered officer. Jianna looked at the man. He had tired eyes. He bowed to her and waited.

'You have ridden far, sir?' she asked.

'I have, Majesty. Eight hundred miles in fifteen days. Mellicane is on the verge of collapse.'

'What else did you discover?'

'I have brought back all my papers, Majesty; reports on those loyal to your cause, and those we must . . . deal with. I have given them all to Malanek.'

'I shall read them and call for you again,' she said, unable to remember the man's name. 'But why have you waited for me this evening?'

'News of Skilgannon, Majesty.'

'Is he dead?'

'No, Majesty. He had left the church before the riders arrived. He is heading, we think, for Mellicane.'

'Does he have the swords?'

'He killed some men who were seeking to attack the church, Majesty. Our information is that he took sabres from the attackers.'

'He will have them,' she said.

'Hard to believe he became a priest,' said Askelus.

'Why?' countered Malanek. 'Skilgannon brought passion to everything he tackled. And passion is a gift of the Source.'

Askelus shrugged. 'He is a fighting man. Hard to see him mouthing spiritual inanities. Love will conquer all. Forgive those who torment you. Nonsense. Soldiers conquer all, and if you kill those who torment you then you are free of torment.'

'Be silent, the pair of you,' said Jianna, returning her attention to the messenger. 'Who do we have following him?'

'I have sent word to our embassy in Mellicane to watch out for him, Majesty. We also have the original twenty riders in Skepthia, and one skilled assassin we can contact. What orders shall I send?'

'I will think on it tonight,' she told him. 'Come to me in the morning.' With that she waved the man away. When he had gone Jianna sat down on one of the silk-covered couches, lost in thought.

Askelus and Malanek waited silently. At last she glanced up at them. 'Well?' she said. 'Speak your minds.' Neither man said a word. Jianna's heart sank. 'Am I so terrifying, even to old friends?' she asked. 'Come, Malanek, speak.'

The old swordsman sighed, then took a deep breath. 'You are rather hard on those who speak their minds, Majesty.'

'Peshel Bar was a traitor. I did not have him killed because he spoke his mind. I had him killed because he tried to turn others against me.'

'Aye, by speaking his mind,' said Malanek. 'He thought you were wrong, and he said so to your face. Now no-one with any sense will tell you what they really think. They will just mouth the words they think you want to hear. But maybe I'm too old to care. So I *will* answer you, Majesty. I liked Skilgannon. Still do. That man – more than any other – fought to win you this throne. I say leave him alone. Let him be.'

'He murdered Damalon. Have you forgotten that?'

Malanek glanced at Askelus. The tall warrior said nothing. Malanek gave a wry laugh and shook his head. 'I had not forgotten, Majesty. Forgive me if I do not grieve for him. I never liked him.'

Jianna rose from her couch, her expression tense, her grey eyes angry. When she spoke, however, her voice was controlled, almost soft. 'Skilgannon betrayed me. He left without the permission of the Queen. He deserted my army. He stole a priceless artefact. You believe he should escape punishment for those crimes?'

'I have said my piece, Majesty,' said Malanek.

'And what of you, Askelus?' she asked.

'You are the Queen, Majesty. Those who obey your orders are loyal, those who do not are traitors. It is simple. Skilgannon did not obey your orders. It is for you to judge him – or forgive him. It is not for me to offer advice. I am merely a soldier.'

'You would kill him if I ordered it?'

'In a heartbeat.'

'Would it sadden you?'

'Yes, Majesty. It would sadden me greatly.'

Dismissing both men, Jianna saw the councillors who had been waiting, listened to their advice, made judgements, signed royal decrees, then called for Emparo, the blind harpist.

He was an old man, but if she closed her eyes and listened to his music, his soft singing voice, she could imagine what he must have been in his youth, golden-haired and sweetly handsome. She wished he could be young now, and that she could take him to her bed, and banish for a while all thoughts of the man whose

212

face filled her mind, and whose form walked through her dreams.

Lying back on her couch, the sweet music filling the room, she remembered Skilgannon's look as she left the house that day to walk to the market. He had been so young then – a few weeks from sixteen. His handsome features were serious, his expression stern. She had wanted to lean in close and plant a kiss on that grim mouth. Instead she had walked away down the avenue, knowing that his eyes would not leave her until she turned the corner.

Jianna sighed. Tomorrow she would order him killed. Perhaps, when he was dead, she would stop dreaming of him.

CHAPTER ELEVEN

IT WAS AFTER MIDNIGHT WHEN SKILGANNON RETURNED TO THE Crimson Stag. The tavern was almost empty. Druss was still sitting at his table, Diagoras stretched out on the floor beside him, fast asleep. Two Vagrian officers with braided blond hair were drinking quietly some distance away, and an old wolfhound was nosing around beneath the empty tables, looking for scraps.

'Hello, laddie,' said Druss, his speech slurring mildly.

Skilgannon looked down at the unconscious Diagoras. 'The curse of the young,' said Druss. 'Can't hold their liquor. Damn, but I need some air.' Resting his massive hands on the table he half pushed himself upright, then slumped back to his seat. 'On the other hand, it is pleasant sitting here,' he concluded.

'Let me give you a hand,' said Skilgannon. The older man's pale gaze locked with his own.

'I'll manage,' muttered Druss, heaving himself upright, and swaying. Easing himself from behind the table he walked to the front door and out into the night air. Skilgannon followed him. Druss rubbed at his eyes and groaned.

'Are you all right?'

'I am as long as I don't blink,' replied the axeman. 'I need something to clear my head.' There was a water trough close by the wharf's edge. Druss staggered towards it, colliding with one of the

Vagrian officers as they were leaving the tavern. The man fell heavily. 'Apologies,' muttered Druss, moving past them. The Vagrian pushed himself to his feet and glanced down at his cloak. It was smeared with horse droppings. He rushed after Druss, swearing at him. The axeman turned and raised his hands. 'Whoa, there!' he said. 'This noise is splitting my head. Speak quietly.'

'Speak quietly?' echoed the Vagrian. 'You drunken old Drenai fool.'

'Drunk I may be, laddie – but at least I don't smell of horse shit. Is that some new Vagrian fashion?'

The officer swore, then punched Druss full in the face with a straight left. The Vagrian was a big man, with wide shoulders, and Skilgannon winced as the blow thudded home. A second punch, a right cross, followed it. It never landed. Druss caught the man's fist and spun him, hurling the Vagrian into the horse trough. 'That should get the stains out,' he said. The second Vagrian ran at the old man. Druss blocked the punch, and grabbed the man by his throat and crotch. With one heave he lifted him above his head and staggered towards the edge of the wharf.

'Druss!' yelled Skilgannon. 'He's wearing a mailshirt. He might drown.'

The axeman hesitated, then lowered the man to the ground. 'True,' he said. 'And we don't want to be drowning our allies, do we, laddie.'

The first officer had dragged himself from the trough. He was reaching for the hilt of his knife when the skinny form of Shivas, the tavern owner, emerged from the Crimson Stag.

'What is going on here?' he asked. 'Are you fighting in my establishment?'

'You couldn't call it a fight, Shivas,' said Druss, with a smile. 'A little gentle horseplay.'

'Well take it elsewhere – or take your business elsewhere. I'll have no troublemakers at the Crimson Stag. And I make no exceptions. Not even for you, Druss. And what do you expect me to do with that officer sleeping on my floor? If he stays the night he'll pay lodging like everyone else.'

'Put it on my bill, Shivas,' said Druss.

'Don't think I won't,' muttered the tavern keeper, casting a malevolent gaze at the four men before returning inside.

The two Vagrians left without a word to Druss. The axeman walked over to Skilgannon. 'Strange race, the Vagrians,' he said. 'They'd fight to the death on the smallest matter of principle. No threat of pain or injury would stop them. Yet the thought of missing out on Shivas's cooking has them scuttling away like frightened children.'

Skilgannon smiled. 'And how is your head?'

'Clearing, laddie. Just what I needed. A little gentle exercise.' Druss yawned and stretched. '*Now* what I need is a little sleep.'

A figure moved from the shadows. Skilgannon saw it was the strange woman, Garianne. 'You're a little late for that meal, lass,' said Druss. 'But you are welcome to share my room and I'll buy you a fine breakfast.'

'We are very tired, Uncle,' she said. 'But we cannot sleep yet.' She turned to Skilgannon. 'The Old Woman would like to see you both. We can take you to her.'

'I have no wish to see her,' said Skilgannon.

'She said you would say that. She knows the temple you seek. And something else which is very important to you. She told me to tell you this.' She looked at Druss, then half stumbled, righting herself by grabbing the jetty rail. Druss moved in. Garianne took one step and fell. Druss caught her, sweeping her up into his arms. Her head sagged against his chest.

The axeman walked back to the Crimson Stag. Skilgannon moved ahead, opening the door. Moving past the snoring Diagoras Druss carried Garianne to the rear stairs and up to the room he had rented. There were three beds in it. Rabalyn was asleep in the one beneath the window. Druss laid Garianne on a second narrow pallet. She groaned, and tried to rise. 'Rest, lassie,' said Druss. 'The Old Woman can wait for an hour or two.' He stroked the golden hair back from her brow. 'Rest. Old Uncle is here. Sleep.' Lifting a blanket, he covered her. She smiled and closed her eyes.

Druss sat by the bedside for several minutes, then rose and gestured to Skilgannon to follow him. The two men returned to the tavern dining hall.

'What is wrong with her?' asked Skilgannon.

'She'll be fine when she's rested. What do you know of the Old Woman?'

'Too much and too little,' answered Skilgannon. 'I have never believed that evil is linked to ugliness. I have known handsome men who are utterly without souls. But the Old Woman is as evil as she is ugly.'

Druss sat silently for a moment. 'Aye, I expect she is. But she also once helped me bring my wife back from the dead.'

'I'll wager she wanted something from you.'

Druss nodded. 'She wanted a demon that had been imprisoned in my axe. I later found out she had plans to transfer it into a sword she was making for Gorben.'

'Did you give it to her?'

'I would have. But the demon was cast from Snaga when I walked in the Void.'

'So, will you go to her?'

'I owe her. I always pay my debts.'

They sat in silence for a while. 'How did she bring your wife back from the dead?' asked Skilgannon, at last.

'Another time, laddie. Just thinking of Rowena makes my heart heavy. Tell me, did the Old Woman forge those swords you carry?'

'Yes.'

'I thought so. Be wary of them. There is more to her work than simple steel. Do you feel them calling to you?'

'No,' said Skilgannon sharply. 'They are just swords.' Druss sat quietly, holding to Skilgannon's gaze. Finally it was the swordsman who looked away. 'Yes, they call to me,' he admitted. 'They desire blood. But I can control them. I did so tonight.'

'You are a strong man. It'll take them time to eat into your soul. It was one of the Old Woman's swords which drove Gorben mad. The recently deceased Tantrian King had another of them.'

'Are you advising me to be rid of them?' asked Skilgannon.

'You don't need my advice, laddie. You said it yourself. The Old Woman is evil. Her blades mirror her heart. Did she make a weapon for the Witch Queen?'

'Yes. A knife. Jianna said it gave her discernment.'

'It will give her more than that.' Druss pushed himself to his feet.

217

'I'm going to sit in that chair by the fire and doze for a while. Why don't you go up and get some rest?'

'And deprive you of your bed?'

'I am an old soldier, laddie. I can sleep anywhere. Youngsters like you need pillows and blankets and mattresses. You go and lie down. If you can't sleep I'll bring you a goblet of hot milk and tell you a story.'

Skilgannon laughed, and felt all tension ease from him. He strode to the stairs and glanced back. 'Put a little honey in the milk. And I want the story to have a happy ending.'

'Not all my stories have happy endings,' said Druss, settling down into a deep leather chair. 'But I'll see what I can do.'

Skilgannon returned to Druss's room and stepped inside. Garianne and Rabalyn were still sleeping. Moving to the third bed he stretched himself out. The pillow was soft, the mattress firm.

Within moments he had drifted into a shallow sleep.

He was walking through a shadow-haunted forest, and furtive sounds were coming from the undergrowth. Spinning on his heel he caught a glimpse of white fur. His hands reached for his swords . . .

Skilgannon awoke in the pre-dawn and rose from the bed. His eyes felt gritty and he ran a hand over the stubble on his chin. Stripping off his shirt he moved to the rear of the room, where there was a jug of water and an enamelled bowl. He filled the bowl and splashed water to his face, then opened a small flap in his belt and removed a folded razor knife. Flipping it open he shaved slowly and carefully. Back home in Naashan he would have had a servant prepare heated towels to lay upon his face. Then the man would rub warm oils into the stubble before shaving him. Here he had no mirror, and shaved slowly by feel. At last, satisfied, he cleaned and dried the razor before folding it and returning it to the hidden pouch in his belt.

As dawn broke he saw smoke in the east of the city. Pushing open the window, he leaned out. He could just make out the distant sounds of uproar. He guessed the cause. Food riots among the poor.

When he turned away from the window he saw that Garianne

was still sleeping. He gazed down at her face. She looked much younger asleep, no more than a girl. Donning his shirt and jerkin, and looping the Swords of Night and Day over his shoulder, he left the room and walked downstairs.

Servants were already busy in the kitchens and Skilgannon smelt fresh-baked bread. Druss was nowhere to be seen. Skilgannon sat at a table by a harbour window and stared out over the sea. He felt a yearning to be aboard a ship, travelling towards distant horizons; to step ashore where no-one had ever heard of the Damned. Even as the thought came to him he recognized how stupid it was. You cannot run from what you are.

His thoughts swung to the Old Woman, and he felt the familiar surge of distaste and fear. Jianna had used the hag more and more during the civil war. Several enemies had been slain using demonic spells. It was actions such as these that had led to her being known as the Witch Queen.

Shivas strolled towards him, wiping flour from his hands. 'You are too early for breakfast,' he said. 'I can get you a drink, though.'

Skilgannon looked up at the wiry tavern owner. 'Just some water.'

'I am making some herbal tisane. A local apothecary prepares the ingredients for me. Most refreshing. Camomile and elderflower I can recognize, but there are other subtle flavours I cannot place. I recommend it.'

Skilgannon accepted the offer. The concoction was delicious, and he felt fresh energy flow through his tired body. Some time later Shivas returned. 'Now you look better, young man. Good, is it not?'

'Wonderful. Could I have another?'

'You could – if you want to find yourself singing sweet songs and dancing on my table. Trust me, one is enough. Now, I have some smoked fish for breakfast, with a side order of onion bread. Both are delicious. Especially with three eggs, whisked with butter and seasoned with a little pepper.'

Smoke from the riots was now drifting across the water. 'You'd think the city would have seen enough bloodshed,' muttered Shivas.

'Starvation brings out the worst in people,' said Skilgannon.

'I suppose it would. I shall fetch you some breakfast.'

After Shivas had gone Skilgannon's thoughts returned to the Old Woman. If she truly knew the location of the Resurrectionists he would be foolish to ignore her summons. Idly he fondled the locket round his neck. Do you really believe, he asked himself, that Dayan can be returned to life through a fragment of bone and a lock of hair? And supposing that she can, what will you do? Settle down with her on some smallholding and raise sheep? She is . . . was . . . a Naashanite aristocrat, raised in a palace, with a hundred servants to furnish all her needs. Would she live happily on a dirt farm? Would you? You were a general. The most powerful man in Naashan. Would you be content as a farmer, a tiller of soil?

Skilgannon drained the last of his tisane.

Shivas returned with his breakfast and Skilgannon ate mechanically, the exquisite flavours wasted on him, as his mood darkened.

Druss wandered into the tavern and sat opposite him. 'Sleep well, laddie?' he asked.

'Well enough,' answered Skilgannon sharply, feeling his irritation mount.

'Not a morning person, I see.'

'What does that mean?' he snapped.

'Beware of the tone, boy,' said Druss softly. 'I like you. But treat me with disrespect and I'll bounce you off these walls.'

'You'll trip over your guts the moment you try,' hissed Skilgannon. Druss's eyes blazed. Then he saw the empty tankard. Lifting it to his nose he drew in a deep breath.

'Drinking makes you disagreeable, you said. How do narcotics affect you?'

'I don't take them.'

'You just did. Most men who sip Shivas's tisanes merely sit around with happy grins on their faces. You, it seems, slide in the opposite direction. I'll have some water brought out for you. Drink it. We'll talk when the opiates have worn off.'

Druss left the table and walked into the kitchen. A serving girl brought a jug of water and a large blue cup. Skilgannon drank deeply. A mild headache began at his temples. He saw Druss leave the kitchen and climb the stairs.

Suddenly tired, Skilgannon leaned forward, resting his head on his arms. Colours swirled before his eyes. He found himself staring at the blue cup. Light from the window was gleaming upon its glazed surface. Skilgannon closed his eyes. The bright shimmering blue remained in his mind, swirling like the ocean. His thoughts drifted free, skimming across the blue like a seabird – flowing back to the day when blood and horror tore into his life, changing it for ever.

It had begun so well, so innocently. Sashan was holding his hand as they walked in the park at dusk. They had strolled together to the market, and eaten a meal at a riverside tavern. It had been a good day. Spies no longer watched the house, and Skilgannon had begun to believe that his plan had succeeded. The festival was only a week away now, and soon he would take Sashan from the city to seek her destiny among the mountain tribes. This thought was disturbing, and caused his stomach to tighten.

'What is wrong, Olek?' she asked him, as they passed a gushing fountain.

'Nothing.'

'You are gripping my hand more tightly.'

'I am sorry,' he said, loosening his grip. The only time they touched was when they were outside. Skilgannon enjoyed these walks more than any other pleasure he had ever experienced.

Night was falling as they approached the park gates. Two men with fire buckets were moving along the walkways, lighting the tall, bronze lanterns which lit the paths. Skilgannon saw an old woman sitting on a bench. 'You wish your fortunes told, young lovers?' she asked. Her voice grated on Skilgannon. She was extraordinarily ugly, and her clothes were ragged and filthy. He was about to refuse her offer when Sashan released his hand and moved to sit beside the crone.

'Tell me my future,' she said.

'There are many futures, child. Not all are written in stone. Much depends on courage, and luck, and friends. Even more depends on enemies.'

'Do I have enemies?' asked Sashan, the question sounding innocent. Skilgannon was growing ill at ease.

'We should go, Sashan. Molaire will be angry if the meal goes cold.'

'Molaire will not be angry, Olek Skilgannon,' said the old woman. 'I promise you that.'

'How is it you know my name?'

'Why would I not? The son of the mighty Firefist. Did you know that your father is now a demigod among the Panthians?'

'No.'

'They worship courage above all else, Olek. You will need all the courage your blood line can supply. Do you have such courage?'

Skilgannon did not answer. There was something about the crone that chilled him.

'What about *my* fortune?' asked Sashan.

'*You* have the courage, my dear. And to answer your question, yes, you have enemies. Powerful enemies. Ruthless and cruel men. One in particular. He needs to be avoided for now, for his stars are strong, and his standing high. He will cause you great pain.' She looked up at Skilgannon. 'And he will break your heart, Olek Skilgannon, and burden you with guilt.'

'Let's go,' said Skilgannon. 'I need to hear no more of this.'

'I still haven't been told my fortune,' said Sashan. 'I have enemies, you say. Will I defeat them?'

'They will not defeat you.'

'Enough of this nonsense!' snapped Skilgannon. 'She knows nothing, save my name. All else is valueless. Strong enemies, broken hearts. It means nothing.' Fishing a small silver coin from his pouch he dropped it in the crone's lap. 'This is all you desire. Now you have it. Leave us be.'

She pocketed the coin, then looked up at Skilgannon. There was no-one close by when she spoke, and her words lanced into him. 'Your enemies are closer than you think, Olek. The Empress is dead. Your friend Greavas has suffered the most terrible of fates. And the young princess sitting beside me is in mortal danger. You still wish to talk of nonsense?'

The words burned into Skilgannon, stunning him. He stood very quietly, staring at her. Then slowly he turned to scan the park, expecting at any moment to see armed men emerge from the undergrowth. No-one came. He glanced at Sashan. She too was shocked, but showed no grief. 'How did my mother die?' she asked.

'She took poison, my dear. It was hidden in a ring she wore. She did not suffer.'

'And Greavas?' asked Skilgannon.

'They tortured him for hours. He was strong, Olek. His courage was towering. In the end, however, bereft of his eyes, his fingers, he told them everything. Then Boranius continued his butchery for sheer pleasure. It did not sate his appetite for inflicting pain. Nothing can. It is his nature.'

Skilgannon fought to marshal his thoughts. 'How did Boranius find them?' he asked.

'There was a man Greavas trusted.' The old woman shrugged. 'The trust was misplaced – as trust usually is. Now the soldiers are looking for you, Olek Skilgannon. And for the yellow-haired whore who travels with you.'

He stared hard at the ugly old woman. 'Who are you? What is your place in all of this?'

'Hardly the most important questions you need to be asking at this moment. You stand here in a tunic and sandals with . . . what? . . . a few silver coins in your pouch? The princess wears a flimsy dress and has no coins. What are your plans, Olek Skilgannon? And yours, Jianna? A thousand men are searching the city for you.'

'And why do you offer us help?' asked Jianna, her voice cool.

'I did not say I would help you, child. I am merely telling you your fortune. Young Olek has paid me for that. My help comes at a much higher price. One thousand raq seems fair to me. Does it seem fair to you?'

'You might as well make it ten thousand,' said the princess. 'At this time I have nothing.'

'Your word will suffice, Jianna.'

'You could make more by betraying us,' said Skilgannon.

'Indeed. If it suited my purposes, young man, I would have done exactly that.'

'If I survive and succeed I shall pay you,' said Jianna. 'What do you advise?'

The old woman lifted a scrawny hand and scratched at a scab upon her face. 'I have a place near by. First we will go there. Then we will plan.'

Skilgannon suddenly groaned. 'Sperian!' he said. 'What of Sperian and Molaire?'

'There is nothing you can do, Olek Skilgannon. They have followed Greavas on the swan's path. Boranius is leaving your house even as we speak. He has left men behind to watch for you.'

'How many?'

'Four. One you know. A short man, with a long moustache.'

'Casensis.'

'An unpleasant fellow. He also joys in pain. He is not as naturally skilled in the arts of torture as your friend Boranius. But his pleasure in it is equal.'

Skilgannon felt a sick pain gnaw at his stomach. Rage threatened to overwhelm him, and he fought for calm. Darkness had fallen now, and a cool wind was blowing across the deserted park. 'I have no proof that any of this is true,' he said at last.

'You know where to find it, Olek Skilgannon,' she pointed out.

'We must go home,' he said to Jianna.

'That would be senseless,' the princess replied. 'If she is right there are men waiting. I'll not be taken.'

'I cannot leave you with her. She may seem helpful, but I sense the evil in her.'

Jianna rose from the bench, her eyes angry. 'You do not have the right to *leave* me anywhere. Nor *take* me anywhere. I am Jianna. My life is in *my* hands. Despite all you have seen of me you still think of me as a delicate female who needs protecting. Would you be so concerned if I was a young prince? I think not. Well, Jianna is stronger than any young prince, Olek. Malanek trained me well. Go to your house if you must. I shall travel with her.'

'Such wisdom in the young,' said the old woman. 'A pleasure to see it.'

Jianna ignored her. 'Do not be foolish, Olek. They will take you and torture you.'

'It is not foolishness,' said the old woman suddenly, 'for he is not a foolish man.' She looked up at Skilgannon. 'You need to *see* the truth, Olek. And more.' He felt her eyes upon him. She swung to Jianna. 'Let him go, princess. The sights he will witness will make him stronger. The actions he takes will bring him to sudden

224

manhood.' With a grunt she pushed herself to her feet. 'If you survive, Olek Skilgannon, go to the Street of Carpenters. You know it?'

'Yes.'

'Halfway down there is an alley, which runs alongside an old inn. Follow it and you will find yourself in a small square. At the centre is a public well. Wait by the well. I will fetch you, if it is safe.'

'Where will you be?'

'Best you do not know,' said the old woman. 'Boranius carries a number of implements designed to elicit information speedily. One is a beautifully crafted – yet small – set of shears. It can snip a finger with one long squeeze.'

Skilgannon looked into her ugly face and saw the glint of malicious pleasure in her eyes. 'How would you know of his . . . shears?'

'I made them for him, Olek Skilgannon. I make many things. I made the ring the Empress wore, which contained the poison. I cast the runes for the Emperor on the birth of his daughter, and warned him that her life would be fraught with peril. Which is why she was trained like a man, with Malanek as her tutor. I even made a sword for the Emperor Gorben.' She laughed, the sound harsh and dry, like windblown leaves rustling across a graveyard. 'I fear I made that one too powerful. It has gone to his head. But I digress . . . If you survive I shall come to you.'

'I do not like this plan,' said Jianna.

'If he survives he will be more useful to you,' said the old woman. Skilgannon stepped in to Jianna, then raised her hand to his lips and kissed it. He stood for a moment. 'I love you,' he said. Then he turned and loped away into the darkness.

He took a circuitous route back to the house, approaching it from the rear, moving on his belly across the paddock field behind the main garden. The night was cloudy, and he timed his movements to match the moments that the moon was obscured. Reaching the garden wall he rose soundlessly to his feet and paused. Despite everything the old woman had said there was a part of him that could not believe it – did not dare believe it. Once he climbed the wall he would find Sperian and Molaire sitting in

225

the house waiting for him. Doubt struck him. He stood very still, aware that as long as he stood here the world was as he had always known it. The moment he climbed the wall everything might change. His emotions in turmoil, he did not know what to do. For the first time in his life he was truly terrified. You cannot just stand here, he told himself. Taking a deep breath he leapt high, hooking his fingers over the rim of the wall. Drawing himself up, he rolled across the parapet and dropped to the earth below. Lanterns were burning inside the house, but he could see no movement. Keeping low, he crept to the shed where Sperian kept his tools. Inside he found a sharp pruning knife with a short, curved blade and a wooden handle.

Armed with this he darted across the garden and into the building. In the doorway he paused and listened. He could hear no sounds. Moving further inside, and avoiding the windows opening to the front of the house, he checked the main living room. It was empty. Further on he heard strange, gurgling sounds. Taking a deep breath he pushed open the door to the kitchen. A lantern had been set on the table, and by its light he saw the blood-covered, mutilated body of Sperian. Blood had also splashed to the walls of the cupboards, and had seeped across the floor. The dying man made a sound, blood bubbling from a puncture wound in his throat. Dropping the pruning knife Skilgannon knelt beside him. Sperian lifted a hand. It had no fingers. His face had been slashed with a knife, the skin hanging from the wounds. His eyes had been put out. 'Oh, my friend!' said Skilgannon, his voice breaking. 'Oh, what have they done to you?'

Sperian jerked at the sound of his voice, and tried to speak. No articulate sound came. Blood pumped from the wounds in his throat. Skilgannon stared down at the tortured man. Then he realized what he was trying to mouth. It was a single word.

Mo.

In the midst of such terrible pain he was asking about his wife.

'She is fine,' said Skilgannon, tears in his eyes. 'She is well, my friend. Be at peace.'

Sperian relaxed then. Skilgannon took hold of his wrist. There was not enough hand to hold. 'I will avenge this, my friend. I swear this on the soul of my father.'

Sperian lay quietly. The blood ceased to flow. Skilgannon began to weep. 'I thank you for all you have done for me, Sperian,' he said, through his sobs. 'You have been a father to me, and a friend. May your journey end in peace and light.' Struggling to control his grief, he took a silver coin from his pouch and put it into the dead man's mouth. Then he rose and moved further back into the house.

Molaire had been murdered in their bedroom. She had been hacked around the face, and her eyes, too, had been cut out. Her hands had not been mutilated, and Skilgannon placed a coin in her right hand, closing her dead fingers around it. 'Sperian is waiting for you, Mo,' he said, his voice breaking. 'May your journey end in peace and light.'

Then he walked upstairs to his own room. It had been ransacked. Pushing aside the chest in which he kept spare shirts, he reached into the recess hidden in the wall beyond and drew out a small box. From it he took the twelve gold coins and a few silvers. Dropping them into his pouch he opened the chest and pulled out a dark pair of leather leggings. Kicking off his sandals, he donned the leggings, and a brown hooded overshirt. Lastly he tugged on a pair of knee-length riding boots. Once fully dressed he chose other clothes. Stuffing them into a canvas backpack he slung it to his shoulders.

Then he made his way to his father's old room. From a chest in the corner he lifted clear a shortsword in a black leather scabbard. He also found a sheathed hunting knife with a bone handle. Threading a belt through the loops in both scabbards he swung it round his hips and buckled it. Drawing the sword he tested the edge. It was still sharp.

He stood very quietly, thinking out what to do next.

Common sense told him to leave the house the way he had come, and creep back through the fields. But his burning heart and soul had another plan. The old woman said Boranius had left four men to watch the house. One of them was Casensis. They were watching out for an untried youth. Little more than a schoolboy.

Well, they would find him.

Skilgannon walked to the front door and, throwing it open, walked outside onto the narrow, tree-bordered street. As he crossed towards the trees two men came running from cover. Both held swords. Dropping his pack Skilgannon drew his own blade and darted in to meet them, plunging the shortsword into the first man's belly. It went deep, but the blood channel carved into the blade allowed him to drag it clear with ease. The second man's sabre slashed for Skilgannon's head. Ducking beneath the swing he clove his own blade through the man's throat. Before his opponent had fallen Skilgannon ran towards the trees. Another man reared up, scrabbling for his sword. Skilgannon killed him before he could draw it. A shadow moved to Skilgannon's right.

It was Casensis. The man tried to run, but Skilgannon chased him down, cracking the flat of his sword against his skull. Casensis fell heavily. In the bright moonlight Skilgannon could see that the front of Casensis's tunic shirt was covered in blood. Dried spots of blood were also on his face and brow. Grabbing him by the tunic he hauled the semi-conscious man back into the trees. Casensis struggled. Skilgannon struck him again, this time with the pommel of the sword. Casensis sagged back to the ground, groaning.

Skilgannon leaned over him. 'When Boranius returns, tell him that I will find him. Not today, or tomorrow. But I will find him. Can you remember that?' Skilgannon slapped the man's face. 'Answer me!'

'I'll remember.'

'I'm sure you will.' Skilgannon's fist cracked against the man's jaw, jolting his head. Satisfied that he was unconscious Skilgannon stood and looked around. Close by was a flat stone. Dragging it to Casensis's side he laid the man's left hand upon it, then splayed the fingers. He raised the shortsword, bringing it down with all his strength. The blade sliced through the first three fingers, severing them. The smallest finger had curled back and escaped the cut. Skilgannon moved the stone to the other side of the unconscious man, and repeated the manoeuvre, this time cutting away all four fingers and the thumb.

The pain roused Casensis and he screamed. Skilgannon knelt on his chest and drew his hunting knife.

'You also took her eyes, you piece of scum. Now exist without yours!'

The scream that came from Casensis was almost bestial.

It was still echoing in his mind as he felt a hand upon his shoulder. He opened his eyes to see Druss and Garianne standing beside the table. The tavern was almost full now.

'Are you feeling better, laddie?' Skilgannon nodded. 'Then let's go. We've kept the Old Woman waiting long enough. And I have other tasks to complete today.'

CHAPTER TWELVE

SKILGANNON'S HEAD WAS POUNDING, AND HIS MOUTH WAS DRY AS HE walked beside Druss and Garianne. As they moved along the dockside he heard someone running behind them, and swung back. It was Rabalyn. The youth came up to him. 'Where are we going?' he asked.

'To see a sorceress,' said Druss. 'Be careful what you say, boy. I don't want to be carrying you back as a frog.'

'You were right,' replied Rabalyn, 'you are not good at jokes.'

'A man cannot be good at everything,' said Druss amiably.

They walked on. Skilgannon paused at a well, drew up a bucket of water and drank deeply. Bright colours were dancing before his eyes and his stomach felt queasy. He could not shake the memory of that dreadful night back in the capital. Images of the dead Sperian and the mutilated Molaire would not leave him.

'Are you all right?' asked Rabalyn, as they moved on.

'I am fine.'

'Your face looks grey.'

They came at last to the Drenai Gate. Today there were six soldiers there, in bright helms and red cloaks. The guards greeted Druss warmly, and warned the travellers of the riots that had spread through the city in the night. 'You should have brought your axe, Druss,' said one man.

Druss shook his head. 'Not today, laddie. Today is just a quiet stroll.'

The men glanced at one another and said nothing more.

Once into the city Garianne guided them through a series of streets and alleyways. The smell of burning hung in the air, and the people they saw looked at them with undisguised hatred. Some turned their backs and moved indoors, others just glared. Rabalyn stayed close to Skilgannon.

After a while they came to an area of older buildings and narrow streets. The people here wore shabby clothes. Children with filthy faces were playing outside derelict houses, and scrawny dogs delved among piles of discarded garbage, seeking scraps of food.

Garianne led the way, moving across an old market square and down a set of cracked and broken steps, coming at last to an abandoned tavern. The windows were boarded, but the main door had been hastily repaired and rehung with leather hinges. Garianne opened it and stepped inside. Part of the roof had given way, and sunlight filled the interior. Several rats scurried across the rubble inside. One ran over Rabalyn's foot. He kicked at it and missed. Garianne climbed over the fallen roof and made her way to the rear of the building, where she tapped her knuckles on the door that once led to the tavern kitchens.

'Come in, child,' came a familiar voice. Skilgannon felt his stomach tighten, and his flesh crawl.

'Is she really a sorceress?' whispered Rabalyn.

Skilgannon ignored him, and followed Druss across the rubble.

The old kitchen area was gloomy, the windows boarded. The only light came from two lanterns, one set on the warped worktop, the other hanging from a hook on the far wall. The Old Woman was sitting in a wide chair by the rusting ovens, a filthy blanket covering her knees. Her face was partly hidden by a veil of black gauze. Her head came up as the men entered. 'Welcome, Druss the Legend,' she said, with a dry laugh. 'I see the years are beginning to tell on you.'

'They tell on everyone,' he answered. Garianne moved alongside the Old Woman, and crouched down at her feet.

'Indeed they do.' She shook her head and the gauze veil trembled. Then she transferred her gaze to Rabalyn. 'You remember when you were that young, axeman? The world was enormous and filled with mystery. Life was enchanting, and immortality beckoned. The passing of the years meant nothing. We stared at the old with undisguised contempt. How could they have allowed themselves to become so decrepit? How could they choose to be so repulsive? Time is the great evil, the slavemaster who strips us of our youth, then discards us.'

'I can live with it,' said the axeman.

'Of course you can. You are a man. It is different for a woman, Druss. The first grey hair is like a betrayal. You can read that betrayal in the eyes of your lover. Tell me, are you a different man now that you have grey hairs?'

'I am the same. Hopefully a little wiser.'

'I too am the same,' she told him. 'I no longer look in mirrors, but I cannot avoid seeing the dried, wrinkled skin on my hands and arms. I cannot ignore the pains in my swollen joints. Yet in my heart I am still the young Hewla, who dazzled the men of her village, and the noblemen who came riding through.'

'Why did you summon us here?' put in Skilgannon. 'I have no time for such maudlin conversations.'

'No time? You are young yet, Olek. You have all the time in the world. I am the one who is dying.'

'Then die,' he said. 'As it is you have lived too long.'

'I always liked a man who would speak his mind. Lived too long? Aye, I have. Twenty times your lifetime, child. And I have paid for my longevity with blood and pain.'

'Most of that was not yours, I'll warrant,' said Skilgannon, his voice angry.

'I paid my share, Olek. But, yes, I have killed. I have taken innocent life. I have poisoned, I have stabbed, I have throttled. I have summoned demons to rip the hearts from men. I did this for wealth, or for vengeance. I have not, however, taken an army into a city and slaughtered all the inhabitants. I have not killed children. I have not cut the hands and eyes from a helpless man. So save your indignation. I am Hewla, the Old Woman. You are the Damned. You have no right to judge me.'

'And yet I do,' said Skilgannon softly. 'So speak your piece, and let me be free of your foul company.'

She sat silently for a moment, then returned her attention to Druss. 'The man you seek is no longer in the city, axeman. He left some days ago.'

'Why would he do such a thing?' asked Druss.

'To feed, Druss. Simply that.'

'This makes no sense.'

'It will. He came to Mellicane in search of his former wife. She had earlier travelled to Dros Purdol, ostensibly to see her daughter, Elanin. You remember Elanin, Druss. Orastes brought her to see you at your farm. You carried her on your shoulders, and sat beside a stream. She made a crown of daisies, and placed them on your head.'

'I remember,' said Druss. 'A sweet child. And a gentle father. So where is Orastes?'

'Be patient,' she said. 'While Orastes was away from the city his former wife snatched the child and fled from Dros Purdol. She came to Mellicane where she joined her lover. Orastes followed them as soon as he could. Once in the city he sought news of her. He did not know the identity of her lover, and the search proved fruitless. News of the search, however, reached the wife. One afternoon, Orastes and his servant were arrested as they sought information. They were taken to the Rikar cells below the arena. The Rikar cells held prisoners who would be melded into Joinings. That was the fate of Orastes. He was merged with a timber wolf, and the beast that he became fled with the others when the city fell.'

'No!' roared Druss. Skilgannon saw the axeman's face twist into a mask of pain and grief. 'This cannot be!'

'It can and it is,' said the Old Woman. Skilgannon detected something in her voice, a note of malicious glee. In his grief this was lost on the axeman. Skilgannon's anger swelled, but he stood quietly, watching the scene. The huge Drenai warrior turned away, and stood, head bowed, his fists clenching and unclenching.

'How could his wife wield such power in Mellicane?' asked Skilgannon.

'Through her lover,' answered the Old Woman, still facing Druss. 'You met him, axeman, after you arrived in Mellicane. At the banquet held in your honour. Shakusan Ironmask, the Lord of the Arbiters, the Captain of the King's Warhounds. While you drank with him your friend was in chains in the dungeons below.'

For a few moments there was silence. Then Druss took a deep breath. 'If we could find Orastes could he become human again?'

'No, axeman. When the Nadir cast the melding spell they first cut the throats of the human victims, then lay them alongside dogs or captured wolves. Even if the meld could be reversed – which the Nadir say is impossible – I would imagine that only the wolf or dog would survive. The man was, after all, already dead when the meld took place.'

'Then Orastes is lost.'

'He may already be dead. Did you not slay several of the beasts yourself? Perhaps you have already killed your friend.'

'Oh, how you are enjoying this, you hag!' said Skilgannon. 'Does your malice have no ending?' The atmosphere in the room chilled. Garianne looked shocked, and even Druss seemed uneasy. For a moment no-one moved, then the Old Woman spoke.

'The facts are what they are,' she said softly. 'My enjoyment of them changes nothing. I never liked fat Orastes. So stiff and pompous. One of the heroes of Skeln! Pah! The man almost wet himself with fear throughout the battle. You know this, Druss.'

'Aye, I know it. He stood though. He did not run. Yes, he was pompous. We all have our faults. But he never harmed anyone. Why would you hate him?'

'There are very few men I do not hate in this world of violence and pain. So, yes, I laughed when Orastes was melded. As I will laugh when you meet your doom, Druss. At this moment, however, it is not your death I seek. We now share a common enemy. Shakusan Ironmask destroyed your friend. He also caused the death of someone close to me.'

Druss's face was set, and his eyes blazed with cold fire. 'Where do I find this Ironmask now?' he asked.

'Ah, this is better,' said the Old Woman. 'Rage and revenge are such sweet siblings. It does my heart good to feel such purity of emotion. Ironmask is heading into the Pelucid mountains. There is a stronghold there. Be warned, though, axeman. Ironmask has seventy riders with him, hard men and ruthless. At the stronghold there will be a hundred more Nadir warriors.'

'The numbers do not interest me. How far is this place?'

'Two hundred miles northwest. I shall furnish you with maps. Pelucid is an ancient realm, containing many mysteries, and many perils. There are places where all the natural laws are bent and twisted. Your journey will not be without incident.'

'Just give me the maps. I will find Ironmask.'

The Old Woman rose from her chair, and slowly straightened. Taking a long staff she leaned upon it. Her breathing was harsh, and caused the black veil to billow gently. 'You also need to travel northwest, Olek Skilgannon. The temple you seek is in Pelucid, and close to the stronghold. It is not easily found. You will not see it by daylight. Look for the deepest fork in the western mountains, and wait until the moon floats between the crags. By its light you will find what you seek.'

'Can they accomplish what I desire?' asked Skilgannon.

'I have been there only once. I do not know *all* they are capable of. The priestess you will need to convince is called Ustarte. If she cannot help you, then there is no-one I know of who can.'

'Why are you doing this for me?' he asked. 'What trick is there? What evil lurks behind this apparent goodwill?'

'My reasons are my own,' said the Old Woman. 'You will travel with Garianne and the twins.'

'And why would I do that?'

'Because it would be *kind* of you,' she snapped. 'Jared also needs to find the temple. His brother has a cancer inside his head. I have held it at bay with herbs and potions, and even a spell or two. It is now beyond my skills.'

'And why Garianne?' asked Skilgannon.

'Because I ask it. You have reason to both hate and fear me, Olek Skilgannon. But you also owe me the life of the woman *you* love. If you succeed in Pelucid you will also owe me the life of the woman who loved *you*.'

Skilgannon sighed. 'There is truth in that. Although I doubt you wish me to succeed. Be that as it may, I shall take Garianne.'

'I think she will surprise you,' said the Old Woman. 'And now let me fetch you the maps.' Leaning heavily on her staff she made several steps towards an open door. Then her head turned and she stared at the silent Rabalyn. 'What a handsome young man,' she said. 'Can you recite the code, Rabalyn?'

'Yes, mistress,' he answered. 'I think so.'

'Say it.'

Rabalyn glanced at Druss, then drew himself up. He licked his lips and took a deep breath. '*Never violate a woman, nor harm a child. Do not lie, cheat or steal. These things are for lesser men. Protect the weak* . . . I don't remember the rest exactly, but it's something like *don't allow money to make you evil.*'

The Old Woman nodded. '*Protect the weak against the evil strong. And never allow thoughts of gain to lead you into the pursuit of evil.* The iron code of Shadak. The simplistic philosophy of Druss the Legend. And now it is yours, Rabalyn. Do you intend to live by it?'

'I do,' said Rabalyn.

'We will see.' Then she moved away.

At first Rabalyn was pleased to be outside the ruined tavern, and back on open streets under a clear sky. The atmosphere inside had been sinister and more than a little frightening. When the ghastly face under the gauze veil had turned towards him Rabalyn had felt sick with dread.

Now, however, as the small group moved through the crowded streets, Rabalyn was less happy to be outside. He cast nervous glances at the hostile faces of the citizens as they passed. Skilgannon and Druss seemed unconcerned, and chatted quietly. The youth looked at Garianne. She was muttering to herself, and nodding and shaking her head.

They moved on, more slowly now through the mass of people, coming at last to a wider square. Here several men were standing on the back of a wagon and addressing the crowd. The words were angry, and, every so often, the crowd would cheer loudly. The speaker was railing against the iniquities suffered by the populace, and demonstrating how the rich were to blame for the shortage of food, and the anguish of the citizens.

No-one accosted the group, and they eased their way through, and out onto a wider avenue. Rabalyn moved alongside Skilgannon. 'There is so much anger,' said the youth.

'Hunger and fear,' said Skilgannon. 'It is a potent mix.'

'That man back there was saying the rights of the citizens had been taken away.'

'I heard him. A few weeks ago that same man would have been blaming foreigners for their plight. In a few months' time it might be people with green eyes, or red hats. It is all a nonsense. They suffer because they are sheep in a world ruled by wolves. That is the truth of it.'

Skilgannon sounded angry, and Rabalyn fell silent. They walked on, coming at last to the gates of the embassy quarter. Crowds had gathered here too, and they had to force their way through to the front. The gates were locked, and beyond them stood around forty soldiers, some in the red cloaks of the Drenai, others in the thigh-length chain mail and horned helms of Vagria. Beyond the soldiers were bowmen, arrows notched. The gates were tall, and tipped with iron points. On each side were high walls, but already some in the crowd had scaled them and were sitting on the top, shouting down at the soldiers.

Skilgannon tapped Druss on the shoulder. 'They won't open the gates for us,' he said. 'If they did the crowd would storm them.' Druss nodded agreement, and the small group eased their way back through the mob, moving off to the side to a jetty overlooking a canal. Stone steps led down to the water's edge. Skilgannon led them down to the waterside. The angry shouting from above was more muted here, and Rabalyn sat down with his back to the stone wall, and stared out over the water. In the distance he could see more ships anchored in the harbour, awaiting their turn to be unloaded.

'They are going to storm the gates,' said Garianne.

'I don't believe they will during daylight,' Skilgannon replied. 'They may be angry, but no-one wants to die. They will shout and curse for a while. That is all. Tonight may be different.'

Druss stood silently by. Skilgannon approached him. 'You seem deep in thought, my friend.'

'I do not like that woman.'

'Who could? She is a malevolent crone.'

'What did you make of what she said?' The older man's eyes locked to Skilgannon's gaze.

'Probably the same as you.'

237

'Say it.'

Skilgannon shrugged. 'She knew too much about what your friend was seeking. How? My guess would be that Orastes went to her, seeking her help, and that she then betrayed him to this Ironmask.'

'Aye, that would be my reading also,' said Druss. 'Though I cannot work out why. If she hates Ironmask, why would she deliver a potential enemy to him?'

'She is a subtle creature, Druss. She wants Ironmask dead. How better to do that than to make him an enemy of Druss the Legend?'

'There could be truth in that. However, this is a woman who once sent a demon to kill a king. I fought that demon, and, by Missael, it almost had me. Why does she not simply send another after Ironmask? She has the power.'

'The answer to that,' replied Skilgannon, 'probably lies in what she did *not* say. Tell me about this Ironmask. She said you met him.'

'Yes, when I came here three months ago. As she said it was at a banquet. The King did not attend, and Ironmask greeted the guests. He is a big man, but he moves well. There is an arrogance in him – a physical arrogance. I'd say he was a fighting man and a good one.'

'What was his role here?'

'He led the King's bodyguards, and also supervised the creation of the Joinings. The plan was to use them in war, but they could not tame them sufficiently. Ironmask was also the lord of some group calling themselves Arbiters. Strange bunch. Every one of them I met looked at me as if I was a demon. They have a hatred of foreigners. Diagoras thinks it ironic – since Ironmask is also a foreigner.'

'Where is he from?'

'No-one seems to know. Probably Pelucid.'

'Why do they call him Ironmask?' asked Skilgannon.

'He wears a metal mask, which covers his face. Did I not mention that?'

'No.'

'It is a close-fitting and well-made piece, beautifully crafted.'

'He is disfigured then?'

'Not really. I saw him remove it at the feast. It was hot in the hall and he wiped his face with a cloth. He bore no scars. The skin on his nose and the right side of his face is discoloured, dark, almost purple. Like a large birthmark. The mask is just vanity.'

'You say he supervised the creation of the Joinings. Is he a sorceror himself?' Skilgannon asked. Druss shrugged.

'No-one knows. Diagoras thinks not. He says Ironmask brought a Nadir shaman to the city. From what the Old Woman said I would guess he is from this stronghold in Pelucid.'

Skilgannon turned away and gazed out over the harbour for a while. Then he swung back. 'I too know little of magic, Druss, but I would think it is this shaman who prevents the Old Woman sending demons after Ironmask. A summoned demon must be paid in death. If the attack is repulsed the demon will return to the sender and take their life. If this shaman is powerful – and judging by his creation of Joinings he is – then the Old Woman dare not attack Ironmask directly with sorcery. If the shaman repulsed her spell she would die. Therefore she needs a mortal weapon.'

From above them the shouting increased. Then someone screamed. People began running down the steps to the waterside. Others fled along the quayside. Datian soldiers in full battle garb of breastplate and shining helm appeared, swords in their hands. As they marched down the steps the milling city dwellers below panicked and began to hurl themselves into the water. One man put his hands in the air. 'I meant no harm,' he shouted. A short-sword plunged into his belly. A second soldier slashed a blade through the man's neck as he fell.

Several more soldiers, swords drawn, advanced on Druss and Skilgannon. Rabalyn was terrified. Then Skilgannon spoke, his voice calm, his attitude relaxed. 'Is the path to the gate now open?' he asked. 'We have been stuck here for an age.'

The soldiers hesitated. Skilgannon's easy manner made them unsure. One of them spoke. 'You are from one of the embassies?'

'Drenai,' said Skilgannon. 'My compliments on the efficiency of your action. We thought to be waiting here all day. Come, my friends,' he said, turning to the others. 'Let us go through before the mob returns.'

Rabalyn scrambled up, and joined Garianne. Together they

239

followed Skilgannon and Druss. No-one moved to stop them. Soldiers were still massed upon the steps. 'Make way there,' called Skilgannon, climbing upwards and easing past the swordsmen.

On the square above there were bodies lying sprawled upon the stone. One moved and groaned. A soldier stepped alongside him and drove his sword through the injured man's throat.

Skilgannon and Druss approached the gates, which were still shut. 'Open up, lads!' called Druss.

And then they were through.

As they walked on Druss clapped Skilgannon on the shoulder. 'I like your style, laddie. We'd have taken a few bruises if we had had to fight our way through them.'

'One or two,' agreed Skilgannon.

Later that afternoon Diagoras took Druss to see Orastes's servant, Bajin, but they learned little of consequence. Bajin was a gentle man, who had served Orastes for most of his adult life. His mind had been all but unhinged by his experiences in the Rikar cells. Heavily sedated, he wept and trembled as Druss tried to question him. One fact did emerge. Orastes had indeed sought help from the Old Woman.

Diagoras led Druss out into the gardens of the embassy. The Drenai soldier's head was pounding. 'I'm never going to drink with you again,' he said, slumping down on a bench seat. 'My mouth feels like I tried to swallow a desert.'

'Aye, you look a little fragile today,' agreed Druss absently.

Diagoras looked up at the axeman. 'I am sorry, my friend,' he said. 'Orastes deserved a better fate.'

'Aye, he did. One fact I have learned in my long life is that what a man deserves rarely has any bearing on what he gets. As I walked this land I saw burnt-out farms, and many corpses. None of them *deserved* to die. Yet it will go on, as long as men like Ironmask hold sway.'

'You still intend to go after him?'

'Why would I not?'

Diagoras rose from the bench and walked to a well, in the shade of a high wall. Drawing up a bucket, he dipped the ladle into the water and drank deeply. Then he thrust his hands into the bucket, splashing water to his face. '*Why would I not?*' Ironmask had more than seventy men with him, and was heading into a stronghold friendly to him. That stronghold would be packed with Nadir fighters. There were no more terrifying foes than the Nadir. Life was cheap on the steppes and the tribesmen were raised to fight and die without question. Rarely did they take prisoners during battle, and if they did it was to torture them in ways too ghastly to contemplate. He glanced back at Druss. The axeman had walked over to a red rose bush, and was removing those of the flowers that were past their best. Diagoras joined him. 'What are you doing?'

'Dead-heading,' said Druss. 'If you allow the blooms to make seed pods the bush will cease to flower.' He stepped back and examined the plant. 'It has also been badly pruned. You need a better gardener here.'

'So, what is your plan, old horse?' asked Diagoras.

Druss walked across to a second bush, a yellow rose, and repeated the dead-heading manoeuvre, nipping off the faded blooms with thumb and forefinger. 'I shall find Ironmask and kill him.'

'That is not a plan, that is an intent.'

Druss shrugged. 'I never was much for planning.'

'Then it is just as well I'll be travelling with you. I am famous for my planning skills. Diagoras the Planner they called me at school.'

Druss stepped back from the rose bush. 'You don't need to come, laddie. We are no longer searching for Orastes.'

'There is still the child, Elanin. She will need to be taken back to Purdol.'

Druss ran a hand through his black and silver beard. 'You are right. But I think you are a fool to volunteer for such an enterprise.'

'I am also famous for my foolish ways,' Diagoras told him. 'Which I expect is why they didn't make me a general. I think they were wrong. I would look spectacularly fine in the embossed breastplate and white cloak of a Gan. Will the Damned be travelling with us?'

'Part of the way. He has no score to settle with Ironmask.'

'The man makes me uncomfortable.'

'Of course he does,' said Druss, with a smile. 'You and he are warriors. There is something in you that yearns to test yourself against him.'

241

'I guess that is true. Is it the same for him, do you think?'

'No, laddie. He no longer needs to test himself against anyone. He *knows* who he is, and what he is capable of. You are a fine brave fighter, Diagoras. But Skilgannon is deadly.'

Diagoras felt a flicker of irritation, but suppressed it. Druss always spoke the truth as he saw it, no matter what the consequences. He looked at the older man, and grinned as his natural good humour returned. 'You never mix honey with the medicine, do you, Druss?'

'No.'

'Not even velvet lies?'

'I don't know what they are.'

'A woman asks you what you think of her new dress. You look at her and think: "It makes you look fat and dowdy." Do you say it? Or do you find a velvet lie, like . . . "What a fine colour it is" or "You look wonderful"?'

'I will not lie. I would say I did not like the dress. Not that any woman has ever asked me about how she looks.'

'There's a surprise. I see now why you are not known as Druss the Lover. Very well, let me ask another question. Do you agree that in war it is necessary to deceive one's enemy? For example, to make him think you are weaker than you are, in order to lure him into a foolhardy assault?'

'Of course,' said Druss.

'Then it is fine to lie to an enemy?'

'Ah, laddie, you remind me of Sieben. He loved these debates, and would twist words and ideas round and round until everything I believed in sounded like the grandest nonsense. He should have been a politician. I would say that evil should always be countered. He would say: "Ah, but what is evil for one man may be good for another." I remember once we watched the execution of a murderer. He maintained that in killing the man we were committing an evil as great as his. He said that perhaps the killer might have one day sired a child, who would be great and good, and change the world for the better. In killing him we might have robbed the world of a saviour.'

'Perhaps he was right,' said Diagoras.

'Perhaps he was. But if we followed that philosophy completely we would never punish anyone, for any crime. You could argue that to lock the killer away, rather than hanging him, might prevent him meeting the woman who would have given birth to that child. So what do we do? Free him? No. A man who wilfully takes the life of another forfeits his own life. Anything less makes a mockery of justice. I always enjoyed listening to Sieben ranting and railing against the ways of the world. He could make you think black was white, night was day, sweet was sour. It was good entertainment. But that is all it was. Would I deceive an enemy? Yes. Would I deceive a friend? No. How do I justify this? I don't.'

'I think I understand,' said Diagoras. 'If a friend in an ugly dress asks your opinion, you'll give it honestly and break her heart. But if an enemy in an ugly dress comes before you, you'll tell her she looks like a queen.'

Druss chuckled, then burst into laughter. 'Ah, laddie,' he said, 'I am beginning to look forward to this trip.'

'I'm glad one of us is,' muttered Diagoras.

Servaj Das was a careful man, painstaking in all that he did. He had found that attention to detail was the most important factor in the success of any undertaking. Originally a builder by trade, he had learned that without adequate foundations even the most beautifully constructed building would crumble. In the army he had soon discovered that this principle could be applied to soldiering. The uninitiated believed that swords and arrows were the most vital tools to a soldier. Servaj Das knew that without good boots and a full food pack no army could prevail.

He sat now in a high room at the Naashanite embassy, staring out over the harbour, and considering the mission orders he had received by carrier pigeon. He was to locate and kill a man swiftly.

How could one pay attention to detail when the orders specified speed? Speed almost always led to problems. In normal circumstances Servaj would have followed the man for some days, establishing his routines, getting to know and understand the way the man's mind worked. In doing this he would better be able to judge the manner of the man's death. Poison, or the knife, or the garrotting wire. Servaj preferred poison. Sometimes when he followed a man, and observed his habits, he found himself liking the victim. He had never forgotten the merchant who always stopped to pet an old dog at the street corner. It seemed to Servaj that a man who took pity on a mangy, unwanted hound must have a kind heart. Often the man would feed the creature small titbits he had taken along for the purpose. Servaj sighed. He had been forced to garrotte him when the poison failed. Not a pleasant memory. Servaj filled a goblet with watered wine. Sipping it, he rose from his chair and stretched his lean frame. His back gave a satisfying crack. Placing the goblet on the table he interlaced his fingers, and cracked his knuckles. No, poison was better. Then one was not forced to observe the death.

Picking up the small piece of parchment he scanned again the message. 'Kill him. Swiftest. Recover Swords.'

He was not happy.

This was not some offending politician, soft, fat and weak. Nor a merchant unused to violence. This was the Damned.

Servaj had been in the army during the time of the Insurrection. One of the moments he would never forget was when Skilgannon had fought the swordmaster, Agasarsis. As a common soldier Servaj had no intimate knowledge of the reasons for the duel, but gossip among the men claimed that Skilgannon's closeness to the Queen had enraged the Prince Baliel. This jealousy came to the fore when Skilgannon was almost killed at the Battle of the Ford. Baliel's forces had mysteriously drawn back, leaving Skilgannon and his company of horse exposed to an enemy counter attack. Baliel, it was said, maintained he had misinterpreted his battle orders. The Queen replaced him as the Marshal of the Right Flank. Enraged and embittered, Baliel made it known that he believed Skilgannon had engineered the debacle to discredit him. The bitterness grew during the next few weeks, until finally the famous swordsman, Agasarsis – a sworn servant of Baliel – found an excuse to challenge Skilgannon.

He was not the first. During the two years of the Insurrection seven others had crossed swords with the Damned. Only one had lived, and he had lost his right arm. But Agasarsis was different. The man had fought sixty duels in his thirty-one years. His skills were legendary and there was much excitement in the camp as the day dawned. There was also unrest. The Queen's army at this time numbered thirty thousand men, and not all could witness the epic confrontation. In the end lots were drawn. Servaj had been offered twenty silver pieces for his pass to the contest, and had refused. Duels like this one were rare indeed, and he had no wish to miss it.

There was rain in the morning, and the ground was soggy and treacherous, but the sun shone brightly by midday. The one thousand men privileged to witness the fight had formed a large circle some two hundred feet in diameter. Skilgannon was the first of the combatants to arrive. Striding through the ranks of the waiting men he stripped off his battle jerkin and moved effortlessly through a series of exercises to loosen his muscles.

Even then Servaj was a keen student of human behaviour. He looked for signs of nervousness in the general, but could detect none. Agasarsis arrived. He was more powerfully built than Skilgannon, and when he stripped off his shirt he looked awesome. Both men sported the crested plume of hair that signified their swordmaster status, but Agasarsis also had a neatly fashioned trident beard, which gave him a more menacing appearance.

He approached Skilgannon and bowed, and then both men continued their exercises, their movements fluid and synchronized, like two dancers, each mirroring the other. A sudden blaring of trumpets announced the arrival of the Queen. She wore thigh-length silver chain mail, and knee-length cavalry boots, edged with silver rings. Two men carried a high-backed chair into the circle and she sat upon it, her raven hair gleaming in the sunshine.

Servaj was close enough to hear her words to the fighters.

'Are you determined upon this folly, Agasarsis?'

'I am, my Queen.'

'Then let it begin.'

'Might I make a request, Majesty?' said Agasarsis.

'I am in no mood to grant you anything. But speak and I will consider it.'

'My swords are well made, but they hold no enchantment. Skilgannon's blades, however, are known to be spell enhanced. I request that he uses no unfair advantage against me.'

The Queen turned to Skilgannon. 'What say you, general?'

'This fight is already folly, Majesty. But in this he is right. I shall use other blades.'

'So be it,' she said. Turning to the nearest soldiers, one of whom was Servaj, she called six of them forward. 'Take out your swords,' she ordered them. Once they had done so she gestured to Skilgannon. 'Choose one.' He hefted them all, then chose the sabre carried by Servaj. 'Now you,' snapped the Queen, pointing a regal hand at Agasarsis.

'I already have swords, Majesty.'

'Indeed you do. And you have used them so often they are like a part of your body. Your own request was for no unfair advantage. So choose. And do it swiftly, for I am easily bored.'

After Agasarsis had chosen a blade the two men bowed to the Queen and moved back towards the centre of the circle. She gestured for them to begin.

The duel did not start swiftly. The men moved warily around one another, and the first clash of steel seemed more like an extension of the exercises they had undergone before the Queen's arrival. Servaj knew that the duellists were merely accustoming themselves to the feel of the weapons. Neither Skilgannon nor Agasarsis attempted a death strike. They were gauging each other's strengths and weaknesses. The crowd was silent as the two masters continued to circle one another. Sunlight gleamed on the blades, and each sudden attack would see the swords create a glittering web of brightness around the combatants. The ground below their feet was slick and treacherous, and yet it seemed that they remained in perfect balance. Time passed, the action quickened, and the music of clashing steel increased in tempo. Servaj was transfixed, flicking his gaze between the fighting men. Both exuded confidence. Both expected to win. First blood went to Skilgannon, the tip of his sabre scoring a cut to Agasarsis's shoulder. Almost immediately the champion countered, and blood appeared on Skilgannon's torso. It seemed to Servaj that the blood was dripping from the fangs of the panther head tattooed upon his chest.

The speed and skill of the fighters was dazzling. Bets had been placed by the soldiers, but no-one in the crowd cheered or shouted for their favourite. The watchers were all fighting men, and they knew they were observing a classic encounter. Not a whisker separated the talents of the duellists, and Servaj began to believe they would be fighting all day. He half hoped it would be true.

Such a brilliantly balanced contest was rare, and Servaj wanted to savour it for as long as possible.

Yet he knew it could not last. The blades were razor sharp, and they flashed and lunged, parried and countered, within a hair's breadth of yielding flesh.

They had been fighting for some twenty minutes when Agasarsis stumbled in the mud. Skilgannon's sabre lanced into Agasarsis's left shoulder as he fell, then slid clear. The champion hit the ground and rolled, coming up in time to block a vicious cut that would have beheaded him. He threw himself at Skilgannon, hammering his shoulder into Skilgannon's chest, hurling him backwards. Both men fell heavily.

At a command from the Queen the herald beside her blew a single blast upon his curved horn.

Two soldiers ran forward, bearing towels. The combatants plunged their swords into the earth, and took the cloths. Agasarsis wiped sweat from his face, then pressed the towel into the deep wound in his left shoulder. Skilgannon approached him. Servaj did not hear what was said, but saw Agasarsis shake his head angrily, and guessed that Skilgannon was enquiring as to whether honour had been satisfied.

After a few moments the Queen ordered the horn sounded, and the two fighters took up their swords. Once again they circled. Now the duel entered into its last phase. Servaj found it fascinating. Both men were tired, but he could see desperation in the eyes of Agasarsis. Doubt had entered the champion's mind, and was leaching away his confidence. To counter this he launched a series of reckless attacks. Skilgannon defended smoothly for a while. When the death blow came it was so sudden that many in the crowd missed it. Agasarsis lunged. Skilgannon met the attack, blocking the lunge and rolling his blade round the sabre of Agasarsis. The two men leapt back. Blood suddenly gushed from Agasarsis's severed jugular. The champion tried to steady himself, but his legs gave way, and he fell to his knees before his killer. Servaj realized then that, even as he parried, Skilgannon had flicked the point of his sabre across the throat of his opponent.

Agasarsis pitched face forward to the earth.

Skilgannon dropped his sabre and walked back to the Queen. He

247

bowed, and Servaj saw that his face was set, his eyes angry. 'Agasarsis was the best cavalry commander we had, Majesty,' he said. 'This was madness.'

'Indeed it was,' she agreed. 'Behold the man responsible.' She gestured to the herald, who sounded the horn twice in succession.

Two of the Queen's trusted bodyguard, Askelus and Malanek, came into sight, leading a bound man. His eyes had been torn out, and his face was a mask of blood. Even so Servaj recognized the Prince Baliel. The man was sobbing piteously.

Askelus dragged him out to stand alongside the fallen Agasarsis. The Queen rose from her chair and walked out to the centre of the circle. 'Our war is almost won,' she said, her voice ringing out over the seated men. 'And why? Because of your bravery and your loyalty. Jianna does not forget those who serve her faithfully. But this creature,' she cried, pointing to the pitiful Baliel, 'put all your courage at risk. My gratitude to my friends is infinite. My enemies will always find that my vengeance is swift and deadly.' Askelus drew his sword and plunged it into the belly of the blinded man. His scream was hideous. Servaj saw Askelus twist the blade, then wrench it clear. Disembowelled, Baliel fell to the ground, and began to writhe in fresh agony. The Queen let the sounds go on for a while, then signalled Askelus. The soldier drove his sword through Baliel's neck. The silence that followed was total. 'So die all traitors,' said the Queen. Someone began to chant: 'Jianna! Jianna!' Servaj saw it was the former swordmaster Malanek. Other men began to follow his lead, but the cheering was not enthusiastic. Jianna raised her hands for silence. 'When we have taken Perapolis every man in my army will receive three gold pieces, as a sign of my love and gratitude.'

Now the cheering began in earnest. Servaj shouted in jubilation, along with the others. Three gold coins was a fortune. Even as he cheered, however, he glanced at Skilgannon. The general looked troubled.

Shaking himself from his memories Servaj returned to the problem at hand. The Damned had been sentenced to death, and it was left to Servaj to determine the manner of his execution.

He had under his command a number of good swordsmen, but none with the skill of Agasarsis. Skilgannon was staying at the

Crimson Stag. There would be no opportunity to poison his food.

Servaj thought the problem through. There would need to be an attack on the general. Five, maybe six men. And two men with crossbows, hidden close by. Even this was fraught with risk. He would have to visit the alchemist. If the crossbow bolts were tipped with poison, then even if Skilgannon escaped the ambush he would die later.

How, though, could he ensure Skilgannon came to the place of his execution?

CHAPTER THIRTEEN

BACK AT THE CRIMSON STAG SKILGANNON WAS DELIGHTED TO FIND that two merchants had vacated a room overlooking the harbour. He paid Shivas an extortionate four silver pieces for two nights, then went upstairs to the room and closed the door. He had not been aware that his need for solitude was so great. Even the muted noise from the tavern below was welcome, for it emphasized that he was alone now. Lifting the Swords of Night and Day from his shoulders he dropped them to the bed, then pushed open the window and gazed out over the ocean.

The reunion with the Old Woman had been hard – bringing back memories he preferred to forget. Something in him had died that night, along with Molaire and Sperian. In truth he did not know what it was. Childhood perhaps. Or innocence. Whatever the answer, his heart had withered like a flower in the frost.

The planning of the escape from the city had taken days and nights, as each idea he put forward was discussed and dismissed. The Old Woman offered to take them through the gates in the back of a loaded wagon, hidden beneath sacks of grain. Skilgannon disliked this idea. Were he the Captain of the Gates he would search all conveyances. They talked of separating, and meeting later in the forest of Delian, but this was too fraught with the possibilities of becoming lost. Eventually they decided on simple deception. The

Old Woman fashioned a harness that Jianna wore below a torn and colourless knee-length dress. The leather straps of the harness hung down her back. Lifting Jianna's left leg the Old Woman secured a strap to her foot, then bound the ankle tightly to the thigh. Jianna complained of the discomfort. The thigh and calf were then bandaged, leaving the knee exposed. With great skill the Old Woman added to the disguise, using small strips of shaved pig skin, and partly congealed blood, which she pasted to the skin of the knee. Skilgannon watched it all, amazed. By the finish the knee looked like a stump covered in weeping, bleeding sores. The illusion was repeated on Skilgannon, this time twisting his left arm up between his shoulder blades. She also added, using a mixture of white candlewax and a foul-smelling balm, three long scars to his left cheek and eyebrow. Once she had fashioned an eyepatch for him Skilgannon gazed into a cracked mirror. The face he saw looking back at him seemed to have been raked by the talons of a bear. Lastly the Old Woman cut away the dyed parts of Jianna's hair, leaving her with a short, boyish hair style.

She allowed them an hour to become used to their acquired deformities. Jianna spent it practising with a pair of old crutches. Skilgannon merely waited, his crooked and tied arm pulsing painfully.

Finally they set out in the Old Woman's wagon. She stopped some three hundred paces from the East Gate. Already lines of supplicants were queuing there, waiting to be allowed on the two-hour walk to the Maphistan Temple, and the yearly opening of the Chest of Relics. As far as Skilgannon knew there had been no reported miracles for years, but it didn't stop the diseased and the lame from making the annual trip, to kneel before the bones of the Blessed Dardalion, and the faded gloves of the Revered Lady. The richest of the supplicants were allowed to kiss the hem of the robe said to have been worn by the immortal Silverhand, whose death two thousand years ago had caused a dead tree to bloom into life.

It was almost dusk as Skilgannon leapt down from the wagon, then clumsily helped Jianna. She half fell against him and swore. The Old Woman passed down her crutches. Jianna took them and slowly made her way to join the line. Skilgannon fell in behind her, and waited.

Guards were stopping everyone at the gate, and questioning all young women. In the shadows by the gatehouse Skilgannon saw three men standing, watching the crowd intently. He moved alongside Jianna, and tapped her arm. 'I see them,' she whispered.

'Do you know them?'

'One of them. Keep moving.'

As Skilgannon approached the guards he longed to have his hand on the hilt of his sword, but did not. Head bowed, he shuffled forward with the others. A guard stepped in front of him and looked hard at Jianna. Leaning forward he lifted her skirt, then let it go. 'What happened to you?' he asked sympathetically.

'Wine wagon ran over it,' she said, her voice coarse.

'I don't think the relics will grow you a new one, lass.'

'I just want it to stop turning green and stinking,' she said. He stepped back, trying to mask an expression of distaste.

'Keep moving then. And may the gods bless you,' he said.

Jianna leaned on her crutches and followed the people in front. As Skilgannon moved to follow he saw Boranius walk from the gatehouse. A terrible rage flared in him, but he fought it down. Now is not the time, he told himself. Gritting his teeth he walked beneath the gate arch and out into the countryside beyond, keeping his eyes fixed on the distant tree line of the forest of Delian.

Laughter from the tavern below jerked him back to the present. Music had started, and men were clapping their hands, establishing a rhythm. Obviously there was some entertainment going on, but Skilgannon had no wish to observe it.

Stripping off his jerkin, shirt and leggings he stretched himself out on the bed. Only then did he notice the huge mirror fastened to the ceiling. He stared up at the tattooed figure reflected there, meeting the cold stare of his double's bright blue eyes. There was no trace of the idealistic youngster who had fled into the forest with the rebel princess. Idly he wondered what he might have become had he not met Jianna. Would he have been more content? Would Greavas, Sperian and Molaire still be alive? Would Perapolis now be a thriving city, full of happy people?

A great cheer sounded from the tavern below. Then a woman's voice began to sing, the sound high and clear and beautiful. It was an old ballad about a warrior's return to his homeland, in search of his first love. Skilgannon listened. The song was overly senti-mental, the lyrics maudlin, and yet the woman's voice imbued it with a sense of splendour that overcame the mawkish sentiments. It seemed to offer fresh insights into love and its power, giving a magnificence to the man's ultimate, life-giving sacrifice.

When the song ended there was a moment of silence, then a thunderous burst of applause. Skilgannon took a deep breath and closed his eyes.

> *For if love is the ocean, on which sail the brave,*
> *we should welcome the storm winds,*
> *and the wind-driven waves.*

Even now he did not truly know what love was. Jianna had filled his heart. She still did. Was this the love the poets sang of? Or merely a mixture of desire and adoration? Memories of the times of tranquil harmony with Dayan both lifted his spirit and deepened his sorrow. Was this love? If so it was a different beast entirely from what he felt about Jianna. There were never answers to these questions. He had tormented himself with them every day back at the monastery.

Swinging his legs from the bed, he stood up and walked to the basin stand beside the harbour window. He poured himself a cup of water and sipped it, seeking to free his mind of thoughts of the past.

He heard a board creak outside his room and turned. Someone tapped at the door. Skilgannon felt his irritation mount. The tap was too light to be Druss, who would have hammered upon the frame and called out. It was probably the youth, Rabalyn. Skilgannon hoped he would not again request to travel with him.

Walking to the door, he pulled it open.

Garianne was standing there. She was holding a flagon of wine and two empty goblets. Her eyes were bright, her face flushed. As he opened the door she eased past him and walked into the room. Placing the goblets on the bedside table, she filled them with red wine. Lifting one, she drank deeply, then wandered to the window.

'I love the sea,' she said. 'One day I will board a ship and leave them all behind. They can argue amongst themselves. I will be free of them.'

He stood quietly, watching her. She had removed her jerkin and was wearing a thin, figure-hugging shirt. Her leather leggings were also form-fitting, leaving little to the imagination. Skilgannon turned away.

Garianne swung towards him, then brought him a goblet of wine. 'I do not drink,' he said.

'I drink to be alone,' she told him, her voice slightly slurred. 'It is a wonderful feeling to be alone. No voices. No demands. No shrill screeching and pleading. Just silence.'

'I too like to be alone, Garianne. Now I would like to ask what you want of me, but I know that you do not like questions.'

'Oh, I don't mind questions. Not when it is me. Not when I am alone. When they are with me questions make them all speak at once. I cannot think. Then my head swells with pain. It is uncomfortable. You understand?'

'I cannot say that I do. Who is with you?'

She walked to the bed and slumped down. Wine spilled from the goblets in her hands. Carefully she placed them on the bedside table. 'I don't want to speak of them. I just want to enjoy these moments of peace.'

She pushed herself to her feet, swayed slightly, then began untying the waist band of her leggings. Pushing them down over her hips, she sat back on the bed and struggled to tug them over her ankles. Skilgannon moved across the room and sat down beside her. 'You are drunk,' he said. 'You do not want to be doing this. Get into bed and sleep it off. I'll take a walk and leave you to . . . enjoy your privacy.'

Reaching up, she curled an arm round his neck. 'Don't go,' she said softly. 'I want to be alone inside my head. But not out here. Here I need to touch, to hold. To be held. Just for a while. Then I will sleep. Then I will be Garianne again, and I will carry them all with me. I am not drunk, Skilgannon. Or at least not much.' Tilting her head she kissed him lightly on the lips. He did not draw away. She kissed him again, more deeply.

The walls he had built during three years of abstinence crumbled away in an instant. The scent of her golden hair, the softness of her lips, the warmth of her skin overwhelmed him.

All cares and regrets vanished. The world shrank, until all that existed for Skilgannon was this one room, and this one woman. The first lovemaking was intense and swift, the second slower, the pleasure extended. The afternoon faded into evening, and then into night. Finally, all passion exhausted, he lay back, Garianne's head on his shoulder, her left leg resting on his thigh. She fell asleep. Skilgannon stroked her hair and kissed the top of her head. She murmured, then rolled away from him. Rising silently from the bed he covered her with a sheet, then dressed. Looping the Swords of Night and Day over his shoulder he walked from the room.

Earlier that afternoon Diagoras was sitting opposite Druss in the tavern, planning the route to Pelucid and discussing the supplies they would need. One of the difficulties was that Druss did not ride. On foot it would take half as long again to make the journey, and, logistically, require the travellers to carry more food. Diagoras patiently explained this to the warrior, who just shrugged and smiled. 'When I ride it is painful for both me and the horse. In the saddle I can make a sack of grain look graceful. I walk, laddie.'

It was at that moment that Garianne, who had been sitting quietly with them, her expression serene, put down her wine goblet and walked to the dais on the eastern side of the tavern.

'I think she is going to sing,' said Druss, with a wide smile.

'No-one will hear her in here,' replied Diagoras, glancing around at the packed tavern, full of men talking and laughing, or arguing, or pitching dice on several long tables.

'Would you like a small wager?' asked the older warrior.

'No. I always lose when I bet with you.'

Garianne carried a chair onto the dais then stood upon it silently, her arms outstretched towards the rafters. Diagoras gazed at her longingly. The Drenai officer had always been attracted to long-legged women – and Garianne was also strikingly attractive. Several other men noticed her standing there, and nudged their companions. A hush settled on the room.

And Garianne began to sing.

It was one of Diagoras's favourite ballads, and always brought a lump to his throat. But this girl's rendition made it heartbreaking.

255

Every man in the tavern sat entranced. As she finished the song she lowered her arms and bowed her head. For a moment there was silence. Then rapturous applause. Garianne moved back to the table, swept up a flagon of wine and two goblets and walked from the room, the applause following her.

'Where is she going?' asked Diagoras.

Druss shrugged and looked uncomfortable. Raising his hand he summoned a serving girl and asked for another flagon of Lentrian red. 'What does she need two goblets for?' continued Diagoras.

'She's an unusual lass,' said Druss. 'I like her.'

'I like her too. But why don't you answer my questions?'

'Because I don't care to, laddie. Her life is for her to live, as she sees fit.'

'I didn't say it wasn't. And now I'm getting confused.' Realization dawned. 'Oh,' he said. 'I see. She has an assignation. Lucky man.' Then his mood darkened as he guessed the identity of said lucky man. He swore softly. 'Tell me she is not seeking Skilgannon,' he said.

'Don't let it irritate you,' Druss told him. 'If it had been you up in that room, and him down here, she'd have gone to you. It's not about the man. If neither of you had been here she'd have picked someone from the tavern.'

'You?' asked Diagoras.

'No,' answered Druss, with a wry chuckle. 'Damn it, laddie, my boots are older than her. And she's not so drunk that she'd want someone old and ugly. Now what were you saying about supplies?'

Diagoras took a deep breath and tried – without success – to force Garianne from his mind. 'What about a wagon? A two-wheeler. It would travel fast. You could drive it.'

'Aye. A wagon sounds fine,' agreed the axeman.

Diagoras was about to speak when he glanced beyond Druss, and grinned. 'Look what we have here, my friend. A new warrior joins the throng.' The axeman swung in his chair. The youth Rabalyn was moving across the tavern floor towards them. He was wearing a new green tunic of thick wool, and buckskin leggings. Shining leather strips had been added to the shoulders of the tunic. By his side hung a bone-handled hunting knife and an old short-sword in a ragged leather scabbard.

'Going to war, young Rabalyn?' asked Diagoras. The youngster stood for a moment, looking self-conscious and embarrassed. Then he tried to sit down. The scabbard struck the chair, the hilt of the weapon rising and thudding into Rabalyn's armpit. Adjusting the sword he slumped down into the chair, his face reddening.

'Let me see the weapons,' said Druss. Rabalyn drew the knife and laid it on the table. Druss hefted it and examined the blade. It was double-edged, the tip sharply curved like a crescent moon. 'Good steel,' said the axeman. 'And the sword?' Rabalyn pulled it from its scabbard. The hilt was polished wood, the pommel of heavy brass. The blade itself was pitted and scarred. 'Gothir infantry. Probably older than me,' said Druss. 'But it will serve you well until you can afford better. How did you come by them?'

'Brother Lantern gave me money. I have decided not to stay in the city.'

'Where will you go?' asked Druss.

'I don't know. Thought I might travel with you.' Rabalyn tried to sound confident and assured, but the effort failed.

'It would not be a wise choice, Rabalyn,' said the axeman. 'But I leave it to you.'

'Truly?'

'Go and get some rest. We'll talk more this evening. For now I need to speak with Diagoras.'

'Thank you, Druss. Thank you!' said Rabalyn happily. Sheathing his weapons, he moved away towards the stairs.

'Oh, that was nice,' said Diagoras. 'Perhaps we should also bring a puppy and a troupe of minstrels.'

'This will soon be a city under siege,' said Druss. 'The Naashanites will come. He'll be no safer here. It could be another Perapolis.'

'That is unlikely,' snapped Diagoras. 'They don't have the Damned with them any more.'

Druss's pale eyes narrowed. 'You are an intelligent man. You know that nothing that happened in that city could have taken place without the direct orders of the Queen.'

'You think him innocent then?'

'Pah! Innocent? Are any of us innocent? I was here twenty-five years ago. I took part in attacks on cities. I killed men who were

257

defending their lands and their loved ones. Warriors are never innocent, laddie. I'm not defending Skilgannon. What took place at Perapolis was evil, and every man who took part in the slaughter put a shadow on his soul. Rabalyn is a fine lad. He'll be as safe with me as he will be here. He also has courage. I put him in a tree when the Joinings attacked. He climbed down and came to my aid. Given time he will be a fine man.'

Diagoras leaned back in his chair. 'From what you have told me Ironmask has seventy men with him. From everything we learned of the man while he was here in Mellicane he is hard and ruthless. His men likewise. The stronghold in Pelucid contains a hundred more, mostly Nadir. Ferocious fighters, as you know. They also take delight in torturing prisoners. One hundred and seventy enemies, Druss. How much *time* do you think Rabalyn will have, to become this fine man?'

Druss said nothing. Diagoras pushed himself to his feet. 'Very well, Druss. I'll make enquiries about a wagon, and purchase some supplies. It will take a couple of days. We'll need to wait until the situation in the city has calmed down. I'll see you back here tomorrow evening.'

The young Drenai officer wandered out into the gathering dusk. The air was fresh and cool, a light breeze blowing in from the sea. Several whores were standing at the quayside, ready for the evening trade. Ignoring them, he strolled to the edge of the quay and thought of the trip ahead. You could have been going home, he thought. Back to Drenan and a life of idle pleasure. Instead he was to journey into a perilous wilderness. Druss had called him an intelligent man. There was little intelligence involved in this adventure. But it *was* an adventure, and Diagoras had found little excitement in his life these last four years. Skeln Pass had been terrifying, and there was indeed a large part of him that wished he had never been there. On the other hand it had been the most exciting time of his life. The prospect of death had loomed over him like a storm crow, bringing with it the intense knowledge of the sweetness of life. Every breath was joyful, every moment cherished. And when, in the end, they had won, and he had survived, he experienced a surge of elation and exhilaration unparalleled in his young life. Nothing since had even come close to such a feeling.

Just then, from a window above him, he heard a young woman cry out in ecstasy. Well, almost nothing, he thought, with a smile. The smile faded as he realized the woman was probably the lovely Garianne.

'I could make those sounds for you,' said a voice. Diagoras turned. One of the whores, a girl with long dark hair, had moved nearer to him. Her face was pretty, though her eyes were tired and dull. 'I have a room close by,' she said, giving a practised smile.

Diagoras took her hand and kissed it. 'I am sure you would, my sweet. And I am sure it would be a wonderful experience to treasure. Sadly, though, duty calls. Another time, perhaps.'

Her smile became more natural. 'You are very gallant.'

'Only in the presence of beauty,' he said.

In the room above the woman cried out again. Diagoras suddenly chuckled, and took the young whore by the arm. 'Duty can wait,' he said. 'I yearn for a little time in your company.'

'You'll not regret it,' she promised him.

CHAPTER FOURTEEN

FOR AN HOUR NOW RABALYN HAD SAT ON A BENCH BEHIND THE
Crimson Stag, watching Druss chop logs. Using a long-handled,
single-bladed axe Druss worked methodically, with an extraordinary economy of effort. With each stroke the timber split and
fell apart. Druss would tap the chunks to the left, knocking them
from the large round he used as a chopping block, and then thunk
the axe blade lightly into a fresh round, lifting it to the block. With
a flick of his wrist he would free the axe blade, raise it and bring it
down, splitting the new round. It was rhythmic and impressive to
see. When the timbers to Druss's left began to pile up Rabalyn
would leave his seat and carry them to the wood store by the
tavern wall, stacking them carefully.

As the first hour ended Druss took a break. He was bare-chested,
and his body gleamed with sweat. Rabalyn had known strong men
back at the village. Usually their bodies were sculpted, the muscles
of their chest and belly in sharp relief. Not so with Druss. He was
merely huge. His waist was thick, his shoulders bunched with
muscle. There was nothing remotely aesthetic about the man. He
just radiated power.

'Why are you doing this work?' asked Rabalyn, as the axeman
took a deep draught of water.

'I don't like to be idle.'

'Is Shivas paying you?'

'No. I do it for pleasure.'

'I can't see how chopping wood is pleasurable.'

'It relaxes me, laddie. And it keeps me strong. You'll hear men talk about skill with sword or knife, axe or club. Most people believe it is that skill which makes a warrior great. It is not. Great warriors are men who know how to survive. And to survive a man needs to be strong. He needs stamina. There are many men out there who are faster than me. More skilful. There are few who can outlast me.'

Rabalyn looked at the big man, seeing the old scars on his chest and arms. 'Have you always been a warrior?' he asked.

'Yes. It is my one great weakness,' said Druss, with a rueful grin.

'How can it be weak? That makes no sense.'

'Don't ever be fooled by appearances, boy. Strong men build for the future: farms, schools, towns and cities. They raise sons and daughters, and they work hard, day in day out. See that wood there? The tree it came from is around two hundred years old. It started out as a seed, and had to send roots into the hard earth. It struggled to survive – to live long enough to make its first leaf. Slugs and insects ate away at it, squirrels chewed on its soft bark. But it struggled on, making deep roots and a stronger heart. For two hundred years its falling leaves fed the earth. Its branches became the home of many birds. It gave shade to the land beneath it. Then a couple of men with axe and saw brought it down in less than an hour. Those men are like warriors. The tree is like the farmer. You understand?'

'No,' admitted Rabalyn.

Druss laughed. 'Ah, well, one day maybe you will.'

Rising from the bench, he began to work again. Rabalyn helped him for another hour. Then Skilgannon arrived, and Druss laid down the axe. He still did not seem tired. Skilgannon laid his swords on the ground and stripped off his shirt, exposing the ferocious panther tattoo on his chest. Taking up the axe he lifted a fresh round to the chopping block and split it expertly. Rabalyn sat back, fascinated by the difference in the way the two men worked. Druss was all power and economy. Skilgannon brought a touch of artistry to the labour. Every so often, as the axe swung up, he would twirl it, causing sunlight to flash from the blade. His movements were smooth and supple. Though less strong than Druss he powered through the work with great speed. Where Druss's axe blade would occasionally bite into the chopping block and need to be wrenched clear, Skilgannon would strike each blow with just the right amount of force. The rounds would split, the axe blade coming to rest almost gently on the block.

Both men made the work look easy, and yet when Rabalyn tried it the swinging axe would bury itself in a round and need to be wrestled clear, or else he would miss with his swing, the blade bouncing from the block and jarring his shoulders. 'Keep at it, laddie,' said Druss encouragingly. 'It'll come.'

By the time Rabalyn had successfully sliced around thirty rounds his shoulders and arms were burning with fatigue. Druss called a halt and they moved to the well nearby. Druss drew up a bucket of water and drank.

'We should be ready to leave in a day or two,' he told Skilgannon.

Skilgannon donned his shirt and swung his swords to his back. 'A man at the tavern told me that there are horses for sale in the northern quarter of the city. He said I should seek out a man named Borondel.'

Druss thought for a moment. 'The northern quarter is mostly Naashanite. Will it be safe for you?'

Skilgannon shrugged. 'Nowhere is safe. But we do need horses. Diagoras says the Drenai have none to spare.'

'Did you ask Shivas about this Borondel?'

'Yes. He is a horse trader.'

'But you are not convinced. I see it in your eyes, laddie.'

'No. It seems too . . . convenient that a man should seek me out and ask if I'm looking for mounts.'

'I'll go with you.'

Skilgannon shook his head. 'I'll scout the area. If it is a trap I will seek to avoid it.'

That it was a trap was not in doubt. Skilgannon knew this even as he left the embassy area compound. So why are you going, he asked himself? The man at the tavern had been Naashanite – even though he had tried to disguise his accent. While talking to the man Skilgannon had noted the edge of a tattoo under the long cuffs of his red shirt. He saw enough to know it was the Coiled Cobra, sported by archers and spearmen of the Coastal Army.

As he walked he glanced to his left and right. Once he caught a glimpse of someone darting between two buildings. The man was wearing a red shirt. This is foolishness, he told himself. Why walk into danger?

Why not, came the response? Suddenly Skilgannon smiled and his mood lifted. He saw again Malanek, in his training room back at the compound. 'You look in a mirror and you think you see yourself. You do not. You see a body inhabited by many men. There is the happy Skilgannon, and the sorrowful. There is the proud, and the fearful. There is the child who was, and the man who is yet to be. This is an important lesson, because, when in danger, you need to know – and more important to control – which of these men is in charge at that time. There are moments when a warrior needs to be reckless, and others – far more others – where he needs to be cautious. There are times for acts of great bravery, and times for tactical withdrawals, to regroup and fight another day. Equally there are times when action is needed so swiftly there is little time for thought, and, worse sometimes, where there is too much time for thought. Understand yourself, Olek. Know how to find the right man within, for the right moment.'

'How do I do that?' the fourteen-year-old had asked.

'First you must remove emotion from the arena. Each action is judged on its merits alone, and not from the heart. An example: a man stands before you and challenges you to fight him with your fists. What do you do?'

'I fight him.'

Malanek slapped him on the top of the head. 'Will you think?' he demanded. 'I have no sand timer working here. You have time to consider my questions.'

'Is the man alone?'

'Yes.'

'Is he an enemy?'

'Good question. He might be a friend who is angry with you.'

'Then I would try to reason with him.'

'Excellent,' said Malanek. 'But he is not a friend.'

'Is he bigger or stronger than I?'

'He is – for the sake of this discussion – the same as you. Young, strong, and confident.'

'Then I fight him. Reluctantly.'

'Yes, you do, for a man cannot remain a man if he refuses a challenge. He becomes lessened in his own eyes, and the eyes of his comrades. The important word here is reluctantly. You will fight coolly, using your skill to end the fight as swiftly as possible. Yes?'

'Of course.'

'Now picture this: a man – the same man – has just punched Molaire in the face and knocked her to the ground. He is kicking her as she lies unconscious.'

'I would kill him,' said the youth.

'Now this is what I am talking about, Olek. Who is in charge now? Where is the man who fought coolly and reluctantly, seeking to end the fight as swiftly as possible?'

'If I saw Molaire attacked I would react with anger.'

'Exactly – and this would lessen your effectiveness. Block from your mind all emotion. This will bring you to your true self. When you fight let your body relax, and your mind float clear. Then you will be at your best. I have fought many duels, Olek. Most of the men have lacked my skill. Some of them I managed not to slay. I disarmed them, or wounded them sufficiently seriously to end the fight. Others were almost as skilled. These I had to kill. But a few, Olek, were better than me. One was so far better I should not have survived for more than a few heartbeats. These men should have won. They did not. And why? One died for arrogance. So sure was he of his skill he fought complacently. Another died through stupidity. I managed to make him angry. The one who was infinitely better than I died because he feared my reputation. He was already trembling when we touched blades. Emotion has no place in combat, Olek. This is why I will teach you the illusion of elsewhere. You will learn to float clear.'

As he walked on through the city Skilgannon began to breathe deeply and easily. No longer irritated, no longer tense, he considered the problem.

The assassins knew where he was staying, and therefore could find him. If he tried to hide from them they would continue to seek him, either in the city or on the open road. Better then to seek them. They would have the advantage of numbers, but they would also be expecting to surprise him. The man in the tavern had given directions to the stables owned by Borondel. Therefore the attack would take place either along the route, or at the stables. The most likely place would be at the stables, where, once inside, the murder could be committed out of sight.

That was the strongest possibility, but they could have men stationed along the way. A knifeman, perhaps, or a bowman. Both? Probably. If he himself were planning an assassination – especially that of a known swordsman – he would have at least three units on call. The first would be armed with swords or knives, and would attempt to kill the man as he was on the move through a crowded area. The bowmen would be positioned further back along the route, in case the man escaped the first attempt and ran back the way he had come. The third unit would have been following the victim, some distance back, ready to cut off any line of retreat.

Skilgannon could no longer see the man in the red shirt, and guessed that he had sprinted on ahead to warn the attackers of his arrival.

He strolled on. How many would there be? This was more difficult to estimate. Ten seemed the most likely. Two bowmen, four in the first knife – or sword – attack. Another four following. Emerging from a broad avenue, he crossed the road and entered a small park. There were scores of people here, sitting on the grass, or standing near the fountains. They were better dressed than those he had seen in the mob yesterday. Up ahead was a family, a man and a woman, walking with three children. Skilgannon scanned the area. The park was mostly open ground, with little screening of bushes or trees. There was nowhere for a bowman to hide. Furthermore, the men he could see were dressed in warm weather clothing: tunics, shirts and leggings. None carried weapons. Some way into the park Skilgannon paused on an ornate wooden bridge spanning a stream. He glanced back the way he had come. Three men were strolling some distance back. All wore heavy jerkins, beneath which knives could be hidden.

Three behind.

If the organizer of this attempt believed three could stop him fleeing it was possible that no more than three would be waiting ahead.

According to the directions he had been given the stables of Borondel were beyond the park exit. There was a long alleyway, he had been told, which led on to an area of open ground.

Leaving the park he crossed another road, then cut to the left, avoiding the alleyway. Walking on swiftly, he ducked down a second side street. Out of sight of the men following he broke into a run. This second street was full of market stalls, though there were few goods displayed on them. Several contained clothing, but the food stalls were bare. Halfway along the street was a tavern, with tables set outside. Around a dozen men were sitting there, nursing jugs of black beer. Skilgannon moved past them and entered the building. The interior was dark, and no customers were inside. A thin man approached him. 'There is no food today, sir,' he said. 'We have ale and we have wine. The wine is not high quality.'

'A jug of ale then,' said Skilgannon, moving along the room and sitting by an open window. Shifting his chair to hide himself from view he sat in the shadowed tavern and watched the sunlit marketplace. Within moments he saw the three followers moving past the stalls. They looked tense and angry. One of them approached the group of men sitting outside the inn.

Skilgannon rose from his chair and moved swiftly along the wall of the tavern, halting just beyond the doorway.

'What's it worth?' he heard someone ask.

Skilgannon heard the rasping of metal, and guessed a weapon had been drawn. 'You get to keep your eyes, you slug!'

'No need for that,' said the man, his voice suddenly fearful. 'He just went inside there.'

Shadows flickered across the entrance. Skilgannon's stiffened fingers slammed into the first man's belly. He doubled over, a whoosh of air exploding from his lungs. Before the second could react Skilgannon's fist cracked against his chin, spinning him from his feet. The third man lunged with his knife. Skilgannon grabbed the knife wrist, stepped inside and hammered a head butt to the man's nose, shattering it. Half blinded, the assassin dropped his

266

knife and staggered back. Skilgannon followed in with a straight left and a right cross. The man hit the floor and did not move.

Scooping up the fallen knife Skilgannon turned back towards the first man, grabbing him by his long, dark hair and dragging him into the tavern. The innkeeper, Skilgannon's jug of ale in his hand, stood by anxiously. 'Just put it on the table,' said Skilgannon pleasantly.

'You're not going to kill him, are you?'

'I haven't decided yet. Probably.'

'Would you do it outside? Dead bodies tend to upset my customers.'

The man Skilgannon had hauled into the tavern was gasping for breath, his face crimson. Skilgannon lifted him by his hair into a sitting position. 'Lean forward and breathe slowly,' said the warrior. 'And while you are doing that think on this. I am going to ask some questions. I am going to ask each one once only. If you do not answer instantly I shall cut your throat. Say my name!'

Drawing back the man's head, he laid the blade of the knife on the assassin's jugular. 'Skilgannon,' said the man, between gasps.

'Excellent. Then you know that what I have told you is no idle threat. So, here is the first question. How many are waiting for me at the stable?'

'Six. Don't kill me.'

'How many bowmen?'

'Two. I have a wife and children . . .'

'Where are the bowmen hidden?'

'In the alley, I think. But I don't know. Servaj will have positioned them. We were just told to follow and cut off your retreat. I swear it.'

Skilgannon released the man's hair, then struck him sharply on the back of the neck. The Naashanite slumped forward, unconscious. Skilgannon sliced away the man's money pouch and opened it. There were a few silver pieces inside. He tossed the pouch to the tavern keeper. 'Something for your trouble,' he said.

'Very kind,' said the man sourly.

Skilgannon rose and walked to the entrance. One of the other assassins was beginning to move. The man groaned. Skilgannon knelt beside him and hit him in the jaw. The moaning ceased.

Checking the third man he saw that he was dead, his neck snapped.

The innkeeper leaned over the body. 'Oh, this is pleasant,' he said. 'Another corpse.'

'At least he's not bleeding.'

'Not exactly a silver lining though, is it?' said the man. 'Corpses are not considered good business for an eating establishment.'

'Neither is having no food.'

'You have a point. Does he have money in his pouch?'

'If he does it is yours,' said Skilgannon, rising and walking outside. A small crowd had gathered.

'What went on in there?' asked a round-shouldered, balding man.

Ignoring him, Skilgannon walked to the end of the street and stood by the corner, scanning the buildings close by. Locating the stable, he strolled towards it. The man in the red shirt was in the loft, watching from a hay gate. As soon as he saw Skilgannon approach he ducked back inside. Skilgannon broke into a run, cutting to the left and vaulting the fence around a small corral. As he landed he heard a thunk from behind him. Glancing back he saw a crossbow bolt jutting from a timber. Surging forward, he sprinted across the corral, swerving left and right. Another bolt hit the ground and ricocheted past his leg. Then he was at the stable doors. Drawing the Swords of Night and Day he dived through the open doorway, and rolled to his feet. Three men rushed forward.

And died.

A fourth remained sitting on a bale of hay. He was a thin man, dark-haired and balding, and he wore no weapon. 'Good to see you again, general,' he said affably.

'I know you. You were an infantryman.'

'Indeed so. I have a medal to prove it. The Queen gave it to me herself.'

Skilgannon moved across the stable, eyes scanning the empty stalls. Then he paused with his back to a sturdy column. 'To use such fools as these against me is most insulting.'

'You are not wrong. Speed, they said. It's never a good idea. But do they ever listen? Do this, do that, do it now. Makes you wonder how they reach such high positions, doesn't it? I take it you killed the others?'

'The three who were following? No. Only one. The others will be waking up soon.'

'Ah well, not entirely a bad day then.' Servaj levered himself upright. His sabre was hanging from a hook on the wall. Strolling over to it he drew the blade. 'Shall we end this, general?'

'As you wish.' Skilgannon sheathed the Sword of Night. 'You are remarkably calm for a man about to die. Is this because of some religious belief?'

'You fought Agasarsis with my sword. This sword here. I watched you. You're not that good. Come on. Let me give you a lesson.'

Skilgannon smiled, took one step away from the column, then spun and dropped to one knee. The crossbowman hidden in the far stall reared up. Skilgannon's right hand flashed out. The tiny circular blade sliced into the bowman's throat just as he loosed his bolt. With a gurgling cry he fell back. The bolt flashed past Skilgannon, burying itself in the calf of Servaj, who swore loudly then dropped his sabre. 'A poor end to a bad day,' he said. Looking up he shouted: 'Rikas, can you hear me?'

'Yes, Servaj,' came a muffled voice.

'Forget about your bow and go home.'

'Why? I can still get him.'

'You can still get yourself killed. Just do as I say. Remove the bolt, loose the string and come down.' Skilgannon stood ready as a crossbowman descended the loft ladder steps. He was a young man, fair-haired and slim. He glanced at his wounded leader, then at Skilgannon. 'Just leave, Rikas.'

The young man walked past Skilgannon and left by the rear door.

'Why did you do that?' asked Skilgannon.

'Ah well, there are some tasks which are more onerous than others. To be honest I always liked you, general. And now that I'm dying I don't feel much like completing my mission.'

'Men don't usually die from a bolt in the lower leg.'

'They do if the bolt is poisoned.' The man's speech was beginning to slur and he slumped back to the hay bale. 'Damn. It would be amusing if it wasn't so bloody tragic.' His body arched forward. He groaned, then he pitched to the ground. Skilgannon retrieved the circular throwing blade, cleaned it and tucked it inside his belt. Then he moved back across the stable and knelt beside the assassin. 'May your journey end in light,' he told the dying Servaj.

'I . . . wouldn't . . . bet on that.'

Reaching down, Skilgannon retrieved the man's fallen sabre. 'It was a good weapon that day,' he said. Glancing down he saw that Servaj had died. Rising, Skilgannon lifted the scabbard from the hook on the wall and sheathed the sabre, hooking the sword belt over his shoulder.

There were four horses in stalls at the rear of the stable. All looked thin and undernourished.

Skilgannon saddled them all. Then, mounting a bay gelding, he took up the reins of the other mounts and led them out into the daylight.

As more supplies entered the city the mobs began to disperse. The Datians and their allies proved benevolent rulers, and there were few executions. Some prominent members of the old King's family were hunted down, and a score of his advisers were held in the city prison for interrogation. For the common folk life began to return to normal.

Diagoras took the horses Skilgannon had acquired into the Drenai compound, where they were grain-fed and rested. 'They need more time than we have,' said Diagoras, 'but they'll be in better condition when we leave.'

Skilgannon thanked him, but the officer's response was cool. It was difficult for Diagoras. There was something about the former general that pricked under his skin, leaving him angry and un-settled. Not normally a bitter or resentful man, he found himself uneasy around the Naashanite. What Druss had said about rivalry was partly true, but it was not the main reason for Diagoras's behaviour. He tried to rationalize his feelings, but it was not easy. In company Skilgannon was non-confrontational and pleasant, and Druss liked him. Yet he was also the mass murderer who had ordered and supervised the slaughter of thousands in Perapolis. Stories of his battle triumphs were legion, as were tales of his ruthlessness in war. It was impossible to reconcile the man with the legend. Diagoras knew that if he had met him and been unaware of his past he would have liked him. As it was he could not hold a conversation with Skilgannon without a smouldering anger flaring in him.

'Why do you not like Brother Lantern?' asked Rabalyn, on the afternoon of the third day.

They were taking a break from sword practice on the open ground at the rear of the Crimson Stag. The lad had promise, but his arms needed strengthening. 'Is it that obvious?' asked Diagoras.

'I don't know. It is to me.'

'Then you have a sharp eye, for we have exchanged no angry words.'

'He has been kind to me, and I like him,' said Rabalyn.

'There is no reason, then, why you should not,' Diagoras told him.

'So why don't you?'

'We're here for you to learn swordplay, Rabalyn. Not to discuss my likes and dislikes. You are fast, which is good, but you need to think about your balance. Footwork is vital for a swordsman. The weight must shift from back foot to front foot. Come, let me show you why.'

Moving out onto the open ground Diagoras offered his blade. Rabalyn's sword touched it. 'Now attack me,' said the Drenai. Rabalyn moved forward, slashing his sword through the air. Diagoras blocked the cut, stepped inside and hammered his shoulder into Rabalyn's chest. The youngster tumbled back and fell heavily. Diagoras helped him up. 'Why did you fall?' he asked the lad.

'You shoulder-charged me.'

'You fell because your back foot had come forward alongside your front foot. When weight was thrown against you there was nothing to support you. Stand with your feet together.' Rabalyn did so. Extending his arm Diagoras pushed hard on the youth's chest. He staggered back. 'Now, stand with your left foot pointing forward, knee slightly bent, and your back foot at a right angle to the front.'

'What is a right angle?'

'Point your left foot towards me, twist the other foot to the right. That's it.' Once more Diagoras pushed the youth. This time he hardly moved. 'You see. The weight is pushed onto the back foot, so you remain balanced. When you lunge you extend the left foot first. When you move back it is on to the right foot. They never cross over.'

'It is very complicated,' complained Rabalyn. 'How am I supposed to remember this in a fight?'

'It is not about memory. It is about practising until it is second nature to you. With luck you'll develop into a fine swordsman. Of course it would help if you had a better blade.'

'Then this might be of use,' said Skilgannon. Diagoras spun round. He had not heard the man approach, and this unsettled him. The Naashanite walked past Diagoras and offered a sabre and scabbard to Rabalyn. 'It is a good weapon, well balanced and finely made.'

'Thank you,' said Rabalyn, reaching for it.

'I was just explaining to the lad about the importance of foot-work,' said Diagoras. 'It would be most helpful if he could see it displayed. Would you object to a practice?' He found himself looking directly into Skilgannon's sapphire eyes. The warrior held his gaze for a few moments, and Diagoras felt as if the man was reading his soul.

'Not at all, Diagoras,' he said, retrieving the sabre from Rabalyn.

'Would you be more comfortable using one of your own blades?' asked Diagoras.

'It would not be safe for you if I did,' said Skilgannon softly.

They touched blades as Rabalyn sat down on a bench. Then, in a whirl of flashing steel, they began to fight. Diagoras was skilled. Eighteen months ago he had won the eastern final of the Silver Sabres at Dros Purdol. His assignment to Mellicane had meant missing the national final in Drenan. He was sure, however, that he would have won it. So it was with great confidence that he took on the Damned. The confidence, he soon realized, was misplaced. Skilgannon's sabre blocked every lunge and cut. Diagoras increased the pace, moving beyond that of a practice. He did not do this consciously. His mind was locked now in combat. Faster and faster they moved. Suddenly Diagoras saw his opportunity and leapt forward. Skilgannon parried, stepped inside, and slammed his shoulder into Diagoras's chest. The Drenai officer hit the ground hard. He glanced up and saw Rabalyn staring at him, his expression one of shock and fear. Only then did Diagoras come to his senses and realize that he had been trying to kill Skilgannon. He took a deep breath. 'You see what I meant about balance, Rabalyn,' he said, trying to keep his voice light. 'In my excitement I forgot all about footwork.' The youth relaxed.

'I have never seen anything like it,' he said. 'You are both so fast. Sometimes I couldn't even see the swords. They were just blurs.'

Skilgannon reversed the blade, offering the sabre hilt to Rabalyn. The young man took it, then grinned at Skilgannon. 'It is a wonderful gift. I can't thank you enough. Where did you get it?'

'From a man who had no need of it. Use it well, Rabalyn.'

Diagoras pushed himself to his feet. 'My apologies, Skilgannon,' he said. 'I was so carried away by the contest I almost forgot we were merely practising.'

'No apology is needed,' said Skilgannon. 'There was no danger.'

Anger flared in the Drenai, but he swallowed it down. 'Even so, the apology stands. I should have known better.'

Skilgannon met his gaze once more, then shrugged. 'Then it is accepted. I shall leave you to your practice.'

'Garianne was looking for you,' said Rabalyn. 'She is in the tavern with Druss. I think she's a little bit ... er ... drunk,' he concluded lamely.

Skilgannon nodded, then strolled away.

'He is very good, isn't he?' said Rabalyn.

'Yes, he is.'

'You look angry.'

'You mistake embarrassment for anger,' lied Diagoras. 'But at least you saw how important it is to retain balance.'

'Oh, I saw that,' said Rabalyn.

In the tavern Skilgannon found Druss sitting alone, and eating a double sized meal. Two huge slabs of meat pie had been placed on an oversized banquet plate, with a huge portion of roasted vegetables. Skilgannon sat down.

'You could feed an army on that,' he said.

'I was feeling a little peckish,' said Druss. 'Chopping logs always gives me an appetite.'

'The lad said Garianne was looking for me.'

'Aye, she was. But now she's gone.'

Skilgannon chuckled. 'Druss the Legend is embarrassed,' he said. 'Is that a blush I see?'

Druss glared at him. 'Some Datian officers have been asking questions about a number of dead men found in a stable in the Naashanite quarter,' he said after a moment. 'Best stay low here until we leave.'

'That makes sense,' agreed Skilgannon.

'You think they'll try again?'

'Yes. But probably not until we're on the road. It does not concern me unduly.'

'And why is that?' asked the axeman.

'I must assume Servaj used the best men he had in the first attack. They were really not very skilled. The Source alone knows what the second best will think to accomplish.'

'Beware of arrogance, laddie. I have seen great fighters brought down by an idiot with a bow. Once I saw a fine warrior felled by a stone hurled from a child's sling. Fate has a dark sense of humour sometimes.' The axeman fell silent, and set about tackling the enormous plate of food. After a while he glanced up. 'I saw your bout with Diagoras. Don't judge him too harshly. He's a good man – sound and brave and loyal.'

'I didn't judge him, Druss. He judged me. In all likelihood his judgement is accurate. If I was a warrior told about the deeds of the Damned I would loathe him too. You can't change the past, no matter how much you long to.'

'Aye, there's truth in that. We make mistakes. No point dwelling on them. As long as we learn from them. Garianne went off with a Vagrian officer. Don't judge her too harshly either. She needs what she needs.'

'I know. Have you learned any more about this Ironmask?'

'Nothing good,' said Druss. 'He's sharp, canny and brutal. His men were handpicked for their savagery. Not a nice bunch.'

'And you still mean to take them on alone?'

'Ultimately, laddie, we are all alone.'

'What is your plan?'

'Simplicity itself. I shall walk into the fortress, find Ironmask, and kill him.'

'Simple plans are usually the best,' agreed Skilgannon. 'Less to go wrong. Have you considered the hundred and seventy warriors who are said to man the fortress?'

'No. They'd best keep out of my way, though.'

Skilgannon laughed aloud. 'And you talk to me about arrogance?'

Druss chuckled. 'I might think of a better plan once I've seen the place.'

'That would be wise,' Skilgannon agreed.

'I'm not sure you're the man to be offering lectures on wisdom,' said Druss. 'As I recall you were a general, with a palace and a fortune. You gave it all up to become a pacifist priest – an occupation, I might add, you proved wholly unsuitable for. You are now a penniless warrior, being hunted by assassins. Have I missed anything out?'

'You could add that the person who wants me dead is the woman I love above all else in this world.'

'I take it back,' said Druss. 'Tell me more of your wisdom, laddie. I find it strangely appealing.'

Jianna had been ten years old when first she stumbled on the passageway that led beneath the royal palace. It had been an accidental discovery. She had been playing in her father's apartments while he had been away with the army putting down a rebellion. Her mother had sent servants looking for her, to scold her for some infraction, and Jianna had run into the huge and luxurious bedroom seeking a hiding place. She had sought to conceal herself behind a heavy silk curtain set against the north wall, but when she tugged on it she found that it would not move. A tiny section of it, at floor level, had become wedged in the walnut panelling of the wall behind. The ten-year-old princess found this perplexing. Gently she eased it out, and stepped behind the curtain. The two servants sent to fetch her to her mother soon gave up the search. Jianna heard them move away. Once alone she drew back the curtain and examined the panelling. It was ornately carved, and embellished with gold leaf. Above her head a golden

275

adornment had been set into the wood. It was a lion's head, the mouth open and snarling. On both sides of the head were golden candle holders. Jianna moved back into the room and hauled a chair to the panelling. Standing upon it she studied the lion's head. Suddenly the chair shifted. As she fell the princess grabbed the nearest candle holder. It twisted under her grip. Letting go, she fell to the floor. A cold draught of air flowed across her. The panelling had opened. Beyond was a shadowed chamber. Clambering to her feet she stepped inside. It was no more than five feet deep, ending in a barred iron door. Sliding back the bar, she pushed open the door. Beyond it was a dark tunnel. At ten the princess was too fearful to enter this frightening place. Barring the door once more she returned to the apartment, drew the panelling shut, and pushed the candle holder back into its place, relocking the entrance.

During the following year she thought about the secret passageway often, and chided herself for her childish fears. One hot afternoon, as her servants dozed in the afternoon sunshine, she crept away, back to the royal apartment. Taller now, she could – standing on tiptoe – reach the candle holder and twist it. The panel eased open. Taking a lighted lantern she stepped into the chamber beyond, examining the wall on the other side of the lion ornament. Here there was a simple lever. Pushing shut the panelling she tugged on the lever. A click sounded. The panelling was now firmly shut.

Moving to the iron door, she opened it and stepped out into the passageway. It was cool here, and a flow of air made the lantern flame flicker. Feeling her way carefully ahead she came to a set of steps leading down. The walls glistened with damp, and a rat scurried across her foot. She almost dropped the lantern.

Jianna felt her heart beat faster as fears began to swamp her mind. What if hundreds of rats attacked her? No-one would hear her screams, and, worse yet, her body would never be found. She faltered, and considered going back. But she did not. Instead she recalled the instruction of the swordmaster Malanek: 'Fear is like a guard dog. It warns you when danger threatens. But if you run from all your fears the guard dog becomes a savage wolf, and will pursue you, snapping at your heels. Fear, if unopposed by courage, eats away at the heart. Once you run you will never stop.'

The tunnel seemed to go on for ever. Jianna began to worry that her lantern would splutter out, leaving her in darkness. Eventually though she came to another barred door. The bar had been recently greased, and slid open easily. Opening the door just an inch she saw beyond it an iron ladder set into a rock wall. Chequered light patterned the rocks. Pulling the door fully open, she looked up. A metal grille blocked the shaft some twenty feet above. The shaft continued down beyond the doorway, and she could not see the bottom, though she could hear running water. Leaving the lantern burning in the doorway Jianna climbed the ladder. The grille at the top was too heavy for her to move, but glancing through it she could see the tops of trees, and hear the fountains of the royal park.

The tunnel, she now knew, was an escape route from the palace.

Retracing her steps Jianna made the long journey back to the apartments, re-barring the doors as she went. Her curiosity satisfied, she did not travel that way again until the second year of her triumphant return to the capital. Her face stripped of the paint of nobility, her clothes ordinary, she sometimes escaped to walk the sunlit streets, or shop in the markets alongside ordinary citizens. She would eat in taverns, and listen to the conversations. Had either Askelus or Malanek known of these trips they would have become apoplectic with rage and frustration. Yet it was on adventures like this that Jianna learned what the populace truly thought of her government of their lives. It did not matter to her that she was now known among the nobility as the Witch Queen. To the common people she was a figure of awe, respected and feared. Not loved, though, as Malanek believed. In taverns and eating houses people spoke of her courage, her shrewdness, her battle skills. There was considerably more debate about her ruthlessness.

Crimes were now punished severely; thieves had three fingers of their left hand cut away for a first offence. A second offence led to death by beheading. Killers were taken back to the scenes of their crimes and executed there. Embezzlers and fraudsters were stripped of all assets. In the first year of her reign more than eight hundred people had been put to death in the capital alone. Askelus was not in favour of such extreme practices, even though the numbers of reported crimes plummeted. Jianna listened to his arguments about the need for a compassionate society, about understanding the complexities of the causes of crime. Jianna had been dismissive of his reasoning.

'A man breaks into a house, and kills the owner to steal a few valuables. How many people are affected? The owner may be dead, but he might have a wife and children. He will certainly have relatives, neighbours and friends. His relatives have neighbours and friends. Perhaps a hundred people in all. Like a rock hitting the surface of a still lake the ripples of this crime spread out. People become worried about their own homes and their own lives. When then the murderer is dragged back to the house and killed there people relax. Justice has been done.'

'And what if the wrong man has been killed for the crime?'

'It makes no difference, Askelus. A crime has been punished. A hundred people are satisfied that society will avenge crime.'

'Does the man unjustly killed not have family and friends and neighbours, Majesty?'

'And that is the curse of intelligence, Askelus. Intelligent people always seek to see the other side of the problem. They look for cause and effect, balance and harmony. They focus on the poor man who steals a loaf of bread to feed his family. Oh woe, they cry, that we live in a society where a man can be reduced to such a state. Let us therefore give free food to all, so that no-one will ever steal bread again.'

'I do not see a problem with that, Majesty. There is food enough.'

'There is now, Askelus. But travel a little further down this road and what do you see? Men and women who no longer have to work for food. They breed and they multiply, producing more and more people who do not have to work for food. Where do they then live, these people who do not work? Ah, then we give them free houses perhaps, and horses so that they may travel. What of clothes to wear? How can they afford them, these people who do not work? And who pays for this road to madness, Askelus?'

He had not been convinced and had spoken of building more schools, and the training of the poor to give them new skills. This idea *did* have appeal. Jianna's new empire would need more skilled men and women. So she had allocated funds from the treasury for the creation of more schools and teachers, and even the building of a university. Askelus had been delighted.

As time passed Jianna continued to use the secret passageway, travelling more and more through the city. Shopkeepers and tavern owners came to know her, and she built a new identity. She was Sashan, the wife of a travelling merchant. She even bought a cheap silver wedding band, which she wore on her right wrist. This kept most of the single men from bothering her as she moved through the city. The ones untroubled by the band she sent on their way with harsh words and a flash of her eyes.

An area a mile south of the palace became a favourite haunt for her. There was a square here, and a marketplace. Women would often gather round the well at the centre of the square. There were benches and seats and the women would chat to one another about life and love and the raising of children. It was rare that politics entered the discussion. Even so Jianna found sitting among them hugely enjoyable.

It was there that she met Samias, the wife of a local builder. Often she would have three young children with her, and would watch them run around the square, peeping at items on the stalls. They would squabble good-naturedly, or play. Samias would open her bag and remove parcels of food, and the children would sit by her feet, munching on pies, or cake, or fruit. Samias was a tall woman, heavy around the hips. She constantly smiled as she watched her children. Only on the days when she was alone did her smile fade, and then Jianna saw the sadness in her eyes.

They spoke often. Mostly Jianna listened. Samias was contentedly married. Her husband was 'a good man, sound and caring' and her children were a constant delight. 'Life is good, so I mustn't complain,' she said one day.

'Why do you talk of complaining?'

Samias seemed surprised. 'Did I? Oh, it's just a phrase.'

'You love your husband?'

'Of course. What a silly question. Wonderful man. Very good with the children. What about your man? Is he kind?'

'He's pleasant enough,' said Jianna, suddenly unwilling to create more lies.

'That's good. I expect you miss him when he's away. Travelling merchant, isn't he?'

'Yes. I don't love him, though.'

'Oh, you shouldn't say that. Best to try to love him. Makes life more bearable if you can convince yourself.'

'The man I truly loved went away,' Jianna found herself saying. 'I wanted him more than anyone else I have ever met. He is in my mind constantly.'

'Ah, we all have someone like that,' said Samias. 'What was he like?'

'Handsome, with eyes of sapphire blue.'

'Why did he go away?'

'I wouldn't marry him. I had other plans. We travelled together once, through a forest. Looking back I think it was the happiest time of my life. I can remember every day.' Jianna laughed. 'We were hungry and we came across a rabbit with its leg caught in a trapper's noose. He went to it and knelt beside it. The little thing was trembling, so he stroked it. Then he carefully cut the noose. I looked at him and said: "Well, are you going to kill it and cook it?" He picked the rabbit up and stroked it again. "It has such beautiful eyes," he said, then put the rabbit down and walked away from it.'

'Soft-hearted then? Some men are.'

'In some ways he was. In others he was ruthless. We were attacked in the woods.' Jianna fell silent. 'Ah well, long ago now,' she said at last, realizing she was coming too close to the truth.

'Who attacked you?'

'Robbers,' said Jianna swiftly.

'How awful!' said Samias. 'What happened? Did your lover fight them off?'

'Yes, he fought. He was a fine fighter. I must go now. My . . . husband will be waiting for me.' Jianna rose from her seat.

'Try not to dwell upon the past, dear,' said Samias. 'We can't change it, you know. We can only live with what we have now. Once I loved a man with all my heart. He was the sun and moon of all my desires. He was a soldier of the King. You know, the old King, Bokram. He was sent out into the forest of Delian after a murderer. We were due to be wed within the month. He was killed there. And that was it for me. My life all but ended.'

'I am so sorry,' said Jianna, surprised that she meant it.

'A long time ago now, Sashan. And my husband is a good man. Oh, yes. Very kind.'

'Did they catch the murderer?'

'No. He was an awful man. He murdered the people who raised him after his father died. Cut them up, he did. Tortured them. Can you believe that? Then he fled the city with a young whore. My Jeranon and a group of soldiers almost caught them. That's what I was told. There was a fight and Jeranon was killed. Some others too. And the evil pair escaped. They were never found.'

Jianna felt a sudden chill touch her heart. 'Did he have a name, this murderer?'

'Aye. His name was Skilgannon. I never heard the whore's name.' Samias shrugged. 'The Source will punish them, though. If there is any justice.'

'Perhaps the Source already has,' said Jianna.

As Jianna made her way back to the royal park she thought of how Askelus would have enjoyed listening to her conversation with Samias. Never before had Jianna considered the lives of those soldiers who had almost trapped her in the forest of Delian. They had just been men with swords, ordered to capture her. She tried to remember their faces, but only one came to mind, a bearded man with florid features and savage eyes. He had wanted to rape her, but was overruled by the others.

Skilgannon and she had parted an hour earlier, after harsh words. It was difficult now to recall exactly what the argument had been about. Once they left the city, and were travelling together, they seemed to grate on each other. Looking back with the full wisdom of her twenty-five years Jianna could see now that the tension was sexual. She had longed to be intimate with the young warrior. She smiled. Abstinence had never been agreeable to her. It was much the same for Skilgannon. So they bickered and argued. Finally, two days after escaping the city, they had agreed to separate, Jianna striking out north towards a tribal settlement where she believed she would be safe.

An hour later she had been surrounded, and chased down by soldiers. Fleet of foot, she had almost escaped them. She had been scrambling up a steep slope when she grabbed hold of a jutting tree root for purchase. The root snapped off, and she tumbled back down the muddy slope. They grabbed her then.

'Got to be her,' said the soldier with the florid face. 'Look at her.' Grabbing her by the neck he dragged her head down, and ran his hand over her shorn hair. 'See, there's still traces of the blond dye.'

'What's your name, girl?' asked another man. Jianna couldn't remember his face now, except that he was thin. She didn't answer him.

There were five soldiers in the group and they gathered round her. 'What did she do?' someone asked.

'Who cares?' answered the florid man. 'Boranius said she was important. That's all that matters. Beautiful legs and arse, hasn't she?' he continued, running a calloused hand over her thighs. 'Reckon we ought to sample this one.'

'No, we don't,' said someone else. Jianna wondered now if this was the young man Samias had spoken of. 'We just take her back.'

'I am the Princess Jianna,' she said. 'The tyrant wants me dead. He has already killed my mother and father. Take me north and I shall see you rewarded.'

'Oh, yes, you look like a princess, right enough,' said Florid Face. 'Stupid bitch! You need a better story than that.'

'It is the truth. Why do you think you were sent out? What whore would be worth that trouble? I'll wager you are not the only troops out here.'

'Suppose she's right?' said someone else.

'What if she is?' demanded Florid Face. 'Nothing to do with us. There's a new king now. New kings always kill their rivals. And how would she reward us, eh? There's nowhere safe for her. The only reward she can offer is between her legs. And we can have that now. I never drilled a princess before. Think it's any different?'

'You'll never know,' came the voice of Skilgannon. Jianna still remembered the leap in her heart. It was not because she thought she was rescued. In that instant she believed them both to be ruined. It was merely the sound of his voice, and the knowledge he had come back for her.

The soldiers turned to see the young man. He was standing some ten feet from them. In his right hand he held a short, stabbing

282

sword, in his left a wickedly sharp hunting knife. Sunlight gleamed upon the blades.

'Would you look at that?' said Florid Face contemptuously. 'Be careful with those blades, boy. You might cut yourself.'

'Let her go or die,' said Skilgannon calmly. 'There are no other choices.'

'Will someone take those swords away from him?' said Florid Face. 'He is beginning to annoy me.'

Two men drew their sabres and advanced on Skilgannon. He stood very still for a moment, and when he moved the effect was startling. One man fell back, his throat gouting blood. The second cried out as the hunting knife plunged into his chest, spearing his heart. Before the other soldiers could react he leapt forward, the shortsword cleaving into the belly of another soldier, even as the man struggled to draw his sabre. Jianna's hand reached out, pulling a knife from a scabbard at Florid Face's side. He was too surprised at the sudden violence to notice. He was even more surprised when the blade lanced into his chest just below the sternum. It went deep. He gave a groan and, releasing Jianna, staggered back. The fifth soldier ran for his life. Florid Face clumsily dragged his sabre from its scabbard, and tried to attack Skilgannon. But his legs buckled and he fell to his knees, blood pumping from his chest. Weakly he lashed out with his sabre, but Skilgannon stepped back from the swing.

'Time to go,' he told Jianna. She looked into his face. His sapphire eyes were cold, like ice crystals. She shivered.

'I agree,' she told him.

The story of the rescue in the forest grew in the years that followed. Jianna had heard many versions. In some she had been dressed in armour and had fought and killed three men herself. In others the Damned had defeated six swordmasters. The reality was that the action had been short, bloody and brutal. Jianna had stayed free, and Samias had lost the love of her life.

This was what Askelus had meant when he spoke of a compassionate society. The concentration on individual loss and grief, rather than the effect of an action on society as a whole.

Back at the park Jianna sat on a bench close to the undergrowth which hid the entrance to the secret passageway. She was forced to wait for some time as people were constantly moving along the pathways, or sitting by the fountains. Finally she stood and eased her way back into the undergrowth, squatting down and lifting the grille. The lantern was still burning at the lower doorway. Holding it high she locked the door and moved back along the passageway. She had left instructions that she was not to be disturbed until two hours after noon, but the time was close.

Almost too close.

In the hidden chamber behind the panelling she stripped off her ordinary clothes, then entered the apartment, strolling naked through to her bedroom. Just then two servant girls entered, bowed and told her that Malanek was waiting outside. She ordered them to prepare her bath, then swung a pale blue satin robe round her shoulders.

One of the servants ushered Malanek into the main room. He looked tired, his face drawn. 'I am glad you got some extra rest, Majesty,' he said.

'You should take your own advice, Malanek. You look exhausted.'

He gave a weary smile. 'I keep forgetting I am no longer a youngster.' He sighed. 'There is news from Mellicane, Majesty. Did you have a change of heart about Skilgannon?'

'No. Why would I?'

'There was an assassination attempt upon him. Led by a Naashanite named Servaj Das.'

'It was not by my order, Malanek. Skilgannon is free to go where he wishes.'

Malanek nodded. 'That pleases me, Majesty. But it leaves me wondering who else would want Skilgannon dead.'

She looked at him closely. 'I do not need to lie to you, my friend. When I took your advice to let him go I did so freely. Had I wanted him killed I would have told you.'

'I know that, Jianna,' he said, forgetting himself for a moment. 'Do you mind if I sit?'

Gesturing him to a couch she sat beside him. 'What is worrying you?'

'I have been studying the reports on Mellicane. The man Ironmask made a great many contacts within the Naashanite community. Many of his men are also former soldiers of ours. Most were rebels, though not all. According to our sources in Mellicane Servaj Das worked for him. We have little information on Ironmask, save that he is not from Tantria. His accent showed that he was not Ventrian. It seems he is not known either in Datia or Dospilis. He could be from across the water: Drenan, Gothir, Vagria. But what if he is a Naashanite?'

Jianna shrugged. 'Why should I care?'

'He is a charismatic leader of men. We know this. He has gathered warriors to him, many of whom fought against you. Where did such a man come from? And there is something else. Our sources among the Datian officers say that when they entered the palace he used they found chambers below with blood-spattered walls. They also found severed fingers and hands.'

The Queen sat very still. 'The man whose name we do not speak was killed in battle. Skilgannon slashed away half of his face, and then stabbed him through the heart. I have seen the reports of this Ironmask. The wearing of the mask is merely a conceit. His face is not mutilated, merely discoloured.'

'His body was never found. Supposing he was healed, Majesty? There are reports of a temple in Pelucid, and a priestess who can work miracles.'

'These are not reports. They are rumours. Myths. Like flying lizards, and winged horses.'

'The man whose name we do not speak almost defeated us. If he still lives he is a threat to everything you are trying to build. It may even be that the recent attempts on your life can be traced back to him.'

'Now you are making me uneasy!' she snapped. 'I do not believe the dead can return to haunt me.'

'No, Majesty. Nor would I – had I been able to find his body. But if you did not instruct Servaj Das to murder Skilgannon, and no-one in our embassy did so, then Ironmask is the only other link. That being the case the question is: why would Ironmask seek the death of Skilgannon, a man he does not know, and who is no threat to him?'

'Where is Skilgannon now?'

'Still in Mellicane, but he is preparing to journey north. I have a report from contacts in the Drenai embassy that he intends to travel with the warrior Druss. They are going to Pelucid. Druss intends to kill Ironmask. Why Skilgannon travels with him is a mystery. The Datians are also sending a force to Pelucid. They want to capture Ironmask themselves. Apparently several of his victims were prominent Datian nobles.'

'Then I suspect the mystery will be resolved before long,' said Jianna.

'Until it is, Majesty, we need to be careful for your safety. No unnecessary risks. If the man we do not name is still alive then the danger to you is very real.'

'I do not take *unnecessary* risks, Malanek. And a ruler is always in danger.'

CHAPTER FIFTEEN

DIAGORAS HAD PLOTTED THE ROUTE WITH CARE, AND CARRIED COPIES of maps that showed the mountains, rivers and passes north of Mellicane. By the third day of travel he had begun to enjoy himself. In his saddlebag were copious notes on the positions of villages where they could obtain supplies, the names of headmen to be offered gifts, and details of areas of likely danger. These mostly lay in the mountainous regions close to Pelucid where bands of robbers were known to have hideouts. Diagoras had gathered all known information on the man Shakusan Ironmask. This did not amount to much, though one piece of news interested Skilgannon. Three years before, when Ironmask had first appeared in Mellicane, he had fought a duel. According to the report he used curved swords, which were contained in a single scabbard. The report also said he was a man of prodigious strength, noting that one blow cut through his opponent's breastplate and the chain mail beneath. A second cut had beheaded the victim.

The first day of travel had been taken at leisure. The horses Skilgannon had acquired had indeed been undernourished and, though of good stock, were weak. They needed resting often. In the few days they had been kept at the Drenai compound Diagoras had ordered them grain-fed and gently exercised, but they were still far from fit. By the third day of travel they were already growing stronger.

The twins, Jared and Nian, had met them on the road on the morning of the second day. Both were riding shaggy hill ponies, tough beasts and surly. They would snap at the taller cavalry horses if any rider was foolish enough to come close to them. The brothers took to riding close to the two-wheeled supply wagon, driven by Druss.

As he rode Diagoras would often glance at Garianne. She rode a grey mare, and kept herself a little apart from the company, even at night when they camped. She would sit alone, and occasionally be seen talking to herself. The youth Rabalyn often rode alongside Diagoras, asking constant questions. His joy at being invited on the journey was untainted by any fear of the consequences. He loved to ride, and in the evenings would spend an hour tending to his horse, brushing its back, or stroking its neck. Rabalyn was a natural rider, and would one day be a fine swordsman, Diagoras mused. He had good balance and fast hands. He was also a quick learner.

By the fourth day the land began to rise as they neared the foothills of a western range of peaks. These were the iron-rich Blood Mountains. The landscape was rugged and beautiful, with shimmering, ever changing colours. The morning sunlight glistened upon the red mountains, causing them to glow like old gold. Towards noon dark shadows appeared on the slopes, jagged and sharp. By dusk, with the sun setting behind them, the mountains lost their richness, becoming grey and forbidding.

As they camped that night Druss rose from the campfire and walked back to the wagon, stretching himself out on the ground and falling asleep. Diagoras sat with Skilgannon and the others. 'There is a tribal chieftain who controls the passes here,' he said. 'His name is Khalid. Apparently he is part Nadir, and has around fifty fighting men. My understanding is that the charge he levies is a small one. However, that was when the King and his soldiers were an ever present threat to his authority. It is impossible to say how he will react now.'

'How soon before we reach the pass?' asked Skilgannon.

'By noon tomorrow, I would think,' Diagoras told him.

'I will ride ahead and negotiate with him,' said Skilgannon.

'Be careful,' Diagoras warned him, 'the people here are very poor, but very proud.'

'Good advice,' said Skilgannon. 'I thank you. What else is known of Khalid?'

Diagoras looked back to his notes. 'Very little. He is around sixty years of age, and has no sons still living. He has outlived them all. He pays no taxes. Apparently, some twenty years ago, he and his men joined with the King's forces and defeated an invading force from Sherak in the north. For that he was awarded these lands, free of tribute. It was no more than a gesture, since these mountains would provide little in the way of tax revenue.'

'What is the toll?'

'Two copper coins a head, and one copper for all pack animals or horses.'

They talked on for a while. The twins said little, and Garianne nothing at all. Eventually Diagoras rose from the campfire and strolled to the top of a hill where he sat staring out over the mountains. Rabalyn joined him there. 'Would you like to fence for a while?' the lad asked.

'No, it is too dark. There would be a risk of accidental injury. Tomorrow morning, before we set off, we'll practise a little.'

'What was it like at the battle of Skeln?'

'Brutal, Rabalyn. I do not wish to speak of it. Many of my friends died there.'

'Were you honoured when you got home?'

'Yes, we were honoured. We were the heroes of the hour. It is a phrase that has real meaning, Rabalyn. For a few days we were the toast of the capital. Then life returned to normal and people found other things to amuse them. Those soldiers who survived Skeln, but were crippled, were promised twenty gold raq each, and a handsome pension for life. They never received the gold. Now they struggle to survive on six copper coins a month. Some are even beggars now. Druss helped many of them. He turned over lands he owns to house some of them, and the profits from his farms go to feed veterans.'

'Is he rich then? He doesn't look rich.'

Diagoras laughed. 'His wife Rowena was a shrewd woman.

When Druss returned from his wars he was usually laden with gifts from grateful princes. She used the gold he won to acquire property, and to invest in merchant enterprises. If he chose, our friend Druss could build a palace and live in luxury.'

'Why doesn't he?'

'I can't answer that, lad. Save to say that he has no use for wealth. He is lonely, though. *That* I can see.'

'I like him,' said Rabalyn. 'He gave me his code. I shall live by it. I gave my promise.'

'I know that code. It is a good one. It is dangerous, though, Rabalyn. A man like Druss can live by it, because he's like a tempest, raw, fierce and unstoppable. We mortals, though, may need to be more circumspect. Holding too firmly to Druss's code would kill us.'

Khalid Khan sat in the shade of an overhanging rock and watched the rider upon the road below. The sun was high and hot, the sky cloudless and blue. Yet it was not a good day. This morning Khalid had watched two eagles nesting on the high peaks. It was a long time since eagles had been seen in the Blood Mountains. Normally this would have been a good omen. Not today. Today he knew they were just birds, and they meant nothing.

Khalid was worried.

There had been few merchants on the roads since the start of the stupid war, and Khalid's people had been forced to tighten their belts against hunger. This was not good, and left them morose and complaining. As the leader Khalid would survive only as long as they believed in his power to bring them coin. Last week one Vishinas had led a raid on a northern village, capturing five scrawny cattle and a few sheep. It was pitiful. But Khalid's people, hungry and discontented, had hailed it as a victory, and Vishinas was now more popular among the young warriors. Khalid sighed and scratched his thin black beard. Of late the old wound in his right shoulder had been plaguing him. If Vishinas was to challenge his authority there was no way he could defeat him, sword to sword. Happily Vishinas did not know of the weakness. Khalid's reputation had been built on his prowess with the blade, and the youngster remained wary of him. Not for much longer, thought Khalid bitterly.

This threat alone, though worrying, would have caused him no sleepless nights. But there was something in the air that did not taste right. Khalid's mother had been gifted with the Sight. She was a fine seer. Khalid had not fully inherited that gift, but his instincts were sharper than those of most men. For the last two nights he had woken sweat-drenched and frightened. Not given to dreaming, he had experienced nightmares which left him trembling. He had seen beasts that walked like men, huge and powerful, creeping through the darkness of the mountainside. Disoriented, he had rolled from his blankets, grabbed his sword and run from his tent, standing in the moonlight, his breathing harsh and ragged. Outside everything was silent. There was no threat. No demons.

Just a dream then? Khalid doubted it. Something was coming. Something dreadful.

Pushing aside such dark thoughts, he glanced across to where Vishinas was squatting on a rock. The warrior was also gazing keenly at the oncoming rider.

The man rode well, studying the trail and the rock faces on either side. Vishinas signalled to Khalid, then slipped his bow from his shoulder. Pulling an arrow from his quiver, he cast a questioning look at his chieftain, who shook his head. Vishinas looked disappointed as he returned the arrow to the quiver. Rising from his hiding place, Khalid moved out into the open, and walked down the slope to meet the advancing rider. Vishinas ran out alongside him, and seven other tribesmen emerged from their hiding places.

The rider approached them, and dismounted. Leaving the reins trailing he walked forward and offered a bow to Khalid.

'I am Skilgannon. My friends and I seek to pass through the territory of the renowned Khalid Khan. Will you take me to him?'

'You are not Tantrian,' said Khalid. 'Nor, I think, from Datia. Your accent is from the south.'

'I am Naashanite.'

'How is it then that you have heard of the *renowned* Khalid Khan?'

'I travel with a Drenai officer who spoke of him with high praise. He said it was fitting to offer tribute to the Khan when crossing his lands.'

'A wise man, your friend. I am Khalid Khan.'

The man bowed again. As he did so Khalid saw the ivory hilts of his swords. 'Two blades in a single scabbard,' said Khalid. 'Most unusual. How many men are in your party?'

'Five men and a woman.'

'These are hard times, Skilgannon. War and death are everywhere. Are you prepared for war and death?'

The warrior smiled, and his cold blue eyes glittered in the sunlight. 'As prepared as any man can be, Khalid Khan. What tribute do you deem fair for crossing your land?'

'Everything you have,' said Vishinas, stepping forward. Several young men moved with him. Khalid fought to remain calm. He had not expected a challenge to his authority so soon.

Skilgannon turned to Vishinas. 'I was speaking to the wolf, boy. When I want to hear the yapping of a puppy I will signal you forward.' The words were softly spoken. Vishinas reddened, then reached for his sword. 'If that blade clears the scabbard,' continued the man, 'you will die here.' He stepped in close to Vishinas. 'Look into my eyes and tell me if you think that is not true.' Vishinas backed away a step, but Skilgannon followed him. Trying to create enough distance to draw his sword Vishinas stumbled against a jutting rock and fell. With a cry of rage and humiliation he surged to his feet and lunged. Curiously the lunge missed and he sprawled to the stones once more, his head thumping against a rock as he fell. Half dazed, he struggled to rise, then slumped back. Skilgannon strolled back to Khalid. 'My apologies, lord,' he said. 'We were speaking of the tribute.'

'Indeed so,' said Khalid Khan. 'You must forgive the *boy*. He is callow and inexperienced. It seems to me that I have heard the name Skilgannon before.'

'That is possible, lord.'

'I seem to recall a warlord by that name. The Destroyer of Armies. The victor of five great battles. There are many stories of the warrior Skilgannon. Not all of them good.'

'The good ones are exaggerated,' said Skilgannon softly.

'And the bad also?'

'Sadly no.'

Khalid looked at the young man for a moment. 'Guilt is a burden like no other. It drags upon the soul. I know this. You may pass through my lands, Skilgannon. The tribute is whatever you choose.'

Skilgannon opened the pouch at his side and drew out three gold coins, which he dropped into Khalid Khan's outstretched hand.

Khalid showed no emotion at receiving such a prodigious sum, but he left his hand open so that the men around him could see the bright glint of the yellow metal.

Just then the rest of the party came into sight. One of the tribesmen yelled, then the others surged forward past the dazed figure of Vishinas. Khalid narrowed his eyes against the sunlight, then turned to Skilgannon. 'Why did you not say you travelled with the Silver Slayer?' he asked. He swallowed hard, and offered the gold coins back to Skilgannon. 'There can be no toll for Druss the Legend.'

'It would honour me if you accepted the tribute,' said Skilgannon.

Khalid's spirits soared. He had dreaded the man's consenting to his refusal. 'Ah, well,' he said, 'if it is a matter of politeness then I do accept. But you must come to my village. We will have a feast.'

The chieftain moved away from Skilgannon and walked towards the wagon. Druss looked down at him and grinned. 'Good to see you, Khalid. How is it that a rascal like you is still alive?'

'I am beloved by the gods, Druss. That is why they have blessed me with these verdant pastures and great wealth. Ah, it does my heart good to see you. Where is the Poet?'

'He died.'

'Ah, that is sad. There will be sorrow among the older women when they hear of it. Too many friends have taken the swan's path these last few years. It almost makes me feel old.' Khalid climbed onto the wagon. 'Tonight we will feast, my friend. We will talk and drink. Then we will bore everyone with tales of our greatness.'

For Rabalyn the evening brought a curious mix of emotions. He had been spellbound by the red-gold mountains, and the blazing sunsets in this high country. Everything here was different from what he had experienced at home. The land was harsh, the heat unforgiving. And yet he felt his heart soar as he gazed over the magnificent landscape. The nomads who followed Khalid Khan were also interesting; whip lean and hard, their skin dark, their gaze intense. At any other time Rabalyn would have thought them frightening, but such was their joy at seeing Druss they appeared almost carefree.

The camp of Khalid Khan had been a disappointment to Rabalyn. He had assumed there would be tents of silk, like in the stories. In fact they were a mixture of old hides, linens, and coarse cloth, badly patched and threadbare. The entire settlement sprawled untidily across the mountainside in a shambolic manner. The place reeked of poverty. Naked children ran through the settlement, followed by scrawny dogs, yapping and barking. There was little vegetation to be seen, and no trees. Rabalyn saw a line of women moving down the mountainside, bearing water sacks. He guessed there must be a hidden well close by.

The tent of Khalid Khan, though bigger than all the others, was just as ramshackle. Patches covered the outer skin, and Rabalyn saw a tear just below the first of the three tall poles that supported it.

He glanced around the camp. There were some thirty women and around twenty children in view. They gathered round the company as Khalid led them into the settlement. A few old men emerged from their tents and watched. Some called out to Druss, who waved back. Younger men appeared then, and these did not watch Druss. They were staring with undisguised lust at the golden-haired Garianne, who ignored them. Rabalyn climbed down from the wagon. His shortsword clattered against the wood of the driving platform and he half stumbled. The twins, Jared and Nian, moved alongside him. Nian was smiling at the children close by. One of them approached him cautiously. Nian dropped to one knee and offered his hand. The youngster scampered away. Diagoras dismounted. Khalid Khan shouted an order and several women moved forward to take care of the mounts.

Skilgannon, Druss and Diagoras followed Khalid Khan into his tent. Garianne wandered up the mountainside, followed by the twins. Rabalyn set off after them.

'Where are we going?' he asked Jared. It was Nian who answered.

'We're going to swim in the secret lake, aren't we, Jared?'

Jared nodded. His brother reached out, taking hold of the blue sash hanging from Jared's belt. Nian sighed. 'We like to swim,' he said happily.

Rabalyn had often noticed Nian clinging to the sash, but had not mentioned it for fear of being rude. It seemed odd that the brothers were never more than a few feet from one another. Once, when they were riding, Rabalyn had seen Nian steer his mount alongside Jared's, then reach out and grab the sash. The movement had spooked Jared's horse, causing it to rear and break into a run. Nian had screamed and kicked his horse into a gallop, desperate to catch Jared. Once Jared had control of his horse he halted him and leapt from the saddle. Nian almost fell from his mount and rushed over to his brother, throwing his arms round him and sobbing. It was a disconcerting sight. After that Jared had cut a length of rope so that when they rode he would hold one end and Nian the other.

The brothers scrambled up the rock face, following Garianne. They came to a wide ledge, and a high fissure in the red rock. Garianne entered it, cutting down a steep slope within. Light filtered down from high above them, and glittered on the surface of a deep cave pool. Nian shouted, his voice echoing inside the mountain. Ahead of them Garianne was stripping off her clothing and folding it neatly, laying her shirt, trews and boots on a ledge. Placing the crossbow and quiver atop the garments, she turned and dived into the gleaming water.

Nian and Jared also undressed, then, hand in hand, they jumped into the pool. Rabalyn sat on the rock watching the trio swim. He wanted to join them, but was not comfortable with the thought of swimming naked. Watching Garianne disrobe had caused an embarrassing swelling in his loins, and he had no wish to display it. Instead he sat and surreptitiously watched the woman swim, yearning for the moment she would roll in the water and expose her breasts. Nian shouted for him to join them. 'In a little while,' he answered. He saw Garianne staring at him, and blushed furiously.

Then Diagoras arrived. He stood close to Rabalyn and began to strip off his clothing. 'Can you not swim?' he asked.

'Yes, I can. I will in a moment.'

Diagoras dived cleanly into the water, came to the surface and smoothly swam to the far side of the pool. Ducking beneath the surface he spun, kicked out with his feet and returned to where Rabalyn sat. He grinned at the lad. 'The water is very cold,' he said. 'Trust me. It will cool your ardour.' Rabalyn blushed again. Swiftly he clambered out of his clothes and jumped into the hidden lake. The burns he had suffered during the blaze at his aunt's house had mostly healed, save for a puckered section on his right thigh. The skin there would often split, weeping pus and blood. The cold water felt good upon it. Rabalyn swam to the centre of the small lake, then looked up. Two hundred feet above him, through a sickle-shaped opening in the rock face, he could see open sky. It was the oddest sensation. Like a bright blue crescent moon shining above him.

To his left Garianne was climbing from the water. Rabalyn found himself gazing at the curve of her hips. Despite Diagoras's assurances the cold water proved no match for his arousal. Swinging away he swam back to where his clothes lay. Diagoras was sitting on a ledge nearby. 'Will Druss and Skilgannon be coming?' asked Rabalyn, without leaving the water.

'I expect so, once they have finished questioning Khalid Khan. It seems Ironmask passed through here some ten days ago. According to Khalid Khan there were around sixty men with him. And more at the fortress.' Diagoras frowned, then reached across to his clothes, pulling a bone-handled razor from his belt pouch. Opening it, he began to scrape at the stubble around his trident beard.

'What will Druss do?' asked Rabalyn.

Diagoras dipped his razor into the water. 'He'll go to the fortress. There was a woman and a child travelling with Ironmask. The child is Elanin, the daughter of Earl Orastes.'

'Druss's friend.'

'Yes. The matter is complicated. The woman with the child is Elanin's mother. She is now Ironmask's lover. Druss intends to kill Ironmask to avenge Orastes. He is concerned that the mother will not allow her daughter to be returned to Drenan.'

'Can't he take her anyway?'

Diagoras laughed. 'We're talking about Druss the Legend, lad. Snatch a child from its mother? Not in a hundred years. Anyway, there's the question of a hundred and fifty warriors to consider before we reach that problem. Then there's the Nadir shaman who travels with Ironmask. The man knows magic and may summon demons, for all I know. Then there's Ironmask himself. He carries two swords, like Skilgannon, and is said to be a master. No, I shan't concern myself for a little while over the child's destiny.'

'Will you go into the fortress with Druss?'

'Aye, I will. The man is my friend.'

'I will go too,' said Rabalyn.

'We'll see, lad. I appreciate your courage, but your skills are lacking at present.'

Garianne, dressed now, her crossbow in her hand, walked past them without a word.

More comfortable, Rabalyn eased himself from the water and sat next to Diagoras. 'She is very beautiful, isn't she?' he said.

'She is that. And then some,' agreed Diagoras. The twins had emerged on the far side of the lake and were talking quietly. Rabalyn gazed across at them. Nian rose and Rabalyn saw a long and jagged scar down his right side, the skin around it pinched and puckered. Jared stood. He too had the same awful scar, but on his left side.

Druss and Skilgannon arrived. The axeman sat with Diagoras and Rabalyn, while Skilgannon stripped and dived into the lake. Druss removed his boots and dangled his feet in the water. Rabalyn glanced back at the twins on the other ledge. Nian was asleep, Jared sitting up, lost in thought.

'Have you seen their scars?' Rabalyn asked Druss.

The axeman nodded. 'Are you looking forward to the feast?' he asked, ignoring the question.

'I don't think it will be much of a feast,' said Rabalyn. 'They don't seem to have a lot.'

'True. It's been a bad few years for Khalid. I've given them some of our supplies. Whatever they prepare, be suitably grateful. But don't eat much. Whatever we leave will be shared around the camp later.'

Diagoras chuckled. 'Are you suggesting the boy lie, Druss?' he asked.

Druss scratched at his black and silver beard, then grinned.

'You're like a dog with an old bone,' he said. 'Do you never let up?'

'No,' replied Diagoras cheerfully. 'Not ever. And I too have been wondering about the scars the brothers carry. They are almost identical.'

'Then ask them,' said Druss.

'Is it some dark secret?' pressed Diagoras.

Druss shook his head, then stripped off his jerkin, boots and leggings. Without another word he leapt into the water, making a mighty splash. Diagoras leaned towards Rabalyn. 'Swim over and ask them?' he said.

Rabalyn shook his head. 'I think that would be rude.'

'You're right,' said Diagoras. 'Damn, but I shall lie awake tonight wondering about it.'

Dry now, Rabalyn dressed and climbed from the cave. The sun was setting, the temperature becoming more bearable. He wandered through the camp and sat in the shade of an overhanging rock, staring out over the red land. As darkness began to fall he rose to his feet. As he did so he saw something move across the crest of a distant hill. As he tried to focus it vanished behind a towering rock. Then another figure flitted across the hilltop. The movement was so fast Rabalyn had no chance to identify the creature. It could have been a running man, or even a deer. For a while he stood still, seeking out movement. Whatever it had been it was large. Rabalyn wondered if bears travelled in these high, dry lands.

Then a horn sounded. Glancing down into the settlement he saw people gathering round the large patchwork tent of Khalid Khan.

Hungry now, Rabalyn pushed the thoughts of the figures on the hillside from his mind, and loped down towards the chieftain's tent.

The feast was a poor affair. Two scrawny cattle roasted on a firepit, some salt bread, one keg of thin ale, and some flat baked sweet cake that, as Rabalyn discovered, seemed to have been flavoured with more rock dust than sugar. Khalid Khan was embarrassed, and apologized to Druss, who was sitting beside him on a rug at the rear of the tent.

Druss clamped his huge hand on the nomad's shoulder. 'Times

are hard, my friend. But when a man gives me the best he has I feel honoured. No king could have offered me more than you have tonight.'

'I have saved the best till last,' said Khalid, clapping his hands. Two young women moved out through the throng of men seated close in the centre of the tent, and returned carrying a wooden cask. Placing it on a table they bowed respectfully to Khalid, then backed away. Khalid Khan took an empty goblet, and twisted the spigot of the cask. In the lantern light the spirit flowed like pale gold. Khalid handed the full goblet to Druss. The warrior sipped it, then drank deeply. 'By Missael, this is Lentrian Fire . . . and very fine, my friend.'

'Twenty-five years old,' said Khalid happily. 'I have saved it for a special feast.'

The young men of the clan gathered round and Khalid filled their cups, jugs and goblets. The mood within the tent lightened considerably, and two of the Khan's warriors produced clumsily fashioned stringed instruments, and began to make music.

Within a short time there was a great deal of singing and clapping from the fifty men crowded into the tent of Khalid Khan. Rabalyn tried a sip of the drink, and understood instantly why it was called Lentrian Fire. He gagged and choked, and handed his goblet to a nearby clansman. 'It's like swallowing a cat with its claws out,' he complained to Diagoras.

'The Lentrians call it Immortal Water,' said the Drenai. 'To drink it is to know how the gods feel.' He drained his own cup, then moved away, seeking another. Rabalyn saw Skilgannon ease his way through the revellers and walk out into the night. Tired of the noise, and the press of people within the tent, Rabalyn followed him.

'I see you do not like the brew either,' he said. Skilgannon shrugged.

'I liked it in another life. What are your plans now, Rabalyn?'

'I will go with Druss and Diagoras and rescue the princess.'

'In Drenai culture the daughter of an earl is a lady.' He smiled. 'This is, however, no time to be pedantic. I think you should choose another path.'

'I am not frightened. I mean to live by the code.'

'There is nothing wrong with fear, Rabalyn. Yet it is not fear for yourself that should make you reconsider. Druss is a great warrior, and Diagoras a soldier who has fought in many battles. They are hard, resolute men. Their chances of success in this venture are slim. They will be even less if they have to worry about keeping alive a courageous youngster who does not yet have the skill to survive.'

'You could help us. You are a great warrior too.'

'The girl is no princess of mine, and I have no reason to make war on Ironmask. All I require is to find the temple.'

'But Druss is your friend, isn't he?'

'I have no friends, Rabalyn. I have only a quest, that may yet prove impossible. Druss has made his choices. He seeks to avenge the death of a friend. He was not my friend. His quest, therefore, is not my concern.'

'That isn't true,' objected Rabalyn. 'Not according to the code. *Protect the weak against the evil strong.* The princess – lady, whatever you call her – is a child, and therefore weak. Ironmask is evil.'

'I could argue with almost all of that,' said Skilgannon. 'The child is with her mother, who is Ironmask's lover. For all we know Ironmask loves the child as his own. Secondly, evil is often a matter of perspective. And, more important, even if both criteria you offer are true, the code is not mine. I am not a knight in some childish romance. I do not criss-cross the world seeking serpents to slay. I am merely a man seeking a miracle.'

The noise from the tent suddenly subsided, and, within moments, a voice of almost unbearable sweetness began to sing. Skilgannon shivered. 'That's Garianne,' said Rabalyn. 'Have you ever heard anything more beautiful?'

'No,' admitted Skilgannon. 'I think I will go and swim in the moonlight. Why don't you go in and listen?'

'I will,' said Rabalyn. He watched the tall warrior stride away up the mountainside, then returned to the open flap of the tent. Every man inside was sitting silently, entranced by the magic. Garianne was standing on a chair, her arms outstretched, her eyes closed. The song was about a hunter, who stumbled upon a golden goddess bathing in a stream. The goddess fell in love with the hunter, and they lay together under the stars. But in the morning

300

the hunter desired to go. Angry at being rejected the goddess turned him into a white stag, then took a bow to kill him. The hunter sprang away, leaping high over the treetops, and vanishing among the stars. The goddess gave chase. This was the beginning of day and night over the earth. The white stag became the moon, the goddess the sun. And ever and ever she hunted her lover, throughout time.

When the song finished the silence was total. Then thunderous applause broke out. Garianne stepped down from the chair, and cast her gaze around the tent. She took a few steps towards the entrance and half staggered. Rabalyn realized she was drunk, and stepped forward to assist her. She brushed his hand away.

'Where is he?' she asked, her voice slurring.

'Who?'

'The Damned?'

'He went to the hidden lake to swim.'

'I will find him,' she said.

Rabalyn accompanied her outside and watched her climb the steep slope, then turned away. As he did so the brothers Jared and Nian emerged from the tent. Nian saw him and walked over. 'And who is this?' he asked his brother. 'I feel I should know him.'

'That is Rabalyn,' said Jared.

'Rabalyn,' repeated Nian, nodding. Rabalyn was shocked. Gone was the slack-jawed simpleton with the innocent smile. This man was sharp of eye, and faintly daunting. He looked at Rabalyn. 'You must forgive me, young man. I have not been well. My memory fades in and out. Was that Garianne I saw climbing the slope?'

'Yes . . . sir,' said Rabalyn. He glanced at Jared, who was standing close to his brother.

'Gods, Jared!' Nian snapped. 'Give me room to breathe.'

'I am sorry, brother. Perhaps you should rest for a while. Does your head hurt?'

'No, it doesn't damn well hurt.' He sat down, then looked up at his brother and smiled apologetically. 'I am sorry. It is frightening when you can't remember anything. Am I going mad?'

'No, Nian. We're heading for the temple. They'll know what to do. I am sure they'll bring your memory back.'

'Who was that big old man in the tent? His face looked familiar too.'

'That was Druss. He's a friend.'

'Well, thank the Source I am all right now. It is a beautiful night, isn't it?'

'Indeed it is,' agreed Jared.

'I could do with some water. Is there a well close by?'

'I'll fetch you some. You sit there for a while.' Jared walked back to Khalid Khan's tent.

Nian looked at Rabalyn. 'Are we friends, young man?'

'Yes.'

'Are you interested in the stars?'

'I have never thought about it.'

'Ah, you should. Look up there. You see the three stars in a line? They are called the Sword Belt. They are so far away from us that the light we see has taken a million years to reach us. It could even be that they don't exist any more, and all we are seeing is ancient light.'

'How could we see them if they didn't exist?' asked Rabalyn.

'It is about distance. When the sun first rises the sky is still dark. Did you know that?'

'That makes no sense.'

'Ah, but it does. The sun is more than ninety million miles from the earth. That is a colossal distance. The light that blazes from it has to travel ninety million miles before it touches our eyes. Only when it touches our eyes are we aware of it. An ancient scholar estimated that it takes a few minutes for the light to travel that distance. In those minutes the sky would still appear dark to our eyes.'

Rabalyn didn't believe a word of it, but he smiled and nodded. 'Oh, I see,' he said, confused and even a little frightened by this strange new man inhabiting Nian's body.

Nian laughed and clapped him on the shoulder. 'You think I am mad. Perhaps I am. I have always been curious, though, about how things work. What makes the wind blow, and the tides flow? How does rainwater get into a cloud? Why does it fall out again?'

'Why does it?' asked Rabalyn.

'You see? Now you are getting curious too. A good trait in the young.' He winced suddenly. 'My head is beginning to ache,' he said.

Jared returned with a goblet of water. Nian drank it swiftly, then rubbed at his eyes. 'I think I will sleep,' he said. 'I will see you in the morning, Rabalyn.'

The two brothers walked away. Rabalyn sat for a while, staring at the Sword Belt, and the glittering stars around it. Then he heard Nian cry out, and saw Jared sitting beside him, his arm round his brother's shoulder. Nian lay down, and Jared covered him with a blanket. Rabalyn went over to them.

'Is he all right?' he asked.

'No. The cancer is destroying him,' said Jared, with a sigh. Nian was sleeping now, lying on his back, his arm over his face.

'He talked about the stars and clouds.'

'Yes. He is . . . was . . . a man of great intelligence. He was an architect once. A long time ago. When he wakes he will be the Nian you know. Slow-witted.'

'I don't understand.'

'No more do I, boy,' said Jared sadly. 'The Old Woman says it is to do with the pressure inside his head. Sometimes it shifts or subsides, and for a few minutes he is the Nian he always was. The Nian he was meant to be. It doesn't last. And the moments of clarity are fewer now. The last time he returned was a year ago. The temple will cure him, though. I am sure of it.'

Nian moaned in his sleep. Jared leaned over and stroked his brow.

'I think I'll get some sleep too,' said Rabalyn. Jared was staring down at his brother's face and did not hear him.

As the night wore on many of Khalid's men drifted back to their tents. Others too drunk to move fell asleep on the threadbare rugs. Druss rose from his place, took one look at the sleeping Khalid, then half stumbled as he made his way towards the outside. Diagoras, his mouth dry, his head pounding, followed him out into the night.

Druss stood and stretched out his arms. 'Damn, but I'm tired,' he said, as Diagoras came up to him.

'Did you learn anything worthwhile?'

'Nothing we didn't know about Ironmask. Khalid has never seen the fortress. It's a long way from here. He has heard of the temple Skilgannon seeks. Apparently there was a warrior who went there when Khalid was a child. He said the man had lost his right hand in a battle. He went seeking the temple and when he returned his hand had regrown.'

'Impossible,' said Diagoras. 'Just a myth.'

'Perhaps,' said Druss. 'One interesting detail, though. He said the man's hand was a different colour. It was deeper red, as if scalded. Khalid says he saw it himself, and has never forgotten it.'

'And that makes you believe the story?'

'It tells me there's at least a grain of truth to it. Perhaps the man did not lose the hand, but had it mutilated. I don't know, laddie. But Khalid says the temple cannot be found unless the priestess there wants to be found. He told me he travelled over the area himself, and saw no sign of a building. Not until he was leaving. He had climbed towards a high pass leading home, and he glanced back. And there it was, shining in the moonlight. He swears he walked every inch of the valley floor. There was no way he could have missed it.'

'So, did he go back?' asked Diagoras.

'No. He decided he didn't want to risk entering a building that appeared and disappeared.'

A slender figure moved down the mountainside from the direction of the hidden lake. Diagoras saw that it was Garianne. As she passed them she waved. 'Goodnight, Uncle,' she called.

'Goodnight, lass,' he said. 'Sleep well.'

'Have I too become invisible?' asked Diagoras. Druss chuckled.

'It must be hard for a ladies' man like you, boy, to be so disregarded.'

'I'll admit to that. She never talks to me at all.'

'That's because she knows you are interested in her. And she wants no friends.'

'I'll wager she's just come from Skilgannon,' said Diagoras sourly.

'I expect so, laddie. That's because he has no interest in her whatsoever. What they need from each other is simple and primal. It creates no ties, and therefore no dangers.'

Diagoras looked at the older man. 'Be careful, Druss. Your image as a simple soldier will be ruined if you continue to display such insights.'

Druss was silent, and Diagoras saw that he was staring up into the shadow-haunted hills. 'You see something?'

Druss ignored the question and walked across to the wagon. Reaching in, he drew out Snaga. 'Where is the boy?'

Diagoras shrugged. 'I think he got bored with the revelling and went off to find somewhere to sleep.'

'Find him. I'm going to have a look up that slope.'

'What did you see?' persisted Diagoras.

'Just a shadow. But I have an uneasy feeling.'

With that Druss walked away. Diagoras gazed around at the camp, and the jagged black silhouettes of the rocky hills. The night was quiet and calm. No breeze whispered across the campsite. Bright stars decorated the sky, like diamonds on sable. Diagoras had not felt uneasy before Druss spoke. He did now. The old man had spent most of his life in situations of danger. He had acquired a sixth sense for it.

Diagoras loosened his sabre, then began to scout for sign of Rabalyn.

On the mountainside to the west Skilgannon emerged from the lake tunnel, and out into the moonlight. He took a deep breath. His body, released from tensions by the lovemaking with Garianne, was relaxed, his thoughts untroubled. The woman was a mystery, fey and aloof when sober, passionate and vulnerable when drunk. They had not spoken when she came into the lake cavern. She had walked unsteadily towards him, then looped her arms round his neck. The kiss fired his blood. Garianne was not Jianna, but the touch of soft lips upon his own had brought back the memories of that one, unforgettable night in the woods, after his rescue of her. It was the only time he and Jianna had given in to their passion. He remembered every detail: the whisper of the night breeze in the branches above them, the scent of lemon grass in the air, the feel of her skin pressing against his own. And afterwards the way she cuddled in close to him, slipping her right thigh across him, her arm draped over his chest, her hand stroking his cheek. The memory was almost unbearably sweet. It filled him with both long-ing and regret.

With Garianne there was no affection. She did not stroke his face, or cuddle in close. Her passion exhausted she pulled away, dressed swiftly and left without a word. He made no effort to stop her. They had both taken all they needed from one another. There was no point in prolonging the moment.

Skilgannon stepped from the cave entrance and gazed down at the settlement. He was about to walk down towards the tents when he stopped. His relaxed mood evaporated. The night was silent, and there was no threat in sight. Even so he remained where he was, scanning the hillsides. He saw Druss walking purposefully towards the east, axe in hand. Below he spotted Diagoras moving through the tents. A breath of breeze blew across him. There was a slight scent upon it, musky and rank. Reaching up with his right hand Skilgannon drew one of his swords. Glancing to his left he saw a jumble of boulders, the tallest over ten feet high. He closed his eyes, concentrating his hearing. There was nothing. Yet he did not relax. Reaching back he drew his second sword, and stood, statue still. The breeze blew again, caressing the back of his neck. This time the scent was stronger.

Skilgannon spun.

A massive beast rose up behind him and leapt. Its eyes glittered red, and its jaws spread, showing rows of gleaming fangs.

The Swords of Night and Day flashed out, the first slashing through the huge neck, the second piercing the shaggy chest and cleaving the heart. The weight of the charging beast bore him back-wards, and they hit the slope together and rolled. Releasing his hold on the Sword of Day Skilgannon kicked himself clear of the thrashing beast and came to his feet. Screams began from the settlement below. Skilgannon ignored them, fastening his gaze on the cave mouth.

No other creatures came into sight. He glanced back at the beast he had stabbed. It was no longer moving. Warily he approached it. The Joining was lying on its back, dead eyes open to the sky. Grabbing the hilt of the blade jutting from its chest Skilgannon drew it clear.

From the camp below came more sounds of screaming.

Skilgannon could see three beasts. One had torn through a tent wall and emerged back into the settlement, the cloth of the tent clinging to its back like a trailing cloak. It crouched over a fallen tribesman. Fangs crunched down on the man's skull. A little to the left Diagoras was vainly trying to battle a huge, hunchbacked Joining. The cavalry sabre was having little effect. Skilgannon began to run down the slope towards the fight. As he did so he saw Rabalyn emerge behind the Joining, slamming his shortsword into the beast's back.

Other creatures emerged. Jared and Nian came into view, and charged them. Their longswords were more effective than the sabre of Diagoras, and they drove the Joinings back. Khalid Khan appeared, and began shouting orders to his men. His voice cut through the panic, and some of the warriors ran to gather bows and spears. Skilgannon saw Diagoras attempt a thrust into the chest of an oncoming Joining. The blade failed to penetrate. Diagoras was thrown through the air by a backhanded blow from the creature.

Skilgannon ran in. The beast swerved towards him, its fangs lunging for his throat. He dropped to one knee and sent the golden Sword of Day ripping through the beast's neck. Blood sprayed out and the creature staggered to its right. Nian leapt in, bringing his longsword down in a double-handed chop that split the Joining's skull.

Another beast hurled itself at Skilgannon. A crossbow bolt materialized in its right eye. Its great head jerked, and a terrifying roar burst from its throat. A second bolt thudded into its chest, but did not penetrate deeply. Skilgannon ran in, plunging his blade into the beast's belly, and ripping the blade upwards. Diagoras was back on his feet. Skilgannon saw him bending over the limp form of Rabalyn.

Garianne, reloading her crossbow, strode past Skilgannon, sending a bolt into the back of another creature. The Joining reared up then charged at the woman. Garianne stood her ground. As the beast was almost upon her she raised her arm, sending the second bolt into its snarling mouth. The iron point punched through the cartilage and bone, skewering the brain. In its death throes it lashed out. Garianne was punched from her feet. Then the creature

307

toppled. Skilgannon hurdled the falling body and ran at the Joining still ensnared in the ruined tent. It reared up from the mutilated body upon which it was feeding and sprang away.

Another Joining leapt to the wagon, and let out a roar. Three other beasts ran in. Skilgannon swung to face them.

Then, with a bellowing war cry, Druss the Legend came out of the darkness, Snaga crunching through a first creature's skull. Skilgannon raced in to aid the axeman. Jared and Nian followed him. Druss killed a second, and Skilgannon a third, before the surviving Joining turned and fled into the night. Glancing around the settlement Skilgannon saw the Joining with the tent-cloak was surrounded by tribesmen with bows. Its hide bristled with arrows. It tried to charge, but caught its front paw in the remains of the tent and tumbled over. Khalid Khan leapt towards it, driving his curved sword into the creature's neck. It reared up, throwing the old leader through the air. More arrows thudded into it. The Joining tottered, then pitched to the ground. Tribesmen swarmed over the beast, plunging knives and swords into its flesh.

For a while there was silence. Then some of the women, identifying dead loved ones, began to wail, the sound echoing through the hills.

Skilgannon cleaned his blades and sheathed them. Druss walked back to where Diagoras was kneeling beside the unconscious Rabalyn. 'Does he live?' asked the axeman.

'Aye. His nose is broken. He's lucky. The talons missed him. I think it was the beast's forearm that struck him.'

'That's because he was attacking the Joining,' said Druss. 'Pushing forward. If he'd backed away the talons would have ripped his throat out. Courage kept him alive.'

'He's a brave lad,' agreed Diagoras. 'He's too young and callow, though, Druss. He shouldn't be with us.'

'He'll learn,' argued Druss.

'You've a wound on your back,' said Skilgannon, approaching the axeman.

'It's not deep.' Druss patted the silver steel shoulder guards on his black jerkin. 'These took most of the hit.'

The brothers, Jared and Nian, strolled over. 'You think they'll come back?' asked Jared.

Druss shook his head, and gazed up into the hills. 'Too few of them now. I killed two before coming back here. I think they'll move on, seeking easier prey.' He seemed distracted.

'What's wrong?' asked Diagoras, getting to his feet.

'Damnedest thing,' said Druss. 'I walked up into the hills. Then three of them rushed at me. I killed the first quick, but the second threw me to the ground.' He fell silent, remembering the scene. 'They had me. No question. Then a fourth beast attacked them. Big and grey. He just ripped in, scattering them. I managed to get to my feet. Killed a second. The grey one tore the throat out of the third. Then it just stood there. I knew it wasn't going to attack me. No idea how I knew. We stared at one another, then it gave a cry of pure anguish and ran. Then I heard what was going on here, so I returned.'

'You think it was Orastes?' asked Diagoras.

'I don't know. I can't think of any other reason why it would have saved me. I'm going to find him.'

'Find him?' echoed Diagoras. 'Are you insane? You can't be sure it even intended to rescue you. These are not thinking creatures, Druss. They'll lash out and kill at the slightest provocation. Maybe they were just fighting over who got to eat your liver.'

'Maybe,' agreed the axeman. 'I need to know.'

Diagoras swore. Then he took a deep breath. 'Listen to me, my friend. If it is Orastes there's nothing we can do for him. You said the Old Woman made that clear. Once these poor devils are melded it cannot be undone. So what will you do? Keep him as a pet? Shem's balls, Druss! This is not something you take for a walk and throw a stick for.'

'I'll take him to the temple. Maybe they can . . . bring Orastes back.'

'Oh, I see. That's all right then,' said Diagoras, his voice angry. 'So, let me get this clear. Our new plan is to capture a werebeast, find a temple which may or may not exist, then ask the priests to heal a tumour, and unmeld a wolf and a man? And all this before the two of us attack a fortress and despatch a couple of hundred warriors and rescue a child? Have I left anything out?'

'I am hoping they can raise the dead,' said Skilgannon. Diagoras looked at him and blinked.

'Is this a jest of some kind?'

'Not to me.'

'Ah, well then . . . I shall ask for a winged horse and a golden helm that makes me invisible. I'll fly over the fortress and rescue the child without anyone seeing me.'

'They can do amazing things,' said Jared, stepping forward. Nian moved alongside him, taking hold of the sash at Jared's belt. 'I know this. We have been there before.'

'You've seen the temple?' put in Skilgannon.

'I don't remember much of it,' said Jared. 'Our father took us there when we were very young. No more than three years old.'

'Were you sick?' asked Diagoras.

'No, we were healthy enough. But we were joined at the waist. Born that way. Our mother died in childbirth. The surgeon cut us from her dead body. We were freaks. I don't remember much of those early years. But I do remember being stared at, laughed at, pointed at. All I recall of the temple was a woman with a shaved skull. She had a kind face. Her name was Ustarte. One morning I awoke, and Nian was no longer joined to me. He was lying beside me, and we were both bandaged. I recall the pain from the wound.'

For a moment there was silence, then Diagoras spoke. 'I have seen your scars, and they tell me the priests at the temple must have cut your flesh in order to separate you. That was an incredible feat.' He swung back towards Druss. 'But they cannot cut Orastes clear of the wolf. They have become one. If they could separate one from the other without slicing flesh they would have done that with the brothers.'

'On the other hand,' put in Skilgannon, 'Orastes and the wolf were joined magically. Perhaps that magic can be reversed. We won't know until we get the beast to the temple.'

Diagoras looked around the group. He saw Garianne sitting on a rock close by. 'You haven't offered anything,' he said, careful to avoid framing a question.

'We would like to see Ustarte again,' she said.

At that moment Rabalyn groaned. Druss knelt beside him. 'How are you feeling, laddie?'

'Can't breathe through my nose, and it hurts.'

'It's broken. Can you stand?' Druss helped the boy to his feet.

Rabalyn swayed slightly, then righted himself. He looked around. 'Did we beat them off?'

'Aye, we did,' said Druss. 'Stand still and lean your head back.' Reaching up, Druss clamped his fingers to the boy's misshapen nose, then gave a sharp twist. There was a loud crack. Rabalyn cried out. 'There, it's straight now,' said Druss, patting Rabalyn on the back. Rabalyn groaned and staggered away, falling to his knees and vomiting.

'Always good to see the gentle touch,' observed Diagoras. 'So how do we capture Orastes?'

'I'll go and find him,' said Druss. 'The rest of you wait for me here.'

'It would be folly to go alone, axeman,' said Skilgannon.

'Maybe so, but if we go in a group Orastes will avoid us. I think some part of him still recognizes me as a friend. I might be able to reach him.'

'There is sense in that. However, there are still more of the beasts out there, Druss. The group can remain behind, but I'll go with you.'

Druss stood quietly, thinking. Then he nodded.

'You want me to stitch that cut in your back before you go?' asked Diagoras.

'No, the blood will help draw Orastes to me.'

'Oh, good plan,' said Diagoras.

CHAPTER SIXTEEN

THE MOON WAS HIGH AND BRIGHT AS THE TWO WARRIORS TRUDGED UP the hillside. Skilgannon glanced at the axeman. Druss looked tired and drawn, his eyes sunken. Skilgannon himself was weary, and he was half Druss's age. They walked in silence for a while, coming at last to a rocky outcrop close to a high rock face, pitted with caves.

'My guess is they are in there,' said Druss.

'You want to go in?'

'Let's see what transpires.' Druss slumped down on a boulder, and rubbed his eyes. Skilgannon looked at him.

'This Orastes means a lot to you?'

'No,' said Druss. 'He was just a fat boy I knew back at Skeln. I liked him, though. He should never have been a soldier. I was amazed when he survived. War is a curious beast. Sometimes it will swallow the best and leave the worst alone. There were some great fighters at Skeln. Cut down in their prime. I'll give Orastes his due, though. He stood his ground.'

'No more can be asked,' said Skilgannon.

'You'll get no argument from me. I didn't see him many times after that. His father died and he became Earl of Dros Purdol. Another role to which he was not suited. Poor Orastes. A failure in almost everything he ever did.'

'Everyone is good at something,' said Skilgannon.

'Aye, that's true. Orastes was a fine father. He adored Elanin. Just to see them together made the heart soar.'

'And the wife?'

'She left him. I'd like to say she was a bad woman, but my guess would be that Orastes was a poor husband. I suppose that she must have regretted leaving her child. Hence she stole her back while Orastes was away from Purdol. That would have torn him apart.'

A slight breeze whispered across the rocks. Upon it Skilgannon could smell the rancid scent of fur. Druss was right. The beasts were close.

Constantly alert, his eyes scanning the rocks, he sat beside the axeman. 'So, Orastes came to Tantria and sought help from the Old Woman. And she betrayed him. Tell me, why did you not take vengeance on her?'

'I don't make war on women, laddie.'

'And yet they have just as great a capacity for evil.'

'True, but I'm too old to change now. Ironmask destroyed Orastes. It is Ironmask who will pay.'

'So you think that Orastes is still following his daughter?'

'Aye, I do. I don't know how much of Orastes survives in the beast. He probably doesn't even know why he is heading into Pelucid. But that's why he's here. The child meant everything to him.'

The two men fell silent, each lost in his own thoughts. The sky was cloudless, the moon high and bright. Something moved upon the rocks. The Sword of Day slid into Skilgannon's hand. He relaxed as he saw a small lizard scurry into the shadows.

'Why are you here, laddie?' asked Druss suddenly.

'You know why. I am hoping to bring my wife back from the dead.'

'I meant why are you *here*? With me now. In this place. I could be wrong about Orastes. There could be more of the creatures than we can handle. This is not your fight.' Skilgannon was about to say something light when Druss spoke again. 'And don't be flippant, laddie. 'Tis a serious question.'

Skilgannon sighed. 'You remind me of my father. I was too young to be alongside him when he needed me.'

'Death always brings guilt,' said Druss. He pushed himself to his

313

feet. 'I am a good judge of men, Skilgannon. You believe that?'

'I do.'

'Then believe me when I tell you that you are a better man than you know. You can't put right the evil you have done. All you can do is ensure it never happens again.'

'And how do I do that?'

'You find a code, laddie.' Druss hefted Snaga. 'And now it's time to enter those caves. I don't think Orastes will be coming out to us.'

Skilgannon stared at the nearest entrance. It seemed to him then that it resembled a gaping mouth. Fear touched him, but he drew his second sword and followed the axeman towards the cliff face.

Beyond the cave mouth was a twisting tunnel. Moonlight did not pierce the gloom for more than a few yards. Druss took several steps towards the darkness. 'There'll be light further on,' he said. 'The whole of the cliff face is pockmarked with caves and openings.'

'Let's hope so,' said Skilgannon, following him into the dark. Within a few paces they could see nothing, and Druss moved warily, feeling ahead with every footfall. The stench of animal fur was stronger now, and some way ahead they heard a low growl.

Skilgannon sheathed one of his swords, and placed a hand on Druss's shoulder. Ahead they saw a faint gleam of moonlight, shafting down at a forty-five-degree angle. Slowly they approached it. They rounded a slight bend. Several shafts of moonlight could now be seen, coming from fissures in the rock face.

The tunnel opened out into a cavern. Stalactites hung from the domed roof. 'You could try calling his name,' offered Skilgannon. 'Maybe some part of his mind still remembers it.'

'Orastes!' shouted Druss, his voice booming and echoing. 'It is I, Druss. Come out, my friend. We mean you no harm.'

A movement came from the right. Skilgannon turned towards it. A massive creature lunged from the shadows, jaws open. Skilgannon leapt aside, the golden Sword of Day slashing in a wide, glittering arc. The blade sliced into the creature's shoulder, and down through the powerful collar bone, exiting at the chest. It did not halt its charge, and its powerful body cannoned into Skilgannon, knocking him from his feet. Snaga swept up and down, cleaving through the Joining's skull. It slumped to the cavern floor.

Skilgannon rolled to his feet, drawing the Sword of Night as he did so. The dead beast was covered in thick, black fur. Skilgannon did not know whether to be relieved that it wasn't Orastes, or disappointed. Had it been Orastes they could have left this grisly tomb.

'Orastes!' called out Druss. 'Come forth. It is I, Druss.'

Another shadow moved. Skilgannon readied himself for an attack. Moonlight fell on a great grey beast, with huge hunched shoulders. It was standing beside a stalactite, and staring at the two men, its golden eyes gleaming in the moonlight.

'We have come to help you, Orastes,' said Druss, laying down his axe and stepping forward. The creature gave out a low growl, and Skilgannon saw it tense for the charge.

'Druss, be careful,' he warned.

'You are looking for Elanin,' said Druss. At the sound of the girl's name the beast seemed to shudder. Its massive head twisted, and it gave out an ear-splitting howl. 'We know where she is,' said Druss. 'She has been taken to a citadel.' Now the creature backed away a few paces. Its eyes narrowed. It was preparing to attack.

'Say the girl's name again, Druss,' advised Skilgannon.

'Elanin. Your daughter Elanin. Listen to me, Orastes. We need to rescue Elanin.' The beast roared again, and Skilgannon almost believed he could hear anguish in the sound. Then it smashed its fist against a stalactite, shattering it to shards. The beast backed away into the shadows.

Druss took another step away from his axe. 'Trust me, Orastes. We know of a temple where they may be able to bring you back. Then you could come with us when we rescue Elanin.'

The grey beast roared and charged. Its shoulder struck Druss, sending him hurtling to the ground. Then it bore down on Skilgannon, who hurled himself to his right, landing on his shoulder and rolling to his feet. The swords came up. Orastes or no he would kill it if it came for him. But it did not. The Joining ran off into the darkness. Druss made to follow, but Skilgannon stepped into his path.

'No, Druss,' he said. 'Even a hero should know when he has lost.'

Druss stood for a moment, then gave a deep sigh. 'It *was* Orastes. I know that for sure now.'

'You did all you could.'

'It wasn't enough.' Druss walked to where Snaga lay and recovered it. 'Let's get back to where the air is clean,' he said.

For the next two days Druss continued to walk the mountains seeking Orastes. This time he went alone. The company remained in the settlement of Khalid Khan. Diagoras, who had some skill with wounds, helped with the injured. Seven men and three women had been killed by the beasts, and eight others carried injuries, five from bites and slashes, three from broken bones. The nomads made no attempt to skin the dead beasts. Instead they were dragged from the camp, covered in brushwood and set alight. On the morning of the third day Khalid Khan's men began dismantling their tents.

'We are moving further into the mountains,' Khalid told Skilgannon. 'This is now a place of ill omen.'

Garianne came into the settlement, a bighorn sheep across her shoulders. She left it with several of the nomad women, then walked to a spot in the shade and sat down alongside Skilgannon.

'We need to leave,' she said. 'The Old Woman spoke to us. She told us in a dream that enemies are coming.'

Skilgannon glanced at the young woman. She was staring ahead, her face set. He had learned not to ask questions of her, so merely waited. 'The Nadir shaman with Ironmask is now aware of Old Uncle. He has sent riders to waylay him. Many riders. They will be here by tomorrow morning. The Old Woman says to head northwest. To leave Old Uncle to his fate.'

'She told Druss she wanted Ironmask dead,' he said, choosing his words carefully. 'That is . . . Old Uncle's . . . quest. Yet now she is content to see him killed, so that we may survive. That seems strange to me.'

'We do not know what she desires,' said Garianne. 'We only know what she told us.'

'Perhaps it was just a dream, and the Old Woman did not appear to you.'

'It was the Old Woman,' said Garianne. 'It is how she speaks with us when we are far away.'

Skilgannon believed her, but the Old Woman's advice made little sense. If she wanted Ironmask dead, as she had indicated, then why encourage the company to split up? Leaning back against the rock wall Skilgannon closed his eyes. The Old Woman was a dark mystery. She had come to the aid of Jianna, ensuring her escape from the capital. Yet never, to Skilgannon's knowledge, had she come for the gold she had requested for the service. Perhaps Jianna had paid her secretly. In all the stories of the Old Woman that he knew there was one common factor. Betrayal. Yet Jianna had suffered no such fate. And why did the hag want Ironmask dead? What had he done to earn her hatred? There were no answers. He had insufficient information. Her request for the company to leave Druss to his fate meant that she desired them to survive. Why? Irritated now, he opened his eyes and stared out over the encampment. Most of the tents were down, and rolled. The few pack animals owned by the nomads were being loaded.

'I will not leave Druss,' he said.

'We are glad,' Garianne told him. 'We love Old Uncle.'

Still being careful with his words, he spoke again. 'Yet had I gone away you would have come with me.'

'Yes.'

'Not, I think, because you love me.'

'No, we do not love you. We hate you.' The words were said without passion or regret. They were merely spoken. It seemed to Skilgannon that she might as well have been talking about a change in the breeze.

'You stay with me because the Old Woman requires you to.'

'We do not wish to speak further,' said Garianne, rising smoothly to her feet and walking away. He sat where he was. Her hatred was not a surprise. As the Damned he had seeded hatred across three nations. Every man or woman or child who had been killed by his troops would have had relatives or friends. Far easier for them to hate a single general than a vast, faceless army. He had heard it before. Once, on his travels, he had sat quietly in a tavern. Men were sitting close by discussing the war. 'The Damned killed my son,' he heard a man say. Skilgannon had listened carefully. As the conversation went on he learned that the boy had been killed in a skirmish some twenty miles from the battlefield where

Skilgannon had fought. Wherever he went he heard people discussing the evils of the Damned. Some of the stories were hideously twisted, others merely ludicrous. The Damned had filed his teeth to sharp points and dined on human flesh. His eyes had become red as blood after he sold his soul to a demon. The stories grew and grew, becoming mythic. It was one of the reasons he could travel without being recognized. Who would suspect the handsome young man with the eyes of sapphire blue? He had learned that people needed evil to have an ugly face.

Skilgannon sighed, his spirits low.

A month ago he had been a novice priest in a quiet community, believing the days of war and death were behind him. He realized he had no longing any more for those peaceful days, and yet there was an edge of regret that they had passed. Idly he stroked the locket round his neck. Would anything change if he managed to restore Dayan to life? Would his guilts be lessened? Skilgannon didn't know. 'You deserve life, Dayan,' he said aloud. As always thoughts of Dayan merged into memories of Jianna. He pushed himself to his feet. The Old Woman's advice was good. He *should* leave Druss to his fate.

Skilgannon strode up the mountainside and into the cavern of the hidden lake. Here it was cool and he swam for a while. Levering himself from the water he sat on a rock. After that one night of lovemaking with Jianna in the forest his life had changed. He had lived only for the day when he could restore her to her throne. Looking back he felt both foolish and naïve. He had believed that once she was safe, and the realm was hers, they would be together once more. Skilgannon did not care if she could not wed him. He had allowed himself to dream of being her consort, and her lover. And that's what it was. A wishful dream.

The truth was that – if she loved him at all – she loved power more. Jianna would never be content. If she became queen of all the world she would stare longingly at the stars and dream of conquering Heaven.

The harsh reality had come home to him on the day they defeated Bokram. Skilgannon could still recall the fear he had experienced on the night before the final battle. Yet again it was the Old Woman who had given birth to it. She had walked into the

318

battle camp, past the guards and the sentries, and entered the Queen's tent. Skilgannon had been with Jianna, Askelus and Malanek, discussing the proposed course of the battle. Malanek had leapt to his feet, drawing a dagger. Jianna told him to sit down. Then she had stood and walked to the Old Woman, taking her hand and kissing it. The thought still made Skilgannon shudder. That those beautiful lips should have touched the skin of something so vile. 'Welcome,' said Jianna. 'Come, join us.'

'No need for that, my dear. I have no head for battle plans.'

'Then why are you here?' Skilgannon had asked, his voice harsher than he intended.

'To wish you well, of course. I have read the runes. Tomorrow will be a bad day for Bokram. It may even be a bad day for you, Olek. Did you know that Boranius employed a seer? He cast the bones for him. According to his prediction Boranius will kill you tomorrow. Still, I expect you are willing to die for your Queen, Olek.'

'Indeed I am.'

'Boranius also has swords of power. Ancient blades given to him by Bokram. They are called the Swords of Blood and Fire. I would love to have acquired them. Much of the magic I used to create your own swords was based upon spells woven around blood and fire. The two of you will meet on the battlefield. That much I *have* seen.'

'And was the seer correct?' asked Jianna. 'Will Boranius . . . conquer?' she added, clearly unwilling to speak openly about Skilgannon's death.

The Old Woman shrugged. 'The seer has been right before. Perhaps this time he is wrong.'

'Then you must stay back tomorrow,' said Jianna, turning towards Skilgannon. 'I do not want to lose you, Olek.'

The Old Woman smiled. 'That is touching, my dear. But if Olek does not fight then I fear the battle will be lost.'

It was in that moment that Skilgannon learned that Jianna loved power more than she loved him. He saw her face change. She looked at him, waiting for him to speak.

'I shall fight,' he said simply. Jianna protested, but weakly, and he saw the relief in her eyes.

'Such a fight it will be,' said the Old Woman happily. Then she had bowed to Jianna and left the tent.

'You will beat him, Olek,' said Jianna. 'No-one is as good as you.'

Skilgannon had glanced at Malanek, who had trained Boranius. 'You have seen us both. What do you think?'

Malanek looked uncomfortable. 'In a fight anything can happen, Olek. A man may stumble, or be more tired than his opponent. His sword might break. It is too close to call.'

'Do you have no respect for me, old friend?'

Malanek seemed shocked. 'Of course I have.'

'Then do not use weasel words. Speak your mind.'

Malanek took a deep breath. 'I don't think you can beat him, Olek. There is something inhuman about the man. His great strength, the weight of his muscles, should limit his speed. Yet it does not. He is ferociously fast, and utterly fearless. You should take the Queen's advice and stay back tomorrow. The Old Woman is wrong. We *can* win without you.'

Fear had been strong upon him the following morning. He was on the verge of fulfilling his dream. Today, if they won, the Queen would regain her father's throne, and he, Skilgannon, would take her in his arms once more. Yet a seer had prophesied that Boranius would kill him. The thought made him shudder.

With the battle at its height Skilgannon had seen Boranius. He was fighting on foot, cleaving his swords left and right, men falling before him. Time froze in that moment. Every instinct told him to avoid the man. He was surrounded by soldiers who would eventually drag him down. Let them do it. Then you will be free!

The coward is never free, he told himself, spurring his horse and riding towards his enemy. He had leapt from the saddle and shouted for the soldiers to fall back. They had parted then, and he had looked into the eyes of Boranius. The golden-haired warrior had grinned at him. 'Have you come to race me again, Olek? Be careful. I have no injured ankle this time.' Skilgannon had drawn his swords. Boranius laughed. 'Pretty. They are copies, you know. In my hands are the originals.' He raised the Swords of Blood and Fire. 'Come to me, Olek. I will kill you a piece at a time. Like I killed your friends. Oh, you should have heard them squeal and beg.'

'Don't tell me. Show me,' said Skilgannon.

Boranius had attacked with blistering speed. Even with Malanek's warning the awesome speed of the man was a surprise. Skilgannon parried desperately, weaving and moving. He knew in those first moments that Boranius was a better swordsman, and that the seer was right. He fought on, blocking and swerving, the Swords of Blood and Fire glittering as they sought his flesh.

Many of the soldiers watching could see their general was doomed. One of them raised a spear and hurled it. It struck Boranius high on the right shoulder, surprising him. Skilgannon launched an attack, the Sword of Night flashing in a searing arc for Boranius's throat. The blond warrior threw himself back. The blade struck his cheekbone, shearing through his lips and nose. The Sword of Day plunged into Boranius's chest, and the man fell.

The relief Skilgannon felt was colossal. Enemy cavalry began a counter attack. Skilgannon ordered the waiting soldiers to regroup and ran to his horse. Within an hour the battle was over. Bokram was dead, his head raised on a pike, his surviving soldiers in flight through the valleys.

It should have been the day of his greatest triumph. He had avenged Greavas, and Sperian and Molaire. He had returned Jianna to her rightful place. And yet he had not attended the feast of celebration that night. Instead the Queen had sent him out, harrying the fleeing troops. That night, as he had learned later, she took another general to her bed, the Prince Peshel Bar, whose cavalry had held the right, and whose power had allowed Jianna to raise her army.

The same Peshel Bar she later had murdered.

Rising from the waterside, Skilgannon dressed and returned to the open air. A convoy of nomads was heading deeper into the mountains. Khalid Khan had remained behind, and was talking to Druss. Skilgannon strolled down to join them.

Khalid Khan embraced the axeman, then turned and walked away. Diagoras, Rabalyn, Garianne and the twins were close by. Skilgannon approached Druss. 'Have you spoken with Garianne?' he asked.

Druss nodded. His face was grey with exhaustion. He had not slept in days. 'Nadir warriors are coming. She says the Old Woman advised you to move on. Good advice, laddie.'

'I don't live my life on her advice. We know which direction they are coming from. I'll ride out and scout the land. I'll find a battleground that suits us.'

Druss grinned. 'She says there are around thirty of them. You plan to attack?'

'I plan to win,' said Skilgannon. With that he strode after Khalid Khan and questioned the old nomad about the roads and passes to the northwest, and the water holes and camping places the Nadir would seek out on their way here. They talked for some while, then Skilgannon saddled his gelding and told the company to follow Khalid Khan to a campsite some eight miles northwest. 'I will meet you there later tonight,' he said.

Then he rode into the hills.

Following Khalid Khan's advice Skilgannon rode the mountain paths towards the north, the route rising steadily. It was searingly hot in the open, the air heavy and soporific in the shade. Concentration was difficult. Skilgannon struggled to maintain his focus. He rode on, picking a path towards a sharp summit rearing high above the surrounding mountains. From here the land dropped away sharply towards the northwest, the mountain road – such as it was – snaking in a series of half-circles round the flanks of the peaks. Skilgannon dismounted and scanned the land, recalling the descriptions Khalid Khan had given him, fixing the terrain in his mind.

Far below him he could see where the road emerged onto flat land before rising again, twisting and curving up into rugged, dusty hills. Here and there were small stands of gnarled trees, too few to offer cover or a line of safe retreat. Remounting, he moved on, seeking out places which offered concealment, or a defensive perimeter; somewhere from which he could organize a surprise attack. He could rely only on the fighting talents of himself, Druss, Diagoras, Garianne and the twins. The boy Rabalyn was too young and inexperienced. Any Nadir warrior would cut him down in seconds. Then there were other complications. Druss and the twins would be fighting on foot, the Nadir mounted, and probably armed with bows. Garianne might well be deadly with the small crossbow, but that only accounted for two enemies, not six, in the

322

first moments of conflict. It would be necessary for Garianne to scramble to a place of safety to reload.

Bearing all these things in mind Skilgannon rode on, scanning not only the immediate countryside, but also the distant road, seeking sign of the Nadir. If they were to be at the campsite by morning that probably allowed for a night camp and some rest. It was unlikely they would ride all day and all night before tackling a man like Druss. Though not impossible, he conceded.

Skilgannon had never fought the Nadir, but like most professional soldiers he had studied histories of their race. An offshoot of the Chiatze people, they were nomads, living on the vast steppes of northern Gothir. Vicious and warlike, they had not proved to be a danger to civilizations like Gothir, or the richer nations to their south, because they were constantly at war with one another, living out ancient blood feuds that sapped the strengths of the tribes from generation to generation. They fought mostly from horseback, their mounts being small, hardy steppe ponies. Preferred weapon was the bow. In close quarters they used shortswords or long knives. Lightly armoured – a breastplate of hardened leather and a fur-rimmed helm, sometimes of iron, but again mostly of leather or wood – they could move fast and fight with a fury unequalled. It was said they had no fear of death, believing that the gods would reward a warrior with great wealth and many wives in the next life.

Locating a hiding place for his mount Skilgannon crawled out to the edge of a high ridge and watched the road. The sun was setting now, and there was still no sign of the enemy. He waited, allowing his mind to relax. Not so long ago he had twenty thousand soldiers under his command: archers, lancers, spearmen, infantry. Now he had five fighters. Druss was not a concern. If he could get close enough to the enemy he would create carnage among them. Diagoras? Tough and skilled and brave. But could he take out five hardened Nadir warriors? Skilgannon doubted it. Then there were the twins. Good men, but – in truth – nothing special in terms of combat. They would fight hard, and maybe account for two each. Again, if they could get close enough. Garianne was harder to judge, but Skilgannon's instinct was that she would prove sufficiently deadly.

He saw dust to the northwest. Shading his eyes against the sun setting to his left, he focused on the distant band. A column of riders was moving down the mountainside. Flicking his gaze left he located the jutting rocks, within which Khalid Khan had said there was water. Did the Nadir know of it? The column slowed as it neared the rocks. Two riders split off from the column and rode out of Skilgannon's sight. A few moments later they returned, and the men in the column dismounted, leading their ponies into the rocks.

Skilgannon counted twenty-seven men in the party.

Easing himself back from the ridge he rose and walked to where his horse was tethered. Darkness was gathering now. Skilgannon sat down with his back against a rock and rested for half an hour. Then he mounted the gelding and set off down the slope to the desert floor, heading slowly towards the distant oasis and the camp of the Nadir.

With a fighting force of six his options were few. They could retreat, and seek to avoid the enemy. This would only delay the inevitable. Or they could fight. The harsh reality, though, was that a Nadir force of almost thirty, once engaged, would win. Skilgannon had made his name as a general not merely by his prowess with a blade. He had a sharp mind, and an instinctive grasp of tactics. His ability to spot a weakness in enemy formations had become legendary. This situation, however, offered few opportunities to use such skill.

He rode on. Would the Nadir put out scouts to watch for enemies? It seemed unlikely, but even so he held to the low ground, riding through high brush where he could. Pulling up in a small stand of pine some two hundred yards from the entrance to the rocks he dismounted, tethering his horse. The scent of woodsmoke was in the air. The Nadir had lit a fire. Skilgannon squatted down and closed his eyes, sharpening his senses. After a while he caught the aroma of cooking meat.

Moving out on foot he approached the rocks, climbing silently above the Nadir camp. There were two fires, a dozen men round each. This left three. Skilgannon waited. Another man emerged from the shadows. After a while a second came into sight. This one was naked, carrying his clothes in a bundle. Skilgannon guessed he had been swimming.

So where was the last man?

Was he even now creeping towards Skilgannon's position?

The answer was not long in coming. A second naked man came in from the rock pool. There were ribald comments from his friends. The man dressed swiftly and approached the fires.

All twenty-seven Nadir were in sight. Skilgannon settled down to wait.

An hour drifted by. Some of the warriors, having eaten, stretched out on the ground and slept. Several others squatted in a circle and began to gamble with knuckle-bones. This told Skilgannon a great deal about them. They had set no sentries, and therefore were confident that no danger threatened. Why should it? They were hunting – at worst – a few travellers, and at best a single, ageing axeman and his companion. Why would they be worried? It was vital, Skilgannon knew, that warriors remained confident. Only confident men achieved victory. The good leader, however, watched out for the subtle movement between confidence and arrogance. An arrogant army carried the seeds of its own destruction. The secret to defeating them lay in the ability of the enemy to nurture those seeds; to introduce doubt and fear.

He knew then what he had to do.

But it bothered him. It would be high risk, and the chances of surviving were low. For another hour he worked through other strategies, but none would yield such high rewards. Having exhausted all the possibilities he began to prepare, sitting quietly, eyes closed, settling himself into the illusion of elsewhere. Fear and stress melted away. Rising, he drew both swords and made his way down the rocks.

The Nadir had set one night sentry at the entrance to the oasis. The man was sitting with his back to a tree, head down. Skilgannon knelt in the shadows watching the man for some minutes. The Nadir did not move. He had fallen asleep. Rising from his hiding place Skilgannon crept forward. His left hand clamped over the man's mouth. The Sword of Night sliced across the Nadir's throat. Blood spurted. The man jerked once – and died.

Moving through to the centre of the campsite Skilgannon stood for a moment among the sleeping men. Then he took a deep breath. 'Awake!' he bellowed. Men rolled from their blankets, scrambling to their feet. Skilgannon stepped towards the first. The Sword of Day slashed through his neck, decapitating him. A second man was disembowelled as Skilgannon spun and sent the Sword of Night plunging into his belly. Nadir warriors dived for their weapons. Several grabbed swords and rushed at the newcomer. Skilgannon leapt to meet them. Blocking and parrying. The Sword of Night sliced open a man's jugular, and he fell back into his comrades. Then Skilgannon was among them, swords cutting into flesh and severing bone.

They fell back from his fury. Spinning on his heel Skilgannon darted back towards where the Nadir had tethered their ponies. A warrior ran to head him off. Skilgannon dived below a ferocious cut, rolled on his shoulder, and came up running. The ponies were in two lines, each row held by a picketing rope. Slicing his blade through the first tether, he spun in time to parry a lunge. His riposte plunged the Sword of Day into the Nadir's chest. The Nadir ponies whinnied and reared, breaking free. Moving back Skilgannon slashed his sword through the second picket rope, then pushed himself in among the nervous mounts.

Sheathing one of his swords he gave a high-pitched wolf howl. This was too much for the ponies. The sudden movement around them, and the smell of blood, had made them skittish. The bestial howl was enough to send them running. Nadir warriors, still trying to reach Skilgannon, made an effort to block the ponies' escape. Skilgannon grabbed the mane of one mount as it passed and vaulted to its back. An arrow slashed past his face. Giving another howl he slapped the flat of his sword against the pony's rump and galloped through the camp. Two more arrows flashed past him. A third sliced into the pony's shoulder, making it stagger. It did not go down, but followed the rest of the herd out onto the desert floor.

Skilgannon rode to where his own horse was tethered and jumped down from the pony. Mounting his gelding he swung round to see Nadir warriors racing from the rocks. 'Come to me tomorrow, my children,' he called. 'We will dance again!'

Kicking his horse into a gallop, he rode away from the furious Nadir.

He had been lucky, but even so he was disappointed. He had

hoped to kill at least ten of the enemy, reducing the odds for to-morrow. Instead he had slain five or six, maybe seven. Several others were wounded, but their cuts could be stitched readily enough. He doubted the wounds would stop them. Riding south-east he came up behind a dozen or so of the Nadir ponies, and continued to herd them away from the rocks, forcing them further and further from their riders. Several of them were still saddled, and hanging from the saddles were horn bows and quivers of arrows. Skilgannon rode alongside the mounts, lifting clear the weapons and hooking them over his saddle pommel. Then he left the ponies, and set off up the snaking mountain road to where the others would be waiting.

The Nadir had been tough and fast. They had roused from sleep more like animals than men, instantly alert. This had surprised him. He had expected to be able to kill more of them as they blundered from sleep to awareness.

Skilgannon rode on, still scanning the land, and planning the next attack. Only one important question remained. What sort of losses would the Nadir need to suffer before they pulled back from the fight? There were, at most, twenty-two fighting men left. How many would the companions need to kill. Another ten? Fifteen?

He saw Druss and the others waiting on a wide section of the road. Stepping from the saddle he approached the axeman.

'You're bleeding, laddie,' said Druss.

In the shelter of a concave depression in the cliff face Diagoras knelt behind the standing Skilgannon, stitching the cut in his lower back. Moonlight shone down on the blue and gold tattoo of the eagle, its flaring wings rising across Skilgannon's shoulder blades. There were old scars on the young man's body, some jagged, some clean and straight. There were old puncture wounds from bolts or arrows. Diagoras pulled close the last stitch, knotted it, then sliced his dagger through the twine. Skilgannon thanked him, and donned his shirt and sleeveless jerkin.

Diagoras placed the crescent needle and remaining twine in his pouch and sat back, listening as Skilgannon outlined his plan for the morning. He had said little of his fight with the Nadir, merely telling them that he had entered the camp and killed five. He made it sound undramatic, almost casual. Diagoras was impressed. He had not fought the Nadir himself, but he knew men who had. Ferocious and brutal, they were enemies to be feared. Skilgannon asked Druss if he had any idea how many men the Nadir would have to lose before they withdrew. The old warrior shrugged. 'Depends,' he said. 'If their leader is a bold one we might have to kill them all. If he is not . . . another ten, maybe twelve, dead will convince him to pull back. It is hard to say with Nadir fighters. Their chief back at the fortress may be the kind of man who will kill any survivors who have failed him.'

'Then we must plan to take them all,' said Skilgannon.

Diagoras swallowed back a sarcastic comment and remained silent. He glanced at the others. The twins were listening intently, though the simpleton had a puzzled look on his face. He had no idea what was really going on. Garianne seemed unconcerned at the prospect of defeating twenty Nadir warriors, but then she was a fey creature, and more than a little insane. The boy, Rabalyn, sitting with his back to the far wall, looked frightened, but resolute.

Skilgannon outlined his strategy. It sounded, at first, breath-takingly simple, and yet Diagoras, who prided himself on his tactical skills, had not thought of it. Few men would have. Skilgannon called for questions. There were a few from Druss, and one from Jared. They were all concerned with timing. Skilgannon glanced at Diagoras, who shook his head. This was not the time to point out that there was no fall back plan, and no line of escape. Which, of course, was the danger with a strategy of such stunning simplicity. It was win or die. No middle ground. No safety factors.

Skilgannon moved to where a water skin had been placed. Hefting it, he drank deeply. Then he gestured to Diagoras and walked out onto the road. Diagoras joined him there.

'I thank you for your silence back there,' said Skilgannon.

'It is a good plan.' He gazed down over the sickening drop to the valley floor below, then stepped back. 'But you know what General Egel once said of plans?'

'They survive only until the battle starts,' replied Skilgannon.

Diagoras smiled. 'You are a student of Drenai history?'

'A student of war,' corrected Skilgannon. 'Yes, there is much that could go wrong, and even if it goes right we are likely to take losses.'

Diagoras laughed suddenly. Skilgannon eyed him curiously. 'What is amusing you?'

'Isn't it obvious? A mad woman, a simpleton and an unskilled boy make up almost half of our fighting force. And here we are talking of what *might* go wrong.'

Skilgannon was about to answer, but then he too laughed.

Druss wandered out to join them. 'What are you two discussing out here?' he asked.

'The stupidity that comes with war,' said Diagoras.

'Diagoras believes our force is not as good as it might be,' offered Skilgannon.

'That's true,' said Druss, 'but then you can only fight with what you have. I've seen Garianne and the twins in action. They'll not let us down. And the boy has courage. Can't ask for more than that.'

'This is all true,' said Diagoras, with a grin. 'So we're not worried about them. It's you. Let's be honest, Druss, you are a little too old and fat to be of much use to young and powerful warriors like us.'

Druss stepped in and Diagoras was hauled from his feet. Even as he began to struggle he was hoisted above the axeman's head. Druss grabbed his ankle then swung him upside down. Diagoras found himself hanging head first over a six hundred foot drop. Twisting his head he looked up. Druss was standing, arms out-stretched, holding him by his ankles. 'Now, now, Druss,' he said, 'no need to get angry.'

'Oh, I'm not angry, laddie,' said Druss amiably. 'We old folk have difficulty hearing sometimes, and with you speaking out of your arse I couldn't catch what you were saying. Now, with your arse where your mouth was, it should be much easier. Speak on.'

'I was telling Skilgannon what a privilege it was to be travelling with a man of your renown.'

Druss stepped back and lowered Diagoras to the rock. The Drenai breathed a sigh of relief, then stood. 'I fear you don't have much of a sense of humour, old horse,' he said.

'I wouldn't say that,' offered Druss. 'I laughed so much I nearly dropped you.'

Diagoras was about to say more when he looked into the axeman's face. In the moonlight there was a sheen of sweat upon his brow, and he was breathing heavily. 'Are you all right, my friend?' he asked.

'Just tired,' said Druss. 'You are heavier than you look.' With that he turned away from the two warriors and walked back to where the others waited. Diagoras saw him kneading his left forearm, and frowned.

'What is worrying you?' asked Skilgannon.

'Druss does not seem himself. At Skeln his complexion was ruddy. These last few days he has looked ten years older. His skin is grey.'

'He is an old man,' said Skilgannon. 'He may be strong, but he is still a half a century old. Travelling these hills and fighting werebeasts would sap anyone's strength.'

'You are probably right. No man can fight time. When do we need to get into position?'

'An hour. No more than that.'

Druss had stretched himself out on the ledge and appeared to be sleeping. Diagoras and Skilgannon walked further along the road. Here and there were fissures in the rock wall, some shallow, others deep. At one point the road narrowed, then widened. To the left was the sheer red rock face, to the right an awesome drop. Diagoras scanned the area and shivered.

'I have always been nervous about heights,' he said.

'I don't much like them myself,' said Skilgannon. 'But in this situation the terrain is to our advantage. And we need all the advantages we can get.'

'The Nadir are said to be superb horsemen.'

'They will need to be,' observed Skilgannon grimly.

For some time they discussed the plan, and then, as warriors will, they spoke of gentler days. Diagoras talked of an aunt who ran a brothel. 'She was wonderful,' he said. 'I liked nothing better as a child than to sneak off into the city and spend a day with her. My family never spoke of her – except my father. He went into the most terrible rage when he discovered I'd been seeing her. I don't

330

know what annoyed him the most, the fact that she was a whore, or that she was richer than all the rest of the family.'

'Why did she become a whore?' asked Skilgannon. 'My guess is that you are from a high-born family.'

'I really don't know. There was some scandal when she was young. She was sent to Drenan in disgrace, and then ran away. It was before I was born. It was some years later that she appeared. She had wealth then, and she bought a huge house on the outskirts of the city. It was beautiful. She hired architects and gardeners and turned it into a palace. The gardens were a sight to behold. Pools and fountains, and rooms there created from bushes and trees. And she had the most gorgeous girls.' Diagoras sighed. 'They came from everywhere – Ventria, Mashrapur, Panthia. There were even two Chiatze girls, dark-eyed and with skin the colour of ivory. I tell you that place was like paradise. Sometimes I still dream of it.'

'Does your aunt still own it?'

'No. She died of a fever a few years back. Just after Skeln. Even in death there was a scandal. My aunt's closest friend was a woman named Magatha. She was Ventrian, and, like my aunt, had been a whore. She killed herself on the same day my aunt died. Sweet Heaven, that caused a ripple in polite society.'

'So, the whorehouse is closed now?'

'Oh, no. She left it to me, along with all her wealth. I promoted one of the women there, and she manages it for me.'

'This must please your father.'

Diagoras laughed. 'It pleases almost every other man in the community. It is – and I say this with great pride – the best whorehouse in the south.'

Dawn was not far off. 'It is time,' said Skilgannon.

CHAPTER SEVENTEEN

FOR RABALYN THE NIGHT WAS SPENT IN A STATE OF PANIC. HE SAT quietly as the others discussed the fight that would come tomorrow. His hands were trembling, and he clasped them together tightly, so that Druss would not see he was frightened. The attack by the beasts on the camp had been sudden, and he had reacted well. Druss had praised him for his courage. But now, sitting waiting to be attacked, he found his stomach churning. He saw Diagoras and Skilgannon joking together by the ledge, and then watched as Druss picked up the struggling Drenai officer and dangled him over the edge. These men had no fear.

Rabalyn had no understanding of military tactics, and he had listened to Skilgannon outline the plan of attack and it seemed so perilous. Yet no-one else had pointed this out, and he felt, perhaps, that his own lack of knowledge was preventing him from seeing just what a fine plan it was. So he said nothing.

The Nadir would ride up the mountain road, past where Diagoras and the brothers were hiding in a shallow fissure. Then Skilgannon and Druss would attack them from the front. He and Garianne would shoot arrows at the riders from the shelter of a stand of boulders above the road. Once Skilgannon and Druss were engaged Diagoras and the twins would rush in from behind. Apparently these five fighters would then overpower twenty or so savage tribesmen. It made no sense to Rabalyn. Would the Nadir not ride over the men attacking them on foot? Would they not be trampled to death?

Rabalyn had been afraid to ask these questions.

All he knew now was that this might be his last night alive, and he found himself staring longingly at the beauty of the night sky, wishing that he could sprout wings and fly away from his fears.

Druss had walked back to the rock wall, stretched himself out, and fallen asleep. It was incomprehensible to Rabalyn that a man facing a battle could just sleep. He found himself thinking of Aunt Athyla, and the little house back in Skepthia. He would willingly have given ten years of his life to be back at home, worrying about nothing more than a scolding from old Labbers for not doing his homework. Instead he had a sword belted at his side, and a curved bow with a quiver of black-feathered arrows.

Time drifted by, and the fear did not subside. It swelled in his belly, causing the trembling to worsen. Skilgannon came back with Diagoras, and they woke Druss. The old man sat up and winced. Rabalyn saw him rubbing at his left arm. His face seemed sunken and grey. Then the brothers approached. Once again Nian was holding on to the sash at Jared's belt.

'Are we going to fight now?' asked Nian.

'Soon. But we must be quiet,' answered Jared, patting his brother on the shoulder.

Diagoras and the twins left the company then, walking back down the road and out of sight. Skilgannon came and knelt beside Rabalyn. 'How are you feeling?' he asked.

'Good,' lied Rabalyn, not wishing to shame himself by admitting his terror. Skilgannon looked at him closely.

'Follow me. I'll show you where I want you to shoot from.'

Rabalyn pushed himself to his feet. His legs were unsteady. As he made to follow Skilgannon Druss called out to him. 'You've forgotten the bow, lad.' Blushing with embarrassment Rabalyn swept up the bow and the quiver and ran to catch Skilgannon. They walked to the site of a recent landslide, where several huge boulders had fallen across the road. Skilgannon scrambled up the first, hauling Rabalyn up behind him. 'There is good cover here, Rabalyn. Do not show yourself too often. Shoot when you can, then duck back.'

'Where will Garianne be?'

'She'll be on the ground below you. She is a better shot.' He smiled. 'And less likely to send an arrow through one of us. Keep your shafts aimed at the centre of the riders.'

'The centre. Yes.'

'Are you frightened?'

'No. I am fine.'

'It is not a crime to be frightened, Rabalyn. I am frightened. Diagoras is frightened. Anyone with any intelligence would be frightened. Fear is necessary. It is there to keep us alive; to warn us to avoid danger. The greatest instinct we have is for self-preservation. Every ounce of that instinct is telling us that it would be safer to run than to stay.'

'Then why don't we run?' asked Rabalyn, with more feeling than he intended.

'Because it would only save us today. Tomorrow the enemy would still be coming, and the terrain would be more suitable for them than for us. So here we stand. Here we fight.'

'We could die here,' said Rabalyn miserably.

'Yes, we could die. Some of us may anyway. Keep yourself safe here. Do not venture down for any reason. You understand?'

'Yes.'

'Good.'

'Is Druss all right?'

Skilgannon looked away. 'I am concerned about him. Something is troubling him. I cannot worry about that now. The Nadir will be here soon, and I must ride to meet them.'

'I thought you were going to stand with Druss.'

'I will. Try not to shoot me as I ride back.'

Skilgannon climbed down the boulders, leaping the last few feet to the ground. Garianne was waiting at the bottom, her crossbow hanging from her belt, a Nadir bow in her hands. Rabalyn heard Skilgannon speak to her. 'Protect Old Uncle,' he said.

Then he was gone. Moments later he rode by them.

The dawn was breaking.

Skilgannon rode back along the rocky road, moving past the fissure in which Diagoras, Jared and Nian were hidden. As he did so Nian called out. 'There's Skilgannon! Hello!' As he rode on Skilgannon heard Jared telling his brother to keep quiet. Anger flared fleetingly in his heart, and then the dark humour of the situation relaxed him. Diagoras was right. A simpleton, a mad woman and a frightened boy made up half of Skilgannon's army. Then there was Druss. Old and weary. Somewhere the old gods were laughing.

He slowed his horse on a steep downward stretch, then halted him where the road widened. Looking down over the edge he could see the Nadir on a bend of the road far below. There were only nineteen of them. This was a small relief. The men he wounded must have been more badly hurt than he had guessed.

Lifting the stolen Nadir bow from his saddle horn he notched an arrow. It was unlikely that he would cause any damage from this range, but he wanted them to know he was there. Drawing back the string he let fly. The arrow flew straight, but his aim was faulty. It struck the road just ahead of the lead rider. The Nadir drew rein, and glanced up just as Skilgannon loosed a second shaft. This also missed. 'Good morning, my children,' he called down. Several of the riders drew their own bows, sending black shafts hissing towards him. The elevation made the range too great, the arrows falling short. 'You need to come closer,' he shouted. 'Come up here.' He sent another arrow hissing through the air. This one sliced through a warrior's forearm. The Nadir heeled their mounts and galloped towards the sharp bend in the road that would bring them to him.

He waited calmly, another arrow notched. He was getting used to the bow now. It was far more powerful than he had first supposed. As the Nadir rounded the bend he sent a shaft at the lead warrior. The man tried to swerve his mount, but only succeeded in making it rear. The arrow sliced into the pony's throat, and it fell.

Swinging the gelding Skilgannon rode up the road, the Nadir close behind. Arrows flew by him. Up ahead he could see Druss standing, axe in hand. Then Garianne stepped into sight. She shot an arrow that flew past Skilgannon. Then another. Coming alongside Druss he threw himself from the saddle, slapping the gelding on the rump and sending him running back along the trail.

Drawing both swords he turned and ran at the oncoming tribes-men. An arrow tore through the collar of his jerkin, slicing the skin. Druss bellowed a war cry and charged into the Nadir, his axe cleaving through a man's chest, catapulting him from the saddle. Skilgannon plunged his sword through the belly of another. The Nadir threw aside their bows and grabbed for their swords. Skilgannon cut and thrust. A pony swung into him, hurling him from his feet, but he came up fast. Druss hammered his axe into another warrior. Skilgannon heard loud shouts coming from behind the milling Nadir horsemen, and knew that Diagoras and the others had attacked from the rear. The Nadir tried to reform, but the new attack unnerved some of the ponies, which, in trying to escape, came too close to the edge. Four Nadir horsemen plunged over the side. Some of the tribesmen jumped from their saddles and began to fight on foot. Skilgannon killed one with a reverse cut across his throat. A second leapt in. An arrow appeared in his chest and he stopped in his tracks, before dropping to his knees. Three horsemen rode at Druss. Skilgannon saw the old warrior stagger as he waited to meet them. Then he fell to his knees. The riders thundered past him towards Garianne.

She shot the first. Then the other two were on her. One threw himself from his mount. He and Garianne went down together. Skilgannon wanted to go to her aid, but he was himself now being attacked. Blocking wild cuts and slashes from two tribesmen he backed away – then leapt forward and to the right. The Sword of Day clove through the first Nadir's breastbone, while the Sword of Night blocked an overhand cut from the second warrior. The first Nadir went down, his hands grabbing at the sword impaling him, trying to drag Skilgannon down with him. Releasing his grip on the hilt Skilgannon parried a fresh attack from the second man, then killed him with a riposte that opened his throat. Druss had forced himself to his feet and was staggering back towards Garianne.

Skilgannon killed another warrior then spun to follow the axe-man. Garianne was lying on the ground. Beside her was the still form of Rabalyn, his tunic covered in blood. Three dead Nadir were close by.

Skilgannon swore, then turned back to the fight.

Only there was no fight.

Diagoras and the brothers were walking towards him, past the bodies of twelve Nadir warriors. There was blood flowing from a cut on Diagoras's brow. Jared was wounded in the arm. Nian was untouched.

Skilgannon ran back to where Druss was kneeling by the boy. The axeman's face was grey, his eyes sunken. He looked in pain and his breathing was ragged. 'Couldn't . . . get . . . to them,' he said. Skilgannon knelt by Garianne. She had a lump on her temple, but her pulse was strong. Rabalyn had been stabbed in the chest. Sheathing his sword Skilgannon pulled open the boy's tunic. The wound was deep, and blood was bubbling from it. Diagoras came alongside.

'Pierced his lung,' he said. 'Let's get him out of the sun.'

Jared and Diagoras lifted the boy, while Nian knelt down beside Garianne. Stroking her face the simpleton called her name. 'Is she sleeping?' he asked.

'Yes,' said Skilgannon. 'Carry her back into the cave. We'll wake her then.' But Nian saw his brother move away carrying Rabalyn. He cried out.

'Wait for me, Jared!' His voice was panicky. Dropping his sword he ran to Jared and took hold of the sash at his brother's belt. Skilgannon looked at Druss, who was now sitting on the roadside.

'What happened?' he asked.

'Pain . . . in the chest. Like there's a bull sitting on it. I'll be all right. Just need to rest a while.'

'Is there pain in your left arm?'

'It's been cramping lately. I'm feeling better already. Just give me a moment.'

Skilgannon lifted Garianne and carried her back to the shallow cave, laying her down in the shade. Despite the blood still flowing from the cut to his head Diagoras was working on the wound to the boy's chest. He and Jared had hauled Rabalyn into a sitting position. The lad was still unconscious, his face ashen grey. Jared was holding him upright.

Skilgannon walked back into the sunlight, retrieving the Sword of Day from the chest of the dead Nadir. Several of the ponies were still standing on the roadside. Two of them carried saddlebags. Skilgannon walked to the ponies, speaking softly. They were still skittish. Searching the saddlebags he found that one contained an engraved silver flask. Uncorking it, he sniffed the contents. Then he sipped it. It was fiery and hot. A spirit of some kind. He walked back to where Druss still sat. 'This might help,' he said, offering the flask. Druss drank deeply.

'Long time since I've tasted this,' he said. 'It's called lyrrd.' He drank again. 'I couldn't get to the boy in time,' he said. 'I saw him jump down to help Garianne. He killed the first Nadir. Caught him by surprise. The second stabbed him. I got there too late. Will he live?'

'I don't know. The wound is a bad one.'

Druss winced and groaned. 'Pain in the chest is getting worse.'

'It is a heart seizure,' said Skilgannon. 'I have seen them before.'

'I *know* what it is!' snapped Druss. 'It's been coming on for weeks. I just didn't want to accept it.'

'Let me help you into the cave.'

Druss shrugged off Skilgannon's hand and pushed himself to his feet. 'I'll rest awhile,' he said. He took two steps, then staggered. Skilgannon came alongside him. Reluctantly Druss accepted his help into the cave.

Diagoras approached Skilgannon. 'I have sealed the boy's wound, but he's still bleeding inside. I don't have the skill to heal him.'

'Let's see to you,' said Skilgannon. Together they moved out into the light. Blood had drenched Diagoras's tunic on the right side, and was still flowing from the deep cut on his head.

'It is not so bad,' Diagoras told him. 'A little blood goes a long way. Most shallow wounds look worse than they are.'

Skilgannon smiled at him. Diagoras looked suddenly sheepish. 'But then I suppose you already knew that, general.' He opened his pouch and removed his crescent needle and a length of twine, handing them to Skilgannon. Then he sat down, allowing Skilgannon to examine the cut.

'It extends into the hairline. That's where most of the blood is coming from. I'll need to shave the area around it.'

Diagoras eased his hunting knife from its sheath. Skilgannon took it. First he sliced away the long dark hair, leaving a stubbled area three inches long and two inches wide. The skin had split here, and there was some swelling. Skilgannon worked on the wound, needing to draw the skin tightly into place. It was not easy.

'Pull much harder and my ear will end up on top of my head,' complained Diagoras.

Jared walked out to join them. 'Garianne is awake,' he said. 'I think she is all right.' Then he gathered up his brother's sword and returned to the cave.

'What's wrong with Druss?' asked Diagoras, as Skilgannon completed the last stitch.

'A seizure. His heart all but gave out. He's been suffering for some weeks, he said.'

Diagoras rose to his feet and walked out among the dead. Skilgannon followed him. 'With a sick heart he killed five Nadir. Damn, but he is a phenomenon.'

'Six,' corrected Skilgannon. 'He made it back to kill the man who stabbed Rabalyn.'

'That is one tough old man.'

'He will be a *dead* old man if we do not find the temple. I have seen these seizures before. His heart is barely holding out. That massive body needs a healthy heart to feed it. In the condition he's in he'll have another attack before long. He won't survive it.'

'How far to this temple?'

'Khalid Khan says two days. But that was a man travelling across rough country on foot. With a wagon? I don't know. Three perhaps.'

'The boy won't last three days,' said Diagoras.

They heard the rumble of a wagon coming down the road. Skilgannon glanced up to see Khalid Khan driving it. Several of his men and two women were following behind. Skilgannon walked to meet him.

'These women know wounds. Does the Silver Slayer live?' said Khalid Khan.

'He does.'

'That is good to hear,' said the old man. 'I had a bad feeling when he sent me away. Is he sick?'

'Yes.'

Khalid Khan nodded. 'I will guide you to where I saw the temple. We must pray to the Source of All Things that it is there this time.'

Elanin had long given up hope of rescue. Even if Uncle Druss did find this fortress in the middle of the wilds the men here were of appalling savagery, Nadir warriors in clothes of stinking goatskin, and hard-eyed soldiers who stared at her with cold indifference, their voices harsh, their eyes cruel. Uncle Druss would not be able to take her away from them. A man who could bend horseshoes would be no match for these terrible warriors.

And then there was Ironmask.

He had not struck her again, for she was careful around him. He had beaten Mother, though. He had blackened her eyes and split her lip. There were bruises on her body. And he yelled at her, calling her a 'useless sow' and a 'stupid whore'.

Elanin sat in her room, high in the citadel. She had not seen Mother now for five days, nor been allowed out of the room. A cold-hearted Nadir woman brought her two meals a day, and took away the chamber pots, emptying them and replacing them. Elanin no longer dreamed of being free. In the last two weeks she had developed a trembling in her hands and arms, and would spend much of the time finding places in which to hide. There were cupboards, and spaces behind tall chests. Once she even found her way into a wine cellar, and hid behind the barrels. Each time they found her, and now she was locked into a small room at the top of the citadel. The room was not large enough for a good hiding place. But she discovered that if she crawled into the closet and pulled shut the door, the darkness was welcoming and gave her a sense of protection. She would cower in this small place for hours. Then she began to pretend that this was all a terrible dream, and that if she tried hard enough she would wake up in her sunny room in Purdol. And Father would be sitting by the bed. The days drifted by, and her fantasies increased. She ate mechanically, then returned to her sanctuary.

Today Ironmask had come to her room, wrenching open the closet door and dragging her out into the light. Twisting his hands in her now greasy blond hair he pulled back her head and stared into her face. 'Not so proud now, are we?' he said. 'Are you going to tell me you hate me?'

Elanin began to tremble, her head twitching. Ironmask laughed at her. 'I want my mother,' she managed to say, tears spilling to her face.

'Of course you do, little one,' he said, his voice suddenly gentle. 'That is only natural. And I am feeling generous today. So I have left a little gift by your bed. Something for you to play with. Something of your mother's.'

He left her then, pulling the door to behind him. She heard the bolt clang shut.

Still trembling, Elanin went to her bedside. There was a pouch there. She lifted it, and opened the drawstrings, tipping the contents onto her bed. Then she screamed and fled back to the closet.

On the bed, blood from her mother's severed fingers began to seep through the dirty sheets.

The forest was dark and gloomy, but up ahead Skilgannon could see an angled shaft of moonlight. Slowly he made his way towards it, heart beating fast, fear swelling. Movement from his left caused him to spin, and he caught a glimpse of white fur. His hands snaked for his swords, but he stopped. The yearning to grip the ivory blades was almost overpowering. He walked on.

And there, illuminated by the shaft of moonlight, sat an enormous wolf, its fur glistening white as virgin snow. The beast stared at him. Its eyes were huge and gold. Then it rose and padded towards him. The fear roared back at him, swirling into panic. The swords were in his hands now, and he raised them. A savage exultation fired his blood. He screamed a war cry – and the swords swept down . . .

A hand was pulling at his shoulder, and he surged upright, pushing Diagoras away. 'What are you doing?' he yelled.

'Calm yourself, man. You were shouting in your sleep.'

'I almost had it,' said Skilgannon. 'I could have ended it.'

'What are you talking about?'

Skilgannon blinked and rubbed his hand across his face. 'It doesn't matter. It was just a dream. I am sorry for disturbing you.' He glanced around. Druss was still sleeping alongside the wounded Rabalyn. Garianne was awake, and staring at him, her face emotionless. On the far side of the camp the twins were sitting close together, and talking in low voices. Khalid Khan walked across to Skilgannon, handing him a cup of cool water.

'Are they dreams or visions, warrior?' he asked.

'Just dreams,' said Skilgannon. He drained the water and took a deep, calming breath. Then he rose and walked across the rocks to a flat area, where he began to stretch. Then, with Diagoras and Khalid Khan watching him, he eased his way through a series of slow movements, like a dance. He felt his lungs expand, and his body loosen.

Khalid Khan returned to his blanket, but Diagoras walked over and sat close by. 'What is it that you do?' he asked.

'It is an ancient discipline. It brings the body back into harmony.' Skilgannon continued for a while, but being observed prevented him from achieving complete oneness. Even so he was more relaxed as he joined Diagoras. 'The boy is holding up well,' he said.

'I am more optimistic tonight,' said Diagoras. 'He is young, and it seems the bleeding is slowing down.'

The day had been a long one. Diagoras had driven the wagon, while Druss sat in the back, talking to the stricken Rabalyn, encouraging him, and telling him stories. Skilgannon had ridden alongside for a while, listening to the old warrior talking. His stories were not about warfare, but about different lands and cultures. He spoke of his wife, Rowena, and her talent for healing. She could lay her hands on the sick, and within days they would be up and working in the fields. Skilgannon looked at the axeman, noting the grey face and the dark, sunken eyes, and wished his wife could be here now. Soon after that Druss lay down and slept, as the wagon slowly trundled on, ever deeper into the mountains.

According to Khalid Khan they had one more day of travel. They would arrive at the temple site around dusk tomorrow.

Skilgannon walked away from the campsite, climbing a ramp of rocks and staring back over the rocky trails they had covered that day. 'You think we will be followed?' asked Diagoras, coming up beside him. Skilgannon glanced round.

'I do not know. There were fewer Nadir in the attack than I expected.'

'It is a shame about the boy, but your plan worked well.'

'Yes. Though it shouldn't have,' said Skilgannon. 'Any plan that depends on the stupidity of the enemy is flawed. They could have attacked us in two groups. They could have dismounted, and moved in on foot. They could have sent a scout ahead. Even better, they could have held back until we were forced to leave the mountain road and enter open country.'

Diagoras shrugged. 'But they did none of these things, and we survived.'

'True.'

'What were you trying to catch in your dream? You said you almost had it.'

'A wolf. It is not important.'

Diagoras reached up to the shaved part of his skull, gingerly touching his fingers to the ragged stitches. 'Damn thing itches,' he said. 'I hope the hair grows back. I knew a warrior once who had a long scar on his skull. Hair turned white around it. Damn, but he was ugly.'

'The scar made him ugly?'

'Not entirely. He was mildly unattractive before. The scar tipped him into downright ugliness.' Diagoras laughed. 'He was a most unfortunate fellow. Always complaining about how fate hated him. He could cite a litany of bad luck that had dogged him since childhood. One night, when he was severely depressed, I got him to walk with me. I explained how important it was to have a positive outlook on life. Rather than dwell all the time on the bad things, a man should look at the blessings. For example, we were returning from fighting the Sathuli. Now *they* are a fighting race. We'd lost twenty men. However, as I pointed out, he was not among them. He had survived. And that was lucky. I tell you I worked hard during that walk, and by the time we got back to the camp he was much cheered. He thanked me profusely, and said that from that moment on he would look at life differently.'

'And did he?'

'No. We got back to our tent to sleep and he was bitten by a snake that had crawled into his blankets while we were walking.'

'A poisonous snake?'

'No. I think he wished it was. It bit him in the balls. He was in agony for weeks.'

'Some men are just unlucky,' said Skilgannon.

'True,' agreed Diagoras. They sat in silence for a while. Then Diagoras spoke again. 'How did you earn the enmity of the Witch Queen?'

'I ceased to serve her. It is that simple, Diagoras. I walked away. Men don't walk away from Jianna. Everything but that. They flock around her, vying to catch her eye. If she smiles at them it is as if they have imbibed some narcotic.'

'She casts spells on them?'

Skilgannon laughed. 'Of course. The greatest spell of all. She is beautiful, Diagoras. I do not mean pretty, or attractive, or sensual. She is stunning. I mean that in the fullest sense. A man who gazes upon that beauty has his senses stunned. He cannot drink it all in. When I first knew her she was being hunted. She disguised herself as a whore, dyed her hair yellow and streaked it with crimson. She wore a cheap dress, and no paint upon her face. Even then she would turn heads.' He took a long breath. 'She turned mine. I have never been the same since. When you are with her you have eyes for nothing else. When you are away from her you can think of little else. In my years as a priest I thought of her almost hourly. I tried in my mind to dissect her attraction. Was it the eyes, or the mouth? Was it the beauty of her breasts, or the curve of her hips? Was it her legs, so long and luscious? In the end I realized it was something far more simple. You cannot have her. No man can. Oh, you can sleep with her. You can touch and kiss those breasts. You can hold her close, skin on skin. But you cannot possess her. She is the unattainable.'

'I know that feeling,' said Diagoras.

'You knew a woman like that?'

'No. It was a horse. I went to an auction in Drenan, to buy a stallion. There were some wonderful beasts there. I was hard pressed to choose one to bid for. I had almost eighty raq to spend, and that would have bought just about any horse in Drenan. Then they led out a Ventrian pure bred. It was magnificent. The crowd went silent. It was a grey, with an arching neck, and powerful shoulders. It was perfect in every line. Flawless. The bidding started at fifty raq, but it was like a joke. Within minutes it had reached two hundred raq, and was still climbing. I kept bidding, even though I could never raise the money. I managed to pull out at three hundred raq. It went for four hundred and thirty. I've never forgotten that stallion. Never will. The moment I saw it I knew I could never own it.'

Skilgannon looked at the Drenai officer. 'You Drenai are an interesting people. I talk of a fabulous woman, and you speak of a horse. Now I know why all your fables and stories are about wars, and not about great love.'

'We are a more pragmatic race,' agreed Diagoras. 'But then no stallion ever sent assassins to kill someone who walked away from it. No stallion ever metamorphosed from an angelic lover to a harridan. And with a good horse you get a fine ride every time you mount. The horse won't tell you it has a headache, or is angry with you because you were late home.'

Skilgannon laughed. 'You have no soul, Drenai.'

'Having been raised largely in a whorehouse I am not easily captivated by mere beauty. Though I will admit I find Garianne more than a little becoming, and I have been known to feel the tiniest pang of jealousy when she seeks you out.'

'It is hardly a compliment when a woman needs to be drunk to seek your attention,' observed Skilgannon, rising from the rock. Diagoras joined him as they walked back to the campsite. Everyone was asleep now.

'I'll keep watch,' said Skilgannon. 'Get some sleep.'

'Gladly,' said the Drenai, moving off into the darkness.

For Rabalyn the journey across the mountains was difficult. He could only breathe when propped up, and there was some dull pressure pain in his chest and upper belly. It was not, however, insufferable. He'd once had a toothache that had been considerably more painful. Yet, as they moved on, faces would constantly appear above him, asking how he was, and looking grave and concerned. Diagoras, Jared and Skilgannon would check on him. Even Nian came over as Rabalyn was lifted down from the wagon for a noon stop in the shade of some high rocks.

'Lots of blood,' said Nian. 'Your tunic is very wet with it.'

'You . . . remember . . . the stars?' asked Rabalyn, having to take swift shallow breaths in order to speak. Nian looked nonplussed. He sat beside Rabalyn, his head tilted on one side.

'Don't get stars in the daytime,' said Nian. 'Night time is for stars.'

Rabalyn closed his eyes, and the bearded simpleton ambled away. The most talking came from Druss. Rabalyn enjoyed it when the axeman sat beside him in the back of the wagon. It was relaxing to close his eyes and listen as Druss told him of far-off countries, and hazardous journeys by sea. On one occasion, when Rabalyn opened his eyes and looked at the Drenai, he saw his face was pale, and covered in a film of sweat.

'You . . . are . . . in . . . pain?' he asked.

'I've known pain before. It usually goes away, I find.'

'Is it your heart?'

'Aye. I have been thinking on it. Two months ago I passed through a village that had suffered some sickness or another. Mostly I don't get sick. This time, though, I did. Headaches, chest pain, and an inability to hold food down. I've not been myself ever since.'

Rabalyn gave a weak smile.

'What's so funny, laddie?'

'I saw you . . . kill those . . . werebeasts. I thought . . . you were the . . . strongest man . . . ever.'

'And so I am,' Druss told him. 'Don't you forget it.'

'Will . . . I . . . die . . . from this?'

'I don't know, Rabalyn. I've seen men killed by tiny wounds, and others survive when they should not have. It is often a mystery. One fact I do know is that you must desire to live.'

'Doesn't . . . everyone?'

'Yes, of course. That desire, though, has to be focused. Some men will scream and beg for life. They exhaust themselves and die anyway. Others, though wanting to live, look at their wounds or their sickness, and just give up. The secret – if there is truly any secret – is to hold close to life, as if you were gripping it in your palm. You tell your body, quietly, firmly, to hold on. To heal. You stay calm.'

'I . . . will.'

'That was brave of you, laddie, to jump down and help Garianne like that. I am proud of you. Because of you she is still alive. You were thinking of the code, weren't you?'

'Yes.'

Druss laid his huge hand on Rabalyn's arm. 'There's some would say what you did was foolish. There's many would tell you that it would have been best had you stayed on that rock and remained safe. They would tell you that it is better to live a long lifetime as a coward, rather than a short one as a hero. They are wrong. The coward dies every day. Every time he runs away from danger, and leaves others to suffer in his place. Every time he watches an injustice and tells himself: "It is nothing to do with me." Every time a man risks himself for another, and survives, he becomes more than he was before. I have seen you do that three times. Once, back in the woods when you took up my axe. Once in the camp when the beasts attacked. But, best of all, when you leapt from that rock to help Garianne. We none of us live for ever, Rabalyn. Better by far, then, to live well.'

Blood was flowing once more from the pressure pad strapped to Rabalyn's chest. Druss's fingers were too thick to untie the bandage. Diagoras came over, and as he unwrapped the bandage Druss applied pressure to the wound. 'I can ... smell cheese,' said Rabalyn. He saw Diagoras glance at Druss, but neither man spoke. Sitting him up they applied a new pad, and strapped the bandages tightly. Diagoras gave him a drink of water. Then they lifted him back into the wagon.

'We need to press on,' said Diagoras. The others were mounting their horses. Diagoras swung into the driver's seat. Druss grunted as he eased himself alongside.

Rabalyn drifted off to sleep. It was a warm and comfortable sleep. He saw his Aunt Athyla calling to him. She was smiling. He ran to her, and she put her arms round him. It was the most wonderful feeling he had ever known. He fell into her embrace with the joy of homecoming.

'Damn you, Druss!' shouted Diagoras. 'You should never have allowed him to come!'

Druss the Legend stood wearily by the wagon, gazing down at Rabalyn's body. The lad looked smaller in death, hunched over by the wagon wheel, a blanket around his thin shoulders. Jared moved to Diagoras, trying to calm him, but the Drenai officer had lost control. Shrugging off the restraining hand he strode to stand before the axeman. 'It was your code that killed him. Was it worth it?'

Skilgannon stepped in. 'Leave it be, Diagoras!'

The officer swung round, his face ashen, his eyes angry. 'Leave it be? Why? Because you say so? A dead boy may not mean much to the man who wiped out an entire city of men and boys and women and babes. But it means something to me.'

'Apparently it means you can behave like an idiot,' said Skilgannon. 'Druss didn't kill him. A Nadir sword killed him. Yes, he could have been left behind. Mellicane will be a city under siege before long. Food will run short. How would he have survived? And if he had managed to scrape a living, who is to say what would have happened when the Naashanite army swept inside? Perhaps the Queen would once more have ordered the massacre of all within. You don't know. None of us know. What we can be sure of is that the boy was brave, and he stood by his friends, even though he was terrified. That makes him a hero.'

'A dead hero!' snapped Diagoras.

'Yes, a dead hero. And all the wailing and recriminations will not change a thing.'

Garianne moved to Druss, who was leaning against the wagon, his breathing ragged. 'Are you all right, Uncle?'

'Aye, lass. Don't concern yourself.' The old warrior glanced once more at the boy, then swung away. He moved off slowly into the rocks and sat down some distance from the group, lost in thought.

Khalid Khan approached Skilgannon. 'This is where the temple was,' he said. 'My oath upon it.'

Skilgannon gazed around at the towering cliffs. There was no sign of any building. 'I was walking back up that ridge yonder,' said Khalid Khan, pointing back the way they had come. 'When I glanced back I saw the temple, shimmering in the moonlight. It was nestling against the mountain. I do not lie, warrior.'

'We will wait for the moon,' said Skilgannon. Garianne moved across to sit with Druss, her arm round him, her head upon his shoulder. Jared and Nian walked to Rabalyn's body. Nian knelt down and stroked the boy's hair. Diagoras sighed.

'I am sorry, Skilgannon,' he said. 'Anger and grief got the better of me.'

'Anger will do that, if you give it a chance,' said Skilgannon.

'You never get angry?'

'Sometimes.'

'How do you control it?'

'I kill people,' said Skilgannon, stepping past the officer. Walking away he glanced at the sky, recalling the words of the Old Woman. *'The temple you seek is in Pelucid, and close to the stronghold. It is not easily found. You will not see it by daylight. Look for the deepest fork in the western mountains, and wait until the moon floats between the crags.'*

He could see the fork in the mountains, but the moon was not yet in sight. Just then something moved at the edge of his vision. Skilgannon did not react with any sudden movement. Slowly he turned and scanned the jagged rocks.

A gentle breeze blew. There was a scent upon it. Skilgannon walked to where Druss was sitting. 'Can you fight?' he asked.

'I'm alive, aren't I?' grunted the axeman.

'Fetch his axe,' Skilgannon told Garianne. For a moment she glared at him angrily, then ran to the wagon. She could not lift the massive weapon over the side. Jared helped her. Garianne returned with the axe, and Druss took it from her. In the moment of passage between them the axe seemed to lose all weight. Druss hefted it, then stood.

'Nadir?' he asked.

'No. The beasts have returned.' Skilgannon drew his swords. Garianne notched two bolts to her bow.

Some twenty paces to the south a huge grey form rose from behind a jumble of boulders. It stood, massive head swaying from side to side. Garianne lifted her crossbow.

'No, girl,' said Druss. 'It is Orastes.' Laying down his axe he took a deep breath, then walked slowly towards the creature. Skilgannon fell in behind him, but Druss waved him back. 'Not this time, laddie. It doesn't know you.'

'What if it comes for you?'

Ignoring him, Druss continued to walk towards the creature. It gave out a ferocious roar, but remained where it was. Druss began talking to it, his voice low and soothing. 'Long time since I've seen you, Orastes. You remember the day by the lake, when Elanin made me that crown of flowers? Eh? Have I ever looked more foolish in my life? I thought you would laugh fit to bust. Elanin is close to here. You know that, don't you? We will fetch her, you and I. We will find Elanin.'

The beast reared up and howled, the sound echoing eerily in the mountains.

'I know you are frightened, Orastes. Everything seems strange and twisted. You don't know where you are. You don't know what you are. But you know Elanin, don't you? You know you must find her. And you know me, Orastes. You know me. I am Druss. I am your friend. I will help you. Do you trust me, Orastes?'

The watching travellers stood stock still as the axeman reached the beast. They saw him raise his hand slowly, and lay it on the creature's shoulder, patting it. The beast slowly sagged over the face of a boulder, its great head resting on the rock. Druss scratched at the fur, still speaking.

'You need to have the faith to come with me, Orastes,' said Druss. 'There is a magic temple, they say. Maybe they can . . . bring you back. Then we'll find Elanin. Come with me. Trust me.'

Druss stepped away from the beast, and began to walk back towards Skilgannon. The Joining reared up, letting out a high-pitched scream. Druss did not look back, but he raised his hand. 'Come on, Orastes. Come back to the world of men.'

The beast stood for a moment, then shuffled out from behind the rocks and padded after the axeman, keeping close to him, and snarling as they neared the others. Up close he was even larger than he had appeared. Garianne approached him, and he reared up on his hind legs and roared. He towered over Druss, who put out his hand and patted him. 'Stay calm, Orastes,' he said. 'These are friends.' Then he glanced at Garianne and the others. 'Best stay back from him.'

'You don't have to tell me twice,' said Diagoras.

As the moon cleared the western crags the spell faded away.

Skilgannon gazed in amazement at the massive building, with its windows and columns and turrets.

The gates opened, and five golden-clad priests began to run towards them over the rocky ground.

Half an hour earlier the priestess Ustarte had stood at the high tower window, gazing down over the gloomy, dusk-shrouded valley. Her heart was heavy as she saw the people there, gathered round the wagon.

'They do not see us yet,' said her aide, the slender, white-robed Weldi. She glanced at him, noting the lines on his careworn face.

'No,' she said. 'Not yet. Not until the moon is higher.'

'You are tired, Ustarte. Rest a little.'

She laughed then, and the years vanished from her face. 'I am not tired, Weldi. I am old.'

'We are all getting old, priestess.'

Ustarte nodded and, gathering her red and gold silk robes in her gloved hands to raise the hem from the floor, slowly shuffled to the curiously carved chair at her reading desk. There was no flat seat, merely two angled platforms, one against which she could kneel, while the other supported her lower back. Her ancient bones would no longer bend well, and her legs were stiff and arthritic. Not all the vast range of medicines she knew, or had perfected, could fully keep the ravages of time from her body. They might have done, had her flesh not been corrupted and altered, genetically twisted and melded in those dreadful long-ago days. She sighed. Not all her bitterness had been put behind her. Some traces had escaped the vaults of memory.

'Do you remember the Grey Man, Weldi?' she asked, as the servant brought her a goblet of water.

'No, Ustarte. He was in the time of Three Swords. I came later.'

'Of course. My memory is not what it was.'

'You have been waiting for these travellers for some time now, priestess. Why do you make them wait for the moonlight?'

'They are not yet complete, Weldi. Another is coming. A Joining. You know, I miss Three Swords. He made me laugh.'

'I only knew him when he was old. He was crotchety then, and he did not make *me* laugh. To be honest he frightened me.'

'Yes, he could be frightening. We went through much together,

351

he and I. For a while we thought we could change the world. Such is the arrogance of youth, I suspect.'

'You have changed the world, priestess. It is a better place with you in it.' Clumsily he took her gloved hand and kissed it.

'We have done a little good. No more than that. Yet it is enough.'

She gazed around the room, at the scrolls and books on the shelves, and the small ornaments and keepsakes she had gathered during her three hundred and seventy years. This tower room was her favourite. She had never really known why. Perhaps it was because it was the highest room in the temple. Closer to the sky and the stars. 'You will remember at least two of the travellers,' she told Weldi. 'The conjoined twins?'

'Ah, yes. Sweet children. That was a wonderful day, when they walked in the garden, separate but hand in hand. I shall never forget that.'

'Hard to imagine those babes with swords in their hands.'

'I find it hard to imagine *anyone* who would choose to have a sword in their hands,' said Weldi.

'Garianne is with them too. You said she would come back one day.'

'You never did answer my question about her affliction.'

'What question was that? I forget.'

'No you don't. You are teasing me. Are the voices real, or imagined?'

'They are real to her. They could not be more real.'

'Yes, yes! But are they real? Are they the spirits of the dead?'

'The truth is,' said the elderly priestess, 'that I do not know. Garianne survived a dreadful massacre. She lay hidden, and listened to the screams of the dying. All that she loved, all that loved her. When she emerged from the hole in which she had been concealed she felt a terrible guilt for having survived. Did that guilt unhinge her mind? Or did it open a window in her soul, allowing the spirits of the dead to flow in?'

'Why did you let her steal the Grey Man's crossbow? You went through many dangers to bring that here.'

'You are full of questions today. I have one for you. Why is the priestess still hungry, when her servant promised her a meal some time ago?'

Weldi grinned and bowed low. 'It is coming, Ustarte. I shall run all the way to the kitchen.'

Ustarte's smile faded as soon as he had left the room. She felt terribly tired. The magic needed to maintain the cloak of confusion over the temple took a heavy toll on an ageing priestess. It had been such a simple spell two hundred years ago, using merely a fraction of her power. It was merely a matter of reshaping and blurring refracted light so that the red stone of the temple appeared to merge with the towering mountain of rock from which it had been carved. Only in the brightest moonlight did the spell fade sufficiently for men to be able to observe the vast building. Even then the gates were strengthened by spells which – when activated – caused immense forces to build up in metal. Swords would stick to shields, battering rams could not be swung. Men in armour would feel as if they were wading through the thickest mud. Ustarte knew that no castle on earth was completely impregnable. The Temple of Kuan did, however, come close. No-one could enter uninvited.

Her legs rested, she eased herself to her feet and returned to the window. Closing her eyes she concentrated her power, reaching out until she could feel the life forces of the travellers flickering around her, gossamer moths drawn to the light. Gently she examined each of them, coming at last to the youth. His heart had failed. Poison had entered his bloodstream, carried there by the filthy sword blade and the small sections of cloth from his tunic which had been driven into his body. Staying calm and focused Ustarte sent a bolt of energy into the still heart. It flickered, then failed again. Twice more she pulsed energy into the stricken muscle. It began to beat – but irregularly. Ustarte's spirit flowed through Rabalyn's lymphatic system, boosting it with her own life force. The adrenal glands, overworked and undernourished, had also failed. These too she worked upon. The eerie howling of a wolf cut through her concentration momentarily. Ignoring it she continued to replenish Rabalyn's energy. The dead youth was alive once more, and would survive until she could work on him inside the temple.

The moon was beginning to rise.

Ustarte drew back from Rabalyn and pulsed a message to Weldi. He was climbing the lower stairs, carrying a tray of food for her.

Leaving the tray upon a step he ran back to the inner hall to summon four priests, clad in yellow robes, who were dining there. Together they made their way swiftly through the corridors and halls of the temple, pushed open the gates, and ran across the open ground towards the travellers.

The travellers – all except Druss and Khalid Khan – were taken to an antechamber on the first floor of the temple. There were chairs and leather-cushioned benches here, and a wondrously fashioned table of twisted metal, upon which had been set fruit and goblets of sweet juices. Nian sat on the floor, running his hands over the undulating metal of the table. Jared knelt by him. Garianne lay down on a couch. Diagoras moved to a high window and leaned out, gazing down upon the valley below.

'Druss and Khalid are still there,' he told Skilgannon. 'It looks like Orastes is asleep at the axeman's feet.'

Skilgannon joined him. Priests had gathered round the giant beast and were struggling to lift it. The door behind them whispered open. Skilgannon turned. An elderly man, with small, button eyes, bowed to the company. He shuffled forward, his long white gown rustling on the terracotta flooring.

'The lady Ustarte will be with you presently,' he said. 'She is engaged at present with your companion, Rabalyn.'

'He is dead,' said Diagoras. 'She can bring him back to life?'

'He was dead, yes, but had not yet passed the portals of no return. Ustarte's magic is very strong.'

Garianne rolled to her feet, a wide smile on her face. 'Ho, Weldi! It is good to see you.'

'And you, sweet one. I told the priestess you would come back to us.'

The elderly priest moved to the table where Jared and Nian waited. 'You will not remember me,' he said. 'We played in the inner gardens when you were young.' Jared looked uncomfortable, and merely shrugged. Nian looked up at the old man.

'There is no beginning,' he said, running his fingers along a length of metal in the centre of the table.

'It is one piece, interwoven again and again. Very clever.'

'Yes,' said Nian. 'Very clever.'

Weldi turned to Skilgannon. 'Please rest here for a little while. You will each be assigned rooms later, after Ustarte has spoken with you individually.'

'And the axeman?' asked Diagoras.

Weldi gave a crooked smile. 'The beast would not leave him. So we have sedated it. It will remain asleep while you are guests here. Druss will be with you presently. Khalid Khan refused our invitation. He has returned to his people. Is there anything you require in the meantime?' Skilgannon shook his head. 'Very well then, I shall leave you. The door at the far end of the apartment leads to an ablutions chamber. Its workings are not complicated. The main door leads out into the main temple. The passages and tunnels are very much like a maze to those who do not know the paths. I would therefore request you remain here until Ustarte calls for you. That may be an hour – perhaps a little longer.'

'We wish to go to the gardens,' said Garianne. 'It is very peaceful there.'

'I am sorry, sweet one. You must remain here. I do not have happy memories of the last time you wandered free.' Garianne looked crestfallen. 'I still love you dearly, Garianne. We all do,' he said.

After he had left, Garianne returned to the couch and lay down once more. 'Found it!' said Nian happily. He had squirmed under the table and had his hand on a section of folded iron. 'Look, Jared! I found the join.'

Druss came in. He seemed in better spirits as he strode to a deep chair and stretched himself out in it. 'Rabalyn is alive!' he said.

'We heard,' Diagoras told him. 'This is truly an enchanted place.'

'Everything here is good,' said Garianne. 'No evil – save that which comes in from the outside,' she added, staring at Skilgannon. 'Ustarte can read the future here. Many futures. Many pasts. She will take you to the Vanishing Wall. There you will see. We saw. So many things.'

'What did you see?' asked Nian.

Garianne's grey eyes clouded over, and her face hardened. Closing her eyes again she lay down.

'I don't care much for magic,' said Druss. 'But if it saves the boy I'll put aside my doubts.'

'You are looking better, old horse,' said Diagoras. 'You have colour in your cheeks again.'

'I feel more like myself,' admitted Druss. 'The pain in my chest is less now, and I have a little strength flowing back into my limbs. They gave me a drink of something when first I entered. Cool and thick, like winter cream. Tasted fine, I can tell you. I could do with another.'

Diagoras moved back to the window. The moon was high and bright over the mountains. Skilgannon joined him. 'There was something odd about that Weldi,' said Diagoras.

Skilgannon said nothing, but he nodded. 'You saw it too?' persisted Diagoras.

'Yes.'

'I can't quite put my finger on what was wrong about him.'

'I saw nothing threatening,' said Skilgannon. 'He moves oddly. But then he is old and may have crystals in his joints.'

'For me it was the eyes, I think,' said Diagoras. 'You don't often see that red-gold colour. In fact I have never seen it – save in a dog or a wolf. Sometimes a horse.'

'He is an odd-looking man,' agreed Skilgannon.

'Good news about Rabalyn, eh?'

'Let us hope there is more good news to follow,' said Skilgannon, idly stroking the locket round his neck.

CHAPTER EIGHTEEN

JUST OVER TWO HOURS LATER SKILGANNON WAS LED TO A ROOM ON A higher level. As he followed the slow-moving Weldi he saw several other priests moving along the corridors. They passed a dining room. Through the open door Skilgannon saw a large group of people sitting and eating. 'How many of you are there?' he asked Weldi.

'More than a hundred now.'

'What is it you do here?'

'We study. We live.'

Climbing another set of stairs they came to a leaf-shaped door. The wood was dark, and there were gilded inscriptions upon it that Skilgannon could not read. The door opened as they approached. Weldi stepped aside. 'I shall return for you when your visit is concluded,' he said.

Skilgannon stepped inside. The room was large, the ceiling domed. The plastered walls had been adorned with paintings, mostly of plants, trees and flowers, against a background of blue sky. There were also real plants here, in earthenware containers. In the lantern light it was difficult to see where the real greenery ended and the paintings began. The sound of tinkling water came to him. Stepping further into the room he saw a tiny waterfall bubbling over white rocks to a shallow pool. There were many

357

scents in the air, jasmine and cedar and sandalwood. And others more heady. He felt himself relax.

As he moved past the waterfall the room narrowed, then widened again, leading out onto a balcony above the valley. Here, in the moonlight, he found Ustarte. The shaven-headed priestess was leaning on an ebony staff, tipped with ivory. He stood for a moment, transfixed by her beauty. Her features were Chiatze, fine-boned and delicate. Her large, slanted eyes, however, were not the deep golden brown of that race. In the moonlight they shone like silver, though Skilgannon guessed them to be blue. He bowed low. 'Welcome to the Temple of Kuan,' she said. The music of her voice was extraordinary. He found himself suddenly speechless in her company. The silence grew. Angry with himself, Skilgannon took a deep breath.

'Thank you, lady,' he said at last. 'How is Rabalyn?'

'The boy will survive, but you will need to leave him here with us for a while. I have placed him in a protective sleep. There was a deal of sepsis and gangrene had begun. He will need a week or more before he can rise from his bed.'

'I am grateful. He is a courageous lad. And you brought him back from the dead.'

Ustarte looked at him and sighed. 'Yes, I did. But I cannot accomplish what you would ask of me, Olek Skilgannon. This is not the Temple of the Resurrectionists.'

He stood silent for a moment, struggling with his disappointment. 'I did not really believe that you could. The one who sent me to you is evil. She would not wish me to succeed.'

'I fear that is true, warrior,' said Ustarte softly. She gestured to a table. 'Pour yourself a goblet of water. You will find it most refreshing. The water here has enhancing properties.' Skilgannon lifted a crystal jug and filled a matching goblet.

'Shall I pour for you, lady?'

'No. Drink, Olek.'

Raising the goblet to his lips he paused. Her laughter rang out. 'There is no poison. Would you like me to taste it first?'

Embarrassed, he shook his head, and drained the goblet. The water was wondrously cool. In that moment he felt like a man who had crawled across a burning desert and had discovered an oasis.

'I never tasted water like it,' he said. 'It is as if I can feel it flowing through every muscle.'

'As indeed you can,' she said. 'Let us go inside. My old legs are aching and tired. Give me your arm.'

Together they moved back to the garden room. By the light of the many lanterns he saw that her eyes were indeed of a dazzling blue, flecked with gold. He helped her to a weirdly carved piece of furniture. It seemed a cross between a chair and a stool. She slowly knelt upon it, then handed him her staff. He laid it down close to her, then, lifting his scabbard from his back and placing it on the floor beside him, he sat himself on a high-backed chair opposite her.

'So, why did the Old Woman send you here?' she asked.

'I have been giving that a great deal of thought,' he said. 'Almost from the moment she sent us on this quest. I think I know the answer – though I hope I am wrong.'

'Tell me.'

'First I have a question of you, lady. If I may?'

'You may.'

'Is it true that you grew a new hand for one of Khalid Khan's tribesmen?'

'The body is a far more complex and wonderful piece of machinery than most people realize. Each cell contains details of its master plan. But to answer your question simply: yes. We helped him to grow a new hand.'

'Some years ago was a man brought to you whose face had been cut away?' Even as he asked the question Skilgannon felt the tightness of fear in his belly.

'You are speaking of Boranius. Yes, he was brought here.'

'A shame it was you healed him,' he said bitterly. 'The man is evil.'

'We do not pass judgement here, Olek. If we did would we have allowed you inside?'

'No,' he admitted.

'When did you suspect Ironmask was Boranius?'

'Something inside me said he was alive. When we couldn't find his body after the battle I knew. Deep down, I knew. Then when I heard of Ironmask I wondered. But then Druss told me he was not mutilated, he merely had an ugly birthmark. Only when I heard of the tribesman with the discoloured hand did the thought recur. The fear of it has been growing in my mind ever since.'

'That is why the Old Woman did not tell you. She knew you feared this man, and yet she desired you to go after him. She guessed that – once set upon this road – you would not let Druss tackle the evil alone. Was she wrong?'

'No, she was not wrong. Though how Druss can tackle him with a ruined heart I do not know.'

Ustarte smiled. 'There is nothing wrong with Druss's heart – though Heaven alone knows why, considering his love of alcohol and red meat. He contracted an illness in a village south of Mellicane. It attacked his lungs. Any ordinary man would have taken to his bed for a while and given his body the opportunity to rest and defeat the virus. Instead Druss marched around the country seeking his friend. He exhausted himself and put his heart under enormous strain. He has been given a potion that will eradicate the . . . illness. Tomorrow morning he will be strong again.'

'And the twins?'

Ustarte's smile faded. 'We cannot heal Nian. A year ago perhaps. Six months ago even. Tumours are now erupting all over his body. We cannot deal with them all. He has less than a month to live. We will reduce the pressure on his brain, and he will be himself for a while. Not long, though, I fear. Maybe days. Maybe hours. Then the pressure will increase again. The pain will swell. He will fall into a coma and die. It would be best if he stayed here, where we can administer potions to quell the pain.'

'This will break Jared's heart,' he said. 'I have never seen two brothers so close.'

'They were conjoined for the first three years of their lives. That creates a special bond,' she said. 'I performed the operation which separated them. Part knowledge, part magic. It is the magic that is killing him now. In order for them both to survive I had to re-engineer Nian's life codes. They shared a single heart. I manipulated his genetic foundations, causing his body to create a second heart. This manipulation resulted, finally, in the mass of cancers that are now killing him. It grieves me greatly.'

Skilgannon did not understand much of what she told him, but he could see the anguish in her face. 'You gave them a chance at life,' he said. 'A life they could not have enjoyed without your help.'

'I know this, though I thank you for saying it. What else do you wish to ask of me?'

'What of Garianne?'

'I cannot help her. She is either possessed or insane. You know, of course, that she is in the thrall of the Old Woman.'

'I know.'

'Then you know also her purpose on this quest?'

'She is here to kill me.'

'Do you know why?'

He shrugged. 'It is what the Old Woman wants, ultimately. That is reason enough. I doubt she will attempt an assassination until Boranius is dead. I will deal with that when it happens.'

'You will kill her.'

'To save myself? Of course.'

'Ah, yes, of course. That is what warriors do. They fight. They kill. They die. Do you know where Garianne was born?' she asked suddenly.

'No. She does not take well to questions.'

'That is because she was tortured and abused for some weeks by vile men. They wanted information. They wanted pleasure. They wanted pain. But that came after. Garianne was a normal, healthy young girl. She lived with her family and her friends. She dreamed of a future in which she would be happy. Like all young people she built fantasies in which her life was enriched by love and success, fame and joy. Her tragedy was that she had these dreams in Perapolis.' Skilgannon shuddered, and could no longer gaze into Ustarte's blue and gold eyes. 'When the Naashanite soldiers first breached the walls Garianne's father – a stonemason – hid her beneath some rocks behind his workshop. She lay there terrified all that day, listening to the screams of the dying. She heard people she loved begging for their lives. Old men, women, children, husbands, fathers, sons and daughters. Priests, merchants, nurses and mid-wives, doctors and teachers. The loveless and the loved. When night fell she was still there. Only now she was not alone. Her head was filled with voices that would not go away. They just carried on screaming.'

They sat in silence for a few moments. 'You must hate me,' he said at last.

'I hate no-one, Olek. Long ago hatred was burned out of me. But I have not yet finished the story of Garianne. I shall not tell you of the horrors she later suffered, when captured by Naashanite troops. When she was brought here there seemed no hope for her. We did all we could to restore some semblance of normality to her. What you see now is a result of our best efforts. She ran away, and somewhere came under the sway of the Old Woman. She managed to give her purpose. She gave her a goal. It may even be that this goal will give her back her life. You see, Garianne believes that the ghosts will find peace when they have been avenged. The ghosts will sleep when the Damned is dead.'

'And will they?' he asked.

'I wish I could say. If the ghosts are real then perhaps they will find peace through revenge. I have never believed that vengeance brings peace, but then I have never been a ghost. If her mind is unhinged it may be that completing her mission will free her. It is doubtful – but possible. So you see, if you do kill her you will merely be completing the horror for which you are so aptly named.'

'A fine set of choices,' he said, rising from the chair and gathering up the Swords of Night and Day. Swinging the scabbard to his shoulder, he bowed to her. 'I thank you for your time, lady.'

'Those blades are of evil design, Olek. Eventually they will corrupt your soul. They carry as much responsibility for Perapolis as you yourself.'

'My chances of defeating Boranius are not good. Without the Swords of Night and Day they would be non-existent.'

'Then do not fight him. I do not have the skill to bring back Dayan. Others will. The code of her life is contained in the hair and the bone you carry. There are those who could activate that code. They might also have the skill to draw her soul back from the Netherworld to re-inhabit a new body.'

'Where would I find such people?'

'Beyond the old lands of Kydor, perhaps. Or deep in the Nadir steppes. The Temple of the Resurrectionists does exist. I believe this. There is too much evidence to ignore. Leave Boranius behind. Leave Garianne behind. At least then your quest will be wholly unselfish.'

'That would also mean leaving Druss and Diagoras behind. I cannot do that. What of Druss's friend, Orastes? Can you bring him out of the beast?'

Ustarte lifted her hand and peeled off her glove. Then she drew back the sleeve of her silk robe. Skilgannon stared at the soft, grey fur which covered her arm, and the talons that glinted on the ends of her fingers. 'If I could do that for Orastes, would I not do it for myself?' she asked him. 'Go now, warrior. I wish to speak to the Legend.'

There were thirty-three windows and three doors in the Citadel. The Nadir shaman, Nygor, checked each one of them before retiring to his pallet bed on the fourth level. The ward spells on the main doors were the simplest to re-energize, for here he had hung an ancient relic, the withered hand of Khitain Shak. The dried bones retained much of the power the legendary priest had wielded in life. The windows were more tiring and time-consuming. Some were wide, others mere murder holes – slits through which archers could shoot down on enemies below. Each of these needed a fresh spell daily, fuelled by a drop of Nygor's blood. The wounds on the palms of his hands were troubling him now, itching and irritating. This annoyed him.

For a few days he had managed to use the blood of the stupid woman Ironmask had brought to the Citadel. But then the Naashanite had lost his temper and killed her. A waste. He could at least have allowed her to live until Nygor's hands healed. The child would do. Ironmask would have none of it. He wanted the girl alive until Druss the axeman was in his power. Then he would kill her in front of the Legend. 'Can you imagine,' said Ironmask, 'how sweet that will be? Druss the Invincible. The Captain of the Axe. The Victor of Skeln. Trussed and chained, and watching the slow death of the child he had come so far to rescue? It will drive him mad.'

'I think you should just kill him, lord,' warned Nygor.

'You have no understanding of the exquisite,' Ironmask had told him.

This was obviously true. Nygor took no enjoyment at all from the suffering of others. Death was sometimes necessary in the pursuit of knowledge. Now, at sixty-one, Nygor was close to understanding the secrets he had yearned for decades to unlock. He had mastered the Meld, one of the greatest of the ancient spells. The concentration needed for the creation of Joinings was prodigious. Soon he would unravel the mysteries of rejuvenation. He would have achieved that already had it not been for the Old Woman, and her constant seeking for ways to kill him. He could feel her power even now, pushing at the ward spells, tugging upon them, ever searching for a gap in his defences.

He knew she did not hate him for his own sake. Her true target was Ironmask. Nygor was merely an obstacle in her way. It was a thorny problem. If he left Ironmask she would probably leave him alone. However, if he did quit the service of the warrior he would have no wealth, and no way to pursue his dreams. He could not return to the steppes. Ulric's shaman, Nosta Khan, would have him killed the instant he set foot on Nadir lands.

So he remained – for the moment – trapped between the hammer of her hatred, and the anvil of Ironmask's ambition. Not for much longer, though. Ironmask had hoped to build the Tantrian nation into a force strong enough to oppose the Witch Queen. He had dreamed of leading an army back into Naashan. Those dreams had withered now. They had begun to fail the moment the Old Woman gave the Tantrian King that cursed sword. It had corrupted his mind, filling him with delusions of greatness. Nygor could see now that this had been her intention all along. When Tantria declared war on Datia and Dospilis it served only the Witch Queen. Ironmask had been ruined. Nygor sighed. He should have quit him when the war went bad, and the Datians were at the gates of Mellicane. But Ironmask had escaped with a large portion of Mellicane's treasury, and that wealth might still serve Nygor. If he could find a way to steal it.

The shaman moved to the next level and revived the spell on the windows there. His right hand was aching now.

He stood at the murder hole and stared out at the stars. In that moment he sighed, as he thought of his bond woman, Raesha. It was not until she was dead that he realized how great an affection he had for her. Last year Ironmask had demanded the death of the Witch Queen, and Nygor had summoned a demon to slay her. Not a great feat. Not even a difficult one. He had used Raesha as a vessel of summoning, to enhance his own power. The demon had sped off in search of its prey. All had been well. What they could not know was that the Old Woman had placed powerful ward spells around the Queen. Rebuffed, the demon had returned, seeking blood. Raesha's heart had been torn from her body. Nygor shuddered at the memory.

There were also ward spells around Druss the axeman and his companions. They made it impossible for Nygor to track them. Now the more traditional attempt on Druss's life had also failed. Nygor had an ill feeling about Druss. It was surely impossible for the ageing axeman to assault a fortress manned by ferocious warriors. And yet . . . There was something indomitable about the man, a force that was not entirely human.

Nygor climbed the stairs to the circular battlements, and added fresh ward spells to both doors. They would last three days, but he would revive them after two.

Returning to the main building he almost trod on a large black rat, which scurried past him. Nygor cursed, then made his way down to his own rooms.

The black rat vanished into a hole and emerged out onto the battlements. From here it ran along the edge of the crenellated wall and through another hole that brought it onto one of the domed roof timbers. Its sleek black form scuttled along the wood, coming at last to a torn section of tarred felt. The rat began to gnaw at the felt, creating enough of an opening to squirm beneath. Here there were interlocking planks, and several dead rats.

Tugging aside one of the bodies the rat began to gnaw at the splintered end of one of the joints, its sharp incisors nibbling at the edges of the wood, pulling them clear.

Tirelessly it worked, ripping and gnawing, until its heart gave out and it slumped dead beside the timber. Minutes later another black rat appeared. It too began to bite at the wood.

Finally a sliver of light from below pierced the darkness beneath the roof felt. The rat blinked and shook its head.

It sniffed around for a while, confused. Edging back from the light it scurried away.

Jared returned to the antechamber where the others waited. He sank to a chair, ignoring them. Garianne moved to him, putting her arm round him and kissing his cheek. Diagoras scratched at his trident beard and shivered.

'What is wrong with you, laddie?' asked Druss.

'I am fine, axeman. Never better.'

'You look like a man with a scorpion in his boot.'

'Well, that's a surprise,' said Diagoras. 'I am sitting in a mystic temple, which, it transpires, is entirely manned by Joinings. How curious of me to find this unsettling.'

Druss laughed. 'They have done us no harm. Far from it.'

'Up to now,' said Diagoras. 'They are animals, Druss. They have no souls.'

'I never was much of a debater,' said Druss. 'So I won't argue with you.'

'Please argue!' insisted Diagoras. 'I would love to have my mind put at ease.'

'Far too complex a question for a single debate,' said Skilgannon. 'If men have souls then it follows that Ironmask has one. His life has been spent torturing and maiming innocent people. I had a friend once who had a dog. When their house caught fire the dog ran up the stairs, through the smoke and flame, and awoke my friend and his family. They all escaped. The door downstairs was open. The dog could have fled to the safety of the street. It did not. So if the dog was heroic and selfless without a soul, and Ironmask is vile and evil with one, then what use is it?'

Druss laughed. 'I like that,' he said. 'In my view Heaven would be a better place if only dogs dwelt there.'

'They cannot cure him,' said Jared suddenly. 'They can relieve the pressure on his brain. He will be as he once was. They cannot even say for how long. Hours. Days. And he is dying still. Ustarte says he has less than a month.'

'I am sorry, lad,' said Druss.

'You'll understand, axeman, why we won't be coming with you to the Citadel. I want to spend some time with my brother. We'll stay here. When the time comes they will have medicines to ease the pain.'

'Ah, it wasn't your fight anyway, Jared. Don't concern yourself.'

'We would like to come with you, Uncle,' said Garianne. 'We want to see the little girl safe.' Skilgannon saw that Garianne was looking directly at him as she spoke, her grey eyes unflinching. Druss saw it too, and said nothing.

'You desire my company on this journey, I think,' said Skilgannon.

'You must come now,' she said. 'You must face Boranius. It is your destiny.'

Skilgannon felt anger stirring in him, but swallowed it down. 'The Old Woman does not know my destiny, Garianne. Any more than she knows yours. However, I will travel with you, for my own reasons.'

'Glad to have you, laddie,' put in Druss. 'Is there something between the two of you that you'd like to share?' he went on.

Skilgannon shook his head. The door opened and the servant Weldi entered. 'I have come to bring you to your rooms,' he said. 'You will find clean beds, a little food and water, and a fresh breeze through your windows.'

Later, as Skilgannon lay in his bed, staring up at the stars outside his window, the door to the bedroom whispered open, and Garianne entered. She walked to the foot of the bed without a word. In her hand was the crossbow, a single bolt notched.

'You would like to do it now,' he said.

Extending her arm she pointed the weapon at him. 'We would like to do it now,' she agreed. With a sharp twang the bolt hammered into the bedhead less than an inch from his skull. She lowered the bow and set it down upon a night stand. 'We cannot yet,' she said. 'Uncle needs you.'

Lifting her shirt over her head she tossed it to the floor, then slid out of her leggings. Pulling back the sheet she snuggled into bed alongside Skilgannon, her head upon his shoulder. He felt her fingers stroke the side of his face, then her lips sought his.

*

Boranius sat upon a wicker chair, watching as the Nadir woman bathed the child, Elanin. The little girl was sitting in the copper bath tub, staring ahead, expressionless, as the Nadir scrubbed the dirt from her pale skin. There were sores upon her shoulders and back, but she did not flinch when the harsh cloth scraped across them.

'You know who is coming to get you, little princess?' said Boranius. 'Old Druss. Uncle Druss. He is coming here for you. We must make you clean and pretty for when he gets here.'

There was no change of expression. Irritation flickered in Boranius. The spectacle would be of little merit if the child did not react. 'Slap her,' he ordered the Nadir woman. Her hand cracked against the child's face. Elanin did not cry out. Her head drooped a little, then she stared ahead again. 'Why does she feel no pain?' he asked.

'She is not here,' said the Nadir woman.

'Bring her back then.'

The woman laughed. 'I do not know where she is.'

Boranius rose from the chair, and left the room in search of Nygor. The little shaman would know what to do with the child. It would be such a waste if she couldn't scream for Uncle Druss. He strode through the armoury, and up to the roof hall. Here he found Nygor, sitting in a window seat, scanning some old scrolls. 'The child's mind has snapped,' said Boranius.

'You gave her the mother's fingers to play with,' said Nygor. 'What else do you expect?'

'I thought it amusing. How can we bring the child back?'

Nygor shrugged. 'Opiates, maybe. We'll find a way when the time comes.'

'The girl is soft like her father. His wife told me he was one of the heroes of Skeln. You saw him, Nygor, blubbing away about his little girl. How could such a man have taken part in the defeat of the Immortals?'

The shaman sighed and put aside his scroll. 'I knew a warrior once who tackled a lion with a knife. Yet he was afraid of rats. All men have their fears, their strong points and their weaknesses. Orastes was terrified of the dark. The dungeon was dark. You told him you were going to kill his daughter, cut her into little pieces. The girl was everything to him. He loved her.'

'I have no weaknesses, shaman,' said Boranius, moving to a chair and sitting down.

'If you say so.'

'I do say so. You wish to disagree?'

'I need my fingers, Ironmask, so, no, I will not disagree. You are a strong man. Cursed by the stars, though.'

'That is true enough,' said Boranius, with feeling. 'I never met a man with such ill luck. Bokram should have won, you know. We did everything right. He panicked in that last battle. Had he not been a coward he would now have ruled all of Naashan. And as for the Tantrian King . . . his stupidity was beyond reason. I wish I had taken longer to kill him.'

'As I recall he screamed for several hours.'

'It should have been days. I warned him not to invade Datia. We weren't ready. If he had but waited.'

'The Old Woman got to him with that cursed sword. We could not have predicted that. It corrupted his mind.'

Boranius swore. 'Why does that hag haunt me? What did I ever do to her?'

'My guess would be that you killed someone she had some use for.'

'Ah, well, it matters not. If the best she can do is to send an old man with an axe then I see little to fear.'

Nygor's face darkened. 'I feel her presence at all times. She constantly tests my defences. Do not take her lightly, Ironmask. She has the power to kill us all.'

A cold breeze rippled through the roof hall. Two of the lanterns went out. Boranius leapt from his seat. Nygor cried out and sprang towards the open door. It slammed shut in his face.

A hooded, translucent figure appeared in the shadows by the doorway. 'So pleasing to be appreciated,' said the Old Woman. Boranius drew a dagger from his belt and threw it across the hall. It passed through the figure and clattered against the wall.

'How did you breach my spells?' asked Nygor, his voice echoing his despair.

'I found another opening, Nadir. Up there in the roof. A tiny hole I forced some rats to make. And now it is time for you to join your friend Raesha. Burn, little man.' The hooded figure pointed at Nygor. The shaman tried to run to the window, to hurl himself to the stones far below, but a holding spell closed around him. Flames leapt up from his leggings, igniting his shirt. He screamed and screamed. Boranius watched as Nygor's hair flared away, his scalp and face turning black, the skin bubbling. Still the screams filled the hall. Men began pounding on the door. Finally the screams ended. Nygor's blackened corpse fell to the floor. It continued to burn, filling the hall with acrid black smoke. At the last there was nothing left upon the floor that was remotely human.

The pounding continued. 'Be silent,' said the Old Woman, flicking her hand towards the entrance. The pounding ceased.

'You want to see me burn, whore?' shouted Boranius. 'Come then! Work your magic! I spit on you!'

'Oh, I shall watch you die, Boranius. I shall take great pleasure in it. First, however, you will do me a service.'

'Never!'

'Oh, I think you will. Druss the Legend is coming for you. And with him a man you have not seen for some time. An old friend. What a merry meeting that will be. You remember Skilgannon? How could you not? He cut your face off, as I recall.'

'I'll kill them both, and piss on their corpses.'

The Old Woman's laughter rang out. 'Ah, but I could like you, Boranius. Truly I could. Such a shame we are enemies.'

'We do not need to be.'

'Ah, but we do. I was not always as you see me now. A few centuries ago I was young and men considered me comely. In that heady time of youth I had a child. I left it to be raised by others. I have never been maternal. As time passed I watched over that child, and the children she had. There were not many. Easy to keep track of. At first it was an amusement for me. My gift to the future. The fruit of my loins. Quietly – so quietly – I manoeuvred their lives, bringing them a little luck when they needed it. I could not watch them all the time, however. They got old and died. Despite my best efforts the line ran thin. Until there was only one. A girl. Sweet child. She married the Emperor of Naashan after I slipped him a love potion. There was no way he would ever betray her. She then had a daughter. The last of my line. And you, Boranius, killed the mother and hunted the daughter. In your wildest imaginings can you believe I will forgive you?'

'I care nothing for your forgiveness. I'll kill Skilgannon for the pleasure of it. I'll kill Druss to avenge the Immortals and their defeat at Skeln Pass. If I live long enough I'll kill Jianna – and rid the world of your get.'

'But you will not live long enough, Boranius. And I will be here, in the flesh, to see your soul torn screaming from your body. Until then, something to remember me by.'

Fire swept across Boranius's face, searing lips and nose and cheeks. With a strangled cry he fell back.

'A man with a soul as ugly as yours has no right to a second face,' said the Old Woman. 'So let us remove the flesh Ustarte gave you.'

When Skilgannon awoke he was alone. He yawned and stretched. His arm brushed against the splintered wood of the bedhead. The bolt had gone – as had Garianne. Rising from the bed he pulled on his leggings and boots, and then his cream-coloured shirt and fringed jerkin. Lastly he hooked the ebony scabbard over his shoulder. The dawn was breaking, the land outside the window bathed in gold.

Moving to the door he stepped out into the corridor beyond, making his way back towards the antechamber. He passed a yellow-robed priest and stopped him, asking where he might find the boy, Rabalyn. The shaven-headed priest said nothing, but indicated that Skilgannon should follow him. They walked through a bewildering series of tunnels, down circular stairs, and along corridors, until, at last, they came to a wider hall. At the end of the hall the priest opened a door, and gestured for Skilgannon to enter.

Druss was sitting at Rabalyn's bedside. The lad was asleep. Skilgannon leaned over him. Rabalyn was pale, but he was breathing well. Pulling up a chair Skilgannon sat down beside the axeman.

'He is deeply asleep,' said Druss. 'It does my heart good to see him well.'

'He is a fine lad.'

'He is that. Too many shirkers and cowards in this world,' said

Druss. 'Too many people who live life selfishly and care nothing for their fellows. It grieved me greatly when I thought the boy was dead. Did I tell you that he leapt from a tree and took up my axe to fight a Joining?'

'Only ten or twelve times.'

'That kind of courage is rare. I think this boy will achieve something in his life. Damn, but I hope so.'

'Let us hope he achieves more than we have,' said Skilgannon.

'Amen to that.' The axeman glanced at Skilgannon, his piercing grey eyes holding to the sapphire blue gaze of the Naashanite warrior. 'So why are you coming with me, laddie?'

'Perhaps I just enjoy your company.'

'Who wouldn't? Now tell me the truth.'

'Boranius killed my friends. He threatened the life of the woman I love.'

'And what else?'

'Why does there need to be something else? You are going after Boranius because he . . .' Skilgannon struggled to find an adequate description of the horror that had befallen Orastes '. . . because he destroyed your friend. He also killed all who loved me.'

'Aye, they are good enough reasons. I don't quibble with them. There's something else, though. Something deeper, I think.'

Skilgannon fell silent. Then he took a deep breath. 'Why do you play the simple man, Druss? You are far more subtle and intuitive than you generally let others see. Very well then. The full truth. He frightens me, Druss. There, it is said. Skilgannon the Damned is afraid.'

'You are not afraid of dying,' said Druss. 'I have seen that. So what is it about this . . . this Boranius that causes such terror?'

Quietly Skilgannon told the axeman about the mutilations suffered by Sperian and Molaire, the dismemberments and the blindings. 'The strongest of men would be unmanned and mewling like a babe under his ministrations, Druss. He would end his life as a wretched, broken, bleeding piece of flesh. Everything in me screams to run away. To leave Boranius to his own fate.'

'Every man has a breaking point. I don't doubt that,' said Druss. 'With luck you'll get to meet him blade to blade. You are perhaps the best swordsman I ever saw.'

'Boranius is better. Stronger and faster – or at least he was when last we met. He would have killed me, but one of my men threw a spear at him. It did not pierce his armour, but it broke his concentration. Even then he managed to avoid the first death blow.'

'Maybe you should just let me have him, laddie. Snaga will cut him down to size.'

Skilgannon nodded. 'Perhaps I will.'

They sat with Rabalyn for a little while, but the boy did not wake. The door opened and Weldi entered, bowing low. 'Good morning,' he said. 'I trust you slept well.' Before they could answer he spoke again, this time to Skilgannon. 'The priestess Ustarte has requested your presence, sir. Come, I shall take you to her.'

Druss looked up as Skilgannon rose. 'I'll stay awhile with the boy. He might wake.'

Skilgannon reached out his hand. 'Thank you, Druss. You know, you would have made a fine father.'

'I doubt that, laddie,' answered Druss, taking the offered hand in the warrior's grip, wrist to wrist. 'The most important thing for a father is to be there when his child needs him. I am never anywhere for long.'

Skilgannon followed Weldi to the upper chamber of greenery, where Ustarte was waiting upon the balcony. In the bright morning sunshine Skilgannon could see beyond her beauty, to the weariness and age she carried. The tiniest of fine lines etched her fragile Chiatze features. She smiled at him as he walked out onto the balcony.

'You sent for me, lady?'

'I thought you might like to travel with me, warrior. To the Citadel.'

'Now?'

'If you wish.'

'You will travel with us?'

'No. Just you and I, Olek. It will take but a matter of moments.'

Skilgannon was uneasy. 'And how are we to do this?'

'Merely sit in the chair there, and relax. I will lead your spirit there.'

Nonplussed, he removed his scabbard and sat down, leaning his head back against a cushion. He heard the rustle of her robes, then felt the warmth of her hand upon his brow. Instantly he was asleep.

He rose from the welcoming darkness, towards a bright and shining light. He became aware that someone was holding his hand. For some reason he thought it was Molaire, and he wondered where they were going. Then he recalled that Molaire was dead. Momentary panic touched him as the light neared.

'Do not be afraid,' the voice of Ustarte whispered inside his head. 'Do not struggle or you will wake too early. Trust me.'

Suddenly he was above the clouds, and the bright light was that of the sun, shining in a sky of unbelievable blue. Below him were the red mountains through which he had travelled, and a long, winding river that glittered brilliantly as it snaked towards the distant sea. He felt his hand tugged and his spirit soared towards the northwest, away from the rising sun. Far below he saw villages and farming communities, and two small towns, the largest of which had grown up around the crossing point of four major roads. Just beyond this was an ancient fort. A crumbling, rectangular outer wall enclosed an area of around a mile. Within it were warehouses and tall buildings. At the centre of the fortress stood a circular keep, four storeys high. A domed wooden roof had been added.

'It was built hundreds of years ago to guard the trade roads,' said Ustarte. 'But when the kingdom of Pelucid fell the fortress became derelict for decades. Lately it has been used by robber bands, who control the trade routes. They levy taxes upon the land caravans passing through from the coastal cities. The silks of Gothir, the spices of Namib, gold and silver from the mines to the west. All these fall under the sway of those who control the Citadel. Ironmask captured it over a year ago, ostensibly to allow free trade to flow into Tantria.'

The Citadel loomed closer. 'As you can see it is still a formidable castle. It could withstand a besieging enemy for some time. A few willing fighters, however, could enter the outer wall largely unnoticed.'

'What of the Nadir shaman? Would he not see us coming?'

'The Old Woman killed him last night. Burned him alive. He tried to jump to his death to avoid the pain, but she fixed him with a spell of holding. She is like Boranius. She lives to enjoy the suffering of others. Now let us see the inside.'

For some while their spirits flowed through the Citadel, and Skilgannon mentally noted the rooms and halls, the corridors and exits. Finally they came to an upper room, small and cramped. 'What is here?' he asked, seeing only a shabby bed, and an old wooden closet.

'Here is sadness and pain of the worst kind,' she told him. They passed through the thin door of the closet and Skilgannon saw a small, blond-haired child, sitting against the closet wall. She was hugging her knees and swaying back and forth. 'This is the child Druss seeks to rescue.'

Pulling back from the gloom of the closet they floated within the room beyond. 'Look there,' said Ustarte, 'by the bed.'

He saw the blackened, rotting fingers, and the insects crawling across them. 'Her mother's fingers,' said Ustarte. 'Boranius cut them away before killing the woman. He gave them to the child as playthings.'

'She will never recover from this,' said Skilgannon. 'He has destroyed her future.'

'You may be right, but it is best not to be hasty in these judgements. The child has fled in her terror. She needs to be found and comforted *before* the rescue. She needs to know that help is coming. She needs to feel that she is loved.'

'How would that be possible?'

'I can take you to her, Olek.'

'I am not much of a comforter, Ustarte. It would be better if you went.'

'If I did, do you know what she would see? A wolf woman, with bright golden eyes and sharp claws. She needs someone of her own species, Olek.'

'She knows Druss. Let us go back. You can bring Druss to her.'

'I wish that I could. What you say is true. The mere sight of Druss would lift her. It is not possible. Druss cannot be *reached* in this way. Last night as you all slept I flowed into your dreams. Jared is full of grief, and, though warm-hearted, could not bring the child what she needs. Druss's mind is like a castle. He guards his inner privacy with great resolution. When I reached out to communicate I was met by a sudden wall of anger. I retreated instantly. Diagoras would have been my next choice. He is too fearful of me, and what he sees as my kind. He would not have trusted me as you did. At some point he would have panicked and tried to flee. He might even have succeeded, and his soul would have been lost. Then there was Garianne. I would not even try to enter the scream-filled labyrinths of her mind. In there I could have been lost. So there is only you.'

'What must I do?'

'I will take you to her. She will have built a world around herself that is familiar. You must reach her, and find a way through the elaborate – and perhaps dangerous – place she inhabits.'

'Dangerous for her – or for me?'

'For both of you. Do not give her false hope. It will seem helpful at the time, but will make the return impossible. Do not tell her that Orastes is alive. Be honest, but loving with her. That is all I can advise.'

'I am not the man for this task, Ustarte.'

'No, you are not. And you may fail, Olek. But you are the only one I can use.'

'Take me to her,' he said.

Skilgannon found himself standing before an immense thicket of thorns. He felt disoriented. The sky above shifted and swam with swirling colours, clouds of purple and green, shot with lightning streaks of yellow and crimson. The ground below his feet writhed with long roots, squirming up from the earth like questing snakes.

Moving back from the thorns he sought out firmer ground. Ustarte had told him that the world he now inhabited was entirely the creation of the eight-year-old Elanin. It existed only in the depths of her subconscious. 'It is her last defence against the horrors of the real world,' the priestess had said.

'What can I do there?'

'You have no ability to change her world. Everything you do must be consistent with the world she has created. If there is a stream you can drink from it or bathe in it. If there is a lion you can run from it, or battle it. I cannot help you there, Olek. If you cannot find her, or you are in danger, merely speak my name and I will draw you clear.'

Moving back from the writhing roots he stared at the forest of thorns. He felt the weight of his swords upon his back, and considered cutting his way through. It seemed the most logical course. Yet he did not.

Instead he looked around, and saw an area of flat stone. He walked to this and sat down, staring at the thorns. Some of the limbs of the forest were as thick as a man's thigh, the thorns sprouting from them long and curved like Panthian daggers. He looked more closely. In fact they were daggers.

This was a quandary. The child had created the thorn barrier as a defence. Were he to slash and cut at them he would be attacking her, causing her even more fear. She needed to believe in her strength. Swinging the scabbard from his back he laid it down on the stone. Then he removed his fringed jerkin and his shirt. Leaving the weapons behind he carefully picked his way through the writhing roots until he reached the first of the thorn limbs. These too were moving.

'I am a friend, Elanin,' he said aloud. 'I need to speak to you.'

A wind picked up. The thorns swayed and slashed. 'I am coming through the thorns,' he said.

With great care he eased himself past the first of the limbs. A thorn dagger slashed across the top of his shoulder, the wound burning like fire. 'You are hurting me, Elanin,' he said, keeping his voice soft. 'My name is Brother Lantern. I am a priest from Skepthia. I mean you no harm.'

Pushing further into the thorns he struggled to stay calm. A dagger sliced across his thigh. Another embedded itself in his forearm. 'I have come to help you. Please do not hurt me.'

Gripping the dagger thorn in his arm he prised it loose and moved on. Pain roared through him, igniting his anger. Fighting to hold it back he stepped over a low limb. Searing agony shot through his back. Looking down he saw a long dagger thorn protruding from his belly. Panic touched him. This was a death wound. He was about to utter the name of Ustarte when he saw that the deep gouge on his arm had disappeared now. 'Please take this thorn from me, Elanin,' he said. 'It hurts greatly.'

The dagger was ripped from him. He screamed in pain and fell to his knees. Looking up, he saw a narrow pathway between the thorns. Touching his fingers to his belly he found no blood, nor any sign of a wound. Pushing himself to his feet he moved down the winding path. A savage roar made the ground tremble beneath his feet. He walked on. The thorn wall ended. Before him was a clearing. At its centre stood a huge bear with slavering fangs. Skilgannon stepped to meet it – and saw that he once more held his swords in his hands.

'No!' he shouted, hurling them from him. 'I don't want them!'

The beast charged. Skilgannon instinctively dived to his right, rolling on his shoulder and coming smoothly to his feet. 'I will not hurt you, Elanin,' he shouted. 'I am here to help.'

The beast reared and moved towards him. Skilgannon stood very still. 'I have come with Uncle Druss to find you,' he said, scanning the undergrowth for signs of the child.

The bear loomed above him, and he looked up into its huge brown eyes.

'Where is Uncle Druss?' it asked, with the voice of a small girl.

'He is coming to the Citadel.'

'Does he have an army?'

'No. I am with him. And Diagoras and Garianne. Two friends of Uncle Druss.'

The bear sat down. Its shape shimmered and changed. The ground shifted. Walls reared up around the clearing. Within moments Skilgannon found himself sitting in a high room, with a wide window overlooking the sea. It was a child's room, full of toys and books. On the bed by the window sat a blonde girl, with large, blue eyes. 'Hello, Elanin,' he said.

'Where is my father?' she asked. 'I cannot find him.'

Skilgannon sighed. 'May I sit with you?' he asked.

'You can sit in the chair.'

He did as she bid. 'I am Brother Lantern,' he said. 'I am . . . I was . . . a priest. I am also called Skilgannon. I do not know your father. I have never met him. Uncle Druss tells me he is a fine man.'

'They killed him, didn't they? They killed Father. Ironmask told me. He said they turned him into a wolf and he was killed in the arena.'

'Ironmask is an evil man. But you must be strong. We will come for you.'

'He wants to kill me too. But he won't find me here.'

'No, he won't.'

The little girl looked into Skilgannon's eyes. 'If you haven't got an army you won't win. There are lots of soldiers with Ironmask. Big men with big swords. More than a hundred. I saw them from my window.'

'I have seen them too. It will be difficult. Tell me, little one, do you know the way back to the Citadel?'

'I'm not going there! You can't make me!' The room shimmered, thorn limbs sprouting from the walls.

'No-one is going to make you do anything,' he said swiftly. 'Is that the harbour outside? Do you have a boat there? I have always liked boats.' The thorns withdrew. Elanin rose from the bed and walked to the window.

'Father doesn't like boats. They make him feel sick.'

'I sometimes feel sick in boats. But I still like them.' He knelt down in front of her. 'When we come to rescue you in the Citadel we need to be able to call you home. We need . . . a secret password so you know it is safe.'

'I am not coming home. Father isn't there. I shall stay here.'

'That is one plan,' he agreed. 'I think it will make Uncle Druss sad.'

'Then he can come here.'

'And what of your friends back in Dros Purdol? They can't come here. This is your special place. I only came because I have a special friend who showed me the way.'

'Ironmask killed Mother too. He cut her up.' Tears welled in the child's eyes. Instinctively Skilgannon reached out and drew her into a hug. He stroked her hair, and patted her back.

'I cannot bring her back,' said Skilgannon. 'I cannot take away your suffering. But you are strong. You are a very brave girl. You will make your own decisions. Let us agree on a password. You can then decide whether to stay here, or come back to Uncle Druss and me.'

'I think you should go now,' she said. 'It is getting late.'

The room spun. Skilgannon was flung through the air, in total darkness. He landed heavily on the ground – just in front of the thorn forest.

'I will see you soon, Elanin,' he called. Then he whispered the name of Ustarte.

Skilgannon opened his eyes. Ustarte was standing by the balcony's edge, looking at him intently. 'How do you feel?' she asked.

'Weary.'

'Drink a little of our water. It will revive you.' The sun was shining brightly, and a cool breeze flowed across the balcony. Skilgannon filled a crystal goblet and drained it. His limbs felt leaden, as if he had run a great distance.

'You suffered much,' said Ustarte. 'I will be honest, you have surprised me, warrior. You almost died in there.'

'You warned me it could be dangerous.' Strength was seeping back into his limbs.

'That is not what surprised me. Even Druss, I think, would have taken his axe to that thorn thicket. He would certainly have fought the bear.'

'It doesn't matter. I failed. She is too terrified to come out.'

'You have planted a seed. You could do no more. You should rest for a while.'

'Not yet,' said Skilgannon. 'Can you take me to the Citadel once more? I need to see exactly how many soldiers there are, and what their duties.'

'I can tell you the numbers.'

'With respect, lady, I need to see for myself. Four warriors cannot attack the Citadel. If we merely needed to enter and kill Ironmask we could do it. However, I have now seen the child, and the most important duty we have is to rescue her, to bring her safely home. If that is to be even remotely possible I need to know the movements of their troops, their methods and their duties. I need to understand their loyalties. Do they fight for love of Boranius, or for plunder? Everything is against us at this moment. Had we arrived in secret we might have spirited the child away, and then returned for Boranius. But we are not arriving in secret. He knows we are coming. And I know Boranius. He is not a fool. From what I saw of the Citadel there are only four approaches. He will have scouts out, watching for us. Once we are seen on the open road he will send riders to intercept us. Even with twenty Druss the Legends we would be overcome, by arrows and spears, if not by swords.' He looked up at her. 'So I ask again that you take me back.'

'Would it make a difference to your plans if I told you that you cannot win, Olek?'

'No,' he said simply.

'And why is that?'

'Not an easy question to answer, lady, and I am too weary to debate it.'

'Then I shall take you back to the Citadel, Olek. Close your eyes.'

CHAPTER NINETEEN

MORCHA SAT OUTSIDE THE BEDROOM. THE GROANS OF PAIN WERE easing now as the surgeon applied narcotic salves to Boranius's ruined face. The burns were severe, and yet strangely had only affected the discoloured skin. The rest of his face and his eyes were completely untouched. After a while the surgeon Morcha had brought from the market town emerged from the bedroom. 'He is sleeping now,' he said. 'I have never seen a wound like it.'

'Nor I,' said Morcha. The sandy-haired officer rose from his seat. 'I thank you for coming,' he said. The surgeon, a thin-faced man with rounded shoulders, looked at him curiously. Morcha felt embarrassed suddenly. The man had had no choice. When Ironmask issued a command you either obeyed or died. Sometimes you did both.

'I will need a room close by. When he awakes the pain will return. I need to be here.'

'Of course,' said Morcha.

'I am amazed his sight is not affected. There are no burns to the skin around the eyes. How did this accident occur?'

'I was not present, sir. The Nadir was burned to ashes. Not a bone remained. My lord was mutilated as you saw. Some of the men heard screams from the roof chamber and ran to the room. The door was barred. They heard voices from within – one of

382

them a woman's. When they finally broke in the woman was gone.'

'Were there other exits?'

'No.'

The surgeon shivered. 'I need to know no more about this,' he said, making the sign of the Protective Horn. 'Show me where I may sleep.'

Morcha took him to a small room on the ground floor. 'I shall send you some food and drink,' he said. 'I hope you will be comfortable.' Once again the surgeon looked at him strangely.

'If you don't mind my asking, young man, how is it that you are here?'

'I do mind your asking,' said Morcha, giving a short bow and leaving the surgeon.

As he walked out into the night the question continued to burn in his mind. He strolled across the open ground then wandered past the warehouses and storage areas, coming at last to the low barracks which housed the soldiers who still followed Boranius. Alongside the barracks was the Long Tavern, where the men relaxed at day's end. The sounds from within were raucous. Morcha did not feel like joining them. He walked on, coming to the now near deserted Nadir area. The death of Nygor had been seen by most of the warriors as an evil omen – especially coming so soon after the killing of the men sent after Deathwalker. Of the hundred Nadir warriors who had inhabited this section only four scouts now remained. The rest had saddled their ponies and ridden off towards the north.

Morcha made his way to the outer defensive wall, and climbed to the ramparts. He found the two sentries on this section in deep conversation. One of them saw him, and leapt to his feet. The other merely stared at Morcha, and remained where he was. 'There are still enemies out there,' said Morcha. 'We need to be alert.'

'Sorry, sir,' said the standing soldier. 'We were just talking about the attack on Ironmask.'

'And the fact that we're all out of luck,' said the second. 'We should be quitting this place, Morcha. If we don't we'll die here.'

'There are merely a handful of warriors out there, Codis. Druss may be a legend, but even he cannot defeat us all.'

'No, he can't,' agreed the man, rising to his feet. 'But what next?

A few years back we were soldiers of the King. Shem's balls, man, we were the elite. Then we lost, and barely got out with our lives. What have we been since then? Truth to tell, Morcha, I wish you had never come to me and said Boranius was still alive. I wish with all my heart that I'd stayed quietly in Dospilis. Not one of the promises has been met.'

Morcha sat down on the crenellated battlement. 'You weren't saying that, Codis, while we were gathering riches in Mellicane.'

'Does this look like Mellicane to you?' sneered Codis. 'This is a crumbling ruin. What is the point of having sentries on the walls, when there are at least ten full breaches, and other areas where a man could just walk in unobserved? We have trees which come almost to the edge of the walls. When the enemy get here they will just walk in. We'll see them only when the bloodletting starts. I say we take off and head into the hills. We can plunder a few caravans, make some money, and then strike east towards Sherak. They are hiring mercenaries. We could do well there.'

'Aye, we could. Perhaps you would like to put that view to Boranius?'

'Perhaps we all should,' said Codis. 'Perhaps we should go to him now and put him out of his misery.' Codis fell silent, and the words hung in the air. He looked into Morcha's eyes. 'He's never going to win back power, Morcha. He had a chance in Mellicane, but not now. What are we? A band of robbers. Sooner rather than later the Datians will come for us. We used to be part of an army of thousands. Now there are seventy of us. We're out of gold, out of opportunities, and out of luck.'

'Luck can change,' said Morcha.

'Aye, it can. For us, though, it's likely to move from bad to worse. I spoke to the three Nadir who survived the attack on Druss. Have you heard?'

'I heard they were massacred.'

Codis suddenly chuckled. 'Ah yes, you've been in the north. You haven't heard the best news then?'

'Just tell me.'

'Well, the Nadir made camp the night before the attack. A lone swordsman walked in, killed a bunch of them, then rode out on one of their ponies. The swordsman had two curved blades, with white ivory hilts. One of the Nadir recalled he had a tattoo of a spider on his forearm.'

'So?'

'So?' echoed Codis. 'Who do you think that is likely to be? We're not just facing Druss the Legend. Skilgannon is coming.' He stared intently at Morcha, then his expression hardened. 'You knew. You damned well knew!'

'He is one man. As you said yourself, we are seventy.'

'Oh yes, one man! If he was to walk in here now how many of us would he take down before we stopped him. Five? Ten? I don't want to be one of those ten.'

'You won't be, Codis,' said Morcha, with a smile. Easing himself off the battlements he suddenly laughed. 'I can guarantee that.'

'Oh yes, and how exac—' Codis grunted. His knees buckled. Morcha powered the dagger further into his chest. The soldier sagged against his killer. Morcha stepped back. Codis fell face first to the stone. The other soldier stood by silently. Morcha rolled the body onto its back and retrieved his dagger.

'Keep watch,' said Morcha. 'I'll send another sentry to join you. Best you don't fall into conversation again.'

'I won't, sir.'

'I believe you.'

Morcha wiped his dagger clean on the dead man's tunic, then sheathed it. Descending the rampart steps he walked back to the tavern, where he located an officer and ordered him to send some men to retrieve Codis's body.

Then he returned to the Citadel. Remembering the surgeon he ordered one of the cooks to take the man some food, and sat alone in the deserted dining hall. The cook returned after a while, and brought Morcha a tankard of cold beer. Morcha thanked the man.

His mind flowed back over the years, recalling the day that he and Casensis had followed the youth, Skilgannon. He still remembered fondly the time at the bathhouse. How neatly the boy had fooled them, and how priceless had been the disguise the princess had adopted. The whole city had been searching for Jianna, and there she was, dressed as a whore, and standing before two of the men charged with capturing her. Morcha smiled at the memory.

How cool the young Skilgannon had been. Morcha admired

him. More than that, he had liked him. He had even been secretly pleased when the lad escaped the city with the girl. With luck they would have kept on moving, and drifted out of the pages of history. But no. The rebellion had begun. Boranius had been delighted. The prospect of battles and glory had thrilled him. Thoughts of defeat had entered no-one's head. The forces of the princess had been small, offering mere pinpricks and irritation to Bokram. A few outlying forts were taken, a few caravans seized. The attacks were hit and run and small in scale. The first year had seen little more than bee stings against the body of Bokram's army. The second year much the same. Then two more tribal leaders had joined Jianna's army. They had blocked the high passes in the west of Naashan, effectively liberating a region containing two cities and a score of silver mines. Looking back that was the beginning of the end for Bokram. Though none of us saw it at the time, recalled Morcha.

Even up to the last battle we believed we would conquer. A sudden shiver rippled through him. The day, begun in high spirits, had ended with Morcha and five others carrying the mutilated Boranius from the field.

Now, years later, Boranius was mutilated again, and once more Skilgannon was coming. Codis had been right. The only sensible course was to ride away now.

And yet he could not.

In a world of shifting values Morcha believed in loyalty. He had pledged himself to Boranius, and he would stand by him.

'Have you seen enough?' asked Ustarte. Skilgannon struggled to open his eyes. His body felt as if it had been without sleep for a month. Every muscle ached. He could not raise himself from the chair. Ustarte's gloved hand stroked his face. 'Humans without training find the journey of the spirit exhausting,' she said. 'Water will help.' It was all Skilgannon could do to raise the goblet to his lips. His hand trembled. He drank, then fell back into the chair and closed his eyes.

'I feel I have aged twenty years,' he said.

'It will pass when you have rested. Sleep a little. I will come back in a while.'

Skilgannon needed no urging. He fell asleep immediately, deep and dreamlessly. When he awoke the new dawn was breaking. Ustarte was standing by the balcony's edge, the sunlight glinting on her red and gold gown.

'Do you feel better?'

'I do, lady. It was the best sleep I have had in years.'

'You did not see the White Wolf?'

He smiled. 'It seems my curse to meet people who know my dreams. But, no, the wolf did not come to me. I almost slew it the last time.'

'It is as well that you did not.'

He sat up, and drank some more water. 'I feel it would stop it disturbing my sleep.'

'Indeed it would. Which is why you must not.'

'You think I need troubled dreams?'

'I think you need to understand the nature of the wolf. Has it ever attacked you?'

'No.'

'It is you who hunt the wolf, yes?'

'That is true. Whenever I see it I draw my swords. Usually it disappears. The last time, though, it padded towards me.'

'It did not charge? Its fangs were not bared?'

'No. It just walked towards me. I raised my swords to kill it, but Diagoras woke me.'

'The swords again. Did you know that the Old Woman conjured demons and trapped them within the blades?' Skilgannon shook his head. 'The demons give them power. It is a trade, however. Slowly the demons will exert an influence over you. They will corrupt you, increasing your angers and your hatreds. It is they who wish to kill the White Wolf. That is why whenever you see it in your dreams they leap to your hands.'

'Why do they need to kill the wolf?'

'That is for you to answer, Olek. The White Wolf is usually driven from the pack. He is different, and the other wolves fear him. So this wolf stands alone. He has no mate, no pack to follow or to lead. Does he remind you of anyone?'

'The wolf is me.'

'Yes – or rather your soul. He is all that is good in you. The

387

swords need him dead before they can overcome you. Did the journey to the Citadel help you?'

'I believe that it did. The troops there are demoralized. The Nadir have fled. More will desert as the days pass. They fear Druss. Merely knowing he is coming is filling the soldiers with terror.'

'And you, Olek Skilgannon. They fear you mightily.'

'Yes, that is true.'

'I sense you knew one of those we saw. You even have affection for him.'

'I knew him years ago. And, yes, I liked him then. Strange to see a man like him following a monster like Boranius.'

She laughed then. 'You humans amuse me. When someone is evil you need to demonize them. He is a monster, you say. No, Olek, he is merely a man who has given in to the evils of his nature. All of you have a potential for evil, and for good. Much depends on the stimuli applied. The soldiers you led into Perapolis butchered and raped, mutilated and destroyed other humans. Then they went home to their wives and their sweethearts, and raised children and loved them. You are all monsters, Olek. Massively complex and uniquely insane. You teach your children that to lie is wrong. But your lives are governed by small lies. The peasant does not tell the lord what he truly thinks of him. The wife does not tell the husband she saw a man in the marketplace who made her loins burn. The husband does not tell his wife he went to the whore-house. You follow a god of love and forgiveness, and yet you rush into war bellowing, "The Source is with us." Need I go on? Boranius is evil. That is true. Yet in all his life he has not ordered as many innocents slain as you.'

'I cannot argue with you, lady,' said Skilgannon sadly. 'I cannot undo the past. I cannot bring them back.'

'You can give them peace,' she said softly.

He looked at her, meeting her gaze. 'By letting Garianne kill me? You said yourself that she is probably unhinged, and that there are no ghosts inside her head.'

'I could be wrong.'

He laughed then. 'One problem at a time, lady. First we need to rescue the child. After that I will consider the problem of Garianne. Where is Druss?'

'He is with Rabalyn. The boy is recovering well.'

'And Diagoras?'

'He and the twins are in the lower gardens with Garianne. Diagoras has discovered much in common with Nian. They argue wonderfully about the nature of the stars.' Ustarte turned and stared out over the red mountains. 'There is something else you should know, Olek. The Old Woman has cast a concealing spell over the lands to the northeast of the Citadel. I cannot penetrate it.'

'The northeast?' he repeated. 'The lands of Sherak?'

'Not all of Sherak. Even she is not that powerful. No, it is merely a . . . mist, if you like . . . over a small area.'

'Her purposes are a mystery to me,' he said, 'save that she wants Boranius dead.'

'There is something more,' said Ustarte. 'I know that she hates Druss. Twice he has thwarted her.'

'She is none too fond of me,' said Skilgannon, 'though, to my knowledge, I have done nothing to cause her harm.'

'She has sent Garianne to kill you. Of that I have no doubt. So, at the very least, she requires three deaths. Boranius is obviously the most important. Otherwise Garianne would already have tried to slay you. The Old Woman's actions are most odd. She slew the Nadir shaman with a fire spell. His body became a living candle. This is powerful magic, Olek. To achieve it, while in spiritual form, is awesome indeed. What it means, though, is that, if she desired it, she could kill you and Druss in precisely the same manner. Or indeed Boranius. The question then is: why does she not? Why this elaborate quest?'

'Our deaths alone are not sufficient,' said Skilgannon.

'I don't understand.'

'Take Boranius, for example. You might ask why, when he kills, he does it so slowly. He takes pleasure in torture and pain. The Old Woman is no different. To merely kill us holds no attraction for her. Druss is a proud man. He wants to rescue the child. Imagine how he would feel if that rescue were to fail. Worse, if he were to arrive and watch her die.'

Ustarte shuddered. 'I do not want to understand such depths of evil. If what you say is true, then what is it she requires of you?'

'That is more simple, I think. I fear Boranius, more than I fear death. It would please her to see Boranius cut me to pieces.'

'And the concealment spell she has cast?'

He fell silent for a while, thinking the problem through. 'Someone else is coming,' he said at last. 'If she wants Boranius to kill Druss and myself, then she will need another weapon to dispose of Boranius. More warriors drawn into her web.'

'And knowing this you will proceed against the Citadel?'

'The child is the key to it all,' he said. 'That is the beauty of her plan. We cannot now walk away. This she would have known. Even if we survive – which is doubtful – the child will be slain before our eyes.'

Ustarte took a deep breath. 'We do not usually take part in the affairs of this world,' she said. 'I shall make an exception now. I will help you, Olek.'

Diagoras was enjoying the conversation with Nian. They had moved from the nature of the stars and the planets to the fundamental complexities of nature. So engrossed did the Drenai officer become that he quite forgot, for a while, that Nian was under sentence of death. Jared, meanwhile, sat back, taking little part in the discussion. He watched his brother, his expression showing a mixture of admiration and sadness. Garianne was sitting by the banks of a stream that flowed through the indoor garden. She was staring at the water as it bubbled over a bed of glistening white rocks.

Nian walked over and kissed her golden hair. 'It is good to see you again, my friend,' he said.

'We are happy that you have come back,' she told him. Nian looked over her shoulder at the stream, then walked to the edge of the water, squatting down and pushing his hand into the pool at the base of the stream. Then he rose and examined the five foot high waterfall that bubbled from the rocks by the north wall.

'What do you find so fascinating?' asked Diagoras, moving to join him.

'Do you not see? Watch the waterfall.' Diagoras did so.

'What am I supposed to be seeing?'

'The pink rose petals swirling on the water's surface.'

'What about them? They are coming from the rose bushes on the other side of the stream,' said Diagoras, indicating the small floribunda bushes.

'Yes, they are. How then are they also falling from the waterfall, which appears to be coming from the rock wall?'

'Obviously there are more rose bushes above us somewhere.'

Nian shook his head. 'I think the water just comes down the waterfall, and then is drawn back from the pool to go round again and again. Intriguing.'

'Water does not flow uphill, Master Nian,' Diagoras pointed out. 'It is impossible.'

Nian chuckled. 'Master Diagoras, you are sitting in a temple that magic has made invisible, which is run by creatures half human and half beast, who have brought Rabalyn back from the dead, and have brought me back to the living. And you speak of the impossibility of water flowing uphill?'

Diagoras gave an embarrassed laugh. 'Put that way I can only agree with you.'

Garianne rose lithely to her feet. 'Hello, Uncle,' she called. Diagoras saw Druss striding across the garden. The Drenai grinned.

'Ah, that is better, Druss. *Now* you look like the man I knew.' It was true. Druss's grey eyes were sparkling and his skin glowed with health.

'And I feel it, laddie. The water here is almost as good as Lentrian red – and that is saying something. Have you seen Skilgannon?'

'No. He went off with the priestess last night. I've not seen him since.'

'They are making a journey of the spirit,' said Nian. 'It is called *soaring* by some. It is a feat said to have been first mastered by the Chiatze thousands of years ago. The spirit is loosed from the body and can travel vast distances. I believe Ustarte is using her powers to allow your friend Skilgannon to examine the Citadel.'

Diagoras looked doubtful. Nian laughed. 'Truly, my friend. I would not lie to you.'

'I believe you, laddie,' said Druss. 'My own wife had that talent. It is good to see you looking well.'

'You have no idea how good it is to be myself. All I have had for these past few years are snatches of coherence, and odd memories of foolishness, or downright stupidity. It embarrasses me to think of what I became.'

'You shouldn't be embarrassed,' said Druss. 'You were a good companion, and a faithful friend. That counts for much.'

Nian smiled, and reached out to shake Druss by the hand. 'I thank you for that,' he said, 'though, truth to tell, I would sooner be dead than live as I did. And, though Jared has not admitted it thus far, I fear that death is waiting for me rather sooner than I would like.' He glanced at his twin. 'Not so, brother?'

Jared said nothing, and looked away. Nian returned his gaze to Druss. 'You will tell me the truth, axeman. I am a good judge of men, and you are no liar.'

Druss nodded. 'They couldn't remove your cancers. That is the truth of it.'

'How long do they give me?'

'A month. Maybe less.'

'As I thought. Jared's long face was proof enough. You will understand, I hope, why I will not be travelling with you on your quest? I would like to stay here. There are books in the library that are filled with wonders. I'd like to read as many of them as I can before I die.'

'Of course,' said Druss. 'I wish they could have helped you, Nian. You're a good man. You deserved better.'

'It has always been my belief that this stage of our existence is merely the beginning of a great journey. I am saddened – and a little frightened – to be facing the second stage so early. But I am also excited by the prospect. I wish you well, Druss. I hope you rescue the child.'

'I usually do what I set out to do.'

'I don't doubt it.' Nian turned to Diagoras and Garianne. 'Excuse me, my friends. I have a little reading to catch up on.'

As he walked away Jared rose to follow him. Nian placed his hand on his brother's shoulder. 'No, brother. Stay here with your friends. I need a little solitude.' With that he left the gardens.

The following morning the travellers assembled outside the temple. The beast that was Orastes was awake now, and clambered

392

up on the back of the wagon, staying close to Druss who was in the driving seat. Skilgannon, Diagoras and Garianne were all mounted, and the priestess Ustarte was standing beside Skilgannon's gelding.

'I will watch over you all,' she said. 'When the enemy is close I will lay a spell over you. It will confuse those who gaze upon you, in much the same way as the temple deceives the eye. I will not be able to hold the spell for more than a few minutes. But it should suffice. When you are stopped say you are travellers bound for the market town. Say you are looking for work.'

'I thank you, lady, for all you have done for us,' said Skilgannon.

'It was little enough. We will meet again, I think, Olek. Perhaps then I can do more.'

As Skilgannon swung his horse the gate of the temple opened. Jared came out, leading his horse, followed closely by Nian. Diagoras rode back to them.

'I'm glad you changed your mind, Nian,' he said. 'I would have missed your company.'

'Going to Citadel,' said Nian happily. 'Chop up the bad people.' Seeing that Jared had mounted, Nian scrambled onto his own mount.

Reaching out, he took hold of the sash at his brother's belt.

Morcha had slept for no more than three hours of the last forty-eight. Everything was falling apart. Eighteen men had deserted, and morale among those remaining was low. Boranius himself seemed unconcerned. He spent most of his time in the roof hall, high in the Citadel, his bandaged face now permanently covered by the ornate black mask. Morcha had tried to interest him in the scouting reports, and the slow erosion of their fighting force. Boranius just shrugged.

'Let them all go. I care not,' he said, his voice muffled by the mask.

This morning Morcha had found Boranius stripped to the waist and practising with his swords. He had stood and watched. The man was extraordinarily lithe, his movements lightning fast. At the rear of the hall sat the Nadir woman. On the floor before her was the Drenai child, Elanin. She was crouched down, hugging her knees and swaying slightly, her head cocked to one side, her blue eyes staring sightlessly into the distance.

Morcha and the rest of the men had been told the child was being held for ransom. Morcha was beginning to doubt it. No message had been sent to Earl Orastes at Dros Purdol. It was mystifying.

Boranius saw Morcha and paused, sheathing the Swords of Blood and Fire. They were handsome blades, the ivory hilts superbly crafted.

'Well?' asked Boranius, draping a towel over his sweat-drenched shoulders. 'Are our guests close?'

Morcha strode forward, then began to refer to the sheaf of notes he carried. 'It is most odd, lord. The enemy has been sighted in several places, some of them thirty miles apart. Our best Nadir scout sent word he saw Druss in the mountains, at the camp of Khalid Khan. I sent out twenty men to set up an ambush.' Morcha shuffled through the notes. 'Now I have had word he and the others have been sighted far to the west. I have sent two more riders to scout the high pass, and have another ten bowmen positioned at the only entrance to the lowlands. An hour ago a rider came in saying he had seen them going in to the Temple of Ustarte.'

'They will come, regardless of your efforts, Morcha. I know this in my soul.'

'With respect, lord, there are only four routes to the Citadel. All of them are now watched. We will have word when they approach.'

'They will come,' repeated Boranius. 'I shall kill Skilgannon. It is my destiny.'

'Are your wounds still troubling you?'

'The surgeon has done well. My face is numb to pain. See that his body is removed from my quarters. I don't want it starting to stink.'

'You killed him? Why?'

'Why not? I had no further need of him.' Boranius strode to a window and gazed down at the land below. 'At dusk bring twenty of our best swordsmen into the Citadel. The rest can man the walls. Their screams will alert us when the enemy attack. Go now. I need to practise.'

Morcha bowed and left him. In his own office on the ground floor he sat by a window and went through the reports. There was increased movement into the market towns, but this was to be expected at this time of year. Many of the poorer hill people travelled down seeking work. No armed men had been reported travelling the roads. There were no reports from the east. This was hardly surprising, since it was the one direction that the enemy could not have taken. Having been with Khalid Khan it would have been impossible for them to cross the high peaks. They would first have to travel past the Citadel. Even so, Morcha made a mental note to send a rider to find out why the daily report had not been made. Maybe the eastern scouts have also deserted, he thought. He swore softly, and returned to studying the reports.

A wagon had been seen on the road above the town. It was driven by a large old woman. Five children had been riding alongside. Their mounts were described as shaggy hill ponies. The wagon had contained a large bundle of furs. Morcha flicked through the reports. They should have been reported twice, once on the High Road, and once when they approached the town below the Citadel. Yet the only other wagon noted was driven by a crippled old man, travelling with four women and a simpleton. This wagon had three wolfhounds in the back.

Noting the names on both reports Morcha strode from the office and walked back to the buildings being used as a barracks. He found the first of the men eating a meal in the tavern, and asked him if he recalled the wagon with the furs.

'Yes, sir. Strange bunch. They had no weapons. Just the furs.'

'What do you mean by strange?'

'Hard to say. Just odd, really. The sun was very bright. Hurt the eyes. Then this family rode through. No problem at all. Called for them to stop, and they did. Didn't say anything. We checked the wagon, saw they weren't armed, and let them through.'

'So what was strange?'

'I feel foolish saying it, sir. One of the children said something as they went by. And just for a moment everything blurred. I think it was just the sunlight being so bright. I thought I saw two eyes staring at me from the furs. I ran up to the wagon, but there weren't any eyes. See what I mean? Just odd. Strange moment.'

'But you saw no other wagons?'

'Just that one, sir, during my watch. It came in around noon yesterday.'

The second of the men named on the report sheets rode in an hour before dusk. Morcha had left word for him to report to his office. He stepped into the room and saluted. Morcha questioned him about his report.

'Nothing special, sir. Crippled old man and four women. Oh yes, and a simpleton. Thought he was a woman at first, and when he spoke it was quite a shock. Don't know how I could have missed the beard.'

'What did he say that made you realize he was a simpleton?'

The soldier shrugged. 'Just his manner of speaking, sir. You know how they sound. Don't recall what he said.'

'And there were dogs in the back of the wagon?'

'Yes, sir. Thought they were furs at first. I poked at them and then one of the dogs snarled at me. I jumped like a startled rabbit.'

'You walked up to the wagon and did not recognize three dogs?'

'Yes. Odd, isn't it? The sun was very bright about then. Could hardly see.'

'And this was when?'

'A little after noon yesterday.'

Morcha shuffled through the reports, coming at last to the note concerning Skilgannon and the others reaching the temple. The Nadir scout said he had seen a large arena beast, a Joining. It was crouched down alongside the old axeman.

'Are you finished with me, sir? I could do with a meal.'

'Did you see all three dogs in the wagon?'

'Of course.'

'Think for a moment. You heard a snarl and jumped back. What happened then?'

'I saw the first dog snarling. The others were behind it.'

'You saw all their heads?'

'Yes.' The man hesitated. 'Well . . . no. But there must have been at least three.'

'Forget the meal,' said Morcha, rising. 'Saddle a fast horse, and take a spare. Find Naklian. He is with twenty men, guarding the nomad road. Tell him to bring his men back here as soon as possible. What you saw was not three dogs. Nor was it a bale of fur, as the other report stated. It was a Joining. It is travelling with Druss and Skilgannon. The enemy is here.'

'With respect, you are wrong, sir. There were no fighting men. Just the old cripple.'

'They came from the temple. There was a spell put upon you. That is why the sun seemed so bright. Trust me. The enemy is close.'

The soldier looked bemused. He was one of the newer recruits, from the Naashanite community in Mellicane. 'Am I wrong, sir?' he asked. 'There are only a handful of men coming after us, aren't there?'

'Yes. Though two of them are more deadly than I could make you understand.'

'I appreciate that, sir. I have listened to the men talking about Skilgannon and Druss. But even so, they can't attack the Citadel, can they? If they are hunting Lord Ironmask, they'll have to wait until he leaves the fortress. They'll be looking for an ambush, surely?'

'I cannot anticipate what they'll do,' admitted Morcha. 'I fought against Skilgannon for years. What I learned was that he always found a way to attack. In every battle we were always, somehow, *reacting* to him. You understand? Action and reaction. Action is what usually wins battles and wars. Reaction is almost always defensive. You think six men cannot attack a fortress? I agree with you. But what I think does not matter. The question is this: does Skilgannon think he can attack the Citadel.'

'It would be madness. They couldn't survive.'

'Perhaps survival is not uppermost in their minds. There is no more time to debate, soldier. Find Naklian, and get him and his men back here as soon as possible.'

Survival *was* uppermost in the mind of Diagoras, as he waited for the sun to drop behind the mountains. The Drenai officer was standing in a grove of trees no more than a quarter of a mile from the Citadel. From here the fortress looked impressive. True, the walls around it were crumbling and in disrepair, but the tall, round Citadel itself, with its murder holes, through which archers could shoot barbed shafts down at attackers, and its ramparts, from which defenders could hurl down rocks and hot oil, seemed particularly daunting.

Diagoras had listened as Skilgannon outlined his plan. It was a good plan – if you were talking of it theoretically. It was a dreadful plan if you actually had to carry it out. There was no way they could accomplish what was required and escape unscathed. Diagoras gazed at the others. Jared and Nian were sitting apart from the rest. Nian's head was causing him pain, and Jared had given him some powder, and was sitting alongside his brother, his arm round his shoulder. Garianne was lying down, apparently asleep, and Druss and Skilgannon were talking in low voices. Diagoras stared at the huge, grey beast crouched down at Druss's side. He kept trying to tell himself that this was Orastes, but it was almost impossible to hold on to this thought. Fat Orastes was a jolly and timid fellow, the butt of many jokes when they had soldiered together. He never seemed to take offence. This massive beast, with its slavering jaws and its coldly glittering, golden eyes, made Diagoras's blood run cold. It amazed him that Druss could be so calm around it. Diagoras believed that at any moment it might rend and rip at them.

Returning his gaze to the Citadel he shuddered. I might be looking at my tomb, he thought. A rider emerged through the gateway. Diagoras ducked further back into the trees. The horseman galloped past the stand of trees, heading back towards Khalid Khan's mountains.

One less, thought Diagoras, trying to force himself to be cheerful. You survived Skeln, he reminded himself. Surely this can't be any worse. No, of course it can't. All you have to do is walk into an enemy fortress, and defend the Citadel entrance against around seventy swordsmen. Diagoras glanced across at the brothers. Nian had said he would sooner die than live as a simpleton. Now Jared was aiming to grant him that wish. They weren't here to rescue Elanin. They were here to die together.

Dusk was less than an hour away.

Diagoras strolled over to where Skilgannon and Druss were talking. Carefully he skirted the beast. 'Would it not be better to wait until full nightfall?' he asked Skilgannon. 'At least some of them will be sleeping then.'

'Dusk will be better,' said Druss.

'Why?'

'Less traditional,' said the axeman.

'What does that mean?'

Skilgannon stepped in. 'Night attacks are standard. They know we are coming. Because we are so few they will expect either that we stay close to the Citadel and ambush them, or that we attack at night and seek to surprise them. Therefore night is when they will be ready for us.'

'I don't wish to sound critical at this late juncture,' said Diagoras, 'but how many of us do you expect to survive this plan?'

'I would be amazed if any of us did,' said Skilgannon.

'That's what I thought.'

'I intend to survive,' said Druss. 'That little girl needs to be taken home. I think it a good plan.'

'If we are still discussing its merits tomorrow I will agree with you,' said Diagoras.

'Cheer up, laddie. Nobody lives for ever.'

'Oh, I expect you will, Druss, old horse. It's the mortals around you who always seem to kiss the granite.'

'Once Boranius is dead his men will be less likely to want to go on fighting,' said Druss. 'Simple fact of life among mercenaries. No-one to pay them, then they don't fight. We just need to get to him fast. Anyhow, there won't be seventy men inside. They've got men in the hills scouting for us. I'd say there were around forty inside. Maybe less.'

'I am hugely comforted,' muttered Diagoras sarcastically.

Druss grinned at him. 'You can always wait here, laddie.'

'Don't tempt me!' He glanced at the setting sun. Just under an hour to wait. Diagoras guessed the time would race by.

CHAPTER TWENTY

IPPELIUS WAS NINETEEN YEARS OF AGE. HIS FATHER HAD BEEN A CAPTAIN in the King's army, killed in the last battle, when Bokram fell. The months following the Witch Queen's victory had been harsh for the families whose men had served the King. Ippelius's mother had been driven from the family home, her goods and wealth seized by the crown. A crowd had gathered outside, hurling dirt and dung at the family as they were marched away. Ippelius had been thirteen years old, and hugely frightened. Many of the widows had left the capital, seeking sanctuary with relatives in outlying towns and villages. Others had journeyed to Naashanite communities in other lands. His mother had gone to Mellicane.

Ippelius had finished his education there. It was a fine city, and the horrors of the past, though powerful in his nightmares, seemed insubstantial in the city sunlight. When Ironmask had come to power he promised a chance for revenge. One day the outcasts would return to Naashan. The Witch Queen would be overthrown. It seemed to Ippelius a golden opportunity to avenge his father's death, and his mother's shame.

Now, as he sat in the miserable tavern, with some twenty or so soldiers, he realized the dream was dead. As dead as poor Codis on the walls. He had been stunned when Morcha stabbed his friend.

The action was sudden and murderous. Codis had been dead before he knew it.

Ippelius sipped his ale. It was sour and he did not like the taste. Yet all men drank it, and Ippelius did not wish to seem less than the men around him. Also if he forced himself to drink enough of it his fears did, at least, lessen. Codis had been like a brother to the young soldier, helping him in the early days, when he made a fool of himself during training. Ippelius was constantly tripping over his sword, and falling flat on his face. His horsemanship was not of the highest quality, and he would bounce around in the saddle like a sack of vegetables. Through it all Codis had offered advice and support. As had Morcha, who had always appeared to be good-natured and understanding. Ippelius felt his stomach churn. Codis had liked Morcha and respected him. How terrible it must have been to be killed by a man you liked.

Then there was Boranius. How impressed Ippelius had been when first he had been introduced to the general. A man of power and courage, who radiated purpose. When this man said they would overthrow the Witch Queen it sounded a certainty.

Ippelius shuddered. A little while ago he and Codis had been ordered to remove a body from the Citadel. It was wrapped in canvas, which had been hastily stitched. Blood was seeping through the cloth. Halfway down the stairs the canvas had split. What fell from it was the hideously mutilated body of a woman. Ippelius had vomited at the sight. He was no help to Codis, who forced the remains back into the canvas.

Later, after they had buried her, Ippelius had sunk to the ground in tears. 'How could any man do that to a woman?' he asked Codis.

'Boranius is not any man.'

'That is no answer.'

'Gods, man, what do you expect me to say? I have no answers. He always was a torturer. Best to put it from your mind.'

Ippelius had gazed down on the grave. 'There's not even a marker,' he said. 'I thought they were lovers.'

'They *were* lovers. Then he killed her. End of story. Now get a grip on your emotions, lad. We are not going to talk about this to anyone. You understand that? Boranius tortures men

401

too. I don't want to have my fingers cut off or my eyes put out.'

'You think he killed the little girl too?'

'I don't know and I don't care. Neither should you. We are going to bide our time and then get out of here.'

'Why can't we leave now?'

'What, with patrols everywhere looking for Druss? How far would we get? No. When Druss is dead, and things calm down. Then we'll slip away east. Head for the coastal cities.'

Ippelius drank more of his ale. The bitterness of the taste was passing now. He looked around him at the other soldiers. There was little laughter in the tavern this evening. The murder of Codis had affected them, as had the news that Skilgannon was coming. Some of them had fought against the man in the past. They all had stories to tell.

A burly soldier named Rankar came into the tavern. He strolled through the dining area and came to where Ippelius sat. Easing himself down he waved his hand at the barman, calling out for a jug of ale.

'How goes it?' he asked Ippelius.

'Fine. You?'

'Fine. Barracks is empty. They've moved a lot of the men into the Citadel. I'm heading there after I've eaten.'

Ippelius looked at the man. His heavy face was pockmarked and a jagged white scar cut down from his brow to his cheekbone. His left eyelid drooped over a bright green eye. Ippelius found himself staring at the scar. 'You were really lucky,' he said.

Rankar rubbed at the drooping lid. 'Didn't feel lucky at the time. But I guess you are right. You eaten?'

'No. I am not hungry.'

Rankar nodded. 'Codis was a good man. We fought our way across Naashan together – and then fought our way out. They don't come better.'

'I can't believe that Morcha killed him.'

'Me neither. Goes to show you can't trust anyone.'

At that moment the door at the far end of the tavern opened, and a powerful figure entered. Ippelius stared at him. He was wearing a round, silver-ringed helm, decorated with silver axes flanking a skull. His once black beard was heavily speckled with silver.

Upon his enormous torso he wore a black jerkin, the shoulders reinforced by silver steel. And in his right hand he carried a shining, double-bladed axe. The man walked into the middle of the room and paused by a table at which sat four soldiers. Spinning the axe he thudded it into the table top. 'Let's have a little quiet, lads!' he bellowed. 'I'll not take much of your time.'

Silence fell, as the twenty or so men stared at the newcomer. 'I am Druss,' he said, laying his gauntleted hand on the black hilt of the axe, '. . . and this is Death.' His gaze swept the room. Ippelius shuddered as the winter grey eyes fastened on his own. 'Now I have come here to kill Boranius. I shall be doing that presently. I don't much care if I have to kill every man in this room first. But I have always had a soft spot for soldiers. Good men, in the main. So I'm giving you an opportunity to live a while longer. I suggest you finish your meals, then gather whatever wealth there is in this fleapit of a fortress, and ride away. Any questions?'

The silence continued, as men stared at one another.

'Then I'll leave you to your food,' said the man, wrenching the axe clear. As he turned to leave two soldiers drew knives from their belts and leapt at him. The silver axe clove through the chest of the first, and a left hook thundered into the face of the second. He flew across a table, hit the floor and did not move.

'Anyone else?' said the axeman. No-one stirred, though Ippelius could see a number of the men surreptitiously reaching for their weapons.

The axeman moved towards the door. At that moment it burst open and a creature from Hell loomed in the doorway. It was an arena beast, one of the largest Ippelius had ever seen. Its jaws opened and it gave out a long, bloodcurdling howl. Soldiers leapt from their seats, scattering tables as they drew back from the abomination in the doorway.

The axeman walked up to it, and patted it on the shoulder. The beast dropped to all fours and stared malevolently at the soldiers. Then Druss left the tavern, the creature following.

Ippelius sat very still. Rankar swore softly.

'What should we do?' asked Ippelius.

'You heard the man. Finish our food and then leave.'

*

Diagoras and the twins passed through the gate. The Drenai officer glanced up at the body of the dead sentry on the parapet steps. Garianne was kneeling over him, tugging at the black bolt in his chest. Swiftly Diagoras crossed the open ground to where Skilgannon was waiting at the Citadel entrance. Druss came loping towards them, the Joining alongside.

'Now it begins,' said Skilgannon.

Suddenly the Joining gave out a howl. Running past Druss it leapt through the wide doors of the Citadel entrance and on up the first flight of stairs. Druss called out to it, but the beast was gone.

'It has scented the child,' said Skilgannon.

Hefting his axe Druss ran through the doorway. Skilgannon swung to Diagoras. 'Hold the doors for as long as you can.'

'Rely on it,' said the Drenai, drawing his sabre, and a razor-edged hunting knife. Then Skilgannon followed Druss into the building. There were two sets of stairs. Druss was climbing those on the right. Skilgannon took the left.

Diagoras moved back into the doorway, scanning the buildings and alleyways that led out past the warehouses towards the tavern. Jared and Nian stepped alongside him, longswords in their hands. Garianne remained on the rampart steps, some thirty feet away, her double crossbow in her hands. The howling of the Joining came from above, followed by screams.

No soldiers had emerged from the tavern. This astonished Diagoras. When Druss had said he was going in to talk to them he had been incredulous. 'Are you mad? They'll come down on you like rabid wolves.'

'Probably not,' was all Druss had said.

Diagoras had waited with Skilgannon. 'You agree with this insanity?' he asked the Naashanite.

'It has a good chance of working. Picture it yourself. You are having a meal and in walks the enemy. He has absolutely no fear of you. We expect fear from our enemies in certain situations. Where he is outnumbered, for example. Or trapped. By contrast there are places where our own fear is much less. Like inside our own fortress. Now, you have a single warrior, striding in, hugely outnumbered and yet fearless. It will give them pause for thought. Bear in mind also that their morale is low.'

'So, you think he will just tell them to leave and they'll do it?' asked Diagoras.

Skilgannon thought about the question. 'I'd say he might have to kill a few. The rest will not interfere.'

Diagoras shook his head. 'You are a different breed, you two,' he said.

Now, as he stood in the shadows of the entrance, he began to feel more relaxed. Druss and Skilgannon were inside the Citadel, and his own role seemed far less perilous. No soldiers were attacking him. No flashing blades, no piercing of his flesh. Jared obviously had the same thought. He grinned at Diagoras. 'So far, so good,' he said.

Diagoras was about to reply when Garianne suddenly waved at them, and pointed out beyond the gates.

That was when Diagoras heard the pounding of hooves. The first of the twenty riders galloped through the gates. He pitched from his saddle, a crossbow bolt through his neck. His horse reared. A second bolt thudded into a man's chest. Then Garianne was running along the ramparts above them.

A group of riders saw Diagoras and the twins, and spurred their mounts forward. The Drenai officer swore, and hefted his sabre.

Other Naashanites jumped down from their mounts and ran up the rampart steps towards Garianne, who was reloading her crossbow. Diagoras backed up the steps to the Citadel doors. A horseman galloped at him. Diagoras ducked under the mount's neck, plunging his sabre into the rider's unprotected left side. The man fell back. The horse reared, dumping him from the saddle.

Jared and Nian charged into the milling horsemen.

On the ramparts Garianne shot the first man running at her, then turned and sprinted towards the roof of the gate. Several of the riders at the rear of the group lifted bows from their saddles. An arrow slashed past Diagoras. Other riders had dismounted and were running towards the Citadel. Diagoras leapt to meet them. Garianne scrambled up to the gate roof, then turned and shot a man through the head. Two others were climbing towards her. Running forward she kicked the first in the head, hurling him back to the ramparts. The second lashed out with his sword. The blade twisted in the man's hand, the flat of the steel thudding against

405

Garianne's ankle. She fell heavily. The man grabbed at her. Savagely she struck him in the face with her bow. Losing his grip he slipped back to the ramparts.

Diagoras had three men attacking him, and was backing away, parrying furiously. Nian raced to his aid, his longsword cleaving through the back of a Naashanite's neck. Seeing his chance to attack Diagoras leapt in. His sabre glanced from a breastplate, but his hunting knife plunged home between collarbone and neck. A sword slashed across his shoulder. With a grunt of pain Diagoras let go of the hunting knife and spun to meet this fresh attack. Blocking a second wild cut he twisted his wrist, sending his own blade in a deadly riposte that opened his attacker's throat.

Horses were screaming and rearing, and the cries of wounded men filled the air. Diagoras was under attack again. A blade tore into his side. Diagoras stumbled. Before the death blow could be struck the Naashanite grunted and staggered back, twisting as he fell. Diagoras saw a crossbow bolt in his back.

Now the Naashanite archers turned on Garianne. Shafts struck the rampart wall close to where she was crouched. Rising she coolly shot a rider from the saddle then ran along the wall.

Diagoras forced himself to his feet. He felt light-headed. He saw Jared go down, a lance through his back. Then Nian hacked the lancer from his saddle and, dropping his sword, ran to his brother. Diagoras charged across towards them, slashing his sword across the face of one man, and plunging the blade through the chest of another. Nian hauled Jared to his feet. 'Pick up your sword!' he heard Jared yell. Nian ran back towards the weapon. A black arrow materialized in his back. He stumbled and fell. His fingers curled around the hilt of the sword and he half rose. Another arrow slammed into him. With a roar of pain Nian gained his feet. Turning he ran at the archer on the horse. The man tried to loose another shaft, but his mount reared. Then Nian was upon him. The longsword clove through the man's side. As he fell from the saddle Nian brought the sword down on his skull. Jared was facing two men. He no longer had the strength to hold them back. One ran in. Jared weakly lashed his blade at the man. The blow was blocked. The second dived in, plunging a long dagger into Jared's belly. Nian, seeing his brother's plight, screamed at the top of his voice.

He charged the men, who fell back. Instead of chasing them Nian dropped his sword once more, and knelt beside his fallen brother. He kept shouting his name, over and over.

Diagoras could see Jared was dead. The two men Nian had attacked rushed in. One stabbed Nian in the neck, the other slashed his sword down onto Nian's skull. Diagoras charged them. One tried to defend himself, and died with Diagoras's sabre through his neck. The other backed away, and was joined by four others. They advanced on Diagoras. 'Come on then!' yelled the Drenai. 'Which of you whoresons wants to die first?'

They stood for a moment, swords ready. Then, as one, they backed away a few steps, before turning and running back towards the tavern. Diagoras blinked sweat from his eyes, trying to make sense of their flight.

Then he heard sounds behind him. Slowly he turned.

A large group of heavily armoured horsemen were sitting their mounts. Their armour was black, their helms full-faced, with high horsehair plumes. Each man carried a lance, and a sword, and a small round shield, bearing the sign of the Spotted Snake.

The line of horsemen parted and a woman rode in. Diagoras found his pain forgotten as he gazed on her. Her hair was raven dark, and held back in a single braid, through which silver wire had been entwined. She wore a white, flowing cloak, and silver chain mail. Her legs were bare above knee-length riding boots of black leather, embossed with silver. Lightly she leapt to the ground and approached Diagoras.

Stupidly he tried to bow, but his legs gave way. Stepping in, she caught him.

'If this is a dream,' he said, 'I never want to wake.'

'Where is Skilgannon?' she asked.

Skilgannon stepped across the bodies of the two soldiers and moved forward warily. There were a number of doors on the landing, all of them open. Coming to the first room he stood outside, listening. Hearing nothing he took a deep breath and stepped quickly through the doorway. The first man rushed at him from across the room, sword raised. In that moment Skilgannon heard a whisper of movement from behind. Dropping to one knee he reversed the Sword of Day, ramming it backwards. The curved blade sliced up through the second attacker's belly and clove his heart. The Sword of Night slashed out, half severing the leg of the first man. The man screamed and pitched to the floor. Another soldier loomed in the doorway, holding a crossbow. Skilgannon rolled to his right as the string twanged. The bolt ripped into the carpeted floor. Rising swiftly Skilgannon leapt at the crossbowman, who dropped his weapon and ran for his life. Out on the landing several more soldiers had arrived. Skilgannon tore into them, spinning and leaping, his blades flashing. Blood-spattered, he ran on to the second staircase.

The howling of the Joining had ceased now, and Skilgannon guessed it had been cut down.

He ran up the stairs. Another crossbow bolt hissed by his head. Two swordsmen blocked his path. They died. The crossbowman tried another shot. Skilgannon dived forward, rolled on his shoulder, and rose to his feet in one smooth motion. The crossbowman grunted as the Sword of Day plunged into his heart.

A long corridor connected the third landing to the stairs Druss had taken. Skilgannon could hear the sounds of battle. Taking no time to check the rooms as he passed he sprinted along the corridor. He came to two open double doors, leading to a large dining area. Druss was battling furiously against a dozen opponents. Several bodies were already sprawled on the timber floor. The survivors were seeking to circle him, but the axeman spun and whirled, the huge axe glinting in the lantern light. Blood flowed from a cut on Druss's face, and his jerkin had been slashed in several places. His leggings too were damp with blood. A soldier more daring than the rest darted in. His head bounced to the floor, a gush of blood pumping from his severed neck.

Skilgannon ran to Druss's aid. Seeing this new enemy the soldiers tried to reform. Two went down swiftly under the slashing Swords of Night and Day. Another died, his spine smashed to shards by Druss's axe. The remaining men broke and ran towards the double doors.

Skilgannon stepped in towards Druss. 'How badly are you hurt?' he asked.

'Hurt?' responded Druss. 'Pah! Scratches only.' He was

breathing hard and once more looked weary and grey in the face. Only days ago he had been close to death. Skilgannon looked at him, and shook his head. 'Don't be concerned about me, laddie,' said Druss. 'I can still climb the mountain.'

'I don't doubt it, axeman.'

'Then let's find Boranius.'

Druss hefted his axe once more, but Skilgannon paused. 'The child will be with him, Druss,' he said.

'I know.'

'He will seek to make you suffer. It is likely he will kill her in front of you.'

'I know that too.' The old man's eyes were cold now, like polished steel. 'Let's find the whoreson, and finish this.'

Together the two warriors headed for the final staircase.

CHAPTER TWENTY-ONE

IN THE ROOF HALL MORCHA WAITED WITH FIVE SWORDSMEN. Boranius, bare-chested, and wearing his ornate mask of black iron, was sitting on a high-backed chair, the catatonic child Elanin in his lap. There was blood on Boranius's chest, seeping from the four talon marks that scored his skin from shoulder to belly. The huge grey Joining lay on the floor before him, its own body pierced by a score of wounds. It was still breathing, and its golden eyes were open and fixed on Boranius. Its spine was severed and it could not move.

'See the hatred there?' said Boranius, with a harsh laugh. 'How it would love to come at me again.' A large pool of blood was spreading from beneath the dying beast. Boranius took hold of the child's blond hair and tilted her head towards the Joining. 'See there, little one. Daddy has come for you. Isn't that sweet?'

Morcha looked away.

So, he thought, it all ends here. All the dreams, all the hopes, all the ambitions. He looked around at the decaying roof hall, then back at the blood-smeared man in the black mask. Boranius was stroking the child's hair, but there was no reaction. Her eyes were open and unblinking. Morcha drew his cavalry sabre. It was a beautiful weapon, with a filigree fist guard and a pommel stone of emerald. It had been given to him by Bokram, as a reward for his loyalty and bravery. He glanced at the five swordsmen, and saw the fear on all their faces. They had all run here from the hall below, where they had faced Druss and Skilgannon. They knew they were going to die.

Morcha swung back to Boranius. 'Lord, if you will just put the child down. We will need you to fight.'

'Oh, I will fight, Morcha. I will kill them both. First, though, you can tire them for me.'

'Tire them? Are you insane? Do you not know what is happening here?'

'Skilgannon is coming, and the axeman. Of course I know. How is it that two warriors have breached our defences and are now climbing my stairs? I will tell you, Morcha. It is because I am surrounded by dolts and cowards. After today I will raise a fresh force. Only this time I will pick the fighting men myself. Your judgement has proved to be sadly defective.'

Morcha stood silently for a moment. 'You are right, my lord. My judgement has for years been defective.' Before he could go on the sound of horses' hooves echoed up to them from the courtyard below. Morcha ran to the window and looked out. When he turned away there was a grim smile on his face.

'It seems, Boranius, that you will not be raising a new army – even if you kill Skilgannon and Druss. The Witch Queen is here, with a company of her guards.'

'I'll kill them too,' said Boranius. 'I'll cut the bitch's heart out.'

Skilgannon stepped into the hall, followed by the black-clad axeman. The five Naashanite swordsmen backed away, dropping their blades. Morcha sighed, then glanced at Skilgannon.

'You have done well since those early days,' he said. 'I still have fond memories of the bathhouse.'

'Put up your sword, Morcha. There is no need for you to die here.'

Morcha shrugged. 'There is every need. Defend yourself!' He leapt forward, his sabre slashing through the air. Skilgannon swayed. A piercing pain shot through Morcha's chest. He stumbled and dropped his sabre, watching it clatter to the floor. Then he slumped against the wall, and slid down.

'Oh, neatly done,' said Boranius. Rising from his seat, still holding the child, he drew one of his own swords. Resting the blade against Elanin's waist he stepped away from the chair.

'It is good to see you, axeman,' he told Druss. 'I have heard so much about you.'

Druss slowly advanced on the masked figure. Blood seeped through the child's thin blue dress.

'One more step and I will slice her open, and you can watch her entrails fall to the floor.'

Druss paused. 'Excellent choice,' said Boranius. 'Now be so good as to lay your axe down.'

'He will kill her anyway, Druss,' said Skilgannon. 'He is just prolonging the moment.'

'I know what he is doing,' replied Druss, his voice cold. 'I have met his like before. Weak men. They are all the same.' Even as he spoke Druss let Snaga fall to the timber.

'Now step forward so that I may savour this moment,' said Boranius. Druss did so, moving within range of the sword Boranius held at the girl's side. 'You know what happens now, axeman?'

'Of course I know. You are going to die. I am going to kill you.'

'If you move I shall kill the child.'

'That's what I am waiting for,' said Druss coldly. 'The moment that sword slides into her you won't be able to use it against me. And then, you whoreson, I will break every bone in your body. So let us not wait. Do it!' he thundered, stepping in. Shocked, Boranius instinctively stepped back. The dying Joining growled, its jaws snapping towards Ironmask's leg. The sword in Boranius's hand flashed down, striking the Joining across its snout. Blood sprayed out. In that moment Druss dived forward, snatching Elanin from Boranius's grasp. The silver blade swept out. Druss turned his back, protecting the child, and threw himself to the floor. The sword sliced through the back of his jerkin, scoring the flesh. Boranius screamed in fury and charged towards the axeman.

The Sword of Fire lunged towards Druss's unprotected body.

The Sword of Day parried it.

Boranius leapt back, drawing his second sword from the

scabbard hanging between his shoulders. Then he faced Skilgannon. 'Oh, I have waited long for this, Olek,' he said, his voice muffled by the iron mask. 'I shall carve you like a banquet swan.'

The Swords of Blood and Fire glinted in the lantern light as the two men circled. Boranius sprang forward and their swords clashed. Time and again the music of the steel rang out.

Morcha watched them, his pain forgotten. The two warriors seemed to glide across the timbered floor, their swords creating glittering arcs of light. The fighters spun and moved, ever faster, and yet perfectly in balance. The deadly blades clanged and clashed, hissed and sang, the razor sharp steel seeking to sheathe itself in soft flesh. Back and forth across the hall the two men fought without pausing for breath.

Morcha became aware that others had entered the hall. Looking up he saw Jianna, the Witch Queen. Alongside her was the old swordsman, Malanek. Black-clad guards thronged the hall, and beyond them stood an old woman, leaning upon a gnarled staff. Morcha knew he was dying, but he prayed to be allowed to see the end of this incredible contest.

Both men had suffered wounds. Skilgannon was bleeding from a shallow cut to his face, Boranius had been sliced across the left bicep, the skin flapping, blood flowing. They fought on.

Inevitably they were slowing now, and once more circling one another. Then Boranius spoke. 'You remember Greavas, Olek? Ah, you should have heard him squeal. He was brave enough when I cut away his fingers. But when I sawed away at his arm his cowardice came through. He begged me to kill him.'

'Don't let him goad you, laddie!' called Druss. 'Stay cool and cut his heart out!'

Boranius leapt to the attack. Skilgannon parried desperately, then spun away. Boranius followed. The Sword of Blood lunged towards Skilgannon's throat. He parried it, then blocked a cut from the Sword of Fire. Off balance now Skilgannon went down on one knee. Boranius launched a fresh assault. Skilgannon hurled himself to his right, rolled and came up, just as Boranius swung his right-hand blade in a murderous arc. The Sword of Night came up, the blade chopping through Boranius's fingers. With a scream he fell back, the Sword of Fire dropping from his mutilated hand. Boranius backed away.

Skilgannon followed. 'Now tell me about Greavas!' he said. 'Now tell me about his pleading!'

Boranius screamed in pain and fury and rushed in. Skilgannon parried, leapt aside and sent a slashing cut across Boranius's back as he blundered past. The Sword of Night sank deep, slicing into Boranius's spine. His legs gave way and he fell to his knees, his remaining sword slipping from his hand.

Skilgannon walked around the man. The Sword of Day sliced through the leather straps holding the iron mask in place. It fell away, exposing the horror of Boranius's mutilated face. The man's blue eyes blazed with undisguised malice and hatred. 'You are nothing, Boranius,' said Skilgannon, his voice emotionless. 'You never were. Greavas was ten times the man you are.'

With that he walked away. Boranius screamed insults after him. His body jerked as he tried to force his legs to obey him, but his fractured spine could no longer send messages to his muscles. He tried to reach for his sword, but his arm spasmed and twitched.

He looked up to see the Witch Queen walking towards him, a slender dagger in her hand.

She knelt down before him, and he looked into her eyes. 'You killed my mother,' she said.

The dagger came up slowly, the tip moving towards his eye.

Boranius screamed as the cold steel slowly, so slowly, pushed its way into his brain.

Skilgannon did not watch the tortured finish to Boranius's life. Instead he moved to where Morcha was sitting by the wall, his hands trying to stem the flow of blood from the wound to his lower chest.

'You were too good a man to follow such a wretch,' said Skilgannon. 'Why did you do it?'

'I wish I could answer that,' said Morcha. 'I'm glad you beat him. Didn't think you could. Didn't think anyone could.'

'There's always someone better,' said Skilgannon. Wearily he rose and walked back to where Druss was sitting with the child.

'You did fine, laddie,' said the old warrior. 'You think Elanin will ever recover?'

Skilgannon lifted her from Druss's arms and carried her to where the Joining lay. The golden eyes were still open, but its breathing was harsh now, and ragged. Kneeling down he laid the child alongside its huge head. A low moan came from the beast, and it pressed its muzzle against her face.

'I don't know if you can hear me, Orastes,' said Skilgannon. 'But your daughter is safe now.' Druss came and squatted down by the beast. He laid a huge hand upon its brow, stroking it as if it were a dog. The golden eyes remained fixed on the delicate features of the child for a while. Then they closed, and the breathing ceased.

For a while no-one moved. Then the child's eyes flickered, and she took a deep, shuddering breath. She blinked and sat up. Druss reached for her, drawing her into his arms.

'It is good to see you, pretty one,' he said.

'Daddy came for me,' she told him. 'He told me you were here.'

Jianna stood back, gazing down at the man who had haunted her dreams for what seemed almost half a lifetime. Her thoughts fled back to those early, perilous days when she had posed as a prostitute, and had lived with the youth Skilgannon. The memories were sharp and vivid, tinged with many sadnesses. Yet they were also golden, and bright. Her dreams then had been simple. First there was survival, and then revenge. Nothing complicated. And always by her side was the swordsman Skilgannon.

He was kneeling now beside a golden-haired child, his hand gently brushing back her long fringe. She remembered when his hand was upon her face. She felt the first warning signs of tears, and angrily shut off the memories. Turning away from the scene she saw the Old Woman leaning upon her staff by the far wall. She wore a heavy black veil, and there was no way to read her expression.

She had appeared by the quayside as Jianna was leading her personal bodyguard onto the ship that would bear them up the coast to Sherak, on the first leg of the journey to the Citadel.

'Are you travelling to kill Boranius or to rescue Skilgannon?' she had asked, as they stood on the aft deck.

'Perhaps both,' she had replied.

'He is wrong for you, Jianna. He will destroy you.'

Jianna had laughed then. 'He loves me. He would do nothing to harm me.'

'It is love which is dangerous, my Queen. Love blinds us to peril. Love leads to foolishness and sorrow.'

'And what if I love him?'

'You *do* love him, Jianna. I have known this since first we met. And that is the peril of which I speak. You are wise now, and ruthless as a leader must be. You are loved and you are feared. You can achieve greatness. It is there ... just ahead ... beckoning you.'

'Why do you hate him so?'

'I do not hate him. He is a fine, courageous man. I wish him dead because he is a threat to you. No more than that. Have you not also tried to have him killed? Can you not understand why? Your secret self, the true you, the centre of your soul, knows he must be dealt with. Thoughts of him torment your mind.'

Jianna watched as the ship's sails were unfurled, and sailors ran along the quay, letting slip the ropes. 'Perhaps it is my true self telling me that I need him,' she countered.

'Pah! You need no-one. I have lived long, Jianna. I know what you are experiencing. I was there myself once. You love him too much and too little. Too much ever to love another, and too little to change for his sake. He wants a wife and a mother to his children. You want an empire and a place in history. Do you believe these ambitions can be linked? He feels the same, my Queen. He cannot love another, and your image is constantly in his mind. Yet he will not change either. He will not become your general again – even if it means sharing your bed and your life. As long as he lives he will be a rock in your heart.'

'I will think on what you have said,' Jianna had told her.

Now, in this crumbling citadel, she realized more than ever before how much she had missed this tall man, and the joy of his company. She longed to walk across to him, and lay her hand upon his shoulder. To take a cloth and wipe away the blood that ran from the cut on his face.

A movement came from behind her. She turned to see the Drenai warrior she had first noticed in the courtyard below. His face was grey, and blood was drenching his tunic and leggings. He paused before her. 'What are you doing climbing stairs, idiot?' she asked him. 'I told you to wait until our surgeon attended you.'

'Thought I might die before seeing you again,' he told her.

'You fool. You could have died climbing those stairs.'

'Worth it, though.' The man swayed. Malanek stepped forward, taking his arm.

'Make sure his wounds are seen to,' she said. The soldier leaned in to Malanek and gave a crooked, boyish grin.

'Oh, I'll not die now,' he said. As Malanek led him away, he swung his head. 'Are you married?' he called back. Jianna ignored him.

A young, golden-haired female came into the hall, and spoke in low tones to the Old Woman. She was carrying an ornate, small double-winged crossbow. The Old Woman waved an arm at her, pointing to a door across the hall. The young woman walked across to it, glancing back once. Then she was gone.

Skilgannon rose to his feet, and turned. His sapphire blue eyes held to her own. Jianna allowed no expression to show. She merely waited. He strode towards her, and bowed deeply. Then he looked up, saying nothing.

'No words for me, Olek?' she asked him.

'None could do justice,' he said. 'In this moment, standing here, I am complete.'

'Then come home with me.'

A spasm of pain crossed his features. 'For more wars and death? For more destroyed cities and orphaned children? No, Jianna. I cannot.'

'I am a queen, Olek. I cannot promise no more wars.'

'I know.'

'Do you wish you had never met me?'

He smiled then. 'Sometimes. In the depths of despair. If I could go back I would change many things. But meeting you? I would never change that. You might as well ask a man with sunstroke if he wished he had never, ever seen the sun.'

'So what will you do?'

He touched the locket round his neck. 'I'll travel on.'

'You still think you can bring her back?'

He shrugged. 'I won't know unless I try.'

'And what then? Will you live with her on some arid farm?'

He shook his head. 'I have not thought that far ahead.'

'Such a quest is a waste of life, Olek.'

'My life is already a wasteland. This at least gives me some purpose.'

A soldier appeared alongside Jianna. He bowed. 'The rebels have gathered together in the courtyard, Majesty. They have plundered the warehouses and are seeking to leave. They say the man Druss promised them their lives. Should we kill them?'

'Let them go.'

'Yes, Majesty. Also our scouts report a large contingent of Datian cavalry are less than two hours from here. We should be gone before they arrive.'

Malanek stepped forward, and also began to speak to her. Jianna saw Skilgannon move away towards the Old Woman, who was beckoning him. Malanek was also urging swift departure.

'Very well. There is no more to achieve here.'

Glancing towards Skilgannon she saw him walk through the small doorway at the rear of the hall, followed by the Old Woman. Before the door closed she saw that there were stairs leading upwards towards the battlements.

'Is he coming with us, Majesty?' asked Malanek, presenting her with the scabbarded Swords of Blood and Fire. Jianna shook her head and saw the old swordsman was disappointed. He sighed. 'He's a good man. I didn't believe he could defeat Boranius. Nice to find that life can still surprise me.'

'There is no-one he cannot beat. He is Skilgannon.'

She glanced again towards the small door. Beside it lay the body of a man who seemed familiar to her. 'You recognize him?' she asked Malanek.

'Yes, Majesty. It is Morcha, one of Boranius's officers.'

'I cannot place him. Ah well, no matter.' Curling her hand round the ivory hilt of one of the swords she slowly pulled it from the ebony scabbard. The blade was etched with swirls of red flame, the hilt beautifully carved, showing intertwined demonic figures. The sword was light in her hands, and she felt a thrill pass through her. Jianna shivered. 'You believe these blades could be possessed?'

418

Malanek looked at her and smiled. 'Time will tell, Majesty,' he said, with a shrug.

As the Old Woman reached the top of the stairs she turned to Skilgannon. 'Are you not curious as to why I asked you to join me here?' she asked him.

'I already know,' he said.

'Ah, you have spoken with the beast-woman, Ustarte. Well, now you intrigue me, Olek. Have you come to kill me?'

'I think your death is long overdue, hag. But, no, I have come to help Garianne.'

The Old Woman's laughter rang out. 'Oh, how sweet! I was hoping you would try to kill me with one of my own swords. I would have enjoyed watching your reaction when the blades failed to pierce my flesh. I may be old, but I am not foolish. I do not make weapons which can be used against me. So,' she said, leaning on her staff, 'how will you help poor Garianne? Will you promise her love and affection?'

Skilgannon eased past her and moved out onto the circular battlements. Garianne was standing on the high wall, balancing on a crenellation and staring out over the land. Her crossbow was in her hand, and Skilgannon saw that it was loaded.

She glanced back at him, her face expressionless. Skilgannon leapt lightly to stand on another crenellation some ten feet from her. 'I have never liked heights,' he said.

'I am not comfortable with them, either,' she said. He noted that she was speaking in the first person. This was something she never did unless drunk. He decided to risk a question.

'Why did you come up here, Garianne?'

'This is where it ends,' she said. 'This is where the voices leave me. I will be free.'

The bright moonlight upon her pale skin made her seem almost childlike. She gazed down at the bow in her hand.

'If it will free you, then do it,' he said, facing her.

'Is the child well again?'

'Yes. As well as anyone can be who has suffered so much. Her mother was killed, her father is dead. She will have to live with those memories all her life. As you have, Garianne. What happened at Perapolis was evil. It was monstrous. For my actions there I am known – will always be known – as the Damned. My guilt is certain. Do what you must.'

'We . . . I . . . cannot live like this any more.'

'Then don't,' he said. 'Aim your bow. Find your freedom.'

The crossbow came up. Skilgannon took a deep breath and prepared for the bolt to strike. Yet she did not release the shaft. 'I don't know what to do. There is a voice I have not heard before.' Turning away from him she looked down at the stone courtyard far below. Skilgannon guessed her intention.

'Don't!' he called, his voice commanding. 'Look at me, Garianne. Look at me!' Her head came up, but she was still perched on the very edge of the battlements. 'Your death would only make the horror of Perapolis complete. You survived. Your parents would have joyed in the thought of you living on. Their lives, their blood, are in you. You are their gift to the future. You leap from here, and their line has ended. Your father did not hide you so that you could end in this way. He loved you, and he wanted you to have a life. To find love as he perhaps found love. To have children of your own. In that way he lives on. I would sooner you sent a bolt into my heart than watch you do this to yourself.'

'He is right, child,' said the Old Woman. 'Kill him and be free. Call it punishment, call it justice, call it what you will. But do what you are here for.'

'I can't,' she said.

'You stupid coward!' shouted the Old Woman. 'Must I do everything myself?' She extended a bony hand towards Garianne. The girl screamed in pain and jerked upright. Her arm spasmed, and the crossbow once more rose.

Skilgannon swung towards the Old Woman. She was chanting now, the words in a tongue he had never heard.

Suddenly a figure appeared in the doorway behind her. A silver blade burst from the Old Woman's chest, then slid back. The crone staggered forward, and fell, her staff clattering across the stone. She struggled to her knees, a large blood stain spreading across her breast. Slowly she turned, and saw Jianna standing in the doorway, the Sword of Fire in her hand. The Old Woman's head dipped and she tugged the black veil from her face. Skilgannon saw blood upon her lips. Then she spoke. 'Love . . . blinds us . . . to peril,' she said. And slumped dead to the battlement floor.

On the ramparts Garianne cried out and began to fall. Skilgannon spun, took two running steps and hurled himself at her. His left hand grabbed at her tunic, his right hit a stone crenellation. His fingers slipped clear and he began to fall. Desperately he scrabbled at the stone, ripping the skin from his fingers. His hand hooked onto an inch-wide ledge some three feet below the battlements. Garianne was a dead weight, and the muscles of his arms were stretched to the point of tearing.

Jianna appeared above him. 'Let the girl go. I'll haul you up.'

'I cannot.'

'Damn you, Olek! You'll both die!'

'She is . . . the last survivor . . . of Perapolis.' His blood-covered hand was giving way. He grunted and tried to cling on.

Jianna climbed over the ramparts, lowering herself to the thin ledge. Holding to a crenellation she reached down, clamping her hand over his wrist. 'Now we all go, idiot!' she said. Her added strength allowed him to hang on, but he could feel his endurance seeping away. All Jianna had bought him were a few moments.

Suddenly he felt Garianne's weight lessen. Looking down he saw that Druss had climbed out of the window of the roof hall, and was standing on the ledge, supporting the unconscious girl. 'Let her go, laddie! I have her.' Gratefully he released his grip. Garianne slid down into Druss's arms. Freed of the weight Skilgannon swung his left arm over the lip of stone and, as Jianna made way for him, climbed back to the battlements.

Jianna took his hand and wiped away the blood. His fingers were deeply gashed, and more blood pumped from the wounds. 'We almost died. Was she worth it?' she asked softly.

'Worth more than the Witch Queen and the Damned? I would say so.'

'Then you are still the fool, Olek,' she snapped. 'I have no time for fools.' Yet she did not move away.

'We need to say goodbye,' he said.

'I don't want to say it,' she told him. Leaning in he kissed her lips. Malanek and several soldiers arrived on the battlements. They stood back respectfully as Jianna put her arms round Skilgannon's neck.

'We are both fools,' she whispered.

With that she swung away from him and, followed by her men, returned to the roof hall.

Skilgannon remained on the battlements. After a while he saw the Naashanites mount their horses and ride from the Citadel.

Druss joined him, Elanin beside him, holding his hand. 'Well, laddie, we did what we set out to do.'

'How is Diagoras?'

'Puncture wound over the hip, and a cut to his shoulder. He'll make it back to the temple.'

'And Garianne?'

'She's sleeping. Diagoras is with her. The twins didn't make it. Died together in the courtyard. It's a damned shame, but I think that's what Jared wanted. They were good lads.' The axeman sighed. 'Will you come with us?'

'No. I'll head north.'

Druss put out his hand, then noticed the gashes on Skilgannon's fingers. Clamping his hand instead to Skilgannon's shoulder he said: 'I hope you find what you are looking for.'

'And you, my friend.'

'Me?' Druss shook his head. 'I'm going home to my cabin. I'll sit on my porch and watch sunsets. I am way too old for this sort of life.'

Skilgannon laughed. Druss scowled at him. 'I am serious, laddie. I'll hang Snaga on the wall and put my helm and jerkin and gauntlets into a chest. By Heaven, I'll even padlock it and throw away the key.'

'So,' said Skilgannon, 'I have witnessed the last battle of Druss the Legend?'

'Druss the Legend? You know I have always hated to be called that.'

'I'm hungry, Uncle Druss,' said Elanin, tugging on his arm.

'Now *that* is a title I do like,' said the old warrior, lifting the child into his arms. 'That is who I will be. Druss the Uncle. Druss the Farmer. And a pox on prophecies!'

'What prophecy?'

Druss grinned. 'A long time ago a seer told me I would die in battle at Dros Delnoch. It was always a nonsense. Delnoch is the greatest fortress ever built, six massive walls and a keep. There's not an army in the world could take it – and not a leader insane enough to try.'

EPILOGUE

USTARTE STOOD ON HER BALCONY, STARING DOWN AT THE INNER gardens. Little Elanin was braiding small white flowers into a crown for the powerful bearded man sitting alongside her at the pool's edge. Diagoras was sitting quietly on a marble bench, watching them.

The servant, Weldi, came up to her. 'Garianne has returned the Grey Man's crossbow to the museum, priestess,' he said. She nodded, and continued to gaze upon the child and the warrior. Elanin reached up and Druss dipped his head, accepting the crown of blooms. 'Why did the voices leave her?' asked Weldi.

Ustarte turned away from the balcony. 'Not all mysteries can be solved, Weldi. That is what makes life so fascinating. Perhaps Skilgannon's offer of sacrifice was enough for them. Perhaps Garianne had fallen in love with him, and that love gave her peace. Perhaps the soul of the child she is now carrying softened her need for revenge. It does not matter. She is no longer haunted.'

'And Skilgannon does not know he is to be a father.'

'No. One day, perhaps . . . Look at the child, Weldi. Is she not beautiful?'

'She is, priestess. A rare delight. Will she be someone important to the world?'

'She already is.'

'You know what I mean. The two greatest warriors in the world came together on a quest to save her. They risked their lives. They battled a sorceress and a villain with magic swords. The result ought to be world-changing.'

'Ah, yes,' she agreed. 'I like those romances too. The return of a golden age, the banishment of evil, the little princess who will one day be great.'

'Exactly. Do any of the many futures show this?'

'They show that Elanin will be happy, and will have happy children. Is that not enough?'

'I don't know,' admitted Weldi.

'In a few years' time Druss the Legend will stand on the walls of Dros Delnoch and defy the greatest army the world has ever seen. He will do this to save the Drenai people from slaughter, and keep alive the dreams of civilization. Is this more to your liking?'

'Ah, indeed it is, priestess.'

She smiled fondly at him. 'And do you think Druss would find that more important than rescuing this child from a place of darkness and horror?'

Weldi gazed down at the warrior below, the absurd crown of flowers on his greying hair. 'I suppose he wouldn't,' he admitted. 'Why is that?'

'Let me ask you this,' said Ustarte, 'if a hero sees a child in danger of drowning, does he need to know the fate of worlds hangs in the balance before leaping in and trying to rescue it?'

'No,' said Weldi. 'But if we are playing this game, what if someone told the hero that the child was destined to be evil?'

'A good question. What then would Druss do?'

Weldi laughed suddenly. 'He would leap in and save the child.'

'And why?'

'Because that is what heroes do.'

'Excellent, my friend.'

'So what will happen at Dros Delnoch?'

Ustarte laughed. 'Your curiosity is insatiable. Why not ask me what you really want?'

He grinned at her. 'I would like to see one of the many futures. A good one, though. Nothing sad or depressing. I know you have

426

delved them, priestess, because your curiosity is no less pro-
nounced than mine.'

'Take my arm,' she said, and together they walked through the
inner corridors of the temple, coming at last to a small room. Soft,
golden light blossomed around them as Ustarte entered. The room
was cool and quiet, and the scent of cedarwood hung in the air. There
were no windows, and no furniture of any kind. Three of the four
walls were of rugged red rock, the fourth was of smooth glass. Ustarte
stood for a moment, staring at their reflections. 'I will show you one
possible future,' she said. 'No more than that. It is one that pleases
me. Though it will only make you the more curious. Are you ready?'

'I am, priestess,' said Weldi happily.

Ustarte lifted her arm and the glass shimmered and went dark.
Bright stars appeared in a distant sky, and they found themselves
staring down at a colossal fortress bathed in moonlight. A vast
army was camped before the fortress. Weldi peered at the campsite.
'What are they doing?' he asked.

'Preparing a funeral pyre.'

'Who is dead?'

'Druss the Legend.'

'No!' wailed Weldi. 'I don't want to see an unhappy future.'

'Wait!' The glass shimmered once more, and now it was as if
Weldi and the priestess were standing inside a large tent. A powerful figure stood there, surrounded by Nadir warriors. The figure
turned and Weldi saw that he had violet eyes of striking power.
Another man entered the tent.

'It is Skilgannon,' said Weldi. 'He is older.'

'Ten years older,' said Ustarte. 'Now listen!'

'Why are you here, my friend?' asked the violet-eyed man. 'I
know it is not to fight in my cause.'

'I came for the reward you promised me, Great Khan.'

'This is a battlefield, Skilgannon. My riches are not here.'

'I do not require riches.'

'I owe you my life. You may ask of me anything I have and I will
grant it.'

'Druss was dear to me, Ulric. We were friends. I require only a
keepsake: a lock of his hair, and a small sliver of bone. I would ask
also for his axe.'

427

The Great Khan stood silently for a moment. 'He was dear to me also. What will you do with the hair and bone?'

'I will place them in a locket, my lord, and carry it round my neck.'

'Then it shall be done,' said Ulric.

Once more the glass shimmered. Weldi saw Skilgannon riding from the Nadir camp, the great axe, Snaga, strapped to his shoulders. Then the image faded. Weldi stood for a moment, staring at his reflection.

'What happened then?' he asked.

'I told you it would only arouse your curiosity further.'

'Oh, this is unfair, priestess! Tell me, I implore you.'

'I do not know, Weldi. I looked no further. Unlike you, I am fond of mysteries. I am also enchanted by legends. And you know that, with all great legends, the same story circulates. When the realm is under threat the greatest hero will return. So we will leave it there.'

'I think you are very cruel,' said Weldi.

Ustarte laughed. 'What else would you expect from someone who is part wolf?'